THE
HANDLER

ALSO BY JEFFREY S. STEPHENS

Fool's Errand
Rogue Mission
Targets of Revenge
Targets of Opportunity
Targets of Deception

Crimes and Passion (A Robbie Whyte Mystery)

THE
HANDLER

A NICK REAGAN THRILLER

JEFFREY S. STEPHENS

Post Hill
PRESS

A POST HILL PRESS BOOK

The Handler:
A Nick Reagan Thriller
© 2022 by Jeffrey S. Stephens
All Rights Reserved

ISBN: 978-1-63758-582-5
ISBN (eBook): 978-1-63758-583-2

Cover design by Cody Corcoran
Interior design and composition by Greg Johnson, Textbook Perfect

Post Hill Press
New York • Nashville
posthillpress.com

Published in the United States of America

For Skip, and all the others
who have risked their lives to protect ours.

PROLOGUE

New York City

It was a bright Tuesday afternoon in early June when two young men, who had never met and never would, approached the same area from opposite directions.

New York City. Where people can be invisible even when they are in plain sight. Where the collective tendency toward short memories leads to a misguided sense of security and superiority. Where size, complexity, and diversity are sources of both strength and vulnerability.

One of the men, named Mustafa Karahan, was the son of a Turkish family that had emigrated to the United States when he was an infant. He was now twenty-three, short, slight of build, and small featured, with a fair complexion and timid affect. He grew up in the Bronx and attended the public schools there but never felt part of the place—something his parents did not understand. They saw their adopted home as a place of opportunity, somewhere their only child could flourish and succeed. But Mustafa did not succeed, and after his father died far too young from lung cancer brought on by a lifetime of smoking, the young man was left without an important male influence. He ultimately found that guidance, and a sense of belonging, when he began spending time at the local mosque. There he found kinship, purpose, and, recently, a mission.

The other young man, Roshan al Ghamdi, was Saudi Arabian. Just under six feet tall, he was dark-skinned with features characteristic of his heritage. He had been sent to America by his family to pursue a college education but encountered the same sense of alienation Mustafa experienced. Failing in both his studies and his attempts to blend with the Americans with whom he attended the university, he also found Islam as his salvation. He too became determined to serve Allah in whatever manner he was instructed.

Today, these two strangers, Roshan and Mustafa, were engaged in the same activities—walking, observing, making mental notes, stopping from time to time, trying to appear as if they were there to enjoy the people around them, the scenery, and the vitality of the place.

When the two passed, neither took notice of the other. Each believed he was on a solitary endeavor, not knowing that a few days from now they would both be returning to this same place at the same time. On that day, Mustafa and Roshan would each be armed with weapons and explosives, determined to murder and injure as many innocent souls as possible.

This, they believed, would ensure their places in *Jannah*.

PART ONE

CHAPTER ONE

Shanghai, People's Republic of China

Mon the Bund in Shanghai was the sort of continental restaurant one would expect to find in Paris, or New York, or London. The lush rooftop setting and pricey menu were geared to occidental travelers, a frequent stop for wealthy Chinese and successful business people on large expense accounts, not the local working class and certainly not CIA agents.

Oh what the hell, thought Nick Reagan when he arrived, *how often do I get to see Weber?*

As he stepped to the reception desk, the attractive young hostess treated him to a warm smile.

"How may I help you?" she asked.

Reagan let the question linger between them for a moment, his deep blue eyes returning her friendly look. "Meeting someone for dinner," he finally said. When her expression betrayed a hint of disappointment, he pointed over her shoulder. "That hefty-looking guy, over there."

Without waiting for her response, he headed to the bar where Chris Weber was standing.

Reagan gave his friend a gentle pat on the gut followed by a warm hug. "Appears life in China isn't treating you too badly."

"As long as you know where to eat in this town," Weber replied with a short laugh, "and where not to." He was forty-one, stood just under six feet, had a beefy build, broad shoulders, and thick, muscular

5

arms. His hair had thinned a bit over the years, and Reagan noticed a few new lines on his face, betraying the strain of the life-and-death profession they had chosen. All the same, Weber still had the same bright look in his eyes and the same relaxed smile Reagan had always known.

He was wearing a gray suit, pale blue shirt, and red tie, and Reagan said, "You're looking very corporate tonight."

"Part of the act."

Reagan was five years younger than Weber, a couple of inches taller, and maintained the fighting trim he developed when they served together in the military. His complexion was tanned from all the time he spent in the field, his rugged features even, his dark brown hair cut short. He had been hardened by combat experience and toughened by a decade spent in the Agency's clandestine service. He was wearing dark gray slacks, a white shirt open at the neck, and a tailored navy blue blazer.

"I'm glad we could get together," Reagan said.

"So am I, although I was surprised you picked *this* place. I'll bet the bean counters on the second floor of Langley are going to have a fit when they see the bill."

Reagan smiled. "I actually had the same thought on the way over."

"Our beloved Deputy Director still doesn't have much of a sense of humor."

"Not a grin's worth. What are you drinking?"

"Bombay straight up, my man. Certain things never change. You still destroying your liver with bourbon?"

"Guilty as charged, although it's tough to find a decent selection of Kentucky nectar over here. Think I'll go with vodka."

They waited for Reagan to be served, then made a toast to the fallen members of their bygone unit in Afghanistan. After that, they spent time catching up on the comings and goings of other colleagues and friends. When they were done with their cocktails, Reagan asked the hostess to take them to the table he had reserved, set in the far corner of the room.

"Backs to the wall as usual," Weber said when he saw where they were being seated. "Always Mr. Tradecraft."

Reagan smiled. "I couldn't eat if I had my back to the door."

"You don't have to tell me," Weber said. Then, after they took their seats, he lowered his voice and asked, "How did it go at the factory today?"

Reagan shook his head. "Not as well as I hoped. You're familiar with the exploits of Anatole Mindlovitch?"

"Sure, big player in Moscow. Putin's buddy until they fell out, so he picked up his marbles and moved to the US."

"With business interests all over the world," Reagan reminded him. "Everything from renewable energy to space travel."

"And the manufacture of microchips," Weber added. "Such as the plant you visited in Suzhou today."

"We're convinced he's doing something there other than building standard microprocessors."

"Based on what?"

"Intel we received back home."

"I wasn't read in on it," Weber said. "You don't have to tell me anything you're not comfortable—"

Reagan held up his hand. "I'm not worried about you, pal."

Weber nodded his appreciation. "So, you see anything interesting?"

"Zero. It's a huge place, and, if you believe what they claim, they're supplying the chips for almost half the smart phones manufactured in China."

"Far as I know, that's accurate. Mindlovitch does things in a big way." Weber paused. "What do you believe he's up to?"

This time it was Reagan who spoke in a whisper. "The Ghost Chip. You've heard about it?"

"I know the theory. Kind of frightening. Would make a phone totally untraceable. Can't tap it, GPS can't locate it, that the general idea?"

"That's only part of it. If it works, it can also send a high frequency signal that can be adapted to ignite explosives, trigger other electronic devices, or destroy the phone itself."

"Sounds like a sci-fi horror film."

"Wish it was."

"You find any indication of that?"

"Nothing," Reagan admitted. "What they showed me I could have seen on their website."

Weber smiled. "They're pretty secretive about business innovations in this part of the world."

"I would say. The highlight was when they had me watch for about fifteen minutes of their elaborate pressing machines stamping out thousands of microchips. It was enough to put an insomniac to sleep."

"I take it they weren't trying to dazzle you with any new technology."

"Not a glimpse," Reagan said. "And I never got near the door of their R and D department."

"Maybe they made you."

"Unlikely. Set up the appointment as an exec with a tech company in the States, claimed we were looking for a new supplier." After a taste of his second drink, Reagan grinned as he said, "I even wore a dull suit and tie."

"They're paranoid about corporate espionage over here. They might have been worried you're working for another manufacturer."

Reagan drew back slightly, feigning outrage. "You think someone could make me as a spy?"

Weber laughed. "What's your next move?"

"I'm going back there and breaking in."

Weber sat up a bit straighter as he had a serious look at his friend. "You know what the Chinese have been up to the last few years? With our people, I mean."

"I have a pretty good idea."

Weber leaned forward again. "Whatever you've seen in the reports won't begin to give you a sense of what's happened in real time."

"I know two of our agents disappeared into the ether."

"Both of them good friends of mine," Weber told him. "And then there were the local sources the Chinese government took down. They've arrested or murdered two dozen of our key informants in the past couple of years. Picked off our best contacts, which scared a lot of the others away, as you'd expect."

"What's your point?"

"My point? You get caught busting into that plant, and we'll never hear of you again. And for what?"

"I have to try and grab this new chip."

"If there even is such a chip." Weber shook his head. "Risk reward, my man. I don't see it."

"What if the Ghost Chip is real? ISIS or al-Qaeda gets hold of it, their lines of electronic communication become impenetrable. Not to mention their ability to wreak havoc with these devices. Murder by remote control."

"I understand the issue, believe me." Weber thought it over. "Isn't Mindlovitch living in California now?"

"A darling of Silicon Valley."

"That might be a better angle, taking a run at him directly."

"You think I should stop by his place and ask him what's new at his factory in Suzhou?"

"I've never known you to run short of, uh, means of persuasion."

Reagan took a moment. "You may be right."

"Mind if I give you some other brotherly advice?"

"Fire away," Reagan said.

"The Chinese secret police play rough. You've been in the game a long time, and no one doubts your survival instincts, but even a cat only has nine lives."

Reagan did not respond.

"There's one other thing," Weber said.

"Only one?"

"We've never identified the informant who gave Beijing the names of our local assets. We think it might be someone at our embassy, but we still haven't found the source. As things stand, the Chinese are watching everyone stationed here, and I mean all of us, twenty-four seven. Their agents probably know I'm meeting with you now."

As it turned out, Weber was not wrong. The Ministry of Security had a man posted in the restaurant during their dinner, and a female agent on site as well.

CHAPTER TWO

Shanghai, People's Republic of China

After a long dinner, they agreed it would be best if they left separately. Weber headed out first, so Reagan went to the bar and ordered a Stoli Elite straight up. The place had begun to empty out, and he noticed the lovely young hostess was gone, but there was an attractive woman sitting alone, a couple of seats away.

"Mind if I join you?" Reagan asked.

She gave him a slow once-over, then smiled. "Why not?"

He slid his martini glass down the polished counter and took the stool beside here. "Come here often?"

She laughed. It was a warm laugh that lit up her large, hazel eyes. *Cat's eyes*, Reagan thought. "You get very far with that old line?" she asked.

"Depends," he said.

She nodded, then held out her hand. "Amanda Whitson," she said.

"Nick Reynolds," he lied. "That accent tells me you're from London, probably Knightsbridge."

She smiled. "You Americans are the ones with an accent. We invented the language."

"Point taken."

She lifted her glass and had a sip of her cocktail. "Been in London for the past ten years. Grew up in Newbury."

"Nice town," he said.

"You've been to Newbury?"

"Been to the track there."

"You must get around. Newbury to Shanghai is an unusual parlay."

Reagan responded with a casual shrug. "I'm in sales, technology sector; I travel quite a bit. What brings you to scenic Shanghai?"

"Queen and country," she told him.

"Government work, you don't say." He took a moment to have a good look at her, from her high heels, up the line of her dark skirt to the white blouse open at the neck. He said, "I'm guessing you're not in the military."

"Diplomatic corps. Always something going on with the Chinese."

"I see. You stationed here now or—"

"Just visiting," she said. "Heading home tomorrow afternoon."

"Me too," he told her, then made a show of looking around the place. "Appears the party's over here, but my hotel has a nice bar that stays open late."

"Looking to make this a memorable last night in China?"

He grinned. "Just looking to make memories."

They had nightcaps at the bar of the Intercontinental, then went upstairs to his room. Whatever Amanda really did for Her Majesty, he quickly discovered that she kept herself in top shape. As appealing as she was fully clothed, she was positively stunning in her panties and bra. She also turned out to be a woman who knew what she wanted in bed.

After more than an hour passionately exploring each other's secrets, they were lying quietly side by side when they heard a loud knock on his door.

Reagan had a quick look at his Rolex Daytona. It was after one. With a smile, he said, "Please tell me you don't have a jealous husband."

Her look betrayed nothing as she asked, "Who would be at your door at this hour?"

After another series of knocks, Reagan got up, pulled on his slacks, and removed his automatic from the night table drawer.

"I thought you were a salesman," she said, sitting up and pulling the sheet to her neck.

"Can't be too careful in the high-tech world," he said, then went to the door. "Who is it?"

"Open up," an accented voice told him. "It's the police."

Reagan turned to Amanda, pointed to the bathroom, and quietly said, "Get in there and lock the door."

She immediately did as he said, which he filed away as another positive for whoever she really was. Then he opened the door as far as the metal security latch would allow, keeping his gun out of view.

There were three men standing in the hallway, all wearing dark suits, white shirts, and dark ties. One of them held out what appeared to be Chinese police credentials in his hand. More persuasive than that, he had a pistol in the other.

"Mr. Reagan," the man said, his face a picture of unpleasant determination.

Since it was not a question, and since Reynolds, not Reagan, was the name on the passport that brought him into the country, he decided if they already knew who he was there was no reason to reply.

"You need to come with us," the man told him.

"Who, exactly, is *us*?" Reagan asked.

The man moved his I.D. closer, but, naturally, it was in Chinese.

"That's not much help to me," Reagan said.

In response, the man raised his weapon and said, "We are police."

"What do you want?" he asked.

"We need to ask you some questions."

"Ask them here," Reagan said.

"If you do not remove the latch and open the door, we will break it down. I will not give another warning."

If the odds had merely been three against one, Reagan might have been tempted to play it out, but he had no idea what sort of backup they had nor any idea why they had come. He also realized a

13

shoot-out with Chinese authorities, or whoever they really were, was not a prudent move.

"I need to finish getting dressed."

"Do it quickly. Bring your papers and passport. We know you have a weapon. Leave it in the room and the woman will remain unharmed."

Reagan left the door ajar, though still secured with the metal security bar, then went to the bathroom. He tapped gently and said, "It's me." Amanda immediately opened up, now dressed in the hotel robe. He held out the automatic, handle first. "Seems the authorities want to have a chat with me. They don't seem to be interested in you, but lock yourself in there until I'm gone. And hold onto this for company."

She nodded. "Are you going to be all right?"

"Always." He smiled. "Can I look you up in London?"

She responded with a probing look, then said "I hope you do, if for no other reason than to tell me what this was all about."

"Fair enough," he said.

Reagan pulled on a dark crew neck sweater, slipped on his socks and shoes, and grabbed his papers. Then he left the room, pulling the door closed behind him, and followed the three men to the elevator. They rode in silence all the way to the underground garage, where two cars were waiting. He was shoved inside the back of the first sedan, where a man was sitting with a gun drawn, immediately leveling it at Reagan's face.

"Welcome," he said. Another man got in from the other side, pulled a sack over Reagan's head, and tightened the cord around his neck as the driver sped away.

CHAPTER THREE

Shanghai, People's Republic of China

Nick Reagan had no idea where he was. The dark hood left him no way to even guess which direction they had gone after they left the hotel. He estimated the drive took less than twenty-five minutes, but that did not tell him much. For all he knew, they could have been driving in circles and ended up around the corner from where they began.

Along the way they had cuffed his hands in front of him, patted him down, removed his watch and cell phone, and emptied his pockets. When they came to a stop, he was pulled out of the car and led forward. He was not forced to walk up or down any stairs nor ride in an elevator, which meant he was on the ground floor or basement of whatever building they entered. That could be helpful if he was going to have any chance to escape. When they finally removed the hood, he found himself in a dimly lit, windowless room with two of his captors. The space was no more than eight feet by eight feet, with cinderblock walls and a ceiling that appeared to be made of concrete.

One of the men shoved Reagan onto an uncomfortable metal chair. The other removed the cuffs, used a plastic restraint to strap Reagan's hands together behind his back, then both turned and walked out. Neither of them said a word.

After waiting for what he judged to be around half an hour, the door opened again. Two different men entered and seated themselves opposite him, a metal table between them. One was the man who had done the talking at his hotel room door. The other was considerably older, and Reagan had not seen him before. Like the others, he was dressed in a dark suit, white shirt, and dark tie.

"Interesting police uniforms you guys have."

The younger man reacted with a scowl that Reagan assumed was supposed to be menacing. "Your real name is Nicholas Reagan," he said.

Reagan did not reply.

The man held up the passport and billfold they had taken in the car. It bore the name of his alias, Nick Reynolds, which was the NOC he was using for this mission. "You have entered our country with a false passport. That is a very serious crime."

Reagan stared at him, his dark blue eyes unblinking as he said, "I want to speak with someone from the American Embassy."

This time the younger man opted for a thin-lipped smile. "Of course you do. Anyone caught engaging in espionage in a foreign country wants to speak with their embassy."

"Espionage? That's what you think?" Reagan stared at the younger man. "Sure, you're right, I'm a spy, you caught me." Then, shaking his head, he said, "You guys must watch too many American movies."

"I would refrain from sarcasm, if I were you."

"If you were me, you wouldn't be under arrest."

The man shook his head. "What were you doing in Suzhou today?"

"That's none of your business."

"Mr. Reagan, please do not confuse the rights you may have at home with your present situation. I will state this as plainly as I can—you have *no* rights here. Whether you even leave this room alive depends entirely on the answers you give to my questions. Is that clear?"

"Very. In fact, I must say, your English is excellent. I can't speak any Chinese at all."

"I'm sure you'll become proficient, after you spend twenty years in our prison system. Now, what were you doing in Suzhou?"

"As you can see from my business card, I'm a sales rep for Spectral Electronics. I was touring a factory we may want to do business with. Is that a crime?"

"It is a crime to lie to an official of the People's Republic. It is a crime to enter our country under false pretenses. It is a crime to spy on duly authorized businesses within our borders."

Reagan smiled. "Are you telling me there are *unauthorized* businesses in your country? How careless of you. Maybe you should spend your time tracking them down."

The man slammed the palm of his hand hard on the table, the sound reverberating in the small room. "Stop!" he shouted. "You either have no idea what you are facing, or you are playing a very dangerous game. I could have you shot right here, right now, and no one will ever know what became of you."

Reagan knew it was true. The Chinese Ministry of Security was not in the business of dragging businessmen out of their hotel rooms in the middle of the night for polite discussions. "What do you want from me?"

"I want to know what you were doing at that factory today."

"I was looking at their products and their systems."

"Why? And please don't tell me you were there as a potential buyer."

"What's so unusual about that?"

"A sales representative does not enter this country with false papers and then report his day's activities to a CIA agent."

Reagan said nothing.

"Do not bother denying it. We had people at the restaurant this evening. Including that attractive young hostess you thought found you charming," he added with obvious satisfaction.

Filing that information away for another time, Reagan said, "Damn, and I thought I was doing so well."

"Come, come, you are wasting our time. You had dinner with Mr. Chris Weber this evening."

Reagan burst out laughing. "Weber? Is that what this is about?"

The man stared at him, stone-faced.

"Feel free to check on me, use whatever channels you have. I served in the United States military with Weber. I was coming to Shanghai on business, knew he worked here, set up a dinner for old time's sake." He paused for effect. "CIA? Weber? Give me a break."

For the first time, his interrogator turned to the older man beside him who, up until now, had neither spoken nor taken his eyes off Reagan.

"You are making serious mistake," the older man said, his English not as good as his colleague's. He got to his feet, and the younger man quickly followed. "We come back."

As they began to walk out, Reagan said, "How about my hands? These straps are cutting off the circulation, and I can't even scratch my nose." When they turned to stare at him, he said, "What am I going to do, claw my way out? In case you forgot, I came with you willingly, right?"

When the superior officer nodded, the other man pulled out a switchblade and approached Reagan. Before moving behind him, he leaned into his face and said, "I hope you give me a reason to use this on your throat."

Reagan smiled at the man as he sliced through the plastic, thinking, *That's your first mistake, because there is no way you're going to cuff me again, pal.*

Then, after the two Chinese were gone, Reagan began to plan his escape.

CHAPTER FOUR

Shanghai, Peoples Republic of China

Left alone in the small, windowless bunker, Reagan got up from the chair and had a look around. There were no cameras anywhere on the walls or ceiling. In fact, there was no evidence of anything at all. It was one of the barest rooms he had ever seen, which is doubtless the way they wanted it.

If they were going to kill him, they wanted no record of the event.

He went to the door and gently tried to turn the knob. It was locked from the outside, with no keyhole on the inside. He stopped and listened for a moment, hoping to hear something, but his effort was met by silence. Either the door was very thick or there was no one nearby.

Reagan checked his pockets, which were empty. They had taken everything. The only thing they had not found when they frisked him was the thin, high-density polymer blade secreted inside his belt. For now, it was his only weapon against the two men who would likely be returning soon, and whoever else they had outside.

He already understood he was not here for a routine interrogation. They knew he was CIA, and Reagan did not intend to become another one of the victims Weber had described. If the plastic blade was all he had, it would have to be enough. In case there was some sort of video system he had not found, he was careful as he removed it, making it appear he was straightening out his pants. Then he sat back on the metal chair, sliding the razor-sharp plastic beneath his right thigh, and waited.

19

Reagan had always hated waiting, but over his years as a covert operative he became good at it. He kept his breathing even and his pulse low. He knew, when they returned, their initial actions would determine what he had to do, and he needed to be ready.

Another twenty minutes or so passed until he finally heard the latch turn. The same two men entered the room and shut the door behind them. He noticed there was no sound of the latch being closed from the other side.

That was good news.

The younger man approached him, saying, "I will bind your wrists again before we speak further."

"Is that really necessary?"

"Put your hands behind your back," the man barked, then stepped behind Reagan and bent down to apply the restraints.

Reagan moved with startling speed and violent efficiency. Drawing the blade from under his leg, he spun to his left, rising from the chair, and lashed out. Although he missed the man's neck, he managed to cut a bloody gash across his left cheek.

The man stumbled back, instinctively grabbing at his face. Reagan lunged forward and made another violent stroke, this time slashing his throat. As the wounded Chinese fell back against the concrete wall, Reagan reached inside the man's suit jacket and pulled out his automatic.

The older man had jumped to his feet and was reaching for his own gun, but his reaction was too slow. Reagan was already pointing the Chinese Type 54 pistol at his head. "Not one word, not one sound—not if you want to live. No one else needs to get hurt here. Just place your weapon on the table."

The older man hesitated, as if weighing his options, but the look in Reagan's eyes made the decision for him. He did as he was told.

"How many men are outside?"

"Two," the older Chinese replied, his gaze locked with Reagan's.

"If you're lying, you're the first one I kill. You understand?"

"Two," the man repeated.

"Right outside the door?"

"Yes."

"Where are we?"

"Inside an empty warehouse."

"How many cars?"

"One."

"What happened to your backup team?"

"They are gone," the man said, then blinked.

Reagan turned quickly to see that the wounded man on the ground was reaching for the knife in his belt, even as blood poured from his throat. Reagan kicked the knife away, then stomped down on the man's head. Turning back to the older man, he said, "Time to go."

Coming around the table, Reagan picked up the second gun and shoved it in his belt. He grabbed the older man by the collar, standing right behind him. "Open the door," he said, "nice and slow."

The man did as ordered. As they stepped outside, Reagan found they were in an empty warehouse, just as he was told. Also as advertised, there were only two other men there, seated in chairs against a wall to the right, waiting.

When they saw what was happening, they both scrambled to their feet.

"Sit down," Reagan hollered at them, showing them the gun and using the older man as a shield. After they reluctantly lowered themselves onto the chairs, he said, "Remove your weapons by the grips, using your thumb and forefinger only, and drop them on the ground."

They looked to their superior number without moving.

"Either of you claim you don't understand English, and I'll shoot you both where you sit."

The older man nodded slightly, and the two guards unholstered their guns and tossed them on the cement floor.

"Where are my things?" Reagan demanded.

One of the men began to get up.

"Don't test me," Reagan barked at him.

The Chinese sat back down and pointed to a table, over to the left. It held a number of items, including Reagan's phone, watch, wallet, and passport, and a laptop computer.

"Stay still," Reagan told them, then moved to the table with his hostage in tow.

As Reagan gathered his things, the older man said, "You are going to die."

"I'm going to die all right, but not today. Where are the car keys?"

"In the car."

"We'll see. Meanwhile, I want some of those plastic restraints you guys are so fond of." When one of the guards went to his pocket, Reagan said, "Easy."

The man pulled out the strips, and Reagan had one of the guards bind the other, hands and feet, face down on the floor. Then he pushed his hostage forward and had him do the same to the second guard.

When the older man started to protest, Reagan said, "Stop grumbling. I could just as easily kill all three of you."

Once the two guards were trussed, Reagan checked that the bindings were tight, then led the older man back into the small room. He checked on the wounded man, who was still on the floor, unconscious.

"I thought about taking you with me," Reagan told the older man, "but I'm going to leave you here to help your friend until I can send you some help."

"This is not over, Mr. Reagan."

"You're right about that, pal." Reagan frisked them both with his left hand, removing their phones, papers, and everything else they had. Then he left them both in the room, locking the door behind him and pocketing the key. He frisked the two men on the floor, ensuring they were also left with nothing. Then, for good measure, he cracked each of them across the back of the head with the butt of the pistol.

The car was just outside, and the key was in the ignition. He retrieved his possessions, then placed all of the things he had taken from the four men into the trunk, tossed their laptop on the driver's seat, and fired up the engine. Then he pulled out his cell and called Weber.

"Chris, we have a problem."

"Where are you? I'm getting messages from the other side of the world. Everyone's looking for you."

"Let's just say I've been indisposed. And now you are too."

"What's that mean?"

"Call Uncle Brian, tell him he needs to organize a Company plane or something private. We're heading stateside, and I mean right fucking now."

"We?"

"You either leave with me or your next visitor is going to be the Chinese secret police."

"How much time do I have?"

"None," Reagan said. "Get back to me on which airstrip we're using, I'll meet you there. I'm on road, and they're going to be on my tail very soon."

CHAPTER FIVE

Baltimore

Mustafa Karahan drove his six-year-old Toyota Camry from the Bronx, heading south on Interstate 95 to Baltimore. He had never been to Maryland, but the Waze app on his smartphone flawlessly directed him to the door of the bar where his meeting was to take place. He had arrived almost an hour early, so he parked across the street and waited.

The neighborhoods of Baltimore are defined by irregularly formed semi-circular rings that spread inland from the harbor. The first, along the waterfront, is comprised of office buildings, retail stores, restaurants, tourist sites, and several high-end hotels. This downtown area, including Fells Point, is bright and pleasant and bustles with the typical daytime activity of a vibrant city. Just a bit inland, however, there is a ghetto filled with old tenement buildings, violence, drugs, and the usual detritus found in too many urban centers in America. This second area virtually surrounds the first, an ever-present reminder of the failure of the American promise. Moving through that Dantesque ring and further inland, one will eventually reach the middle-class suburbs, where the people who spend their days working downtown seek safe haven at night.

Mustafa's meeting was to take place in that second circle of hell.

As he sat and waited, he made sure his car doors were locked. Having lived in the South Bronx since he was eleven, he was alert to the activity around him. The streets were populated by Blacks and

Hispanics and a few Arabic looking people. None of them seemed to be working, and none seemed to be in a hurry to go anywhere. The time passed slowly as he thought about the noble quest he was about to undertake. He was nervous and excited and proud that his life finally had meaning. He was feeling important in a way he had never felt before, and that sustained him as the minutes crawled by.

Just before one o'clock, he got out of the car and headed across the street.

He entered the seedy looking gin mill and looked around. There was a long wooden bar to the right and a dozen small tables in the back. The paneled walls were dark and worn and covered with posters announcing everything from prize fights to music concerts, all of which had occurred long ago. The man he was there to see was already seated at a table in the farthest corner of the room. He appeared just as he had described himself in his text message. Full beard, gray hair, heavy-framed eyeglasses. Mustafa had no way of knowing that the beard was fake, the hair a wig, nor that his eyeglasses were clear. The man remained seated, facing the front of the room, as Mustafa approached. He studied the younger man as he invited him to take the seat opposite him.

"You are right on time," the man said. "Good."

"I was early," Mustafa told him.

The man nodded his approval, then said that Allah should be praised.

Mustafa quietly repeated the blessing.

Despite all he had done to disguise his appearance, the one thing the man could not disguise was the intensity of his dark eyes, which were now fixed on Mustafa. "You have nothing to fear from me," he said.

Mustafa nodded, then looked down, noticing the two glasses on the small table, each filled with whisky and ice.

"I know you do not drink, but we are in a bar, so I have ordered these," the man explained. "As you have been instructed, never do anything to bring attention to yourself."

"I understand."

The place was crowded and noisy, but the man was careful to speak softly. "You have been to the specified location?"

"Yes," Mustafa said.

"Had you ever been there before?"

"No."

"Did you have a thorough look around?"

"Yes."

"No need to return?"

"No."

The man nodded his approval. "Excellent. You should not be seen there again, not until the appointed time."

"Understood," Mustafa told him.

"You have identified the spot where this event is scheduled to take place?"

"Yes, between fourteenth street and—"

The man held up his hand before Mustafa could finish. "We speak of no details. If you tell me you have identified the place, I believe you."

"I am sorry," the young Turk replied with a deferential nod. Then he said, "Yes, I know where it will take place."

The man paused for a moment, having another good look at Mustafa. Then he glanced around to see if anyone seemed interested in their discussion. Satisfied that they were not being watched, he said, "The equipment will be of two types, you understand that?"

"Yes."

"When delivery is arranged you will be given the necessary instructions."

Mustafa waited.

"This will involve great care, both in terms of secrecy and operation. You understand?"

"Yes, I understand."

"When the goods are brought to you, you will be asked a simple question, 'Why are you here?' You will answer, 'I am here to do God's will.' Understood?"

"Yes," he responded solemnly.

The man nodded slowly, taking more time to study Mustafa. That was the only reason he was here, for the opportunity to evaluate the young man, face-to-face. He was risking a public meeting because he had to be certain he had recruited the right person. In two hours he would have the same encounter with Roshan, the other young man he had assigned to carry out this attack, neither of whom would ever know of the other.

Thus far he judged Mustafa to be anxious, but that was appropriate to the actions he had pledged to carry out. Mustafa was also respectful and serious, which was important. The last thing he needed was a quick-tempered zealot. As he had learned through experience, the men and women who successfully carried out these operations were true believers in the cause, not given to panic or nervous mistakes.

"Your father is dead," the man said.

"Yes," Mustafa replied. He was about to say when and how it happened but stopped himself. "I understand, no details," he said with an uncomfortable smile.

The man nodded his approval. "Your mother is devout?"

"A daughter of Allah."

"Good." The man paused again, and Mustafa waited patiently until he was asked, "Do you have any questions?"

Mustafa shook his head slowly. "I am here to serve my God," he said.

The man reached into his pocket and removed a small piece of paper. On it were two names, each followed by a telephone number. He placed it on the table and slid it across to Mustafa. "You will memorize these now. The first is a number you are to call as soon as you receive the signal. The second is only to be used in case of an emergency, only if you have reason to believe you have been compromised.

Each of these numbers will work once, there can be no second call. Is that clear?"

"Yes."

"Take a moment to memorize them. Never write them anywhere."

Mustafa did as he was told. When he looked up the man took the paper back and replaced it in his pocket.

"Go now, back home. Do not spend any more time here. Go, and await my signal."

"*Allahu Akbar,*" Mustafa said in a whisper. When he rose, the Handler remained seated, watching him leave.

Once the young man was gone, the Handler picked up his glass and drained the whisky. He was not one to hold himself to the standards of piety he expected of those who served him. Taking a moment to review this brief meeting, he told himself that Mustafa was an adequate choice, a young man willing to die in a fiery blast that would take the lives of as many infidels as their explosives expert could arrange.

CHAPTER SIX

CIA Headquarters, Langley

The following day, when Reagan and Weber arrived at Andrews Air Force Base, a car had been arranged to bring them directly to headquarters. In short order they were at Langley, in the deputy director's office.

Brian Kenny only stood a trim five foot six, but was one of the toughest men Nick Reagan had ever known. Before becoming the DD of clandestine operations, he had a distinguished Army career serving in the Middle East. Just past fifty, Kenny had the fine features of his Irish-American heritage, dark eyes that Reagan swore could burn through lead and a shock of straight brown hair he could not seem to keep in place no matter how short he had it cut.

"So," Kenny said after patiently listening to Reagan's report, "you cut the throat of one of these Chinese secret police, hog-tied two others, and locked up the lead member of their team so he could play nursemaid to the man you sliced up."

"You left out the part where I called their emergency one-nine-nine line in Shanghai and reported the incident from the airfield. I'm guessing nobody died."

"That should get you another of those Good Samaritan awards you treasure. Anything else I'm missing?"

"If you don't mind me mentioning it, sir, you seem to be glossing over the fact that I was abducted, and they were probably going to kill me if I didn't take action."

"There is that, yes."

"Then there's the matter of how their not so secret police have been treating our people in China for the past few years, not to mention our local assets."

"You're telling me we owed them one, that it Reagan?"

"If that had been my thinking, sir, there would be four fewer bullets in the weapons I took, and four fewer Chinese secret police."

"I see."

"And I did bring home the laptop they were using to vet me, so that might prove useful."

Brian Kenny nodded. "All right. What about dragging Weber home with you? You develop a sudden fear of flying alone?"

"When I was being interrogated, they used his name. They know he's with the Agency."

"Not exactly a news flash, Reagan. We have a roster of their players, and they know who we have working on their home turf."

"But they knew, after my visit to the factory in Suzhou, that I had dinner with Chris."

"They thought you passed some sort of intel to him?"

"That's how I saw it."

"And once you had this little dust-up with the locals—"

"I figured even if I managed to get out, they were coming after him."

Kenny turned to Weber, who had been quiet up to now. "Reagan's recon of the factory in Suzhou, followed by his meeting with you, you think that raised your danger level?"

"Once Nick got away, I was likely to be their next guest," Weber said.

"All right, time for you to pay a visit to your old friends on the third floor."

"The gang in the far east section?"

Kenny nodded. "They'll handle your debriefing, then we'll figure out what's next for you."

Weber and Reagan stood.

"Not you," Kenny said to Reagan. "Sit down, we have more to discuss." After Weber was gone, the deputy director said, "Before we get into what you found at the factory, I want to discuss the policy paper you wrote."

Reagan waited.

"You think it's appropriate for a covert field agent to be circulating a white paper on terrorism?"

Reagan smiled. "A white paper? I don't think so. It's an internal memo, eyes only for our section. That was the extent of my circulation."

"I understand your intention, but you know as well as anyone that when something is reduced to writing in D.C., it becomes impossible to control where it goes and who sees it."

"With all respect, sir, there is nothing in there that divulges company secrets or that I would be ashamed to see on the front page of tomorrow's *New York Times*."

Kenny picked up a copy of the memo that was sitting on his desk. "I frankly do not give a good goddamn what you feel ashamed about, Reagan. This is critical of our stated policies, not to mention the newly appointed head of our agency."

"I'm sorry, sir, but as far as I can see, the newly appointed head of this agency doesn't know his ass from a mole hole when it comes to fighting terrorism. I am sick to death of losing people and seeing innocent souls slaughtered while these paper pushers chase their bureaucratic tails."

The deputy director sat back and studied his agent for a moment. "You have any idea what sort of trouble you'll be in, you start airing that sort of insubordinate bullshit?"

"I'm not *airing* anything. I'm speaking to the man in this agency I trust more than any other." Reagan leaned forward. "As soon as our new director was appointed, he called a press conference to announce the impossibility of preventing every lone wolf terrorist from carrying out their plots. You know what I call that? I call it the ultimate act of prospective ass covering, a civil servant's excuse for failures yet to come. Before he even rolled up his sleeves and got into the job, he was already explaining why we're going to be attacked and why we won't be able to stop it. *That's* the bullshit."

"Is it?"

"There are certainly individuals who act alone, with a gun or rifle or a crude explosive device. But from everything we've witnessed, from before 9/11 and beyond, we know these psychopaths are being recruited, instructed, funded, and equipped. They're being assigned targets by handlers in ISIS or al-Qaeda. Those are the cowards who sit behind their computer screens and direct this murderous traffic, those are the people we're after. Anyone who doesn't see that misses the point."

"You think I don't see that?"

"I know *you* do. But others don't. That's why I wrote the memo. We're not fighting foreign soldiers—we're tracking animals, and we're not going to stop them if we don't begin directing our resources upstream." Reagan shook his head. "It reminds me of the drug trade and the wasted policies of the past fifty years. They rousted local junkies and got them to rat out their neighborhood pushers. The next day another dealer popped up. The only way to win this war is to cut off the head of the snake."

Kenny shook his head. "Even if I agree with most of what you're saying, you can add to your list of problems the misguided notion that there's a short-term solution."

"This administration's disastrous pullout from Afghanistan only worsened the situation and strengthened al-Qaeda. The Taliban released thousands of prisoners we had captured over the years. Now they're on the loose, and they'll be coming at us again. As you know from my memo, I believe it's going to be a multigenerational struggle, whether we like it or not, and we're not going to succeed until we acknowledge that. There's a serious divide between reality and the political perception, and we need to close that gap."

"I suppose you think you're going to be around to battle each of those new generations?"

Reagan drew back slightly, unable to suppress a smile. "Sir, I think you just made a joke."

"Reagan, I'm warning you—"

"Sir, please, this is a special moment for us, don't you think?"

Kenny let out a long sigh, then leaned forward, his elbows on his desk. "Listen to me, Nick. You may be the most talented field agent we have, but at some point the numbers are going to catch up with you."

The smile gone, Reagan said, "Weber told me the same thing in Shanghai."

Kenny sat back. "When I was in command overseas, it was different. I was on the front lines with my men in Iraq and Afghanistan. I took the same risks they did."

"And when you send me out, I'm willing to take the risks. That's never on you. That's the choice I've made."

"I understand," Kenny said. "My concern is that this has all become too personal for you."

Reagan waited.

"You're not going to deny it?"

"You know my history. Some things *are* personal."

Kenny studied him for a moment. "All I ask is that you don't allow what's happened in the past to cause problems for you now. When you're in the field you have no margin for error. Emotions lead to mistakes."

"You think I'm not detached enough?"

"I think revenge is a dangerous motivator."

Once again, Reagan offered no reply.

"Stay focused on the threats we face, and don't let hate corrupt your judgment, all right?"

"Yes, sir."

"And while you're at it, stay the hell out of politics."

"Yes, sir."

Kenny stared at him for a moment without speaking. Then he said, "As for your visit to China, you didn't find any hard evidence, but you believe they're working on the Ghost Chip in Suzhou, and that they may be getting close."

"Precisely."

"All right," Kenny said, sitting back again. "What do you suggest we do?"

"I think I should pay Anatole Mindlovitch a visit. See what he has to say."

Kenny was shaking his head before Reagan could finish the statement. "That would be way off the reservation, jurisdictionally and otherwise."

"Not even a polite chat?"

"Not even hello and goodbye. Anyway, we have other work to do. NSA has intercepted some chatter about current threats, here at home. I've briefed Gellos and Brandt, they'll bring you up to date."

"How real is the intel?"

"Getting realer by the moment," Kenny said. "The White House has elevated the threat level." He stared at his agent. "They're convinced an attack is imminent, and they want us to move on this immediately."

Reagan stood to leave, then turned back. "One more thing, sir. I met a woman in Shanghai."

"How surprising."

Reagan pulled out his phone and brought up a photo. "Don't think she saw me take this. Anyway, you know how I feel about coincidences, especially if they're too good to be true. Said her name is Amanda Whitson, which is questionable. I had the strangest feeling she was there to keep an eye on me."

"Sent by whom?"

"Not sure, but there are two strong possibilities. She's either working for the Chinese or our cousins in the UK."

34

Kenny nodded as Reagan texted him the photo. "Why not just have Erin track her down?"

Reagan grinned. "Sir, I, uh, hate to say that's a silly question—"

The DD nodded. "All right, I'll take care of it. Just get the hell out of here."

CHAPTER SEVEN

Dearborn, Michigan

That day, as Kenny discussed new intel about domestic terrorism, an Arab International Festival was being held in the city that had become the *de facto* center of Sharia law within the United States—Dearborn.

The transformation of this Michigan town over the past decade was unprecedented. Christians and Jews moved away as it became overrun with Arabs. Apartment buildings were acquired and populated by Muslims. Strip mails were purchased, their long-term tenants driven out by demands for exorbitant rents. The shops that replaced them were all owned by Islamic owners, who removed the old signs and installed displays lettered in Arabic. The schools were forced to offer *halal* meals and allow interruption of classes to permit daily prayers to Mecca—even as the Pledge of Allegiance was banned and any mention of a God other than Allah forbidden. The Muslim population refused to adopt the local culture, to speak English, or make the slightest effort to assimilate. To the contrary, Dearborn suddenly became a small Muslim country in the center of the American heartland.

Stories of this radical conversion were generally met with disbelief, especially the further one lived from the city. Only when violent attacks on non-Muslims became more frequent in Dearborn did national news outlets pay any attention to what was happening. There were repeated occasions when local "security forces" resisted the intrusion of outsiders and forbade Christians from preaching their religion or even passing out literature.

In one notable incident, a few young people attended an Islamic festival for the purpose of asking questions, attempting to better understand the strict tenets of Sharia. They also sought a dialogue about how the new occupants of the city intended to move forward as part of the United States.

Five of them showed up, two of them heading for a booth that had a banner proclaiming in English, "If You Have Questions We Have Answers." There were several young men there, offering pamphlets purporting to explain Islam. However, when these outside visitors attempted to videotape the experience with a smartphone, they were confronted by three members of the festival's enforcers.

"Put those away, or we'll take them from you," one of the burly Arabs told them.

"We just want to record our discussion," the young man replied.

"Not happening," another of the Muslims hollered as he reached out and tried to grab the phone.

"Let go of me," the young man shouted.

As soon as voices were raised, more than a dozen other so-called security personnel rushed forward. They did not ask questions or attempt to determine the nature of the dispute. Instead, they began pushing and shoving the two young Americans, who by then had been joined by their other three friends. All five of them were shoved to the ground, kicked, and punched, their phones smashed.

When they were finally allowed to get up and leave, they immediately sought out the local police, who did absolutely nothing. As in other, similar occurrences, the authorities complained they did not have the manpower to deal with the situation. They suggested these young people go to another location it town, far from the festival site, if they wanted to preach their own gospel. But all five told the police they had no interest in preaching. They explained that they had come merely to ask questions, as a result of which they had been beaten and bloodied. The police responded by threatening to arrest them all for breach of the peace if they did not get on their way.

As it turned out, their shattered phones still held the video of what had occurred, and subsequent litigation won these people an award of damages for the abridgment of their free speech rights, not from the perpetrators but from the police department. Consequently, the actions of the Muslims in Dearborn go on unabated, only worsening with time.

On the same day Nick returned from Shanghai, another confrontation had escalated into violence at the current Islamic event in Dearborn. Once again, a group of Christians arrived, this time making an attempt to pass out their own leaflets. The security force met them at the perimeter of the jubilee and told them to leave. The Christians declared that they were Americans and were entitled to their rights of free speech and religion. The Muslims assured them that no such rights existed under Sharia law, which was the only law they followed. The argument intensified and again became violent, in this instance pelting the Christians with rocks and bottles. The police, again bemoaning their lack of available uniformed officers, told the battered Christians that they should disperse because they were the cause of the problem.

"We're the problem?" the organizer of the Christian group asked incredulously. "We've been beaten for no reason, without provocation, and you're telling us we're the problem?"

In response, the police told them to move on, or they would be cited for their actions.

"What about our rights to free speech?" the leader asked.

They were informed by one of the police officers that the town fathers—almost all of whom were now Muslim—had enacted regulations about where and how free speech could be expressed. They were told that, if they wanted to disseminate their religious literature, they would have to move to a park, more than a mile away from the festival, which was currently deserted.

As in the other case, the incident had been filmed, and was immediately downloaded onto the internet where it was viewed more than two million times.

Brian Kenny and his agents were not the only ones watching the video and shaking their heads. Another man, who had more than a passing interest in the details of the melee, was also on his computer, viewing everything that had been posted online.

His upset was for entirely different reasons.

The Handler was sitting at his desk, his fierce gaze focused on the screen, growing angrier with each viewing. He could not care less about the young men and women who were mauled. He was not worried about the public reaction that would come. No, he was focused on one of the members of the squad who had launched the assault.

The young man's name was Yousef Omarov.

Watching the clip for the third time, he shook his head in disgust. How many times had he explained to Yousef and his other recruits that anonymity is critical to the success of any undercover mission? With this footage available to all to see, it was inevitable that everyone involved in the brawl would be added to the FBI's national watch list. Even if the local police did not care, Yousef would surely be identified by any number of federal agencies, and perhaps even brought in for questioning.

Now what?

He had high hopes for Yousef. The young man was smart and strong and devout, but now his temper had done him in. He could no longer be part of the planned attacks. Instead of an asset, he had become a liability.

Cutting off communication with him would be dangerous. The young man would be more than disappointed. He would be angry, and that would pose a risk of its own since he already had too much information, even if he only possessed a small piece of the larger picture. Likewise, telling him his lack of judgment required his removal from the mission might provoke the wrong response.

The Handler sat back, watching the video for the fourth time, staring at the image of the young man from Kazakhstan, knowing something would have to be done about him. He drank his black coffee, which had gone cold, then removed his glasses and rubbed his eyes.

There could be no loose ends.

CHAPTER EIGHT

Islamabad, Pakistan

With the array of other problems facing Pakistan, natural disasters provide an all too frequent complication. Dealing with political unrest, poverty, tribal wars, terrorist influences, and international conflicts is all put on hold when an earthquake hits. The latest measured at 7.6 on the Richter scale and caused damage in both Islamabad and its sister city of Rawalpindi. People were killed, buildings destroyed, utility lines downed, and roads blocked.

Just days after it struck, an international symposium of specialists was organized to address the issues these eruptions cause. While nothing can prevent a seismic event, there are obvious concerns about the long-term consequences. The potential for subterranean instability cannot be underestimated, including the compromise of building foundations and possible fissures in underground gas and water pipes. The damage that might result is almost beyond measure in densely populated areas, and so a group of scientists from around the world agreed to attend the conference in the hope of advising the locals on how to proceed. It was also an opportunity to conduct a first-hand study of the disaster that had just occurred.

Three American scientists from California were among those participating. On their arrival they were taken from the airport by helicopter, which set down on a paved surface in Rawalpindi, not far from one of the hardest hit areas. First responders were still on site, along with Red Cross workers, members of the Pakistani army, and other supporting rescue crews. Men and women were leading trained dogs through the rubble, hoping to locate anyone still alive beneath the debris. Some people were digging furiously with bare hands, their efforts accompanied by frequent wails of despair when dead bodies were discovered, or the occasional shout of joy when someone was found still breathing. Even as lives were being saved, the casualties were mounting.

Triage units were set up on stable sites, which were limited since the last of the tremors had caused a significant mudslide, further thwarting recovery efforts. Still, there was hope that some of those seriously injured could be saved.

As the three Americans emerged from the helicopter, they were overwhelmed by the chaos and carnage. Dr. Peter Reynaud was a well-known geologist. Dr. Ralph Schapiro was a geological engineer. Dr. Mark Finerman was a renowned seismologist. They were all members of the Cal Tech faculty, and all painfully familiar with the hazards of an unstable tectonic fault. As such, they would be among the stars of the seminar.

Their helicopter was quickly commandeered by a medical team who used it to remove several of the badly wounded. After the injured and the medical staff were on board, the chopper took off again.

Meanwhile, the three Americans set up their equipment. Their focus was not on the cause of the earthquake, which was well understood, or the tragic human results that immediately followed, which had been inevitable. They were there to address the stability of the structures that were still standing in the hope that no subsequent catastrophes would occur. They also wanted to determine whether the huge mudslides were caused by the quake or by some other shift, and what might come next.

They were exhausted after their flight from California and grateful for the chopper ride from the airport—traveling the damaged roads into the city by car would have added additional hours to the journey—but they took no time to rest and got right to work. They spent hours examining the site, taking readings, and inspecting some larger buildings and utility lines before they packed up and were driven to their hotel, where they would join the forum that evening.

At that first session, they were surprised when some of the questions from the audience turned to terrorism, and how latent damage to buildings, tunnels, and underground pipes might be exploited by those intent on wreaking additional havoc. None of the three American professors was schooled in such issues, nor were they interested in encouraging the notion of such possibilities. They did all they could to remain empirical, avoiding the political overtones raised by others.

After the second day at this summit, the Americans were invited to dinner by an esteemed local emir, named Kharoti, who had helped organize the hastily convened event. That evening, they were picked up at their hotel in a van and driven to the outskirts of Islamabad, a pleasant neighborhood that appeared unaffected by the recent earthquake. There, they were treated to a sumptuous dinner.

Their host was an elderly, bearded gentleman with a charming affect, an excellent command of English, and a seemingly insatiable curiosity about the United States. He asked about American politics and culture and wanted to know what his guests thought of the current world situation.

"Sad, that's what it is," Schapiro volunteered as he enjoyed the savory curry taste of his kheema. "With so many real problems we could all be solving, we spend endless resources on the military, both for defense and to engage in armed conflict."

Kharoti nodded. "When you say real problems—"

"Take the destruction we're here to study. Imagine the good that could be done, the repairs we could make, if the money being used to fight wars was devoted to repairing your city?"

"Ralph is right," Dr. Reynaud chimed in. "It's wrong that so many countries spend money building armies instead of taking care of a mess like this. Or attending to children around the world who die for want of clean water. Or food that could be provided. Or medicines that are available but not delivered."

"Then there's the issue of terrorism," Finerman said, careful not to offend their host by including any reference to his religion. "Yesterday, at the first seminar, it seemed people were more concerned about someone taking advantage of this situation than the natural risks they face. What kind of world have we created?"

Kharoti nodded his understanding, eyeing each of them in turn. "All you say is true. As for terrorism, it is tragic that my religion has been distorted, used to incite a few radicals to inflict pain and death on innocent souls. And for what? What is the result?"

Schapiro looked up from his dinner. "Exactly. What's the end game? Do they expect us to be so terrified we'll give up our own way of life and become Muslims? Is everything about murder and hate?"

His two friends looked at him, surprised at the outburst from the normally passive engineer. Reynaud, with a slight smile, asked, "Enjoying the local beer, Ralph?"

But Schapiro was undeterred. "It's just as the emir says. They kill innocent people, but what do they expect to accomplish from that, what's their demand? Do they want to force us all to become Muslims and agree to Sharia law? Do they really think that's the way to sell their religion to the rest of us?"

The other two scientists turned to the emir, concerned their associate had gone too far. But the old man slowly shook his head. "America suffered a great loss when New York was attacked on nine-eleven, but in this part of the world we live with that fear of death every day. I know it is difficult for you in the west to understand, but the fighting goes on here as a way of life. For you it is an occasional assault, which I do not mean to minimize. Every death, as they say, diminishes all of us. But look at my country, look at Indonesia, Syria, Afghanistan, Turkey. See how often and how brutally we are subjected to this violence."

"So, what's the solution?" Schapiro asked, as if this old man might have an answer.

"Compassion, my friend. Somehow, we must find the common ground on which to stand together."

They all nodded, as if something profound had been agreed upon, then returned to the damage the Americans had come to inspect and advise upon.

A couple of hours later, as they said good night outside the door to his home, Kharoti thanked them for coming.

"We are so grateful to have met you," Reynaud told him. "And for your hospitality."

"The gratitude is all mine," the old man assured them.

As they walked towards the waiting van, they took no notice of the fact that it was a different vehicle. It was the same make, same color, but there was no hotel logo on the door. Climbing in the back, they were greeted by two masked men, who displayed the business ends of their automatic rifles.

"Say nothing if you want to live," one of the gunmen said.

Fear trumped reason, and Schapiro began to ask, "Why—," but the utterance of that mere syllable resulted in the second gunman lashing out with the back of his hand across his face, then screaming "Silence!"

They drove off, the three scientists looked out the window as if they might find help there, but all they saw was the old emir smiling and waving goodbye.

As if reading their minds, the second gunman said, "You have no hope but to do what we tell you. No one will know where we are taking you. There will be no rescue. You will each agree to do as we say, or you will all die right here, right now."

CHAPTER NINE

New York City

That night, Nick Reagan arrived back in the apartment he kept in New York City, located on East 55th Street. Unlike the rustic home he maintained near the northern shore of the Chesapeake, his place in Manhattan was decorated in contemporary style, a simple refuge in his chaotic life.

It had two bedrooms, one of which was set up as an office; a comfortable dining area he almost never used; and a living room furnished with a large, black leather sectional and Barcelona chairs, also in black leather, with chrome supports. The walls were adorned with framed l'affiche posters.

After pouring a bourbon, Reagan lowered himself onto the sofa and switched on the large monitor that dominated the facing wall. The news broadcast provided background noise he largely ignored as he considered his next move about the intel being gathered. After finishing the drink, he switched off the television and headed inside, pleased to be spending a few hours in his own bed.

He woke early the next morning, had a strenuous workout at the local gym, showered and dressed, then called Erin David.

Erin was one of the Agency's top analysts and Reagan's on-again, off-again lover. Though he had many other brief affairs, he rationalized them as a natural part of his emotional makeup, those hours of passion and release a counterpoint to the tension and danger with which he endlessly lived. But there was no one he loved the way he loved Erin, no woman to whom he felt closer, and in a different world, in a different profession, he figured they would be married with children by now. But this was *his* world, where danger trumped desire, even if she had assured him more than once that she was willing to share those risks.

Erin also topped the short list of people Reagan trusted, which meant she knew his personal history and understood why he held others at arm's length—losing both his father and mother at a young age was obviously traumatic, leaving him wary of getting close to anyone or expressing his feelings. She understood how a brilliant young man with opportunities to pursue a career in politics, law, or diplomacy had instead become an assassin dedicated to protecting his country. Once he followed his father's path in the military, he became forever committed to the fights that needed to be fought.

Erin was familiar with the pivotal events in that evolution, including his military tour in Afghanistan, when his unit was betrayed with lethal consequences. One of the locals, upon whom he had come to rely, and to whom he provided protection from the local warlords, was recruited by an al-Qaeda handler. One evening, when Reagan's squad was on a reconnaissance mission in Kabul, they were all but wiped out by recently planted IED's and a well-orchestrated ambush.

Only Chris Weber and Reagan survived the attack, and they went after the young man who helped to arrange the massacre. The fact that they found and arrested him was less than fully satisfying, since it turned out the traitor did not know the true identity of the man who had planned the assault. Reagan and Weber were consumed with the need to find whoever that was, and to exact the penalty they felt was due—but they had no success with that, and things only became worse when the new administration took power. The president and his advisors tragically bungled an embarrassing withdrawal from Afghanistan, leaving the country to the Taliban and their al-Qaeda associates—one of whom, Reagan felt sure, had been behind the attack on his men.

Receiving his call that morning, Erin asked, "Where have you been?" Then she laughed. "Or is that the wrong question?"

"Right question, wrong timing." Then Reagan said, "I need to see you."

"Chained to my desk, as usual. Come on down."

"Be there in half an hour."

"Anything you want to tell me so I can do some prep?"

"We're having dinner Saturday night. You have enough time to prepare for that?"

Erin laughed. "Not what I meant."

"The chatter about current threats," he said. "And whatever you can get me on Anatole Mindlovitch."

"Interesting," she replied, then hung up.

Thirty minutes later he arrived at her office. It was in one of the nondescript workspaces the Agency maintained in midtown, set in a typical New York skyscraper, all glass and steel and concrete. The majority of the building was occupied by stockbrokers, lawyers, accounting firms, and other businesses. No one there, not even the security staff, knew that the two floors rented to Spectral Advisors was actually home to more than three dozen CIA analysts and their support staff.

Erin greeted him in the reception area on the twenty-third floor and led him to a small conference room down the hall. Once they were alone in the room, they shared a warm hug.

She was dressed in black crepe pants and an ivory-colored silk blouse with long sleeves and French cuffs. She was tall and slender, her devotion to yoga and jogging keeping her firm and fit. She was sexy in an understated way, with no need to flaunt her obvious good looks. Her makeup was minimal but effective, highlighting her soft hazel eyes and full lips, and her straight, light brown hair was cut fashionably short, as always.

He took her by the shoulders and held her at arm's length for a moment, then said, "You look beautiful. And the top you're wearing is just one more open button away from a complete distraction."

Erin smiled one of her indulgent smiles. "You obviously want something from me, Nicholas."

He preferred to be called Nick, by everyone except Erin. He loved it when she called him Nicholas, even when she did it because she was upset with him.

"I always want something from you," he said, "but for this morning, let's stick to business."

She had already placed two files and her laptop on the round conference table. Romance aside, when they worked together it was serious.

"So, what's your interest in our friend Anatole?" she asked as they sat down. "He has so many things going on, I need a little more direction than just his name."

"Let's talk about microchips," Reagan replied.

"Ah, yes," she said, then opened the file.

Mindlovitch was born in Russia, educated in London and the United States, then returned to Moscow where he parlayed his father's wealth from the oil industry into a far-reaching business enterprise that won him both admiration and envy from the most powerful people in the new Russia. He had once been a member of Vladimir Putin's inner circle, but he ultimately became too successful—Putin was not inclined to share the spotlight with anyone—which led to Anatole's decision to relocate somewhere outside his homeland. He left for California, settling in Silicon Valley, not far from where he had attended graduate school at Stanford. Having fallen out of favor with Putin, his move to America was seen as both a defection and a personal betrayal.

Meanwhile, the growing breadth of his business interests was impressive. He had begun in the communications sector, then branched out into other areas, including sources of environmentally friendly power such as solar and wind. He bought up large tracts of real estate in California, invested in apartment buildings in New York City, and, as Reagan already knew, owned one of the world's largest microchip factories, in China.

"So, your interest is his factory in Suzhou."

"Precisely."

"What about it?" Erin asked.

"You're familiar with the Ghost Chip?"

Erin nodded. "Supposed to render a smart phone or computer totally hack-proof and untraceable. Can also be programmed to admit a signal to remotely detonate explosives and even cause the device to explode in the user's hand. So far, it's nothing more than an urban legend."

"May be closer to reality than you think."

"Mindlovitch has people working on it?"

"That's the rumor. I paid a visit to his factory, posing as a prospective customer for their standard chips, but all I got was the cook's tour. I figured they would be proud to show off their research and development department, but I never got so much as a sniff."

Erin shook her head. "Fear of corporate espionage runs pretty high in China."

"Weber mentioned that, but I factored it into the equation. I didn't expect them to describe any of their pending projects, just wanted a quick look inside the lab." Reagan shook his head. "When it didn't happen, I finally asked about R and D, but it was nothing doing."

Erin thought it over. "If anyone can develop that technology, Mindlovitch is certainly a candidate. Some of his countrymen call him the Russian Steve Jobs."

"There's a stretch," Reagan said with a grin. "But let's assume the chip is real. Why would he be doing the work in China? Why not someplace closer to home where he could keep an eye on the progress and monitor security?"

"Labor is certainly cheaper over there, and maybe it's also easier to keep a lid on things. Let's face it, he employs a lot of Chinese in that factory and the size of the operation is a feather in Beijing's economic hat. He might be counting on their cooperation."

"That's possible. I had a run-in with the local authorities after I got back to Shanghai. My guess is that they were being very protective of that factory."

"So now what?"

"I want everything you have on Mindlovitch. Thought I would pay him a visit, have a polite chat. See if he blinks."

"From what I read about him, he's not the blinking type. Did Kenny give this the thumbs-up?"

"Not exactly."

Erin's knowing smile seemed to make her soft eyes sparkle. "What *exactly* does 'not exactly' mean?"

"He told me not to go."

She laughed. "Well you're right then, that doesn't exactly sound like a thumbs-up to me."

Reagan tried to look innocent but failed.

"You're going to see Mindlovitch anyway."

"On my own time."

"What am I going to do with you, Nicholas?"

"I've got several great answers to that. First, can you help me with this?"

She frowned. "Let's talk about the current threats first. Then I'll see what I can do for you about Mindlovitch."

CHAPTER TEN

Dearborn, Michigan

There was a world of difference between the men who were integral parts of the Handler's well-organized network and those he referred to as his "recruits."

The men he trusted were seasoned operatives, committed to *jihad*, and loyal to a cause rather than any one man. They could not be considered an inner circle, since many did not know who the others were, and only a handful knew the Handler's identity. Most lived in their native countries, some in Europe and the Far East, a select few deeply imbedded in the United States. These were not suicide bombers or unstable extremists. They saw themselves as soldiers in the army of Allah, prepared to take whatever actions were necessary to advance their reign of terror as and when instructed.

The recruits, on the other hand, were expendable assets who would carry out the various plans of death and destruction coordinated by the Handler. They were chosen from various circumstances, but, in the end, their basic personality profiles were almost always the same. Disenfranchised loners; young men who did not fit in; losers looking for something that would make them feel important and provide them a sense of belonging, no matter how deranged the purpose of the brotherhood they were invited to join.

To the Handler, they were disposable lives.

The process of enlisting these misfits was similar to the seduction of a lonely, insecure woman. Start by building confidence, instilling trust, and replacing a negative self-image with the assurance of value and desirability. Flatter them, offer them companionship to replace their loneliness.

After that, the recruit would be ready for indoctrination into the cause. They would be told about the unlimited fellowship they would enjoy with like-minded people. They would be enlightened in the ways faith would fill the void within them, and how they would benefit from serving God as well as their new comrades. Their lives would be enriched in a manner they never imagined.

Death, and its true meaning, would come later.

Finding these candidates was simple. Almost all of them had first been identified from visits they made to websites extolling the virtues of Islam and slamming Western values that mocked their religion. They felt trapped within a culture they blamed for their inability to succeed, finding solace in chatrooms on the dark web and blogs in the digital netherworld that was run by those they believed to be dissidents with similar views.

Enemies of Islam, such as the American intelligence services, made attempts to infiltrate these networks. They would create false profiles, visiting the sites and posting inflammatory, anti-Western rants in the hope of being tapped as possible *jihadists*, but these counterfeit insurgents were too easily weeded out.

Contrary to the notion that terrorists are disorganized, the Handler's people conducted detailed background checks of all potential recruits—such as Yousef, the young man in Dearborn. They had dug deep into his personal history, after which he was approached in a most indirect way. One casual meeting led to the next, where they discussed his life, his views, and his aspirations.

After that, they watched him and monitored his emails and texts for several weeks before engaging him in a more pointed conversation.

The Handler was still seated at his desk, shaking his head as he viewed the video of the latest altercation in Dearborn one more time. A great deal of time and effort had been devoted to Yousef's selection and training. His failure to follow instructions came as a great disappointment. He had been ordered to keep a low profile, to all but disappear until he had further instructions. Now he was there on the screen for all the world to see, and, as the Handler well knew, this was just the sort of thing the Americans looked for.

Federal authorities would vet every one of the young men involved in the attack on the Christians who had come to preach in Dearborn that day, and Yousef would certainly be placed on their watch list.

His fate was sealed. The Handler had no choice.

He assigned the task to two of his men from Chicago, Ahmed and Talal, part of the team assigned to Yousef, although the young man had never met them. Ahmed worked part-time in a car repair shop, and the Handler had sent him a coded text early that morning, a benign looking message from a burner phone that said, *Time to change the oil*. Ahmed immediately headed to pick up Talal, and they drove together to Dearborn.

* * *

YOUSEF WAS UNEMPLOYED, LIVING in the basement of his parents' small home. That morning he received a coded text instruction from the Handler, telling him to stay where he was and await further word, which would come soon. It was almost noon by the time the two men from Chicago arrived in Dearborn, and Yousef was still in his small bedroom, sitting at his computer, waiting.

Ahmed drove past the house and parked two streets away. Talal then sent a message, telling Yousef where they were and inviting him to join them for the midday prayer at one of the mosques in town. Yousef promptly left the house, walked the two blocks to where the two men waited, and got in the back of their sedan.

The two older men greeted him warmly. They all exchanged praises for Allah as Ahmed pulled away from the curb and headed into the center of town.

They rode in silence, Yousef knowing better than to ask any questions. Although he still had few details about his role in what was to come, he stifled his curiosity, excited that this meeting might signal a start to the action.

Ahmed reached one of the larger mosques but drove past for several blocks, then turned to the left where he pulled into a parking lot behind a small building. There were no other cars in sight. Yousef continued to resist his urge to ask these men anything as the three of them got out of the car. Ahmed took out a key, unlocked the metal door to the building, and held it open as Talal led Yousef inside. Ahmed followed, locking the door behind him.

The space was a vacant office with a glass wall looking out onto an empty area that once had housed some sort of manufacturing operation. The room had a table, a few chairs, and a metal bookcase off to the right that held a number of loose-leaf binders and papers, stacked in a haphazard manner. Light filtered in through the dirty windows up near the high ceiling of the room.

"Sit," he told Yousef.

The young man did as he was told, choosing one of the chairs beside the table in the center of the room. The two older men remained standing.

Ahmed was tall, thickly built. He had a serious demeanor, and his dark eyes bore an intimidating look. "We are here to ask you a question," he said. "It is a simple question, and we expect you to answer truthfully."

Yousef stared up at him. When he was summoned this morning, he assumed this meeting was being arranged to provide him information about his sacred mission. Why else would these men have come to see him? Up to this moment, his contact with the man he knew only as Mahdi had been limited to coded messages and brief phone calls. Now two of his men had come to speak with him in person. He wanted to believe this was an indication of his importance, a show of respect, but Ahmed's appearance and tone told a different story.

Yousef nodded. "Of course," he said. "I will only speak the truth to you, praise Allah."

Ahmed's voice became even sterner as he asked, "Who have you told about your assignment?"

Yousef began shaking his head. "No one, never. No one."

"We have reason to believe otherwise. We are told you have been bragging about your role in *jihad*," Ahmed said. It was a lie, but he stated it with the certainty of a fact intended to force the young man into betraying himself.

"No, *sidi*," Yousef protested, using a term of respect. "That is not true."

"Are you calling me a liar?"

Fear now mixed with confusion as Yousef said, "No, no. I only meant that whoever would say such a thing is lying to *you*. Who would say such a thing?"

"You are not here to ask questions, you are here to answer them."

Yousef waited.

"Who you have spoken to about your assignment?"

Ahmed's gaze bore down on him with such ferocity that Yousef was forced to look away. "Only a friend at the mosque," he finally admitted in a weak voice.

Ahmed and Talal exchanged a quick glance. The Handler was right about this young man. He could not be trusted.

"Which friend," Ahmed demanded.

"Please, do not ask me. I told him so little—"

"Only to make yourself feel so big," Talal interrupted. "Pride is a sin of the weak."

Yousef turned to face Ahmed again. "Yes, but it was my sin, not his."

"His name," Ahmed shouted at him.

Yousef had no choice. "Fariq," he replied in a hoarse whisper.

"In your mosque."

"Yes."

"What does this Fariq look like? Where does he live, and where does he work?"

Yousef answered their questions.

"Who else have you told?"

"No one. I swear on my life, only Fariq. And I told him so very little," he said again.

For a moment no one spoke. Then Ahmed asked, "Why did you disobey Mahdi's orders? Why did you become involved in that fight with the Christians at the festival of Allah?"

So, that is why they have come, Yousef told himself. "I can explain," he said. "They were defiling our God. I was standing up for the honor of Islam."

"That was not your decision to make. You should have left that to others."

Yousef nodded slowly. "I am sorry if I have done the wrong thing."

He was watching Ahmed and did not see as Talal moved behind him. In one sudden, vicious movement, Talal grabbed the young man by the hair, yanked his head back and drew the sharp edge of a long knife across Yousef's throat. The slash had been so expertly made that it was over in an instant. There was no scream, no time for any reaction except a sickening gurgle as the young man choked to death on his own blood. Talal let go of the partially severed head, and Yousef slumped to the floor.

"Get the things from the trunk," Ahmed said. "We need to clean up here and find this boy Fariq."

CHAPTER ELEVEN

New York City

Reagan spent the rest of the morning with Erin, going over the data on the current threats, as Deputy Director Kenny had ordered.

"Bottom line," she said, "we're looking at the possibility of home-grown fanatics being recruited by al-Qaeda."

"That's what the DD wants me to focus on."

"Without stepping on any toes," Erin reminded him, "such as the FBI, DHS, and the rest of our friends who actually have domestic jurisdiction."

"Would I ever?"

She laughed, then put down the file she had been holding. "On a completely different topic, have you been following Bob's series?"

Bob Nelson and Nick Reagan had been close friends for years. It was an unusual alliance, Reagan a clandestine operative and Nelson a feature editor for the *National Review*. Somehow, they made it work, and along the way Nelson and his wife became close with Erin. In fact, the Nelsons had long encouraged their relationship, but as Reagan explained, "I love her too much to marry her."

Nelson had recently been writing a series on terrorism, examining the distinctions between ISIS and al-Qaeda, and the shifting nature of the dangers each posed in their attacks around the world. The articles were especially critical of the al-Qaeda leadership, describing how they had been routed from their positions in Iraq, Syria, and elsewhere in the Middle East after seizing large areas of land, including oil wells

58

and other assets. Nelson argued that they had been chased from their stronghold due to inept leadership and the superior might of US led coalition forces. Now, however, both groups had been empowered by the Taliban takeover of Afghanistan after the American retreat.

"Of course I've been reading the series," Reagan told her. "Good stuff."

"Incredibly current, too. Someone is feeding him information not generally available to the public, if you catch my drift."

"There were definitely some interesting factoids."

"Any idea who's leaking that information to him?" she asked, her eyebrows rising a bit.

Reagan sat back, doing his best to appear offended. "You think I would do that?"

"To be honest, I don't, but I have to ask."

"Bob and I drew that line in the sand years ago. He knows better than to ask, and I would never play that game."

"Well then, whether the information is coming from our side or theirs, I'm a bit worried about him. He's writing about some dangerous people."

"I'll take another look at the articles, then maybe we can have a chat with him."

Erin hesitated before saying, "Speaking of writing, I heard your memo has been passed around."

"Kenny mentioned that. Do I have a problem?"

"Let's just say it got some traction in the ranks."

"How far into the ranks?"

"Not sure. I just wondered if you were frustrated enough to say something about *that* to Bob."

Reagan held up his hand. "Scout's honor. Never said a word. That paper was intended for Kenny and a few other people on the fifth floor."

Erin tilted her head slightly to the side as she said, "Kenny mentioned it when we spoke the other day. I think he was trying to see if you said anything to me about it."

"And?"

"I told him the truth. Then he asked me to keep it to myself."

"When two people know something, it's not a secret anymore."

"Seems I've heard that someplace before," Erin said. "Especially true in Washington."

"All right, let's get back to our pal Anatole. If you're really helpful, maybe I'll buy you lunch."

"Lunch today and dinner Saturday? Be still my heart."

Reagan smiled. "Lunch is lunch. Dinner has other implications."

Erin went to work on her computer, looking into the work Mindlovitch was doing, the identity of his closest associates, and the details of his lifestyle. As they examined the intersecting lines of his life, they came up with the name of Bruce Levi, a criminology professor at Stanford University specializing in profiling terrorists. He was said to be a close friend and confidant of Mindlovitch, dating back to the Russian's days at the college. He was also someone Erin happened to know well. She had introduced Reagan to him at a conference a couple of years ago, and Reagan found Levi to be both intelligent and well-informed.

After completing their research, Reagan took Erin to Lattanzi, on the West Side. It was a red brick-walled restaurant with linen on the tables, a professional staff, and classic Italian food. Before their appetizers were served, she called Levi's cell.

"Erin, how good to hear from you," Levi said. "It's been a long time. Still fighting the good fight for Uncle Sam or have you opted for a big paycheck in the corporate world?"

Erin laughed her charming laugh, which rendered most men incapable of refusing her anything. "I'm still an underpaid, underappreciated civil servant."

"I'm guessing that might have something to do with that young man of yours on the operational side of things."

Levi was more accurate than she cared to admit. Over the past few years, she had any number of headhunters make attractive offers, trying to lure her into the private sector, but her refusal to leave the agency was about more than her loyalty to the job. "How goes it for you in academia? That's certainly not making you rich."

"It certainly is not, but my consulting work does more than the bills. Otherwise, it's the same old thing. Preparing young men and women to confront the horrors of the criminal mind."

"We can use all the help we can get."

"I'm sorry to say you caught me as I'm just about to start a seminar. Can I get back to you?"

"Sure, but if you have thirty seconds, I'll tell you why I'm calling."

"Shoot."

"Awful choice of words for someone in your line of work."

Levi chuckled.

"You referred to Nicholas Reagan. He needs a favor."

"I'm listening."

"He wants to meet with Anatole Mindlovitch."

The line went quiet. Then Levi asked, "Is this an official visit of some sort?"

"Quite unofficial."

"Subject matter?"

"National security."

"An unofficial visit about national security. I'll take that under advisement."

"Can you arrange it?"

"Let me make a call, I'll get back to you."

Levi knew enough about what Erin did—and by extension, what Reagan did—to realize that if she was making the request it must be important. There were any number of people and governmental agencies interested in Mindlovitch, but this was different.

When he called, Levi was not surprised to find his friend reluctant to grant the interview.

"What good has speaking with anyone in government ever done me?" the Russian asked.

"This is strictly unofficial, Anatole. I have the sense that if you don't see him, the next step is going to be uncomfortably formal."

"Bah! That's how these things always start. A cordial chat, maybe a nice dinner, then a subpoena. Or worse."

"Take the meeting," Levi urged him.

Mindlovitch thought it over. "Only if you're there," he said.

CHAPTER TWELVE

Dearborn, Michigan

Ahmed and Talal placed Yousef's corpse in the heavy-duty plastic bag Talal had brought in from the car, then used bleach to clean up the blood stains on the floor. After confirming the parking lot was still deserted, Ahmed backed the sedan up to the door, making it easy for them to lift the large bag and drop it in the trunk. Talal slammed the lid shut, locked the building door, and they drove off.

Dealing with Yousef's friend Fariq was an unexpected complication.

Picking up Yousef had been carefully orchestrated, with little or no chance of them being seen or identified later. Locating Fariq and luring him to a private location would be another matter. They could not make inquiries in his neighborhood or try to find him at the mosque, there would be too many possible witnesses to describe them after the young man disappeared. There were already going to be enough questions about Yousef vanishing. They needed to act discreetly, get done, and head back to Chicago.

Their first move was to park across the street from the address Yousef had given as his friend's home. It was a four-story apartment building, and although there was activity on the street, they were not concerned about their car being spotted. Ahmed had taken it from a body shop, around the corner from the garage where he worked. Then he switched out the license plates, and once they were done here, the car would be disposed of, along with the two bodies in the trunk.

At the moment, however, they were a body short.

They waited in the hope of spotting Fariq, based on the information Yousef had provided. The description was so vague it could probably describe 50 percent of the Arab men in Dearborn between the ages of twenty and thirty, so they had to be patient.

* * *

MEANWHILE, AS THE HANDLER waited for word that they had completed their assignment, he was tending to another matter—arming the two men in Manhattan who would carry out the first part of his plan.

There are numerous types of explosive devices and materials, from professional grade C-4 plastique to improvised bombs made of household products. For this mission, the Handler was very specific about the type of chemicals to be used.

Incendiary ordnances are designed to start fires that destroy property and injure people. They are made from materials such as napalm, thermite, magnesium powder, chlorine trifluoride, or white phosphorus. Though often referred to as bombs, they are not explosives in the traditional sense. They are intended to promote slower chemical reactions, using ignition rather than detonation to start and maintain their lethal effect. Napalm for example, is petroleum thickened with chemicals that create a gel that will slow, but not stop, combustion. The destructive energy is released over a much longer time than a volatile substance such as dynamite. Napalm gel adheres to surfaces, such as skin and clothing, resists suppression, and therefore maximizes the damage.

The device to be used for this mission would be a combination of explosives and the sort of material that would cause *Death by Fire*. That was what the Handler intended for this first attack—the same way he lost his wife and child when American led forces unleased an air assault in Aleppo. The United States claimed afterward that they had been targeting Assad's forces, but scores of civilians had perished in the flames, including the Handler's family.

Now he would have his revenge. He was arranging to get the appropriate materials to Mustafa and Roshan—the two young men who had never met and never would, at least not until they entered Jannah—and they would be the instruments of his retribution.

The components would be assembled in Dearborn, an unfortunate geographical issue, but a fact with which he would have to deal. The best expert he had in the States was hiding in plain sight, in the middle of the Muslim community which protected their own. He could be counted on to create the devices.

Since Ahmed and Talal were already in Michigan, he decided to use them to transport the finished products to New York, something he had not yet told them—and would not, until they had successfully dealt with their new issue. They reported to him what Yousef had admitted—that he had told this other boy, Fariq, something of his plans. Now he would have to wait until this was dealt with.

Unfortunately, time was becoming a factor.

* * *

AHMED HAD DRIVEN AWAY from their parking spot across from Fariq's building twice, once to visit a service station for gas, to buy some food, and to use the rest room. The second time he left for fifteen minutes because he felt they had been in the same place for too long. Now, back in position, just before five o'clock in the afternoon, they saw a young man, fitting the description Yousef had given them, walking down the street towards the building.

"Could be," Talal said, reading his partner's thoughts.

"Find out," Ahmed said.

Talal was neither as large nor as threatening in appearance as Ahmed. He got out of the car and crossed the street, reaching the front of the building just as the young man approached. He stepped forward and said, "Fariq?"

The young man stopped. Looking Talal up and down, he said, "Who wants to know?"

"A friend of Yousef's," Talal said.

"That right?"

"He needs your help," Talal told him.

Even in the safety of his own neighborhood, even confronted by a man of similar ethnic background, the young man was cautious. "What does that mean?"

"The incident with the Christian infidels," Talal said, as if that were enough.

"What about it?"

"We are here to help."

"Why would Yousef need help?"

"Come with me, to meet Yousef. All will be clear."

Fariq took a small step back. "You're with the group Yousef is working with?"

"That's right. Say no more out here on the street. Just come with me."

Skepticism gave way to curiosity. "Where is he?"

"We are meeting near the mosque. Come."

But Fariq was not so easily persuaded. "Let me call Yousef first," he said, pulling the phone from his pocket.

Talal felt himself begin to tense up, knowing he had already been standing out in the open for too long. He said, "He will not be able to use his phone, he is in the mosque."

But Fariq took a step back. "You said we were meeting *near* our mosque."

Talal opened his jacket, giving the young man a glimpse of the gun perched in his waistband. "You must come with me now." Then he stepped forward and grabbed him by the arm.

His eyes on the weapon, Talal's hand still holding him, Fariq was pulled across the street and into the back of the sedan. Talal climbed in after him, his pistol now in hand.

No introductions were made. The three men remained silent as Ahmed drove to the same warehouse where they had murdered Yousef.

Neither Ahmed nor Talal was happy about returning to the same place, but they had no other viable option. They did not want to kill Fariq in the car, so they took the young man inside the building and yanked the door closed behind them.

As Talal pointed his revolver at Fariq's face, Ahmed demanded, "What did Yousef tell you about us?"

Fariq's eyes widened as he stared at the barrel of the gun. "What?" was all he could bring himself to say.

"Answer me," Ahmed growled.

Fariq turned to Talal, then back to Ahmed. "He told me he was going to work for the jihad." His voice quavered as he fixated on the weapon aimed at the center of his forehead. "He said he had been selected by Mahdi to honor God."

Talal and Ahmed exchanged a quick look at the mention of the Handler's code name.

"What details did he give you?"

"None, I swear it. He said he did not know any details yet."

"You're lying."

"I am not. That was all he said."

Ahmed nodded. "And who did *you* tell?"

"No one."

"Are you sure?"

"On my life," the young man said.

"Yes, on your life," Talal told him. Then he pulled the trigger.

CHAPTER THIRTEEN

CIA Headquarters, Langley

Brian Kenny was in his office with Carol Gellos, watching the television monitor mounted on the wall. It was yet another news report on the three missing scientists in Islamabad, including excerpts from a satellite video. It showed the three men standing outside a large home, then entering a van which drove off into the night. After a fast-forward, there was an image of a second van, the one from their hotel they should have used. These images were followed by clips from the translated interview with the imam, the Pakistani who had hosted their dinner. He claimed to be confused and astonished by what had occurred. He said he never got a look at the driver of the first vehicle. Another view of the satellite feed showed him standing near the side of the van that took them away, waving at his guests as the van pulled away, then turning back to his home.

"They didn't even ask him who knew about the dinner," Gellos said.

With obvious disgust, Kenny turned to her and said, "I'm sure the local authorities made all the appropriate inquiries."

"Satellite reports show the van that took them from the house entered and exited two different indoor garages on its way back into the city."

"So I was told," Kenny said. "Anything could have happened in those garages, probably moved them into a second and third vehicle. Maybe even split them up. After that, tracking in the city became impossible via satellite, especially with the mess the earthquake created."

Gellos agreed. "By the time anyone figured out they were missing, it was too late."

Carol Gellos was tall and lean with short sandy-colored hair, dark brown eyes, and a serious attitude. Kenny's top female operative, she had taken an unusual route to reach that standing. After a troubled high school experience, she dropped out of college in the middle of her second year and joined the Army. It soon became evident that her difficult childhood had masked a keen intellect and a determination to succeed. Her commanding officer saw to it that she completed her education, and she soon rose through the ranks of the Intelligence Division. Several years ago she was recruited by the Agency, quickly advancing to her current status as a clandestine field agent. She had since worked on numerous missions with Nick Reagan, proving herself a fearless and trustworthy partner. And all business.

A British news correspondent in Islamabad came on the screen, and Kenny returned his attention to the monitor. "What now?" he asked as he used the remote to turn up the sound.

The reporter voiced some of the same concerns that Gellos and Kenny had been discussing, but there were no answers. The man finished by posing the most obvious questions—who had taken the three men, where had they gone, and why had no ransom demand been made?

"I have another one to ask," Gellos said. "Why abduct three men who were there to help the local authorities?"

"And why put themselves in that position to start with," Kenny said, still staring at the screen. "God help us from the do-gooders." He switched off the television and turned back to her. "We have no idea what this is about. Our people on the ground are getting nowhere. No calls or emails we can track, no rumors, not a thing."

Gellos nodded.

"I've considered sending you and Reagan there, but based on the priorities from the White House, we may have an even more immediate need for your attention here."

Gellos sat up a little straighter as her boss opened a file on the desk. "Is this about a possible attack in New York?"

Kenny nodded. "The chatter we're intercepting seems unmistakable."

"Any idea of the target?"

"NSA thinks it'll be some sort of gathering place in New York."

"A stadium? Times Square? Central Park?"

"Those are some of the thoughts. The more people you can harm the better, right?" Kenny shook his head. "After the conference I spoke with Fitzgibbon and a couple of his people at the FBI. They're coordinating an upgraded alert level with the NYPD."

"Type of weapon?"

"Nothing on that yet. Could be anything from a suicide bomb to an IED, although there have been references to fire."

"As in firing a gun, or setting a fire?"

Kenny shook his head. "Not clear."

"What can I do to help?"

"I want you up there with Reagan. This is obviously not our jurisdiction, so you'll have to tread lightly, but Reagan has some good police contacts in New York, and the two of you have friends in the Bureau there."

"We do."

"Maybe you can help piece something together."

"Yes, sir."

Gellos stood. "What about the situation in Islamabad?"

"Our station chief in Pakistan is my next call."

* * *

As KENNY AND GELLOS wondered about the fate of those scientists, the three men from California were sitting at a large table in an underground bunker in Islamabad. They were being interviewed by a well-spoken Pakistani, and, to their surprise, the questions being asked had nothing to do with politics, the United States, or the reason they had attended the symposium. The inquiry centered on their respective areas of expertise.

The interrogator was flanked by two men, each of whom was taking notes on everything the three academics said. Behind them stood two armed guards.

"Tell me," the Pakistani said, his tone sounding more like polite dinner conversation than a forced interrogation. "After an earthquake, how would you determine the integrity of the foundation of the buildings in the area. When I say buildings, I obviously mean structures of real height, several stories high."

The three men from California looked at one another. Then the engineer, Ralph Schapiro, spoke up. "It would depend, of course, on the severity of the quake. The more serious the shift, the greater the danger."

The inquisitor waved off the response. "Obviously. Let us assume it is an incident of seven or more on the Richter scale. What would you do?"

"I would begin with test borings," Schapiro said. "There are also sonic devices to determine whether there are serious cracks in the foundations."

Dr. Reynaud, the geologist in the group, said, "What you're asking is highly subjective. It's not just the magnitude of the earthquake that's important. We would also need to know the nature of the tectonic shift and the depth and design of the building's foundation. Are there underground rooms? Pilings? You'd also need to know the composition of the ground. Is it sandy or is it bedrock? That sort of thing."

The Pakistani thoughtfully. "What about underground utility lines?"

Again, the three academics exchanged glances. Reynaud finally said, "That's usually the first concern after a seismic shift. Gas lines, oil lines, water lines. The dangers are obvious."

"What of a man-made event?" the man asked.

"Excuse me?"

"What if it's not a natural disaster? What if major utility lines failed, how would that affect the foundation of a large building?"

"What do you mean *failed*? Do you mean some sort of fissure or leak?"

The man chose his next words carefully. "Let's consider something more traumatic. Say, an explosion that results in a leak in a major gas line."

The three scientists stared at him without speaking.

"Gentlemen, I assure you this inquiry is going to become increasingly specific, and if you expect to leave here alive, you're going to answer all of my questions, regardless of the values or concerns you ascribe to them."

This time, when the three scientists shared a look, the fear in their eyes was evident.

CHAPTER FOURTEEN

Palo Alto, California

Not wanting to discuss his trip west with the deputy director—who had already made his feelings clear—Reagan flew commercial. After landing and retrieving the Walther PPK he had cleared through JFK with his federal documents, he took a cab directly from the airport to the Mindlovitch compound in Palo Alto. He was greeted there by two security checkpoints. The first was at the walled perimeter, where he was required to give up his sidearm—to his amusement he was provided a formal receipt, as if they were expecting a string of armed people stopping by to visit that morning. He was met by the second team in the palm-tree lined courtyard, and he patiently waited while his identification was again thoroughly reviewed, and he was frisked a second time. Only then was he shown into the house.

Reagan had visited any number of spectacular estates, including palaces in Europe and the Middle East, but this was different, a modern-day Xanadu. The press had covered the incredible amenities when it was being built—swimming pools indoor and out, a media room that looked massive enough to host the Oscars, a workout facility the Green Bay Packers could use, and a heliport on the roof that had been the cause of controversy and complaint among his wealthy neighbors. But whatever was described in those news reports was nothing compared to the experience of entering this marble and granite fortress.

He followed two of the guards down a long, art-lined corridor until they reached the double doors that opened into an enormous library. The ceiling was twenty feet high, and the walls were lined with oak bookcases filled with books from top to bottom. Reagan found Mindlovitch and Levi standing near the center of the room.

Levi was short, portly, and wore rimless glasses, more suitable to his role as a college professor than his consulting work as a terrorist hunter.

"Hello, Bruce," Reagan said. "Good to see you again."

Levi smiled as they shook hands, then introduced Reagan to their host.

Reagan stood just over six feet tall, and Mindlovitch had him by several inches. In his late forties, the Russian was known to keep his trim, long limbed physique in top physical shape. He befriended a variety of professional athletes, especially American basketball players, and kept a team of personal trainers on call. The result of all that work was apparent.

His features were plain, his complexion clear, his sandy-colored hair thin and cut short. He was neither handsome nor homely, but his eyes were much like his former comrade Putin's—a killer's eyes. When he spoke he wasted neither time nor energy.

"Welcome," he said. "Bruce is a good friend. When he asked for this meeting I could not refuse."

"I appreciate that," Reagan told him. "It's not every day I get to meet a genius."

Mindlovitch waved off the compliment. "It's not every day I willingly permit a government agent into my home."

Reagan laughed. "*American* government," he said. "From everything I've read about you, that should be an important distinction."

Anatole Mindlovitch allowed himself a slight smile. "A reasonable point," he said, then pointed at a chair to his left. "Have a seat."

As the three men sat, Reagan noticed that the two sentries who had brought him into the room remained standing at the door, legs slightly spread, arms akimbo, combat ready positions. "They going to be part of this discussion?" Reagan asked, nodding his head in their direction. "Not sure they have your clearance for what I want to discuss." When Mindlovitch hesitated, Reagan said, "They've searched me down to my underwear, I think you should feel reasonably safe in having a private discussion."

Mindlovitch stared at Reagan for a moment, then broke into amiable laughter. Without looking at his aides, he said, "You men can wait outside," then waited for them to leave the room and shut the door behind them. "Bruce told me you're a direct man. Not always a pleasant trait, but it certainly saves time."

"It's why I gave up my job in the hospitality industry to work for Uncle Sam."

Mindlovitch smiled. "And why has Uncle Sam sent you to see me?"

"He hasn't. I'm here on my own. I thought Bruce explained that."

"Given my experience with governments, yours and others, I never take such nuances seriously." He had a good look at Reagan. "So, why have *you* asked to see me?"

"I'm here to discuss the Ghost Chip."

Any hint of humor was gone from his expression as Mindlovitch nodded slowly, making it clear this was expected. "You were at my factory in Suzhou."

"I was," Reagan admitted.

"Surveillance photos were sent here. When Bruce asked me to meet with you, I had you vetted. An easy match."

"Well done."

Mindlovitch responded with a look that told Reagan two things— first, the man knew his business, and second, he knew what was at stake in protecting his research.

"You went to the trouble of traveling all the way to China, and now you're here."

"Sources tell me you're working on the chip in Suzhou."

Mindlovitch nodded. "What if I am?"

"To start with, I'd like to know if it's true."

"Why would I be inclined to tell you?"

"Because national security is at stake."

"I thought you were here on an unofficial basis."

"I am, but I don't check my loyalties at the door."

Levi said, "I'm only here as a friendly observer, but could one of you tell me about this Ghost Chip?"

Reagan gave a short explanation of the rumored technology. Then he said, "It would be disastrous if terrorists got their hands on it."

Levi nodded slowly. "There would be no GPS, no way to even triangulate the phone's location?"

"In addition, as I've described," Reagan said, "it could be an instrument of death and serious damage. You can appreciate the risks."

"I certainly can." Levi agreed.

"You're making some rather bold assumptions," Mindlovitch interrupted. "First, that the chip exists, second, that my company has the technology, and third, assuming those two things are true, that someone could take it from us."

"Let's jump to number three," Reagan said. "I admit, I found security at the Suzhou plant to be tight, but no place is impenetrable. And there's no way of knowing if there are spies within your ranks. It is China, after all. The technology could be priceless to the right buyer, which means the price of treachery would be high."

"Unlimited access to money buys unlimited access," Mindlovitch said.

Reagan nodded. "As to whether the chip already exists and whether you have it, well, that's what I'm here to find out."

"And again, I ask why I would be motivated to share that with you, a total stranger who admittedly works for the federal government."

Reagan leaned forward and fixed him with a serious look. "Given what might be at stake, my government can help protect you and the research."

Mindlovitch responded with a thin-lipped smile. "Or steal it. Or attempt to confiscate it through some convoluted legal process."

Reagan sat up a bit straighter. "So, that's why your research and development is being done in China. I wondered about that."

Mindlovitch said nothing.

"You feel safer with their government than ours?"

"Let's just say the PRC deals with immigration and terrorism quite differently than you do in this country."

Reagan grinned. "And I thought you left Putin's Russia because you disliked the totalitarian way of life."

"Not true, Mr. Reagan. Life under a dictator can be extremely rewarding, provided you remain on the leader's good side. Unfortunately, once a shift in favor occurs, well, I'm sure you can fill in the blanks."

Reagan looked to Levi, then back at Mindlovitch. "I don't mean to offend, but that sounds like a morality of convenience."

Mindlovitch gave no hint he was offended. In fact, he appeared to think it over. "Not in my personal dealings, no," he finally replied. "I think you will find that the people who know me best regard me as loyal and honest, a man with integrity who will nevertheless push for what he wants, including the last kopek on the table. When it comes to the geopolitical stage, that is another matter. In that arena, a convenient morality is often synonymous with self-preservation."

"Hence the security teams you maintain at this citadel."

Mindlovitch shrugged without responding.

"So, what happens when you have the Ghost Chip—which, by your refusal to answer my questions about is answer enough. If you don't have it already, you must be close."

Mindlovitch remained silent.

"When the Chinese realize you've developed that technology, don't you think they're going to want in?"

"If it exists, you can assume I have made appropriate arrangements to protect my property." He smiled his thin smile again. "You see, Mr. Reagan, as a young Russian I was tutored in chess. There were some in the federation who even thought I possessed championship potential, but I had other aspirations. Invention, wealth, technology, these were the things that interested me. But the education I received in the game of kings taught me to always think several moves ahead."

"I see."

"I'm not sure you do. There are many reasons the Chinese want me to continue my operation in Suzhou. As you saw, I employ hundreds of their people in the manufacture of conventional microchips. In addition, and without apology for my vanity, an Anatole Mindlovitch facility in China is good for their prestige. They know full well I could relocate at any time on nothing more than a whim, so they are motivated to keep me happy. If at some point they expect me to share information with them, I will deal with it then."

"That's not exactly planning your moves ahead," Reagan said.

Mindlovitch did not reply.

"What about the idea of sharing information with your host country here?"

Mindlovitch looked to Levi and smiled. "A direct man, as observed." Turning back to Reagan, he said, "As with the Chinese, your country is also pleased to have a relationship with me. My companies employ thousands, and we pay our share of your exorbitant American taxes. I feel my contribution to the United States is already quite enough. Furthermore, as you probably know, my philanthropies are designed to help people in distress, not greedy governments." With that he stood. "I believe you have received the answers you came for."

Reagan got to his feet, saying, "No details, no timing, no indication of what you intend to do with the device once you have it?"

"Are you concerned I might sell it to the highest bidder?" Mindlovitch shook his head. "No, Mr. Reagan. If I were to own such technology, I would patent it, keep exclusive manufacturing rights, and make it available to legitimate users."

"Do you consider ISIS a legitimate user? Al-Qaeda? Your old friends in the Kremlin?"

Mindlovitch stared at him without responding. Then, as he made a move to show him to the door, Reagan stopped and held up his hand.

"I'm in the security business," he told Mindlovitch. "There are all types of security. My job is to ensure the safety of the people in this country. I can't ignore what damage the development of this sort of microchip might do."

Mindlovitch crossed his arms, taking a moment to consider his response. "I respect that. You, on the other hand, must respect that a scientist must follow the path his explorations lead."

"That sounds like more rationalization. You're obviously brilliant when it comes to innovation, but I fear you may be ignoring the realities of the geopolitical stage, as you called it. Chess moves are great, until someone reaches across the table and hits you with a two by four."

"It's time for you to leave," Mindlovitch told him.

Reagan stood his ground. "You said something earlier I'd like you to think about. You said that unlimited access to money buys unlimited access, and I believe you're right. Just remember, that cuts both ways, and it only takes one traitor to breach an impenetrable fortress."

Then he turned and left.

Levi walked outside with him. In the courtyard, he said, "That was interesting. Anatole is not used to anyone speaking to him that way."

Reagan nodded. "He'll get over it."

"The chip you're concerned about—"

"It's a game changer. I have no idea how close you are to this guy, but someone needs to move his ego out of the way of his reason."

Levi nodded. "Something tells me he and I are going to have a follow up discussion about this."

"Good. Maybe you can talk some sense into him. Even if the Chinese don't come for the chip, he's still got to worry about his old friend Putin. Not to mention someone on the inside selling it to—"

"You've made your point," Levi said. "How's Erin?"

"She's wonderful."

"She also working on this issue?"

"She is."

Levi took a moment, then said, "I've got to be in D.C. in the next several days, could make it sooner than later. After I speak with him, I'll get back to you."

"I understand who Mindlovitch is," Reagan said, "but this is not just one of his new gadgets we're dealing with. We need to know what he's up to, and we need to know as soon as possible."

CHAPTER FIFTEEN

New York City

Reagan returned to New York, convinced that Anatole Mindlovitch was not only developing the microchip in China, but that he was close to getting it done. He had promised to take Erin to dinner that night, where he would have shared his concerns with her, but his plans changed when he received an invitation from an old colleague.

Yevgeny Durov was a former KGB agent. Like his friend Vladimir Putin, Durov had enough political acumen, feral shrewdness, and a knack for self-preservation to make a successful transition from his position of influence in the Soviet Union to a position of power in the new Russia.

Durov and Reagan first crossed paths years before at a diplomatic function—an ironic setting for two clandestine operatives to meet. Several months after that, they found their interests aligned during a skirmish in Kabul, and a friendship was forged, as it only can be in the fire of battle. A few years later, Durov provided help spiriting Reagan out of Aleppo after an unpleasant encounter obliged the CIA agent to leave the bodies of several terrorists in his wake.

When Durov called, he suggested they meet at Del Posto, a tiny Italian restaurant on the West Side of Manhattan. Beautifully appointed, it provided enough space between the tables to offer the privacy they would want for their discussion.

Durov was a tall, burly man somewhere in his late sixties. His physique betrayed his love for good food and drink, while his avuncular style belied the cold-blooded assassin he could be if the need arose. Nevertheless, his eyes rarely relinquished their look of cynical amusement—he was, above all things, a pragmatist with a healthy perspective on how lucky he was to still be alive.

Already at a quiet table in the corner when Reagan arrived, he rose from his seat, his face breaking into a warm smile. They had not seen each other since a dinner in London, more than a year ago, and Reagan noticed there were a few more wrinkles around his friend's wide mouth and across his prominent forehead. Still, Durov's affable smile was the same, his gray hair full and combed straight back, and, all in all, he looked healthy. He was wearing a pale blue shirt left open at the collar with a dark sport coat, and Reagan found himself wondering what size jacket was required to cover the expanse of the man.

"Good to see you," Reagan said as Durov wrapped him a bear hug.

"You too." Taking a step back, Durov had a look at Reagan, who was dressed in a light gray cashmere polo sweater, dark gray slacks, and a navy blazer. "Don't you ever wear anything that isn't dark?" Durov asked with a chuckle. "You think this costume makes you less conspicuous?"

Reagan smiled. "I'm just trying to blend in with all my ex-KGB pals." As they sat, Reagan had a look around the dining room. "You picked a nice place, as usual."

"Of course. Whenever your government pays, I choose the best."

"Seems to me I picked up a rather large check at our last meeting."

"It was Wilton's, my friend, of course it was expensive. And who could possibly forget the caviar?" Narrowing his eyes, he added, "Or the help I provided to earn the pleasure of that dinner."

"I thought friends don't keep score."

Durov uttered a throaty chuckle. "You're the one who brought up the bill."

Reagan smiled. "Fair enough. So, what are you drinking?"

Durov looked fondly at his martini glass. "Stolichnaya Elite, shaken as cold as they could make it."

"One of my favorites. No olives?"

"Why pollute perfection?" He lifted his glass. "Have one."

"I will," Reagan said as their waiter came by. "Two more of the same," he told the man.

"I'm not even done yet," Durov protested with absolutely no conviction.

"You will be by the time mine gets here." When the waiter walked off, Reagan asked, "What brings you to our fair city?"

Durov squinted, then raised the eyebrow above his right eye and stared at Reagan. It was a look he had perfected over many years. "How did you like Suzhou?"

"Ah, right to the heart of the matter. What happened to your usual repartee, the fun banter you're so good at?"

"We'll have time for that later. I thought it best to lay some of our cards on the table first."

"All right, let's start with Suzhou." Reagan picked up his napkin and spread it across his lap. "One of those small Chinese towns, population roughly three million, give or take a few highly trained scientists. Not much in the way of tourist attractions unless factories are your thing."

"Yes, I understand they make a lot of knitwear and silk there. Noted for the apparel business, am I right?"

"You are."

"Not to mention the manufacture of microchips that power more than half the smart phones coming out of the PRC," Durov said, then polished off the rest of his vodka.

"It seems you've been reading the Suzhou guidebook."

"Let's just say certain information about the subject has been passed on to me."

"What did you say about laying our cards on the table, Yevgeny?"

"I said *some* of our cards."

Reagan laughed. "I think you meant some of yours and all of mine."

The waiter returned with two frosty vodkas and a couple of menus. Durov told him they would be a while before ordering dinner, and the man went away.

"Here's to friendship," Reagan said as he lifted his glass.

The Russian hoisted his fresh drink. "To friendship."

They each had a taste and placed their glasses on the table.

"Did you find what you were looking for over there?" Durov asked.

"Not exactly."

"The Chinese were obviously convinced you did."

"You heard about my detour on the way home?"

"Indeed. It may interest you to know that I personally ensured the situation was being carefully monitored."

"Meaning what?"

"Meaning, if you had not managed to extricate yourself as artfully as you did, I would have reached out to your people through back channels and alerted them to your predicament. Couldn't have the Chinese secret police removing one of my favorite dinner companions."

Even if Reagan did not believe Durov had tracked him in real time, it was clear the Russian knew he had been detained in Shanghai and that he had managed to escape. "My guardian angel," he said.

"Think of me more as an interested spectator," Durov said. Then, after a slight pause, he asked, "Did you confirm the existence of what your people call the Ghost Chip?"

"I did not."

"But then you saw the need to visit my old friend Anatole Mindlovitch."

"You really *are* keeping an eye on me."

"It has become a very small world, Nikolai." He drank some more of the vodka. "What did Anatole have to say for himself?"

Reagan shrugged. "As they say in the media, he would neither confirm nor deny."

"But you believe he is developing this technology."

"Maybe. If he does, I'll be sure to get myself one of those phones, make it tougher for you to keep tabs on me."

Durov responded with a sad smile. "Whatever impact it has on conventional espionage, the effect on global terrorism may be cataclysmic."

Reagan did not disagree.

"It's one thing for nations to track the comings and goings of operatives from other countries, but the exigencies of our global realpolitik can still be civilized. These radicals, the very idea of them becoming invisible to our surveillance, the notion is chilling. Add this device to the equation...." He stopped and shook his head.

"That's an interesting analysis coming from you, since Moscow still supports a genocidal maniac in Damascus."

"Again, there are exigencies that cannot be denied."

"Such as the Russian military base you maintain in Syria, and how that protects your western flank."

"Keep in mind, our support of Assad also helps with the struggle against al-Qaeda and ISIS."

Reagan let out a sigh. "Ever the pragmatist, never the ideologue."

Durov smiled. "I take that as a great compliment."

Reagan had another taste of his drink. "This dinner is about the Ghost Chip?"

"That's part of it, although I knew the answer before you got here. We don't believe Mindlovitch has the technology yet, but we believe his people are getting close. When he has it, which he will, we will want access as soon as possible."

"Not to use it," Reagan said, "but to figure out how to get around it."

"Correct."

"All right, you say that's only part of the reason we're here. What else brings us together this fine evening, other than the opportunity for me to buy you another expensive dinner?"

"Let's order before we get to the other topics. I don't want to discuss any more of this on an empty stomach."

As they made their way through a sumptuous dinner of antipasto, tagliolini Bolognese, and veal marsala, Durov addressed the other subjects on his agenda. One was the increasing threat of terrorist assaults on their respective countries.

"The potential for chemical attacks, they're frightening to me. Trucks filled with explosives, suicide bombers, random shootings, naturally all of that is disturbing," Durov said as he dipped some crusty Italian bread into the marsala and mushroom sauce. "Chemicals though, that's something to lose sleep over."

"You once told me you never lose sleep over anything."

"I'm getting older, my young friend." Then, after a slight pause and without a hint of irony, he said, "I miss the good old days."

"The good old days?"

"The Cold War, when we all spied on each other, politicians made empty threats about their global power to impress their constituents, but we all knew who the enemy was and how to keep the peace. No one slaughtered civilians or set off nuclear bombs or anything close to that." Durov shook his leonine head.

"That may be a slightly idealized version of history, my friend. You're leaving out Vietnam, Laos, and any number of genocidal dictators."

"All true, but your country, my country, the other major powers—we knew how to maintain a delicate balance. Now we have a bunch of lunatics running around, blowing up innocent people, driving trucks onto crowded sidewalks, shooting at children. What has the world become?"

"I wish I had an answer, and I understand your concern about chemical attacks," Reagan said. "But what about nuclear devices available on the black market?"

"Easier to track and identify. Nerve wracking, surely, but despite your Hollywood movies, no one is going to create a suitcase nuke at their kitchen table. Lethal chemicals are another story entirely."

Reagan placed his fork on the plate, sat back, and crossed his arms. "You're dancing around something here, how about we get to the point?"

Durov studied him for a moment, his lips pursed, his look thoughtful. "Your friend Nelson," he said.

"You want to talk about Bob?"

"I know the two of you are close."

"We are."

"Which is the only reason I come to you with this."

"Come to me with what?"

Now Durov stopped eating, which Reagan recognized as an acknowledgment of how serious he was about this next topic. "The series he has been writing on terrorism, including the things we've been discussing."

"I read the first three installments. I think it's quite good."

"I agree. Too good, in fact."

"Meaning what?"

"His information is detailed and accurate and dangerous."

"For whom?"

"For him," Durov said, then went back to the bread basket.

"Dangerous how?"

"He obviously has some well-placed sources. Not just inside your government, but inside the al-Qaeda network. He may be creating a problem for himself."

Reagan waited.

"He has been extremely critical of al-Qaeda leadership, particularly our nemesis al-Zawahiri. I will not say he has mocked him, your friend is a serious journalist, and that is not his style. But he's painted a detailed portrait of Zawahiri as an incompetent, blood-thirsty fool.

Someone with no military acumen or leadership qualities. A lunatic who remains in control only by instilling fear in those around him."

"All true."

"Nelson has also provided names and incidents to back up his claims. Surely you must see how this will play out. He is provoking this maniac into launching an attack, and our intelligence suggests it may involve chemicals. Remember, these people slaughtered the staff of a third-rate magazine in Paris simply because they published an uncomplimentary cartoon of Mohammed. In Nelson's case, they will do whatever is necessary to retaliate against his criticism. Then," Durov said, looking up from his plate, "they will come after him and force him to divulge his sources."

"You have intel that suggests they're making a move to take him?"

"I do not, but I believe he is flying too close to the flame," Durov told him. "If you care about his safety, you need to rein him in." Apparently feeling he had said enough, the Russian went back to eating.

"You make a convincing argument," Reagan admitted, "but I'm curious why you're so concerned about my friend, or an attack on my country."

"Let us just call it a courtesy to you, in exchange for which you will host another dinner sometime soon."

"We'll see about that."

Durov fixed Reagan with a serious stare. "Consider this a word to the wise, as they say. Your friend is in real danger, Nikolai."

CHAPTER SIXTEEN

New York City

Having cancelled his dinner plans with Erin, Reagan picked her up late, took her for drinks in Tribeca, then brought her back to his apartment. It was barely dawn the following day, and they were still in bed together when Reagan received a call from Brian Kenny.

"Good morning, sir. I didn't think the message I sent you last night about my dinner with Durov would get you up this early."

"We'll talk about your Russian friend another time. I have a meeting at the White House at two, and I need an update on the current threat assessments."

"I'm on it."

"Get with Erin David as soon as you can, I'll have Gellos meet you at her office. I want a full report before noon."

Reagan signed off and turned to Erin.

"Kenny?" she asked.

Reagan leaned over and kissed her on the forehead. "The one and only. Seems he wants me to get in touch with you this morning."

"I'm all for it," she said, neither of them eager to give up their time together and face the day.

He took her in his arms, and they shared a long, passionate kiss. Then he said, "Gellos won't get to your office for a while.

"It's too early to go to work," she agreed.

Sliding back under the sheets, they spent the best part of the next hour lost in pleasure. Afterward, they were quiet, enjoying the moment of shared serenity.

The décor in his bedroom was as minimalist as the rest of his apartment. The walls were covered in a gray flannel material that gave a feeling of both warmth and peace, especially with the shades drawn against the light from the rising sun. The king-sized bed was made up with white linens and a pale gray duvet cover, and the night tables were black lacquer, each holding a porcelain lamp with dark green shade.

It was Reagan who finally said, "Time to get to your office."

She sat up, holding the sheet around her. "After your fancy dinner with Yevgeny last night, all I got was a couple of drinks."

Reagan smiled. "That's not all you got."

Erin responded with a narrow-eyed frown. "You're not even taking me to breakfast? A woman could waste away, hanging out with you."

"I promise, as soon as I—"

Before he could finish, she placed her finger across his lips. "We both know by now, it makes no sense for you to promise anything."

Reagan hung his head in mock surrender, then got up, took her by the hand, and led her to the bathroom. "We still don't have to rush out of here, do we?"

After an extended shower together, they took time toweling each other dry as Reagan provided the details of his discussion with Durov, especially the comments concerning Nelson.

"Seems we have similar concerns," she said, "and Durov knows more than he's saying."

"As usual. But the fact that he brought it up at all is reason enough for us to speak with Bob."

Erin hesitated before saying, "You know how Bob is about his journalistic integrity."

"I do know, but this is different. We're not asking who his source is—"

"We're warning him."

Reagan nodded as they finished getting dressed.

*   *   *

By nine, Reagan and Erin were in her midtown office, where Carol Gellos was already waiting for them.

Regardless of their professional partnership, Reagan did his best to keep his private life private from Gellos, and she did the same. Despite their many days and nights on assignments all over the world, they had never shared so much as a kiss. As far as he and her other fellow agents knew, Gellos was single, living alone in an apartment in Arlington that none of them had ever seen, and satisfied to live a cloistered life.

"Even for a spy, you are one secretive lady," Reagan had observed more than once.

Gellos would respond by staring at him without speaking, and that would be that.

Reagan was sometimes amused by the dynamic between his partner and Erin. These were two capable women, each occupying a critical place in his life. Although he and Gellos were all business, she was undeniably attractive, and they did spend considerable time together. Erin was not the jealous type, but she was in love with him and marked her territory carefully, so a hint of their competitive natures sometimes bared its claws.

The three of them were now seated in a small conference room on the twenty-third floor, the décor a blend of utilitarian furniture with high-tech computers and monitors. Gellos had brought a folder from Langley she placed on the table next to Erin's paperwork. "Doesn't contain much in the way of detail, but there seems little doubt the target is New York."

Reagan did not disagree. Turning to Erin, he said, "All we have is a lot of noise you need to help us with."

Erin nodded. "The references to a large meeting place and fire keep showing up in the messages NSA intercepted."

"Fire as in firing a weapon," Reagan asked, "or as in setting a fire?"

"That's what I asked Kenny," Gellos said.

"And we're still not clear," Erin admitted. "We're also coming up empty on the large meeting place."

"NSA picked up a recent text about rail lines," Gellos said, pointing to the folder.

Reagan blew out a lungful of air. "With all their chatter back and forth, you'd think we could grab some of the players."

Erin shook her head. "Everything is generated from burner phones, numbers ranging from Michigan to right here in Manhattan."

"There's got to be some way to triangulate the contact," Gellos said.

"Of course," Erin said, "but by the time we ping the sender and receiver, the phones have been trashed, and they've moved on."

"Let's start with Michigan," Gellos suggested. "Can you be more specific?"

Erin looked up from her screen and said to her, "Take a guess."

"How about Dearborn," Reagan said.

"Give that man an extra donut," Erin replied, still looking at Carol Gellos.

"Dearborn. That place is getting on my nerves," Reagan said.

"Welcome to the wonderful world of Sharia law," Gellos said.

"All of the attackers we could identify from that video the other day have been added to our watch list," Erin told them.

"Our endlessly growing watch list," Reagan said. "Any hits on their personal phones?"

Erin responded with a concerned look. "Not yet. I don't know if they're jamming the local signals in Dearborn or if there's some other issue."

Reagan shook his head, saying, "From what I've learned, there's no way they've gotten their hands on the Ghost Chip. Not yet."

"Let's hope not," Erin said.

Gellos said as she picked up her cell, "I just got an alert from a contact at the FBI, something about the Dearborn incident."

Erin turned to her computer. "I also got it here. A family in Dearborn reported their son missing, name of Yousef Omarov. Kazakhstan national. Left his home day before yesterday, never came back, and they haven't been able to reach him. They've asked the local authorities for help."

"Now there's some bitter irony for you," Reagan said.

"It gets more interesting," Erin said as she continued to read the message. "The police made the usual inquires, including calls to his friends. Turns out a second young man is also gone. Fariq Homsi, a Syrian immigrant, who just happens to be Omarov's best pal. He was seen getting into a car that afternoon, in front of his apartment building. Also hasn't been heard from since. Some neighbors said the car had been waiting there quite a while."

"Any information on the vehicle?" Reagan asked.

"Not according to this report," Erin told him. "Just a dark sedan, no one bothered to get a license plate."

"Or if they did, they're not telling anyone," Reagan said. "Any description of the driver?"

"Negative," Erin told him. "But hang on for the final piece. Both Omarov and Homsi were involved in that attack in Dearborn a few days ago, both prominently featured in the video which happens to be going viral."

"Now that *is* interesting," Reagan said.

"What do you make of it?" Gellos asked.

Reagan sat back. "What if these two are involved in whatever we're chasing? Maybe they've gone to ground, no contact with anyone because they're on their way to New York."

"Which would mean the action really *is* imminent," Gellos said. "Which squares with the DD's opinion."

"And seems consistent with the chatter," Erin said.

"Do we have any photos of these two," Reagan asked, "other than the video of the brawl they were involved in? Any identifying data about them, any goddamned information at all?"

"The FBI has already asked the local police for their cooperation," Erin said. "They're emailing the Bureau everything the parents gave them."

"FBI and the locals should put out a BOLO. Trains, planes, buses, toll booths," he said.

"They're already on it," Erin said.

"I'm going to make sure the DD has all of this before his meeting at the White House," Erin said, then stood and left them alone.

"What next?" Gellos asked.

"I suppose we should do our own checking with the Bureau and NYPD," Reagan said.

"You going to call your friend?" Gellos asked.

Reagan had received help on a prior mission from Rod Williams, a police lieutenant in Brooklyn assigned to narcotics. "Not his area of expertise, but he might be able to help grease the skids. And I just know he'll be thrilled to hear from me."

"Let's do it," Gellos said.

"You go ahead, I'll catch up with you. Kenny will have everything we can give him for now. I have a stop to make first."

CHAPTER SEVENTEEN

New York City

Carol Gellos headed downtown to the FBI office in Federal Plaza, while Reagan invited his friend Bob Nelson for a quick drink. Together with Erin, they met at one of their favorite spots, Esca, on West 43rd Street.

Nelson was a few years older than Reagan, nearly forty-four, a burly man with broad shoulders, a soft middle, and the slightly stooped posture of someone who spent too much time sitting at a desk. That said, he was a street reporter at heart, with a sharp intellect, a droll sense of humor, and an endlessly curious look in his pale blue eyes.

"Good to see you two together," Nelson said as they took their seats.

After glancing at Erin, Reagan said, "I wish this were a social call."

Nelson uttered a short, asthmatic laugh. "Oh boy, that doesn't sound good."

The expression on Erin's face told him it was not. "We need to speak with you about the articles you're writing."

"Ah," Nelson said as he pushed back some of his long, dark, unkempt hair. "Right down to business."

"We don't have much time," Reagan admitted. Then he added, "It's a great series."

"Thanks. Coming from you, that's high praise. No factual corrections?"

95

Reagan forced a smile. "None we can mention. But we do have some concerns."

"Fire away."

"Let's get some drinks first."

They ordered cocktails and spent just a few minutes to catch up on personal matters, including Nelson's wife Claudette, a French national he'd met on assignment years ago in Paris, and their son and daughter. They were served, and Reagan soon returned to the reason they were there.

"I'm not asking for your sources," he told Nelson, "but some of the details in your series border on classified information."

"You're telling me I'm in trouble with the authorities?"

"Quite the contrary. We're worried about the people on the other side of the equation."

"If you think I'm pissing off the boys in al-Qaeda, I regard that as a good thing."

Reagan and Erin exchanged another look. Then she said, "Whoever is feeding you this information is putting you in danger."

Nelson, who was about to have a taste of his scotch, set the glass back on the table. "I'm listening."

"These terrorists are never sure how much accurate data our government has on them, or where it's coming from. But some of the things you've written about could only originate from one of two sources. Either a leak from our side, or a traitor from theirs. If they believe it's the latter, you and your informant are in harm's way."

"Let's start with door number one, then. You both know there are all sorts of leaks that come out of Washington," Nelson said. "Disgruntled employees, people wanting to feel important, others who think it's their right to speak out."

Reagan nodded.

"You also know me well enough to know I would never cross the line. Free speech aside, I would never print anything I thought would be harmful to national security, regardless of the story."

"I know all that to be true."

"Whatever sources I've been using, you can be assured they're not from within our government."

"That's our concern," Reagan said, "which takes us to door number two. Our guess is your intel is coming from people inside their organization, and if that's the case, al-Qaeda is going to do whatever they can to silence them."

"And me," Nelson finished the thought.

"Precisely," Reagan said. "But there's another aspect to this. You've done a real hatchet job on their leader."

"Zawahiri? That's nothing new."

"Agreed," Reagan said, "except you've revealed details he's not going to be happy about. The incident where he flew into a rage and shot one of his lieutenants for simply disagreeing with him, as an example. Or the brutal way he treats novices at their training camps if they don't measure up. Those stories are too close to home."

"Too personal, is what you're saying."

"Not to mention," Erin added with a weak smile, "it may not help his recruiting efforts."

"I'm saying it's a dangerous game to play with a psychopath like Zawahiri," Reagan said. "He and his friends behead people for sport."

"Are you asking me to stop writing the series?"

Reagan sighed. "You know I would never do that, but you need to understand the risks."

Nelson finally picked up his glass and had a long pull of the whisky. Then he put it down, sat back, but said nothing.

Erin said, "You've been working with an al-Qaeda turncoat, haven't you?"

Nelson thought it over. "You know I can't answer that question, or any other questions that have to do with my sources."

Reagan fixed him with a stern look. "You're playing with fire, Bob."

"Story of my life, pal. We all make choices, and we all take chances. You more than anyone, right?"

Reagan shook his head. "How do you even know the intel you're getting is authentic? What possible means of fact-checking would you have?"

Nelson frowned. "I can't tell you that either, but you said yourself you don't have any corrections."

"I said there were none we could mention."

"Hey, if my facts were off why would the bad guys be concerned about me?"

Erin and Nick shared a frustrated look but said nothing.

"Let's get down to it," Nelson said. "You two are here because you think I'm in danger."

Reagan responded with a look that told him the answer was obvious. "Your source is anonymous, but you're not. There are people who are going to want to know who's feeding you the information."

"And they're not going to be as polite as you are in trying to find out."

Neither Erin nor Reagan answered.

"There's something else you're not telling me, Nick."

Reagan paused. "I have a friend, works for the Russian government. He knows all about our relationship, which should tell you his sources are good."

Nelson nodded.

"We had dinner, and one of the items on the menu was you. He believes you may already be in the crosshairs of the people you're writing about."

Nelson had another go at his scotch. Then he said, "I appreciate the concern, I really do. I'll do my best to duck when the shooting starts."

Reagan shook his head as he gave his friend one more disapproving look. "By the time you hear that first shot, it'll be too late."

CHAPTER EIGHTEEN

New York City

Reagan said goodbye to Erin and Nelson, leaving them to have lunch and, hopefully, to have her persuade their friend to watch his back. He picked up his old Land Rover and drove downtown to pick up Gellos. From Federal Plaza they headed over the Brooklyn Bridge.

"You called ahead?" Gellos asked.

"Only to be sure he was in."

"You didn't speak with him?"

Reagan laughed. "I was afraid he'd hide if he heard I was coming."

They entered the precinct in Brooklyn, showed their credentials to the desk officer, and were escorted upstairs to the narcotics division. They found Rod Williams in his office, the door bearing his name and new rank.

"Captain, eh?" Reagan said as they were ushered in by one of the detectives. "You get that promotion for helping me save the city?" Williams had worked with Reagan to prevent an attack on Wall Street a couple of years back.

The NYPD captain could not suppress a grin as he got up and came toward them. He stood a couple of inches under six feet, was thick around the middle with square shoulders and a confident look in his pale blue eyes. Pushing fifty, his full head of hair had already turned silver, his face showing the strain of a quarter century working a tough job in a tough city. "I believe it was in spite of you," he said as he shook Reagan's hand. "The brass probably felt sorry for me, after you almost got me killed."

Reagan laughed. "What an exaggeration."

Williams greeted Carol and invited them to sit as he returned to the chair behind his large metal desk. "I admit this unannounced visit is better than one of those distress calls I get from you at three in the morning, but I'm still guessing you didn't come by just to say hello."

"No," Reagan admitted. "We need your help."

Gellos got up and shut the door, then she and Reagan gave Williams a synopsis of the current threat level and what they needed him to do.

"These people never stop," Williams said.

"That's why we're here," Reagan said. "To stop them."

"You want me to act as your liaison with the terrorist task force, that the idea?"

"That's it. After our adventure together, I figure you know the players over there. I also suspect you're well regarded."

"At One PP? I guess so, but I'm not sure you need me. You flash those federal creds, and they're all supposed to genuflect."

"You know the drill. We're from Langley, which means we're a bit off the reservation far as jurisdiction is concerned. I don't have any direct contact in their unit, hoping you can vouch for us."

"Vouch for you?" Williams said with a brief laugh. "I'll vouch for Gellos. In your case I'll have to warn them you're a wild card."

"That's a start."

"What about the FBI?"

"Just stopped by and said hello," Gellos told him. "We have friends in the New York office and assured them we won't get in the way."

"Reagan? Not get in the way? That'll be the day." Williams turned serious as he asked, "What kind of timeline do you have on this threat?"

"Not sure," Reagan admitted, "but it could be soon." He then told him about the two young men who went missing in Dearborn.

"You think they're flying under the radar because they're on their way here."

"It's possible."

"That means you want to meet the boys at Police Plaza now."

"Right now," Reagan said.

* * *

THE MEETING WITH NEW YORK'S anti-terrorism unit went as predicted. There was a natural resentment toward the intrusion of federal agents, especially those with no real jurisdiction. However, as Reagan also anticipated, Williams was well-known and well-liked after his work two years ago. A couple of officers who were on the task force at the time remembered how Reagan allowed the NYPD to take full credit for the operation after the dust settled, something one of them mentioned as they sat in their large conference room to discuss the latest intelligence.

"Williams makes a better hero than I do," Reagan said with a grin.

"And secret agents don't," another of the officers said, "or whatever you two are."

"Spooks are not supposed to be seen *or* heard," someone else suggested with a laugh.

When the others turned to Gellos, there was obvious curiosity about the tall, attractive woman, but the no-nonsense look in her eyes put a lid on any of that before it began.

"All right," she said, "what have you guys got so far?"

"You show us yours we'll show you ours," said the senior officer, named Ben Jackson. He was a tall, square-jawed African American. His posture was ramrod straight, sitting or standing, and his demeanor was just as stiff. Reagan figured he was former military.

Gellos placed her file on the table. "Hottest lead we have right now has to do with two young men from Dearborn who've gone missing. Could be heading to New York." She spread out some photos and fact sheets as Jackson and his team had a look.

"You have more detail than we do," the commander said as he looked up. "What makes you think they're coming to New York?"

Gellos explained that the NSA had intercepted various communication suggesting a possible attack in the city. Then she described the scuffle in Dearborn and the video that had gone viral.

"We've seen it," Jackson said.

"Both of these suspects were in the middle of that fight," Gellos told them. "Now they're MIA, and even their families don't know where they are. Our people looked into everything we could find. Profilers say they're typical al-Qaeda recruits. Unemployed. True believers in the cause. Violent. And they happen to be best friends."

"There's a federal BOLO out for both," Reagan added. "You probably know that already."

Jackson nodded. "Watching bridges and tunnels, airports, bus stations, the usual drill."

"They may or may not be part of what's coming," Reagan said, "but they're worth trying to find."

"Agreed. You have anything on a location yet, anything about the nature of the attack?"

"Not much," Gellos said. "Our code breakers are working on it. The messages we've intercepted are brief. There are discussions of fire, something happening at a gathering place, a mention of rails. Nothing we can zero in on yet."

"Understood," Jackson said. "Any intel on who's running the show?"

"No, but that's the sonofabitch we want to find," Reagan told him.

CHAPTER NINETEEN

En route New York City

As Reagan and Gellos worked with the NYPD—trying to locate two young men none of them had any way of knowing were already dead—the Handler's henchmen, Ahmed and Talal, were traveling east on I-80, approaching New York City in a rented sedan.

Back in Michigan, Ahmed had disposed of the stolen car with the two corpses in the trunk. Waiting until dark, he had driven to a secluded lake north of Bloomfield, got out, and, putting the car in gear, watched it roll into the water. By the time it disappeared beneath the placid surface, it was as if it never existed at all. Then, using some fallen branches, he did what he could to clean the tire tracks in the mud and made his way through the dense woods where he would leave no footprints behind.

Talal was waiting for him in the car he rented using a counterfeit I.D. and credit card. He was careful to choose a vehicle that did not have Michigan license plates, searching through the lot until he found a Nissan with Ohio tags, as near as he could get to New York from what they had available there.

Together, they traveled back to Dearborn in the darkness, where they had one more piece of business to complete.

Heading straight to the address the Handler had provided, they found a small, ranch-style home. There were no lights on. Parking in the driveway, they walked around to the rear of the small house and knocked on the door.

A few moments later they were greeted by a short man in his late sixties with suspicious eyes and a stern manner.

"We were sent by Mahdi," Ahmed said.

The little man nodded and showed his visitors in.

They were led directly to the basement, where he maintained a makeshift laboratory. On the floor were two parcels, already packed and sealed.

"You must be careful with these," the man told them. "They have not been primed for detonation, but there is always danger in dealing with these materials."

Both Ahmed and Talal nodded.

The man then handed each of them a printed sheet from his work-table. "Two copies of the instructions, one for each device. If they are not followed to the letter, it could be disastrous."

"Understood," Ahmed told him.

"Where are you staying tonight?" the man asked, his tone making it clear they were not being invited to remain with him.

"A motel in Detroit."

"Good. You'll have no problem between here and there. Any difficulty you may have will come when you get close to New York."

"Understood," Talal replied.

"These packages are lined, and should not set off any detectors, not unless they're opened, or a bomb-sniffing dog gets up close."

"You're sure?" Ahmed asked.

With more of a sneer than a smile, the man said, "I have survived for this long doing what I do, and only by being sure."

"Good."

"Stay away from the tunnels. The authorities are always more careful at tunnel entrances than bridges. For obvious reasons."

Ahmed and Talal already knew their route to New York, which would not involve the Lincoln or Holland tunnels, but they said nothing.

"Any questions?"

Ahmed took a moment to study the sheet of instructions he had been given. "Once we deliver these packages, we will not be there for the assembly."

"The steps are clear enough, are they not?"

Ahmed and Talal had another look at the instructions.

"Clear enough," Ahmed agreed.

"Good. Now go."

* * *

HEADING ALONG THE INTERSTATE the following afternoon, Talal said, "I wish there was a better way to hide those parcels. Just sitting there in the trunk—" He didn't finish the thought.

"If they stop and search us," Ahmed said, "they'll find them, regardless of how well he packed them."

Talal frowned.

Fortunately for them, the authorities were not looking for two Arab men in their forties, they were searching for Yousef and Fariq, both in their early twenties, whose photos had been digitally circulated to every transportation hub and agency from Dearborn to New York. Thus far there was no record of either of those young men renting a car or purchasing airplane tickets, either in their own names or using false identification. For that reason, the main focus of the manhunt was now on buses, trains, and the possibility the two young men had stolen a vehicle—the reason the Handler insisted his men rent a car for this part of their mission.

When Ahmed finally reached the access road to the George Washington Bridge, it was late afternoon, and the traffic was building as it always did this time of day across the Hudson River. The congestion was heavy, and they had slowed to a crawl. Ahmed felt his hands growing sweaty as he gripped the steering wheel.

"*Allaena*," Talal cursed as they slowed to a stop.

They could see the large law enforcement presence, even this far from the toll plaza, and the closer they came to the bridge, the more trapped they felt. The number of law enforcement officers and vehicles along the access roads grew as they crept along.

Then they heard the rotors of a helicopter above them.

"*Allaena*," Talal said again.

"If they are going to stop us, it will not be with a helicopter," Ahmed told him.

They inched forward, one excruciating car length at a time, nearing the automatic toll booths ahead. There, they could see cars being stopped, drivers being questioned, and, worst of all, trunks being opened. There was no way to determine how the vehicles were being chosen for inspection. Could it be random selection? The type of car? The look of the people inside? From what little they could see, there did not seem to be any pattern. Some were large sedans, others were compacts, still others were SUVs.

Ahmed and Talal looked at each other but did not speak.

When they finally reached the informally arranged checkpoint, a uniformed officer held up his hand for them to stop, then approached on the driver's side. Ahmed lowered his window.

"Are we in the wrong lane officer?"

The cop shook his head. "Where you guys heading?"

"To work. Hunts Point," Ahmed said, referring to the busy market area in the Bronx, keeping to the script the Handler had given them.

The officer pointed to the license plate on the front of the sedan. "You from Ohio, working in the Bronx?"

Ahmed began shaking his head. "No, we live here in Jersey. My car is in the shop, this is a rental." He reached into the glovebox and began pulling out the papers. "No way else to get there from Cresskill."

"That's all right," the policeman said when he saw the rental agency logo on the top of the folded papers. Already bending down, he took a look at Talal. "You guys look like brothers."

Talal felt himself tense. He wanted to say something to this filthy pig. *Do we all look the same to you?* But before he could speak, he felt his companion slap him on the shoulder.

"This guy?" Ahmed said. "Hell no. Cousin is bad enough," he added with a forced laugh.

The officer was nodding slowly, still looking at Talal. He seemed about to ask something else when another cop, two lanes over, called out his name. He straightened up, slapped the hood of the car, said, "Drive safe," then turned and walked off.

They crossed the bridge, not saying a word until Talal finally broke the silence. "What if he'd read the rental contract? He would have seen we got the car in Michigan."

Ahmed did not disagree. "I had to do something. I hoped he was too busy to look through it. He saw the name of the rental company. That's why I didn't pull the papers all the way out, just enough for him to see that."

Talal said, "He was one question away from having us open the trunk."

Ahmed nodded. "But he did not, my brother. Allah is with us."

They continued east on the Cross-Bronx Expressway, headed north on the Major Deegan Expressway, and found their way to the Cross County Shopping Center, a large outdoor mall in the south-eastern corner of Yonkers. Ahmed parked the car, relieved to finally step outside, stretch his legs, and get something to eat. It was not until dark that he and Talal texted Mustafa Karahan.

Mustafa lived in a small apartment in the South Bronx. He was one of the two young men who had driven to Baltimore for their brief meetings with a man they called Mahdi.

Mustafa received the text from Talal on his burner phone, telling him that the messengers he had been waiting for would be arriving. At the appointed hour, he hurried to his old Toyota and drove to the parking lot adjacent to the Mosholu Golf Course, near the Jerome Park Reservoir. The lot was deserted at this time of the evening, and Mustafa stopped in the far end, turned off his lights, got out, and unlocked his trunk. Climbing back in his car, he waited for less than ten minutes when he saw another car approach. Killing its headlights, it drew close and stopped alongside him.

Talal got out of the car and stepped up to Mustafa's window. Bending down, he said, "Why are you here?"

It was the question the Handler recited when they met at the bar in Maryland. "I am here to do God's will," Mustafa replied.

"Good," Talal said. "Stay in your car. Is the trunk unlocked?"

"Yes, I opened it when I arrived."

Talal said nothing. He walked to the back of the rented Nissan, Ahmed popped the trunk, and Talal carefully lifted one of the two heavy packages. Carrying it to Mustafa's car, he placed it in the center of the trunk and then eased the lid closed. Then he returned to the driver's window and pulled one of the instruction sheets from his pocket. "Read this quickly and let me know if you have any questions."

"Must I memorize this, or may I keep it?"

"You may keep it."

Mustafa nodded, then quickly scanned the instructions, which included some hand-drawn diagrams. "I understand."

"Good," Talal said. "May God's blessing be with you," he said in Arabic.

"*Allahu Akbar*," the young man replied.

An hour later, Ahmed and Talal repeated the same procedure with the second young man recruited for this mission, Roshan al Ghamdi. This time they met in a lot near Van Cortlandt Park in the northwest section of the Bronx.

Once they had fulfilled their responsibilities, Ahmed texted the Handler one word, *Done*.

They abandoned their rental car at a metered spot on Broadway near 242nd Street, rode the subway into midtown Manhattan, made their way inside Penn Station, and boarded the late train to Chicago, leaving behind two young men with weapons and explosives engineered to butcher scores of innocent people.

CHAPTER TWENTY

New York City

Both Mustafa and Roshan lived alone, which was perfect for the Handler's purposes. Of all the traits required of his recruits, their unqualified belief they were outsiders in a hostile country was of primary importance. That was why he did what he could to ensure the people on the lowest echelon of his organization never met. He was not trying to create a spirit of camaraderie among them. He wanted to guaranty their sense of alienation. Loners who were unburdened by family, friends, or social conventions were his ideal candidates.

He wanted people willing to die for the cause, and the fewer reasons they had to live, the better.

As each of these two young men now sat in their dark, cramped apartments—Mustafa in the South Bronx, Roshan in the Kingsbridge section of that borough—they could work undisturbed, assembling the materiel they had received.

The Handler knew this was a critical time in the process, when these men faced the practical realities of what was to come. After all the hours of indoctrination and spiritual discussion, they now had to follow written instructions, attaching wires to the suicide vests they would wear. After so much preparation and all the coded messages and clandestine meetings, they were finally handling the explosives and loading the sidearms that would result in the deaths of countless people—including themselves.

These were the moments when doubt and fear would migrate from the subconscious into active thought. This was the time when the Handler had to risk regular contact with them, taking care to electronically scramble his location as he sent texts and emails to their burner phones.

He had to combat their nerves with calm reassurance. He would refer them to the Koran, not by name and not by quoting particular passages. He sent section numbers that referred them to their holy book, where they would be reminded of some key tenets of their faith:

8:12 terrorize and behead those who believe in scriptures other than the Koran

9:123 make war on the infidels living in your neighborhood

2:191 slay the unbelievers wherever you find them

8:60 Muslims must muster all weapons to terrorize the infidels

And many other similar exhortations.

The Handler would describe the beauty they would experience when they entered Jannah, where they would be celebrated in heaven for their courage and their devotion to Islam. He would discourage any expression of uncertainty, guilt, or anxiety. He would continue to tell them, as he had from the early moments of their recruitment, that they were doing something fine and noble, and that Allah would hold them to his bosom when they arrived in the promised land. He would also repeatedly condemn the infidels and the fate they had brought on themselves.

It was in those moments that the Handler experienced his own intense hatred of his enemies. Innocent people would suffer and die, and he was the instrument of that carnage, determined to wreak vengeance on the people he saw as responsible for deaths of his young wife and children years ago—not to mention all the misery his countrymen and fellow Muslims had endured over these many decades and centuries. He blamed the Israelis, the American Jews, and all the Christians who were complicit in these attacks on his people.

For now, as this first in a series of attacks was about to be launched, he sent another text to Mustafa and Roshan, stating simply *9:5.*

That section of the Koran reads in part: *When opportunity arises, kill the infidels wherever you find them.*

CHAPTER TWENTY-ONE

New York City

Reagan and Gellos stepped outside One Police Plaza and checked in with the deputy director. Sitting on a bench, Reagan used his encrypted cell phone to call the DD's private number.

Kenny had just returned from his meeting on Pennsylvania Avenue. He was with Alex Brandt, a recent addition to the team.

Four years at the University of Pennsylvania led Brandt to the Wharton School of Business, but when he found corporate life both boring and unfulfilling, he was recruited by the Agency. He was tall and athletically built, with light brown hair, dark blue eyes, and an incisive intelligence.

"Nothing new to add from here," Kenny told Reagan. "Any developments in New York?"

"Nothing," Reagan said.

Brandt said, "We've put together a spreadsheet with all of the keywords we've gathered. I'll text it to you now."

"That'd be good," Reagan said. "Still no sign of those two from Dearborn?"

"We've heard nothing," Kenny said.

"I'm beginning to wonder if there's not a different explanation for their disappearance," Reagan said.

"I've had the same thought," Kenny said.

"Maybe they were taken out of play for some reason. We may just be chasing our tails."

"There's been no sign of them anywhere, you may be right," Kenny said.

"I had another idea," Reagan said. "Some of these messages feel like they're too easy for us to decode. What I mean is, we intercept a lot of indecipherable texts, and then suddenly there's one that we can see right through."

"You think we're being manipulated."

"Not completely," Reagan admitted, "but maybe some of these exchanges are part of a misdirection play."

Kenny did not disagree, having learned through experience to trust Reagan's instincts, especially when he was in the field.

"If there's nothing else, we're going to head back inside, sir, we'll keep you posted on anything we hear."

"Before you go," the DD said, "I received an answer on that I.D. you asked about."

Reagan waited.

"She's MI6, as you suspected. And, for what it's worth, Amanda Whitson is her real name."

"I'm guessing she's assigned to their anti-terrorism unit."

"Correct. May have been there keeping an eye on you."

"MI6. Fascinating."

"You want me to make a polite inquiry?"

"Not yet," Reagan said, then signed off.

"Amanda Whitson?" Gellos asked. "Definitely sounds *veddy* British."

"Story for another day," Reagan told her.

They rejoined Williams and the NYPD task force, who were now assembled inside the nerve center of their operation. It was a large room that combined new-age technology with traditional police procedures. There were a dozen computer monitors, each manned by an officer or civilian operator. There were also two large screens on one wall and a transparent screen with virtual images on another. Off to the side stood a dry-erase board on an easel and a corkboard to which various images were pinned, including photos of the two missing young men from Dearborn.

After Gellos told them that Langley had nothing new to report, Reagan explained his concern about being played.

Personnel from the FBI had arrived, and the senior agent spoke up. "The leads indicate a gathering place near rails, and we've been working on the assumption it could be someplace like Grand Central or Penn Station. You suggesting they're not the likely targets?"

"Not sure," Reagan admitted. "There's just something about the way we're reading these messages that doesn't add up."

"Such as?"

"The word 'high,' appears several times. Those two stations have nothing but underground trains."

"Go on."

"If you put 'rails' and 'high' together, what do you get?"

"Elevated trains," Rod Williams said.

"That would be an obvious read," Reagan said. "Which could be anywhere in the five boroughs."

"You're right," the senior FBI agent admitted. "We've looked at that too."

"But what if the word 'rails' doesn't apply to trains?" Reagan asked.

"What else do you think it could mean?" the FBI agent asked.

"The monorail to JFK airport?" Williams suggested.

"It's a thought," Reagan agreed, "but there are other key words the NSA has picked up." He pulled a scrap of paper from his pocket with notes from his session with Erin that morning. "There are also references to an event. Then—and I admit this is a stretch—there are comments that seem to express concern about how the weather would affect their plans."

"Then we're back to an outdoor target," one of the NYPD officers said, "like the elevated trains all over the city."

"Maybe," Reagan said. "But if you're going to set off a bomb at a train station, even an outdoor station, why would you care about the weather?"

The group was quiet until Ben Jackson turned to Reagan. "What do your people in D.C. make of it?" he asked.

Reagan pulled out his phone. "They just texted me a list that pulls together a summary of the intercepted messages. Let's get it up on the screen for everyone to see."

The list was soon displayed on a large, transparent video monitor against the wall.

"Highlight the key words," Commander Jackson told one of his assistants.

"Which ones, sir?"

"Rails, New York, anything relating to height or something high, anything to do with outdoors or the weather."

In short order, all those words were in bold type and organized by category. The group moved closer to see what sense they could make of these disjointed clues.

After a few moments, Reagan said, "This is not about an indoor train station, gentlemen. What we've got is some sort of attack planned for an outdoor location where there are either elevated rails, or rails nearby. That ring a bell for anyone?"

***

ROSHAN AND MUSTAFA WERE DONE with their preparations. Each of them pulled on the vest loaded with incendiary explosives, secured it with the four clasps on the front, and placed an automatic hand-gun into the Velcro holster that was attached to the side. Then, as instructed, they put on a loose-fitting shirt, left it untucked, and covered that with a simple outer garment. Roshan opted for a blue sport coat that was larger than his normal size; Mustafa chose a light, tan zipper jacket.

The Handler had instructed them to arrange for a car service to take them into Manhattan, knowing the long subway ride would be too risky. Once the city was on alert, a young Arab man with a chest too bulky for his size would be easy to spot on a train. There was also the matter of the increasing tension each of them would feel, something that would be etched in their features as they rumbled from station to station, the train stopping and starting, their anxiety growing with every movement, every glance from a stranger—or worse—a transit officer or policeman. The safe play was a gypsy cab, with a driver who cared about nothing except the fare into New York.

At precisely the appointed time, 1:00 P.M., each of them stepped from his apartment for the last time, went out to the street, and climbed into the cars they had called for, which now waited to take them to Manhattan.

* * *

NOT ONLY WERE ROSHAN AND MUSTAFA unaware of the involvement of the other in this attack, but there was another man about whom they knew nothing, a man who would play a critical part in the operation. He was a Saudi, around fifty years of age, riding south on the East Side subway, wearing a bulky sweater that was a bit too large for him or the weather.

Just after 1:20 P.M., as Reagan and the others at Police Headquarters attempted to solve a puzzle with too many pieces missing, this third man reached the Grand Central stop. He got off the train and walked up the stairs toward the huge interior of the famed train station.

Moments later, pandemonium erupted.

It began when shrill warning sounds began to blast within the tiled walls of Grand Central, a piercing, reverberating sound that sent people running with no idea of what to do or where to go. Uniformed police and undercover agents from various federal and local agencies swung into action, ordering people to get on the ground and not move. Some obeyed while others still rushed for the exits, the screaming and hollering from the crowd drowned out by the continuing alarm blasts.

Meanwhile, several agents raced toward the Saudi as he reached the top of the stairs.

* * *

COMMANDER JACKSON RECEIVED the emergency call at One Police Plaza.

"Suspect in Grand Central," he was told. "The Geiger system there lit up like a Christmas tree."

Questions from the group came fast.

"What's the situation?"

"We've got a visual, securing the building and taking the suspect down now."

"Any sign of a device?"

"Negative."

"Only one perp?"

"So far."

"Get the bomb squad in there now. Order every available team to move," the commander said into the phone. "I'm on my way." He cut off the call and turned to the others.

"Someone in Grand Central just set off the radioactivity detector. Let's go."

Several in the group, including Reagan, Gellos, Williams, and the FBI agents in attendance, hurried out with Jackson. Downstairs they jumped into waiting cars and raced uptown, sirens blaring.

"What do you think?" Gellos asked Reagan in a whisper.

"I'm not buying it," he said.

* * *

IN GRAND CENTRAL, TWO OFFICERS had knocked the middle-aged Arab to the ground, shoving his face onto the tile floor, as another pulled his hands behind him.

"Hands are empty," the third officer told the others.

"He feels clean," another said as he roughly frisked the man.

"What is this?" the Arab demanded indignantly.

The officer who was cuffing his hands behind him, hollered, "Shut the hell up."

"Where is it?" the other cop demanded, leaning down so he was nose-to nose with the Arab.

"Where is what?" the Saudi asked in reply.

"Don't give me any bullshit," the officer growled at him. "Where's the device, and where's the trigger?"

"Device?" The man did his best to appear confused, but he was not convincing anyone.

The officer on the ground beside him, lowered his voice. "The nuke," he said. "Where is it?"

The Arab managed a smile. "Nuke? Ah, I see. My back pocket. There's a paper in my pocket."

* * *

REAGAN AND GELLOS WERE in the back seat of an unmarked car with Williams. NYPD Commander Jackson was up front with his driver. When the call came in, Jackson put it on speaker.

"Go," he ordered.

"Damn," they all heard an officer in Grand Central shout into the phone. "He had a paper in his pocket, says he has a heart condition, had a nuclear stress test this morning, he's radioactive for forty-eight hours. We had the Geiger system in GCP tuned for high-sensitivity, that's what set it off. You believe this shit?"

"No evidence of any sort of explosives, nothing?" the commander asked.

"Zero. Turned the bastard inside out."

"He alone?"

"Far as we can tell, but I swear, sir, the look on his face, the way the whole thing went down, I think he knew exactly what he was doing."

118

Reagan exchanged a quick look with Gellos and Williams.

The officer on the line said, "This place is a madhouse, sir, I'll keep you posted."

"Out," said Jackson.

With the call ended, the car was silent for a moment. Then Jackson said, "I've had a nuclear stress test myself, goddamnit. They warned me about the radioactivity, it's in the dye they use. They explained it could set off an alarm. They gave me that same kind of paper this guy had."

Reagan said, "He did it on purpose."

Jackson nodded slowly.

Reagan raised his eyebrows. "If he did, we know why. He has all your units already heading there."

"You're right," Jackson said through gritted teeth.

"Now we need to figure out where the attack is really coming," Reagan said.

CHAPTER TWENTY-TWO

New York City

Captain Jackson told his driver to pull over, then turned to face the rear of the car so he was looking directly at Reagan. "Go on."

"Of all those messages we intercepted, there's not one mention of anything nuclear. I think it's fair to say that would be prominently featured, even in code. Securing and setting off that sort of device is not as easy as people think, there'd have to be much more prep involved, a much higher level of expertise." Reagan paused. "Add to that, we've had no evidence of the movement of radioactive materials, especially not through any of the tunnels or across the bridges. My experience tells me this was a diversion, start to finish."

Jackson stared at him for a moment. "What do you suggest?"

"Not sure," Reagan said, "but I'm thinking we head west or south. This had to be about drawing your resources and attention to Grand Central."

"Agreed," the commander said. "So where are they going, Penn Station?"

"Maybe. Or downtown, one of the terminals between Manhattan and Jersey."

"What about the Port Authority?" Gellos suggested.

Jackson shook his head. "Mostly buses, not rails."

"But it has multiple levels," she said, "and some of the messages talked about elevation."

"Maybe it's not west or south," Rod Williams broke in. "Could be as straightforward as the elevated lines uptown, or even in the Bronx. Maybe near Hunts Point Market, that area is always crowded. Or right next to Yankee Stadium."

"I thought of the stadium earlier," Jackson said, "but they're not playing at home today."

"Citi Field?" Williams suggested.

But Reagan was shaking his head, his right hand in the air to stop them.

"What is it?" Jackson asked. "You thinking someplace uptown?"

"No, sir. I'm thinking the High Line."

"The High Line?"

"It just hit me. Elevated. Outdoors. Built over an old rail yard. They stage events there all the time. And it's far enough from Grand Central to make it worth pulling this misdirection play, which would mean that whatever is going down, it'll be going down right now."

None of the others spoke.

"Anyone have a better guess?" Reagan asked. "If not, send some units to Penn Station, but let's shoot to the west side. Any of your people in that area should get up on the walkway."

The commander did not hesitate. He gave his driver the order, then got on the radio to alert all units. "We're heading to the west side," he told them.

Reagan turned to Carol. "See if there's anything going on there today."

* * *

THERE IS A LONG, WIDE, elevated walkway on the west side of Manhattan known as the High Line. When the weather cooperates, it is a popular gathering spot, one of those urban places where locals and tourists go to see and be seen. Positioned a couple of stories above ground level, it stretches nearly a mile and a half along the Hudson River, from 14th to 34th Streets.

By New York standards the High Line is of fairly recent vintage, constructed in 2009 along the perimeter of an abandoned railway line. It is the city's only park that stands above street level, a concrete promenade overhanging the shore, providing views of the skyscrapers to the east and the New Jersey palisades to the west.

It is a beautiful place to spend a sunny day, featuring all manner of nearby shops, bars and restaurants, and activities that vary from day to day. Weekends are especially crowded, with sightseers wandering up and down the esplanade, attending open air performances, people-watching, and simply taking time to sit and drink up the quintessential New York energy.

* * *

ROSHAN ARRIVED AT THE 23RD STREET entrance to the High Line, the same entrance he had used a few days before. He paid the cab driver and stepped out into the sun-drenched afternoon. Standing on the sidewalk he looked around as if he expected someone to be meeting him there, but, of course, there was no one waiting for him. At least no one that he knew of.

He did not recognize the man positioned across the street who had been assigned by the Handler to ensure that the young man accomplished what he had come to do. The Handler used the man both as a spotter, to witness the events, and an enforcer, if the young man should falter in his resolve.

Roshan checked his watch for what must have been the fifteenth time in the last ten minutes. It was 1:30 P.M. He had gotten there a bit early. In five minutes he would head upstairs and carry out the actions that would be the last of his young life.

* * *

MUSTAFA REACHED THE 14TH STREET entrance just a couple of minutes later. He went through roughly the same actions Roshan had, unaware that he was being watched by another of the Handler's enforcers, positioned on the opposite corner.

Both of these young assassins were experiencing a similar range of intense emotions. There was elation, an adrenaline rush at having reached the moment when they would honor their God by engaging in an act of unspeakable cruelty. There was also fear at the prospect of their own death. All of this was accompanied by uncertainty. Doubt. Guilt.

They each felt the perspiration on their brow and under their arms, the empty feeling in the pit of their stomach and the heaviness of the vest that would be the instrument of the hateful and suicidal destruction they would be delivering just minutes from now.

Neither of them would ever know that the spotters assigned to trail them were armed with remote detonators, each capable of setting off the explosive vests the two young men were wearing.

Just in case.

* * *

As THEY SPED CROSSTOWN toward Manhattan's west side, weaving in and out of traffic and running red lights, Nick Reagan feared they were going to be too late to stop the attack.

Jackson ordered his driver to go faster. He told him to cut into the oncoming lane on 14th Street, then had him cross through an area designated "Pedestrians Only" in the heart of the Meatpacking District.

"The High Line is a mile and a half long," Jackson said, turning to Reagan and Gellos, in the back seat. "Any idea where we should enter?"

Gellos looked up from her cell phone. "Got it," she said. "There's a fashion show today, between 18th and 19th Streets. It's the only outdoor event planned for this afternoon. That's got to be the target."

"When is it scheduled?" Reagan asked her.

"It's going on right now."

"Move it," the commander told his driver, and their tires squealed as they took a sharp left turn.

Gellos was looking at her phone again, bringing up a list of entrances to the High Line. "Drop the two of us at 14th Street, we'll take the stairs up and head north," she said. "There's another access on 23rd, you can make your way south from there."

"Done," the commander said.

Each of them had already fitted earpieces and laser microphones that had been passed out at headquarters, creating an open line of communication. By the time the driver slammed on the brakes at the corner of Washington and 14th Street, Reagan and Gellos had their doors open and were rushing out.

"Good luck," the commander called out as the two CIA agents ran toward the stairway.

Reagan did not reply, his gut still telling him they were too late.

* * *

As Gellos had discovered, the main event scheduled for this sunny spring afternoon was an outdoor fashion show. Attractive young models, male and female, were strutting about, displaying the latest styles for the coming autumn season. It was far less organized or restricted than an indoor runway presentation. Spectators could watch from the edges of the promenade or stroll right through the center of the proceedings.

When Reagan and Gellos reached the top of the stairs, they had no idea who or what they were searching for—they were still not even certain this was the site of the attack—but Reagan was convinced, based on the available intel, that they were in the right place. He also knew, assuming the assault was going to occur on the High Line, it would be where people were gathering, which meant the fashion show up ahead.

Not wanting to attract too much attention or create unnecessary panic, the two agents walked as fast as they could without breaking into a run as they headed north.

Mustafa was just a block ahead of them now, but they had no way of knowing that. Likewise, they had yet to spot the Handler's backup. What Reagan and Gellos *did* see was that the walkway was becoming more crowded the further north they went, people congregating near the fashion show.

* * *

As Mustafa got closer to the activity, he reached into his pocket and nervously took hold of the wireless denotation trigger, holding it tight in his left hand.

* * *

Several blocks further up the High Line, a similar scenario was being played out. Roshan was heading downtown toward the crowd, his spotter keeping a visual on him.

As he walked his deadly path, Commander Jackson and his men reached the 23rd Street entrance and were coming up from behind.

* * *

Reagan and Gellos were alert to everyone they passed. If anyone was capable of spotting a terrorist in the crowd, they had the experience to do so. Each of them had unholstered their weapon, keeping them out of sight. They had no idea how much time they had, but they felt something was going to happen soon.

"We need to split up," Reagan said.

Gellos nodded and, without a word, veered off toward the river side of the wide concrete walkway that overlooked a defunct railway yard. Reagan remained on the eastern side, keeping pace with his partner as they moved north.

The sun was bright, the day was warm, and the crowd ahead of them was growing. It was a typical Manhattan gathering, a cross-section of ages, sizes, and ethnicities. It was not as if a Syrian or a Saudi or an Egyptian would look so out of place that Reagan could simply walk up and take them into custody. New York was the world's most famous melting pot, which added another layer of difficulty to their task.

By the time Reagan and Gellos passed 17th Street, they could see the fashion show ahead and hear the music blaring from outdoor speakers. Since they were moving faster than their anonymous prey, they were drawing closer to Mustafa than they knew.

At one point, Reagan was walking so quickly, with his vision focused on the activity in the distance, he almost tripped over a young woman pushing a stroller. As he began to utter an apology, they made eye contact, then he looked down at her young child.

"You need to get out of here," he whispered.

"What?" the startled woman said.

She was about to say something else, but Reagan held up his hand. "Please, just turn and head south. Please."

Without another word he resumed his hurried pace, and it was in that moment that the Handler's man, who was also trailing behind Mustafa, saw Reagan approaching.

It was the way Reagan was moving, the way he watched the crowd, the way he held one hand out of sight—all of that made it apparent he was not a casual visitor. When the spotter made Reagan, he also recognized what Mustafa did not yet know—they had run out of time. Without changing his gait, the spotter reached for the gun inside his belt, hidden under his dark cotton jacket. In the other hand he held the backup remote detonator, which Mustafa did not know he had.

Reagan had not yet identified the man as a hostile, but Gellos did. She saw that he was not wearing anything bulky enough to contain explosives, but when he slipped his hand inside his coat, Gellos immediately read the move. Speaking quietly into the tiny mic attached to her ear, she said, "Man directly to my right. Does not appear to be wearing explosives. Looks like he's moved for a gun with his right hand. I'm even more worried about what he's holding in his left."

"Roger that," Reagan said, not breaking stride and keeping his gaze forward.

Maybe they were not too late after all.

* * *

With Reagan getting nearer to Mustafa, the spotter's choices were limited. He could run forward, get close enough to Mustafa to detonate the vest and try to shoot his way out, or rush into the crowd and try to evade capture. Whatever decision he made, he had to move now.

From their vantage point, Reagan and Gellos understood that everything depended on whether the man was there merely as some sort of enforcer, or if he had the ability to set off the explosives, wherever they might be.

When the man stole another glance to his right, he saw the look in Reagan's eyes and began hollering, "Now Mustafa, now."

But the man had not seen Gellos, who had already drawn her weapon and was gaining on him in a sprint.

Only fifteen paces or so ahead of the spotter, Mustafa wondered, Who is calling my name? As the young Turk stopped and turned to look, both Reagan and Gellos saw him—a solitary figure, wearing a bulky shirt, standing stock still in the middle of the crowd.

"Everyone, get down!" Reagan yelled, but with the surrounding activity and the music booming through the loudspeakers, he could not be heard. Without hesitation he raised his automatic and pumped two shots in the air, again calling out for everyone to get down.

The gunshots got everyone's attention.

By now, Gellos had reached the spotter, launching herself forward and tackling him from behind. Grabbing him around the legs, she took him down, his weapon clattering to the ground. Before he could flick back the cover of the detonator in his left hand and depress the plunger, Gellos brought the handle of her Glock down on his wrist. She smashed his arm twice, as hard as she could, forcing him to reflexively open his hand, the device rolling harmlessly away. Then she cracked him twice across the back of the head.

But Mustafa, his own detonator in hand, had now turned to the sound of Reagan's gunshots. Trying to make sense of what was happening, he remained frozen in place, encircled by chaos. People in the crowd were rushing in every possible direction. Only Reagan raced directly toward Mustafa, his gun extended, shouting "Do not move!" over and over.

Mustafa pulled out his own pistol, aimed it at Reagan, and held up his other hand, showing the trigger that was connected to the incendiary device wrapped around his chest. "*Allahu Akbar*," he shrieked as he took aim.

Reagan dove to his left as the young man fired a wild shot, hitting a woman who was crouching against the guardrail.

"Stop!" Reagan shouted as he came up on one knee. He was just a dozen feet or so away, his Walther PPK aimed at the center of Mustafa's face.

The young man leveled his gun at him a second time and began to intone the name of his God again, but Reagan realized he was out of options and acted first. He fired three times, shattering Mustafa's face, and dropping him to the ground before the Turk could get off another shot or ignite the explosives.

Reagan rushed forward, pulled the detonator from Mustafa's hand, then felt for any sign of a pulse.

He was dead.

He looked over at Gellos, who gave him a high sign. She had her knee in the small of the spotter's back. The man was nearly unconscious, and she was securing his wrists and ankles with plastic restraints.

But then, before either of them could report their situation to Jackson, the horrific sound of an explosion carried up and down the High Line.

CHAPTER TWENTY-THREE

New York City

Reagan was immediately on his cell, calling for ambulances and emergency backup. As Gellos picked up the second detonator lying beside the spotter she had restrained, Reagan turned back to Mustafa. Opening the dead man's jacket and shirt, he checked to see if there was any backup timing device. When he did not see one, he carefully removed the vest. That done, he hurried over and began administering first aid to the woman who had been hit by Mustafa's errant gunshot. The wound did not appear to be life-threatening, but she was obviously in shock, and he did his best to comfort her as he worked to stop the bleeding.

In the midst of this chaos, Reagan and Gellos received a sit-rep from Jackson, and the news was not good.

Dozens of people had been hit by an explosion, a combination of ball bearings and crude shrapnel launched with lethal, percussive force. There was also a fiery, napalm-like compound that was doing its own damage as the clothing of numerous victims caught fire. The bomber was obviously dead, but it appeared he had not been the one to ignite the blast. There was a second man in the crowd who had apparently detonated the explosives remotely when he heard the gunshots, then fled through the crowd to safety. Thus far they had failed to apprehend him.

Reagan and Gellos watched the people rushing around in panic; saw the ruins of the fashion show; the two dead terrorists on the ground; the injured woman Reagan was still tending to; and the spotter Gellos had in custody. The two agents shared a look of frustration and despair, each wondering when this was all going to end.

As they waited for the first responders to arrive, Gellos nodded at him, the message to Reagan in her sad eyes crystal clear…. *This is why we have to do what we do.*

PART TWO

Three days later...

CHAPTER TWENTY-FOUR

CIA Headquarters, Langley

Deputy Director Kenny was meeting in his office with Reagan, Gellos, and Brandt. Al-Qaeda had taken responsibility for the attack on the High Line, and the team were engaged in yet another depressing post-mortem about a terrorist assault. Seated at the round conference table, their mood was as somber as this group ever allowed things to become.

"We should have been able to do more," Reagan said.

"It always feels that way, after the fact," Kenny said. "If you hadn't convinced Jackson to act on your instincts, none of you would have been there." He paused, slowly shaking his head. There's no telling how much worse the damage would have been."

Reagan frowned. Although he and Gellos succeeded in stopping Mustafa from igniting his vest, Roshan's device had resulted in the deaths of five bystanders and caused severe burns and wounds to dozens of others. Some of those were still in critical condition, and it was feared the death toll might rise. The Handler's enforcer, who had been tracking Mustafa and was apprehended by Gellos, was being held incommunicado by the FBI. The spotter trailing Roshan remained at large.

"The FBI must have completed their interrogation of the man we took down," Gellos said.

"Spoke with Matt Fitzgibbon this morning," Kenny told them. "Says the man is a tough nut to crack, hasn't given them a thing. Keeps asking to make a deal, but the Bureau isn't so inclined."

"Give me ten minutes with him, I'll make a deal," Reagan said.

"They've searched his home and done background checks," Kenny said. "He's an illegal from Syria, only been in the States a couple of months."

"There's a shocker," Gellos said. "Let's hear it for open borders."

"But maybe they *should* offer him something," Brandt suggested. "It might get us to the next level in their organization."

"Not our call," Kenny said. "We did get some news today from Dearborn. They discovered the bodies of those two missing boys."

Reagan forced a bitter laugh. "Pray tell, what happened to the *boys?*"

"The FBI pieced together some footage from a couple of neighborhood CCTV's, matched it with the eyewitness testimony. Seems Yousef Omarov got into a car with two men, was driven into the center of town, and was taken to an abandoned building, not far from his mosque. The other one, Fariq Homsi, was seen getting into what was likely the same sedan a few hours later. He also vanished after being taken to that same location."

"The locals find them in that building?" Brandt asked.

"No, but they found the place had recently been scrubbed with bleach. The bodies were discovered in Bloomfield," Kenny said. "Authorities located a traffic video showing the sedan leaving Dearborn end of that day. Driver and passenger, although no clear images of either man. Other roadside cameras picked it up heading for a park, with no sign of it coming out. FBI tracked it to a small lake. Pulled it out and found both bodies in the trunk."

"Any theories on motive?" Gellos asked.

"Not yet," Kenny said. "The car was stolen from a body shop in Chicago, just a day before Yousef and Fariq disappeared. Which begs the question—why would hitters travel all that way to take out two twenty-somethings, then go to the trouble of dumping their bodies in a lake? Their families claim neither of them ever visited Chicago. According to relatives, they spent all their time in Dearborn."

"What about phones and computers?" Reagan asked.

"The FBI has them. Both men spent time in extremist chat rooms, big fans of radical Islam, Omarov more so than his friend. His phone turned up a few random texts that suggest he was being recruited."

"Maybe that's what got them killed," Reagan suggested.

"It's a theory," the deputy director agreed.

"Which means we should do everything we can to follow those leads upstream," Reagan said.

"Authorities in Chicago are investigating the car theft, but not much is expected from that," Kenny told them.

"If the hitters dumped the car in a Bloomfield lake, how did they get out of there?" Brandt asked.

"Excellent question. Although a few days had passed by the time the car was found, forensics is convinced there was only one set of tire tracks. No evidence of another car nearby. If they were locals, why go to Chicago to steal a car?"

Reagan nodded. "Which means they were from somewhere a lot closer to Chicago than Dearborn. And one of them obviously had a second car, waiting somewhere outside the park while the other drove the stolen car into the lake."

"Makes sense," Kenny said.

"They'd just committed two murders and disposed of the bodies. It's unlikely they were going to steal another car and risk being stopped," Reagan said.

"Which means," Brandt said, "they either arrived in Dearborn in two cars and used one for their getaway vehicle, or they rented another car and used that to leave town."

"Which is more likely?" Gellos asked.

Reagan thought it over. "If they arrived in two cars, they would've had to park one somewhere. Not complicated, but inconvenient to drive two cars from Chicago. Then there was the risk someone might spot the parked car during the day, possibly I.D. it later."

"Especially if it had an Illinois plate," Gellos said.

"The easier option would be for them to split up after they were done in Dearborn, have one of them rent a car somewhere in the area and pick up the second man outside the park, after he dumped the stolen car in the lake."

"That's logical," Kenny agreed. "Alex, call Fitzgibbon's assistant. Get them working on rentals the day the two men went missing."

"The end point may be even more important than where they picked up the car," Reagan suggested. "An Arab man renting a car in the Dearborn area is not likely to be memorable to a desk agent. We should identify every rental car that was dropped off that day in Chicago after being picked up in Michigan."

"Got it," Brandt said, then left the room.

"All right," Kenny said as he turned back to Reagan and Gellos. "I know there's a lot you two want to find out about the High Line. How those two were recruited, where they got those explosives, all of it. But right now we have the short-term problem of additional threats that I don't want to hear about on CNN before we get ahead of the action."

Everyone was quiet until Reagan, with mock indignation, said, "You watch CNN, sir?"

Gellos laughed, but Kenny did not. He said, "We have another problem. Our people in Islamabad are making no progress on the three missing scientists. Their families are all over the news channels demanding action, along with reps from Cal Tech."

"Isn't this something the State Department should be handling?" Reagan asked.

"They're diplomats. Who are they going to negotiate with?" Kenny replied. "No group has taken responsibility for the abduction. There's not even a ransom demand."

"How can we help?"

"You and Gellos need to catch the next transport to Pakistan. You have friends over there, and it's time to call in some favors. I want you to find these three men and get them back, and I want it done now"

"Assuming they're still alive," Reagan said.

"I'm guessing they are," Gellos said. "If they were murdered, the videos would already be going viral."

"You're right," Reagan agreed. "If the kidnapping was some sort of al-Qaeda public relations ploy, we would've heard something by now."

"Any theories on why anyone would grab these three?" Reagan asked.

"A geologist and two engineers," Kenny said. "What do you think?"

"ISIS and al-Qaeda use tunnels for everything," Reagan said. "They hide in them, store munitions in them, use them to make undetectable personnel movements. Maybe they want to up their game."

"You think they would take three American professors to pick their brains about everything subterranean?"

"Could be," Reagan said, "but whatever the reason, if we don't get there before the interrogation is done, they'll kill all three of them for sure."

CHAPTER TWENTY-FIVE

Islamabad, Pakistan

Twenty-four hours after Kenny instructed them to head to Pakistan, Reagan and Gellos were sitting at a table in Al Maghreb, a traditional Middle Eastern restaurant in the Serena Hotel on the Khayaban-e-Suhrawardy in Islamabad. The hotel was one of the buildings that had been spared any serious damage in the recent earthquake.

When Paul Mazaika walked in, he had a quick look around the crowded room, then headed straight for their table, which was set in a small alcove that was partially hidden by a carved wooden screen.

Mazaika was short and dark-skinned, with features that allowed him to pass for almost any ethnic type to be found in the region. It was a useful attribute, providing him the ability to get lost in a crowd or to remain utterly forgettable when that was required. Taking a seat across from his fellow agents, he said, "Just happened to be in the neighborhood?" Then he flashed the easy smile that always seemed to be at odds with the perpetual look of concern in his dark eyes.

"Missed the local cuisine," Reagan said. "So how's it going?"

"Wonderful, as I'm sure you've heard. Had a look around town yet?"

Carol Gellos, who was wearing a long navy-blue dress with a scarf covering her head, told him, "Just got here, but we saw enough photos on the flight to give us the overview. What a mess."

"As if things here aren't screwed up enough already. We definitely did not need another quake."

Reagan nodded. "Then there's the matter of our missing friends."

"Yes," Mazaika said.

"Any news?" Gellos asked.

"Painfully little," Mazaika admitted, "and we've been digging just as hard as the rescue workers scratching through the rubble out there. We can't make any sense of it."

"Because no one has taken responsibility or asked for ransom," Reagan said.

"Right."

"All right, when you say painfully little, what's the little you have?"

Mazaika leaned forward and lowered his voice. "The gentleman who had them to dinner is no friend of ours. Emir Kharoti portrays himself as a moderate, but we have every reason to believe his loyalties are elsewhere."

"You think he set them up?"

"Personally, I have no doubt. Don't have anything to prove it, at least not yet."

"Have we leaned on him?"

Mazaika shook his head. "He's too highly placed. We press him, and we'll have an international incident on our hands. State actually warned us off."

"State?" Reagan repeated with a disgusted look. "If they can't solve the problem, why don't they stay the hell out of our way?"

"Politics, Nick. Who understands that better than you?"

"Which means you're flying blind."

"That's right. We have nothing from the moment they left Kharoti's house."

"What about the van that took them?" Gellos asked. "I know it was lost on satellite surveillance, but do we have any sort of I.D. on the vehicle?"

"A panel van with no visual on the license plate in the midst of all the commotion this earthquake has caused?" Mazaika shook his head. "We have nothing."

"You know the territory," Reagan said. "Any guess where they might've been taken? An ISIS stronghold nearby? An al-Qaeda camp?"

Mazaika smiled again, and again his eyes did not. "Even if we assume they're still in the city, which is a stretch, this town is more than three hundred square miles with a population over two million. Islamabad is like a gigantic rabbit warren, too many places to go, too many holes to search."

"But this Kharoti might be able to give us a lead."

"I'm telling you, Nick, you go at the emir and the locals will throw you in a cell someplace no one's ever heard of."

Reagan and Gellos shared a look, then turned back to Mazaika. "The DD said you had something more valuable to share with us than a warning," Reagan said.

Mazaika drew a deep breath and held it as if he were never going to exhale. He finally let it go. "I'm concerned guys, I really am. This place makes the Wild West look like a church social. They grab you here, there's nothing any of us is going to be able to do. You understand that? It'll be a tactical and diplomatic nightmare."

Reagan stared at him, his gaze cold and unblinking. "Where have I heard that before?"

Mazaika nodded. "I do have one piece of intel. We were able to enhance some of the satellite images."

"We were told you couldn't get the license plate," Gellos said.

"No, but we did get a fairly good image of the driver."

When he hesitated again, Gellos prompted him. "And?"

"And we believe it was the emir's nephew."

"Perfect," Reagan said. "Have you located him?"

"Negative. Hasn't been seen since that night."

Reagan responded with a thin smile. "I guess we really do have to speak with his uncle."

They left Al Maghreb, following Mazaika upstairs to one of the hotel rooms where they were joined by another agent. There, Reagan and

Gellos were briefed on the layout of the emir's home and provided Glock 10 handguns. After changing into the other set of clothes they brought—both now wearing dark slacks and tops with soft-soled shoes—they headed out with Mazaika.

It was less than two hours after arriving in Islamabad when they approached Kharoti's house from the rear. Mazaika brought his car to a stop on a hill that overlooked a tract of manicured land at the back of the large home. From what they could see, and what they had been told, the emir lived well and, as Reagan noted, probably had the requisite security to ensure his safety in these perilous times.

Dusk was falling as Mazaika brought his car to a stop, dropping them off on a narrow street where they were a little more than a hundred yards above the rear of the property.

"I'm not going to tell you again about the risks," Mazaika said. "Just remember, he may actually not know anything about where these men were taken."

"We won't find out unless we ask him," Reagan responded.

Mazaika nodded slowly, then turned to Gellos. "You generally have more sense than he does, so I'm giving this to you," he said, handing her a disposable cell phone. "Not sure what we can do for you if the shit hits the fan, but if it does just punch in nine-nine-nine. No need to speak, I'll know what it means, and I'll track your location."

"Thanks," Gellos said, then she and Reagan got out and watched the car drive off.

"Ah, well," Reagan said, "he travels swiftest who travels alone."

"May I remind you, neither of us is alone."

"Then how about, two's company three's a crowd?"

Gellos shook her head as they began to walk down a steep embankment to the back wall of the property.

It did not appear there were any lookouts posted there, nor did Mazaika's intel indicate that level of alert. Nevertheless, this was Pakistan, and they had to assume someone was on duty. Kharoti was a well-respected leader, and the protection he had in place would likely be the personal kind, such as a bodyguard inside. Whether or not there were cameras in place was another matter.

It was already dark, and there was no reason to wait. When they reached the wall, Reagan gave Gellos a boost that sent her scrambling over the top, then followed her over. They now stood side-by-side amidst some native deodar trees, surveying the situation.

"If they have closed circuit, they'll be on us quickly," Reagan whispered. "Let's split up."

"Even if they don't, it makes sense to come at them from two directions," Gellos agreed. "I'll go left."

They took off on opposite paths along the inside perimeter of the wall, using the heavy vegetation to provide cover, eventually coming around toward the rear of the building from two sides. Once there, they both saw an old, bearded man sitting on a stone bench, reading under the light of a single outdoor lamp.

Without looking up, the man said, "Come, have a seat." He gestured to the chairs facing him, which would put their backs to the house.

They approached from two sides, guns drawn, watching for any sign of activity inside the house.

"I prefer to stand," Reagan said. "This is going to be a short visit."

The man shrugged, then finally looked up. "As you wish," he said in perfect English.

They had seen his photos, and Reagan said, "Emir Kharoti."

"Yes, I am, although you flatter me with that title, young man."

"It's a sign of respect," Reagan replied. "Although I understand it was originally used to identify a military rather than a religious leader. Are you a military leader, Emir Kharoti?"

"Do I appear so?"

Reagan made a motion to Gellos, signaling her to keep an eye on the house, then circled behind Kharoti and conducted a quick frisk. "Sorry to be rude, but one needs to be so careful these days."

The old man did not reply.

Reagan came around and sat on the bench beside the emir, his gun pressed gently into Kharoti's ribs. "Again, forgive my abrupt nature, but I just want to be clear about our intentions. If anyone should interrupt us, you will be the first to leave the conversation. Am I clear?"

Kharoti turned and looked directly into Reagan's eyes. The old man displayed neither fear nor surprise. He simply said, "You have come about your three American friends."

"Yes, I have," Reagan said. "I can see that your reputation as a wise man is well deserved. What can you tell me about them?"

"They are safe."

"How would you know that? Did your nephew call with a report?"

Kharoti's impassive look gave way to the slightest hint of amusement. "Let us say, I am well informed about the goings on in my country."

"Especially when they involve men who were guests in your home. Men who had come here to help your fellow Pakistanis and have now been abducted. Fair statement?"

"Accurate, if not fair."

"So, why not save us a lot of time and tell us where they are? I'll call an Uber, have them picked up, and we can all enjoy the remainder of this pleasant evening."

Kharoti continued to stare at him as he said, "I have all the time in the world. This world and the next. You, on the other hand, do not have that luxury. You see, as soon as my guards saw you approaching the house, they phoned our friends in the local police department. Oh yes, please do not be surprised, we are very efficient here, despite what you Americans think of our backward country. And since it was clear you are Americans, we also phoned associates in the Inter-Service Intelligence. I'm sure you are familiar with our national security force. They will all be joining—what did you call it—our conversation? They should all be here soon."

Reagan gave the barrel of the Glock 10 a hard shove into the man's ribs, their gazes still locked. "Sorry to be rude, but if you're not going to answer my questions, there's no reason for us to wait. I can simply kill you and then leave. I'm sure you can see where that would make sense for me."

"My dear young man, do you think you can frighten someone of my years with death? At this age, death has become a companion, a friend. And to die for Allah, well, you would do me an honor."

Reagan nodded. "All right, then how about we find out what Allah has to say about dealing with pain as one approaches that final reward." Without another word, he lowered the gun and fired a shot into the man's kneecap.

The action in the next few moments, although swift and violent, seemed to occur in slow motion, as it often does in battle. The sound of the gunshot and Kharoti's scream brought two armed men charging out the back door of the house. As Kharoti fell off the bench onto the ground, Reagan stood and fired two shots into the chest of the man on the right, stopping him in his tracks. The gun fell from the attacker's hand as he ripped at his shirt, trying to claw away the two bullets before they dropped him to the ground, leaving him to helplessly bleed to death.

Gellos dispatched the man on the left, also tapping him twice in the chest, then finishing him off with a kill shot to the head.

Kharoti, meanwhile, was writhing on the grass, clutching at his knee, and continuing to holler, using his native tongue to curse Reagan and every other American on Earth. Reagan bent down, leaning with all his weight on the old man's side, then leveled his weapon at Kharoti's other knee.

"You see, this is what I was trying to explain. You may not fear death, but there's a lot that can happen in the journey from here to there, and some of it can be extremely unpleasant. The Koran ever mention that?"

Kharoti glared up at him, his eyes ablaze with anguish and hate.

"You're lucky, though, because you still have a choice. You tell me where the three men were taken, and I'll leave you here to get the medical attention you need when all of those friends of yours arrive. You don't, and, I assure you, that shattered knee is going to be just the beginning of your personal purgatory."

CHAPTER TWENTY-SIX

Islamabad, Pakistan

By the time the authorities arrived at Kharoti's home, Reagan, Gellos, and the emir were long gone.

Despite the searing pain, the old man had persisted in his refusal to tell them anything, and, given the threat of local law enforcement and the Pakistani ISI on its way, Reagan decided their best option was to take Kharoti and leave. They grabbed the cell phones and weapons from the two dead men and removed Kharoti's phone from his pocket. Then they shoved the emir into the back of his car and drove several miles, up into the hills, until they reached a deserted area where they would not be disturbed as they continued their interrogation.

Gellos was driving. When she brought the car to a stop she turned to Reagan, who was in the back seat keeping an eye on their prisoner.

"You're making this hard on yourself," Gellos said to Kharoti. "If you or your men had contact with your nephew, or anyone else involved in this kidnapping, our people will track it through these phones. Calls, texts, emails. We'll find them and trace them."

Kharoti said nothing.

"She's right," Reagan said. "Your heroics, if that's what you think they are, will be for nothing."

When Kharoti did not respond, Reagan took the Glock and placed the business end against the man's left ankle.

148

The emir gritted his teeth, then said, "What you are doing is against every law known to man. Even the barbarians in your country forbid these tactics."

Reagan nodded thoughtfully. "Every law known to man? Such as a law that supports two lunatics who decided to kill themselves while trying to set hundreds of innocent bystanders on fire in New York? You mean, those laws? I suppose I'm in the right place then, since back home we have the misguided notion that human life means something."

Kharoti stared down at the gun. "There is nothing I can tell you that will do you any good."

"Try me."

"I do not know where they are holding these three men, but even if I did and were willing to tell you, you will never reach them."

"I think you should let *me* worry about what I can and can't do." Keeping the gun in place, he turned to Gellos. "Let's have a look at our friend's phone."

Gellos picked the phone up from the front seat and powered it on.

"Give him the security code and your nephew's phone number," Gellos said. "Now."

When Kharoti did not answer, Reagan pressed the barrel of the Glock hard against his shin and began to count to three.

Reagan knew that there are moments in any violent interrogation that define how it will end. Some people face death without breaking, even when confronted with the prospect of great pain. Others reach a point where they can bear no more, still clinging to the hope of survival. The look in Kharoti's eyes revealed that he would be of the latter kind.

Even old men do not want to die.

Kharoti blurted out the four-digit code for his phone, then added, "It will do you no good."

"We'll see," Reagan said as Gellos punched in the numbers, accessed the data, and immediately turned off the location finder. "Now your nephew's phone number."

Kharoti recited the digits, and Gellos went to work on the call history. There were several recent exchanges with that number, assigned in the directory to a man named Qasim.

"It seems you and Qasim are close," Gellos said. Then she pulled out her own cell and phoned Mazaika, who answered on the first ring. "Check out this line," Gellos told him, then gave him the number. "We need to see if you can pinpoint the location for calls made and received in the last two days. We're coming in."

"What happened?" Mazaika asked.

"You don't want to know, just find out where this phone has been used. We'll be back to you." After he rung off, Gellos looked to Reagan. "What do we do with our friend here?"

"I think it's time for us to part company."

"What if this is not his nephew's number? What if he gave us a number of someone else he knows?"

"Good point."

Gellos called Mazaika back. "When you got that I.D. on Kharoti's nephew, did you get a name?"

"Qasim Kharoti," Mazaika told him.

"Good," Gellos said, "the number I gave you is his. Find him." Then she rung off again.

"Well," Reagan said as he pulled his weapon back and looked into Kharoti's furious gaze. "It appears our relationship is at an end." He climbed out of the car, walked around to the other side, and pulled the old man out onto the ground. "I should put two bullets in your head right now," Reagan said. Then, without further warning, he leaned down and smacked the side of the man's head twice with the butt of the Glock. "Pleasant dreams," he said.

Reagan jumped into the passenger seat, and Gellos took a circuitous route back toward the edge of Islamabad where they left the emir's vehicle on a narrow side street. They had to assume the authorities were already looking for Kharoti's sedan by now, so they had no choice but to continue on foot, which posed its own risks. With earthquake damage throughout the center of the city, roads were blocked, and all sorts of government personnel were everywhere, working on repair and recovery efforts as well as enforcing the law. Two Americans wandering through the wreckage would raise too many questions, especially if the ISI was already looking for them.

Just a few blocks away they found a small café, took a table in the back, and Gellos called Mazaika again.

"What have you got?" she asked.

"We've identified two locations where Qasim made and received phone calls. We confirmed one to be his home, the other is a building on the outskirts of the city."

"We're on foot," Gellos told him. "Give us a pickup location, and we'll meet you."

"Hit nine-nine-nine on the other phone I gave you. I'll have your location, and we'll come for you."

Gellos pulled out the burner and did as she was told.

"You get any intel on what we're heading into?" Mazaika asked.

"If you mean how many men are holding them, we have no idea," Gellos admitted. "How many men do you have available on short notice?"

"Me and two others."

Gellos paused for a look at Reagan, then said, "No offense meant Paul, but you're not an active field agent anymore."

"I'll do what needs to be done," Mazaika told her, then hesitated. "Carol, if this is really the location where the three men are being held, maybe we should call in our military."

Gellos shared the idea with Reagan, who shook his head. "We've already created a diplomatic headache, we don't need to start a war. Let's do some recon first."

Gellos relayed Reagan's comments to Mazaika, who responded by telling her he had their location. Then he gave Gellos an address they could walk to in just a few minutes. He would meet them there.

"Done," Gellos said.

Ten minutes later, Reagan and Gellos were in Mazaika's sedan with two other agents. The five of them headed to an area west of the city.

"Did we check to see where Qasim's phone is now?" Reagan asked.

Mazaika gave him a look of pure exasperation. "I may not be a field agent anymore, Nick, but I know what the hell I'm doing."

"Sorry."

"According to the GPS, he's at the building now."

They soon neared the location on the edge of the city Mazaika's people had identified through Qasim's number. Reagan said, "Let's go past it, don't slow down." It was a beige, single-story stone structure, and there did not seem to be any activity outside or in. Two small cars were parked alongside.

The agent behind the wheel did as instructed. Further down the road, Reagan said, "Pull behind that building on the right. We'll hoof it back from here."

The area was quiet, dusty, and almost completely devoid of people. There was no evidence of damage from the earthquake, but Mazaika said many of the locals were probably participating in relief efforts inside the city. The five of them got out of the car and stood behind a two-story cement building, which effectively blocked any view of them from their target location.

"I didn't see any evidence of a lookout," Gellos said.

"Neither did I," Reagan agreed. "No one seemed to be on the roof, but there were enough windows for them to have spotters in place."

Mazaika agreed. "How do you want to play this?"

"We may not have much time," Reagan said. "When they find Kharoti, he'll tell them what happened, maybe even give them this location."

Mazaika nodded. "Let's get some hardware out of the trunk."

Reagan said. "I'll take the direct route back on the right, Carol can head out around the left. Two of you should get up to the roof of this building, that'll give you a clear view of the action. Paul, you trail Carol and take a position across the street once she and I make our move inside."

No one disagreed. One of the other agents opened the trunk and the group removed several weapons, including sniper rifles for the two men who would take positions upstairs.

"We have a couple of tear gas canisters here," Mazaika said.

"No good," Reagan told him. "You toss that through the window, and the first thing they'll do is kill the three hostages."

Gellos found two suppressors, handed one to Reagan, and they them fitted them to their handguns.

"You guys head up to the roof, soon as you get there toss a small rock down so we know you're in place," Reagan said.

When they got the signal, Reagan and Gellos did not hesitate. By now it was possible someone might have warned Qasim that he was going to have visitors. Or a lookout could have spotted their car arriving. Either way, they had to assume a welcoming committee would be there to greet them.

Both Reagan and Gellos stayed close to the two-story building as they came out on the left and right sides, proceeding along the arid street with guns drawn, stopping when they were each directly across from their target. Reagan looked to his left, saw Gellos, and gave her the signal he was going in.

The windows were rectangular openings with no glass. Reagan approached the nearest one in a crouch, then rose up to have a look inside.

There was no one there.

He climbed through the opening, moving quietly, his eyes adjusting since the interior of the building was even darker than the nightfall outside. Moments later he saw Gellos come through the window on the left. They remained still, surveying the area. Then Reagan pointed across the room.

Twenty feet from where he stood, he could see an area of dirt on the floor had been scuffed from repeated movements. He moved forward slowly, his rubber-soled shoes not making a sound as he approached what he was convinced was the entrance to a basement below.

He shook his head so Gellos could see it. They had worked together so many times, the signal was clear. He was saying that something did not make sense. If the three scientists were being held in a basement, why were there no guards at ground level?

Gellos responded by raising both hands together, then quickly pulling them apart. The signal for explosion, meaning the ground level door might be wired.

Reagan nodded, then moved closer, looking for trip wires or an IED pressure plate. There were none, but he now saw that the scuff marks were clearly footprints around a trap door. Bending down he located the handle, then motioned for Gellos, who had brought a loop of synthetic rope from the car.

Gellos tied the cord to the metal handle, and the two of them backed away, extending the rope until they reached the window Reagan had entered. They both climbed back out to the street.

"Should we call the snipers down?" Gellos whispered.

"One," Reagan agreed, then signaled up to the roof behind them that one of the agents should join them. Turning to Gellos, he said, "Ready."

They stood away from the opening as Gellos pulled on the rope, steadily, not with a jerking motion, but it didn't matter. As the door rose up, the explosion went off, sending the door flying across the room as shrapnel scarred the walls.

Mazaika came running, but Reagan motioned for him to stay off to the left, on the opposite side of the building.

Moments later three men emerged through the opening in the floor, moving signal file with automatic weapons in hand at their sides, as if expecting to find bodies scattered across the room. When they saw the room was empty, they paused for an instant, which was all Reagan and Gellos needed. They opened fire, taking all three men out with a combination of nine efficient shots.

Reagan and Gellos climbed back inside, and Mazaika did the same, entering from the left. There was no way of knowing how many other men were still in the basement, but whoever was down there might assume their comrades had dispatched the intruders. The three agents waited for the next move. It came less than a minute later, when a man stuck his head up through the opening, only to have it blown away by a flurry of shots.

Now Reagan moved forward toward the opening, dropping to his hands and knees, and having a quick look over the edge. He saw the ladder that led to the basement below, where lights were on. The man they had just dispatched lay on the floor below, having fallen off the ladder. There did not appear to be any other movement.

Gellos came up beside him and whispered, "You go down there, and yours is the next head that's going to get shot off."

Reagan nodded, then signaled for Mazaika to join them. "You speak Urdu, right?"

Mazaika nodded.

"Tell them all their friends are dead, and if they want to live they need to all get up here with their hands in the air, the Americans first."

Mazaika stared at him. "What if they kill the hostages?"

Reagan gritted his teeth. "I know it's an awful risk, but if they were going to kill them, they could've killed them when the trapdoor exploded, or when their friends up here didn't come back with good news. We've already taken out four men, how many could they have down there?"

Mazaika nodded again.

155

"You said you had photos of Qasim Kharoti. He any of these three?"

Mazaika got up and had a look at the three bodies laying off to the side of the opening. "This one, I think."

"That's good, assuming he's one of the ringleaders. Whoever is left might not be all that eager to die. Give them the message."

But before Mazaika could call out, they heard a muffled voice from the basement, calling out in English, saying, "We're alone," then repeating it over and over.

Reagan and Gellos looked at each other.

"Could be a trap," Gellos said.

"Or they could be tied up somewhere down there." Reagan turned to the opening and hollered out, "How many men were down there with you just now?"

"Four," came the prompt reply.

"Who won the Super Bowl last year?" Reagan called out.

Gellos almost started laughing. "What is this, World War Two?"

"Best I could do," Reagan said with a shrug. "Unless he's an idiot, he'll give the right answer if they're alone. If there's someone down there, he'll call out a different team."

When the voice from below called out the correct team, Gellos said, "Good thing the guy is a football fan."

CHAPTER TWENTY-SEVEN

Islamabad, Pakistan

Down below, they found the three scientists were indeed alone, each tied to a chair in a small, musty room with a single lightbulb hanging from the low ceiling. As the agents cut their bonds away, the men said they were all right, although tired and hungry. They had not been beaten or subjected to any violence, but they had been starved and deprived of sleep. Besides looking pale and haggard, Reagan counted them as lucky.

When they all managed to get to their feet, Mazaika said, "Let's get out of here. Don't be fooled by the deserted look on the street, there has to be someone around, and there's no telling who might make a call about the explosion."

Reagan nodded. "Especially since they're already looking for us."

The three Californians looked at one another, then the geologist, Reynaud, said, "Kharoti was the man we visited, the night we were taken."

"Kharoti is the man who set you up," Reagan explained. "We'll talk later. As Paul said, we need to move out. You guys okay to climb the ladder on your own?"

"Just lead the way," Schapiro said.

Once they were above ground, both of Mazaika's men joined them. He told them to start the cars parked alongside the building, using keys they took from the dead men, and check how much gas each had in the tank. As those agents took care of the transportation, Mazaika advised

Reagan and Gellos against making a run for the US Embassy in Islamabad. With authorities on the lookout, and so many roads blocked as a result of the earthquake, there was too great a chance they would be captured. They were already well west of the city, so he suggested they continue in that direction, toward Peshawar. He said they had assets there who could assist them in leaving the country.

"There's not exactly a six-lane highway between here and there," Reagan said. "What do you figure for driving time?"

"Less than an hour and a half," Mazaika told him.

"That's a lot of time for them to put eyes in the sky," Reagan said.

"I'll phone ahead for help, just in case. Chances are it will be a while before they put all the pieces together. Then they'll still have to guess where we're going."

"Maybe so," Reagan said, not hiding his skepticism, "but Carol and I have not survived this long leaving things to chance."

"I'll line up the support," Mazaika said, "but we need to get going."

Reagan and Gellos agreed.

"We need to split up the three hostages," Gellos said. "In case anything goes sideways, we need one of them to explain what happened, what they were asked, a full debriefing."

"Right," Mazaika said. "We'll take one in our car and lead, you take the other two."

One of Mazaika's agents pointed to the car with the most gas. "That'll get us there," he said.

Gellos nodded.

As they headed for the cars, Reagan said, "I saw a shoulder mounted rocket launcher in your trunk. You come prepared."

Mazaika smiled.

"How many missiles you have for it?"

"Two."

Reagan looked at the other two agents. "You guys know how to use that thing?"

One of them smiled and said, "Hell yes."

"Good. Then get it out of the trunk, and keep it in the car with you."

Then they all climbed into their vehicles and sped away.

Gellos was driving, as usual, which gave Reagan an opportunity to turn toward the two men in the backseat and ask some preliminary questions. He inquired about how they were treated and how much food and water they had been given. For now, he figured the men were running on adrenaline, which would make up for any lack of sleep or nourishment.

"Mind if I ask something?" Reynaud said.

"Fire away," Reagan told him.

"Who are you guys? I mean, we're obviously in your everlasting debt for rescuing us, and if it's something you can't tell us, we'd understand, but—"

Reagan held up his hand. "I get it, and I'm happy to fill you in as we go along. For now, all you need to know is that we're federal agents sent to find you, and we're glad we got here in time."

Both men smiled.

"That's enough information for me," Finerman said.

"Good," Reagan replied. "Now tell me about the interrogation."

"The way it began was odd," Reynaud said. "I mean, as soon as they took us we understood they were some sort of terrorists. What other explanation could there be? We had no idea what they wanted from us, figured they would ask us about our politics, use us as hostages for ransom, or worse. Instead, they seemed interested in how earthquakes happen, and how they affect foundations, utility lines, and other infrastructure."

Finerman chimed in. "At one point, I asked them why they had to take us prisoner to discuss such things. I mean, the information they were seeking was what we had come to help with. We volunteered to attend the symposium, for God's sake. All they had to do was sit in the audience and ask questions. It didn't make any sense."

The geologist agreed. "It didn't make sense at first, but then the questions became more peculiar. For instance, they were interested in how a modern building with a roof supported by piping would react to an explosion or an earthquake."

"What do you mean, a roof supported by piping?" Reagan asked.

"You know how some new buildings have thick translucent roofs, with metal work holding them up, so it almost looks like the top of a geodesic dome?"

"Go on," Reagan said.

"At first they were random questions," Reynaud said, "but they kept pushing it, asking what would happen if the metal struts were compromised, how the roof itself would react, and so on. Why would they want to know? I've never seen a single building like that in Pakistan, and this is my fourth visit here."

"Then they became more and more specific," Finerman said.

"That's right," Reynaud agreed. "They started asking about the easiest way to bring a building like that down."

"Which means you were way beyond any discussion of natural disasters," Reagan said.

"Oh yeah. I think they started with those other topics to make us comfortable, as if there was no harm in answering what they were asking. But it became clear they wanted to know how to create an implosion that would destroy a building like that, and then to gauge the results. What sort of damage there would be to the foundation, the internal structure, and surrounding areas. All of that."

"What did you tell them?"

"We wanted to tell them to go screw themselves," Finerman said, "but we were obviously scared. We just kept saying that we didn't know how to do what they wanted, we didn't have expertise in explosives."

"Did they buy that?"

"Of course not," Reynaud responded. "That's when they began threatening us."

"With torture?"

"No," Finerman said. The two scientists shared a look of mutual relief at being freed from that harrowing situation.

"Our families," Reynaud said. "They kept telling us that they knew who we are, where we lived, where our wives and children were. Said they would kill them all if we didn't cooperate."

"You had to tell them something," Reagan said, trying to sound as sympathetic as he could.

"What do you people call it in your business? Disinformation? We tried to make things sound as technical as we could, because what they were asking was rudimentary. It was like asking how to get a pile of wooden blocks to topple? You pull out the lowest one, right?"

"It was obvious that none of them were any sort of scientist," Finerman said.

"And none would qualify as the sharpest knife in the drawer," Reynaud added. "Our discussions were generally pointless, far as we could tell."

"With one exception," Finerman reminded his colleague.

Reagan waited.

"The four men who were there today, the men you killed, that was not the entire team. Some others came and went, most like the men you saw today. But there was one guy, older, sharper. He was their leader. He was the one who asked the intelligent questions, who knew when we were bullshitting and when we were telling the truth."

Reagan asked for a description of the man, then listened as they provided as much detail as they could.

When they were done, Reynaud added, "You rescued us just in time, I can tell you that."

"Meaning what?"

"This boss, or whoever he was, was done with us. He told us he was coming back, and that when he did, we had better be prepared to answer all of his questions, or he would leave us in that hole to rot while they tracked down our families and so on. You get the idea."

Reagan nodded. "I get it all right. Now let's take some time to go over everything in more detail. I realize this is going to become boring, because you're going to be asked about all this numerous times. You'll find, though, each time you describe what happened you'll remember something else."

The men, physically exhausted and emotionally drained, cooperated as best they could, reliving the harrowing events of these past several days.

Then, when they were more than halfway to Peshawar, Reagan heard the rotors of an oncoming helicopter.

The chopper was approaching from the east. Having a look outside the passenger window, Reagan could see it banking out to the north, then bearing down on them on. The good news was that it was not a heavily equipped military helicopter, such as an American Black Hawk. Reagan knew it had to be carrying armed men, but at least there were no large-caliber weapons or rocket launchers mounted on the sides.

Reagan pulled out his cell and called Mazaika. "Can you guys handle this?"

"Affirmative, but not yet. We need to buy some time, get closer to our drop point."

"You've made the arrangements?"

"All set," Mazaika told him, "but if we take this bird out now, there's enough time for them to send even more serious hardware."

"Copy that. We going to keep running down the road a while?"

"That's the plan," Mazaika said. "Let them get ahead of us, take a position, order us to stop. You know the drill."

Reagan smiled. "I thought you were a desk jockey."

"Not always, old friend, not always."

They followed Mazaika's plan, buying time as the helicopter drew close enough to have a look at them. This was clearly a government operation, so whoever was inside the chopper was not likely to begin firing unless they were either provoked or their orders were disobeyed.

The two cars continued on, as if the chopper had nothing to do with them. Then the pilot made his move, accelerating past both vehicles and banking again, until he turned around, hovering several hundred yards ahead, facing them from less than fifty feet off the ground.

Neither Mazaika's driver nor Gellos slowed as the helicopter began sending out a loud message over a P.A. system that could barely be heard about the roar of blades and rotors.

Reagan got back on the line with Mazaika. "Sounds like they're ordering us to stop."

"Hard to hear, but that would be a good guess."

The cars had already sped past the chopper, which had turned and was again in pursuit. "Let's keep going, force them to come around again, so you have a direct shot," Reagan said.

"Copy that," Mazaika responded, then told the driver what to do.

The pilot caught up and flew past the cars once again. This time, as he came around he lowered the craft so that it was almost touching the ground.

Rather than getting too close, Mazaika's car screeched to a halt, causing Gellos to slam on the brakes. Mazaika and his driver made a show of opening their doors and stepping out, with hands raised. It was enough of a distraction to allow the other agent to climb out the back passenger side with the launcher in hand. Yelling, "Duck," to Mazaika, and using the door as cover, he knelt down and took aim, then sent a missile from his shoulder mount screaming toward the helicopter.

The explosion was deafening, parts of the shattered chopper flying in every conceivable direction. No one in Reagan's car had even opened their doors, and now Gellos threw it into reverse to pull away from the blast zone. The men in front of them jumped back into their sedan and did the same thing, the driver reversing into a flat spin and speeding away, narrowly avoiding the remnants of a rotor blade headed in their direction.

As flames rose into the sky from the remains of what had been a helicopter just a few moments before, Reagan called Mazaika. "Nice work."

"Don't mention it."

"Time for some of us to go home. What about you and your men? You going to be all right?"

"We'll pull over ten minutes further up the road. I'll hand over our guest to you and connect your group with the exfiltration team. Then I'm circling back so we can get to the office and work on plausible deniability."

Reagan smiled. "Loud and clear," he said.

"They're not done with you, Nick. Keep your eyes open."

CHAPTER TWENTY-EIGHT

Washington, D. C.

Through an encrypted message on his computer, the Handler received word of what had transpired in Pakistan. Although the debacle had nothing to do with him, it added to the pressure he was feeling.

The attack in New York City had gone sideways for reasons that were still not clear, but he would be left with the blame. Even with the men he sent as backup, Mustafa was shot before he could detonate his vest. *What pathetic irony*, the Handler thought. *The fate of a coward is to die anyway.* The enforcer assigned to him had also failed, was taken into custody, with no details yet available.

Somehow, Roshan's explosives were detonated, whether by his own hand or by remote detonation. The man assigned to tail him was among the missing, and the Handler was waiting for him to report in. Unfortunately, Roshan had not reached the main crowd at the fashion show, where the Handler envisioned a group of scantily clad women and homosexual men prancing around while others ogled them. *They all deserved to die*, he told himself. The murder of five innocent people was not enough for him.

His superior numbers in al-Qaeda were already pushing for the next attack in the United States, but the Handler warned them about moving too quickly. He argued that taking action without careful preparation would jeopardize the operation and put their entire American network at risk. Their sources of funds and materials might be uncovered. Their recruits could be identified. On a personal level, he was worried about his own safety, but would never give voice to that concern.

But his warnings fell on deaf ears.

Now came this fiasco in Islamabad. The Handler had objected to the plan from the start, never seeing the benefit of abducting these scientists. What information could they possibly provide that could not be obtained elsewhere? Again, his admonitions were ignored, and now a principal asset had been exposed, in the person of Kharoti, with six of his men dead.

The al-Qaeda hierarchy had a very short memory with respect to who took what position on any given mission. For them it was strictly a numbers game, and only results mattered. These recent failures intensified their determination to pursue the next stage of the three-pronged assault the Handler had planned for the United States.

As he considered the safest way to proceed, another encrypted email arrived, this one from a lieutenant close to their leader, Ayman al-Zawahiri, who was presently in Syria. It began with a rant about the Americans, then continued with an exhortation for the Handler to proceed immediately with his plans. There would be no excuses for what had happened in New York, nor was there any mention of the rescue of the three scientists in Pakistan. The note ended with a reference to the glory of Allah.

The Handler understood that his leaders were zealots, whose answer to everything was a vehicle loaded with explosives or a suicide vest. He shook his head as he deleted all their recent exchanges, then removed them from the recycle bin. He realized their tactics might be effective in Aleppo or Damascus, but they would never be as effective here in America. The level of surveillance was too high, the intelligence community far too alert.

He realized that more sophistication and care would be required, particularly since these three attacks were based on a specific ideological theme.

He turned to his list of candidates for the next phase of his plan. Many of them had potential, but there was one whom he had come to mistrust. Nahid Jamal lived in Baltimore, which was why the Handler had chosen that city for his meetings with Mustafa and Roshan. That morning, he had also spent time observing Jamal.

At thirty-six, he was a bit older than the other recruits. He was divorced, currently unemployed, and just the sort of malcontent who fit the profile the Handler usually sought. Jamal had progressed through various stages of recruitment, but lately his behavior raised some red flags. Among other things, they discovered he had a child, something he had never disclosed.

The Handler knew the pain and rage he experienced at the death of his own family. One of the reasons al-Qaeda chose younger men and women was their lack of any such connection to a child or spouse—fewer impediments to committing suicide.

Which, it turned out, did not apply to Jamal.

Just this morning he sent a text with questions about how he might serve Allah without sacrificing his own life and leaving his daughter without a father. As the Handler knew, the question itself was a disqualifier. Not only was the man unlikely to carry out the attack for which he had been chosen, but Jamal now posed a danger to them. As little as he had learned up to now, it was still too much.

After reading Jamal's email again, the Handler sat back, lifted his espresso cup, and drained what was left of the dark, bitter drink. Then he set the cup down again and ran his hand across the top of his carefully combed, straight, black hair.

As his ebony gaze returned to the computer screen, he leaned forward and responded to Jamal with an email providing assurances that there was a role he could play without having to take his own life. He told him to stand by for further instructions.

CHAPTER TWENTY-NINE

CIA Headquarters, Langley

Political repercussions from the incursion in Pakistan came swiftly. The sources of these complaints ranged from the Pakistani embassy, their national police agency, ISI, to America's own State Department. Despite the onslaught, Deputy Director Kenny remained staunch in his defense of Reagan and Gellos. He had sent them to Islamabad to find the professors from Cal Tech. They had done so and brought all three back alive. He had no patience for second-guessers who would have gone on talking and wringing their hands and taking no action while the hostages were murdered.

As the scientists were being debriefed by the FBI at a safe house in Washington, Reagan and Gellos met with the DD, accompanied by Alex Brandt.

"You shot out the man's knee," Kenny said. "That becoming your trademark, Reagan?"

"It's painful, not life-threatening, hobbles the suspect, and tends to get him talking."

"You do recall what we were told directly by the President of the United States? That we do not condone enhanced interrogation techniques? I only mention it because most people would view the destruction of a man's knee with a bullet as something far beyond enhancement. What do you think?"

"We were in a hostile environment with armed men all around, including the possibility that our friend Kharoti was hiding a weapon under his robe. This had nothing to do with torture, sir, this was self-defense." Reagan looked to Gellos, who simply nodded. "As you know, we also had to kill two of his guards. This was a firefight, and we needed to secure the area."

"I see. You shot out his knee to secure the area," Kenny repeated. "And then what?"

Gellos spoke up now. "As our report indicates, we had reason to believe the suspect had information regarding the whereabouts of the three hostages. We removed him to a safe location, where no further physical injury was inflicted during the interrogation."

"What about the two lumps on his head and the concussion they're screaming about?"

"After we were done questioning him, he tried to escape," Gellos said. "Reagan subdued him, which we regarded as necessary to our own safety."

"You're telling me that a seventy-five-year-old cleric with a shattered knee attempted to escape from two armed agents, do I have this right?"

"Yes, sir," Gellos said, her tone and manner deadly serious. "Also keep in mind what might have happened if we allowed him to go free. He could have warned the people holding the three scientists, which might have resulted in their deaths, and he would certainly have put us at greater risk."

"I'd like to add," Reagan said, "that the man we are discussing was complicit in the kidnapping of these three Americans *and* was fully prepared to have his men kill us, rather than allow us to complete our mission."

Kenny sat back and ran a hand through his dark, unruly hair. "I've already heard from the director, who is none too happy about all this. Nevertheless, I told him that I am backing you one hundred percent, largely for the reasons you've just given. You completed your mission, and the collateral damage was suffered only by people involved in the kidnapping. I told him we don't owe an apology to anyone, and if the

Pakistanis don't like the fact that we had to undertake a mission in their country, then they should do a better job of keeping their own house in order."

Reagan began laughing. "I'm afraid Carol and I are becoming a bad influence on you, sir."

"Trust me, that's not possible. And before you laugh too loudly, you should know that I've been told to suspend the both of you."

"What?"

"That's right," Kenny said.

"And what about the current threats we discussed with Erin before we left?"

"That's exactly what I raised with the director. I convinced him that I need all hands on deck, and he backed off. But be assured, the fallout from your actions in Pakistan is not over."

"You've got to be kidding," Reagan said.

"I wish I were," the DD replied. "Believe it or not, Cyla Khoury interceded on your behalf when people in the White House and her own department were calling for your heads. It's a good thing she has access to the President. She managed to calm things down a bit."

Reagan nodded thoughtfully. "Go figure. I suppose we owe her a thank you."

"I think she'll be better off without it. Her assistance, as you can imagine, was totally off the record. Meantime, there's something you should know that you may not have heard while you were traveling back here." They waited. "Anatole Mindlovitch was rushed to the intensive care unit at Cedars Sinai last night."

"What happened?" Gellos asked.

"Not sure. Apparently, he collapsed in his home. We don't have any more information than that right now, but we're working on it."

"Collapsed? That guy works out like a professional athlete," Reagan said.

Kenny nodded. "This is troubling on a lot of levels."

"Principally the fact that I met with him to discuss the Ghost Chip. Just days after I visited his factory in China."

"That's right."

"Should I head out there?"

"Not unless you picked up a license to practice medicine while you were in Pakistan. We have agents in L.A. monitoring the situation. The FBI is also on top of it."

"Any unusual activity at the Suzhou factory?"

"We have assets there trying to find out."

Reagan looked from Gellos to Brandt, then back at their boss. "I have a bad feeling about this."

"Thank you for stating the obvious Reagan." Kenny stood. "Erin David is here, I have her set up on the third floor. I want the three of you to join her and Bruce Levi. He happened to be in town, and, given his relationship with Mindlovitch, Erin invited him."

The three agents got to their feet. "We're on it," Reagan said.

They took the elevator to the third floor, where Erin David, Bruce Levi, and Cyla Khoury were waiting. The conference room was furnished in utilitarian style, a dull mélange of taupe and gray, all function and little comfort.

As Levi told Reagan after their meeting with Mindlovitch a few days ago, he had upcoming appointments that required him to be in Washington. By the time he landed on the red-eye that morning, he already had a text from Erin inviting him here.

Cyla Khoury had been a classmate of Erin David's at Yale, and they remained friends since. Erin had introduced her to Reagan at a couple of functions they attended together. Her parents were long-time friends of President Harmon, and he appointed her to a special team at the State Department. It appeared the choice was a move by the administration to include a Muslim woman in its work against terrorist threats—as if a show of diversity would matter when an attack came, as Reagan observed—but she soon became a respected member of that entourage. The personal access she had to the President also provided her a unique standing.

Her group from State was normally assigned to delegations visiting trouble spots around the world, where they would act as the Chief Executive's eyes and ears for meetings he could not personally attend. Since she was in Washington this week, the White House suggested she attend this meeting—the word "suggested" being a D.C. euphemism for "ordered."

Cyla was a petite young woman, dark-skinned and dark-eyed, with a thoughtful demeanor that rarely gave way to humor. She was married to a Lebanese-born businessman, Walid Khoury, whose business enterprises allowed him wide latitude on where he could work and live, a perfect mate for someone in the diplomatic corps.

Erin made the introductions, then gave the group a summary of what she knew so far about Mindlovitch.

When she finished, Levi said, "My guess is poison." The others waited. "Anatole keeps himself in great physical shape."

"That's what I told the DD," Reagan said, "but what makes you think it was poison?"

"There's always the possibility of some undiagnosed medical condition, but the odds against that are incredibly long. He's got the top doctors in the world on retainer." Levi shook his head. "Without more information, it sounds like a classic KGB move. Putin can carry on a vendetta longer than a mafia don. I'm guessing his people got to someone on the inside. As you saw, Anatole is big on security, so no one would risk any sort of overt attack, he has too many loyal people around him, and the retaliation would be immediate."

"You think someone was bought off?" Gellos asked.

"Pure speculation," Levi admitted, "but I can't see another explanation."

"You really think Putin is behind it?" Reagan asked.

"Putin or someone highly placed in the PRC, but it's just a guess," Levi conceded again. "It might have had something to do with our meeting the other day when we discussed that microchip factory in China. Someone looking to steal the technology might have figured Anatole was going to follow up on what you told him. Beef up security in Suzhou before they could make a move, or maybe bring the whole project stateside. Whatever it was, there are too many coincidences, too short a timeline."

"What do you mean, follow up on what Reagan told him?" Cyla asked.

Reagan exchanged a quick look with Levi, then said, "Bruce and I believe Mindlovitch is working on something new at his factory in Suzhou, and he's closer to getting it done than he would admit. Someone else might have reached the same conclusion, someone who may want to get their hands on the invention. Something like that."

None of them mentioned the Ghost Chip to Cyla, not wanting any more trouble with State than they already had from their adventure in Pakistan.

"Right," Levi agreed. "As I say, we have no way of knowing."

"Let's assume you're close to the truth," Erin said. "What can we do?"

"That's obviously up to you," Levi said.

Reagan shook his head. "The factory is in China, there's no way the White House is going to greenlight an operation like that in the PRC."

"What about a diplomatic approach?" Cyla asked. "We tell Beijing what we know and ask for their cooperation?"

After his recent visit to China, Reagan was about to tell her where she could stick her diplomacy, but it was Gellos who spoke up. "That plant is a huge economic success for both Mindlovitch and China. What motivation would they have to help us? If they do anything to interfere with his operation, he could pull out the next day."

"He definitely could," Levi agreed.

"Then let's look at who benefits if Mindlovitch is gone," Reagan suggested. "The Chinese have more to gain by making him happy than killing him, at least for now."

"Which is why I think the Russians are the obvious choice," Levi said.

"Who else might know about this project?" Erin asked.

"By now? Too many people," Reagan said.

"Meaning ISIS could be behind it?" Erin said.

Reagan thought it over. "They tend to favor slash and burn operations. Al-Qaeda does a better job of long-range planning, fits better with this technology."

"That may be true, but what about the three scientists that were taken?" Erin said. "That was an al-Qaeda move. That would show some sort of down-the-road thinking."

"Point taken," Reagan said. "But why would they bother to go after Mindlovitch?"

No one had a viable answer.

"So where do we go from here?" Erin asked.

"There's one phone call I can make that might help," Reagan said. Then he pulled out his cell and dialed Yevgeny Durov.

"Nikolai, so good to hear from you again," the Russian answered. "Is it possible you're going to buy me dinner twice in one week?"

"That depends entirely on what you have to tell me. Are you in a position to speak freely?"

"In today's world, who knows, but I will take my chances. Let me start by guessing the reason for your call."

"Don't bother, you *know* the reason for my call. I thought these old KGB tactics died with the end of the Cold War."

"Some tactics die harder than others," Durov said.

"Which means poisoning your enemies is still on the table?"

"Who said anything about poison? I believe your new friend had a seizure of some kind. A man his age should not be so rigorous about his workouts. Look at me. I never exercise, and I expect to go on forever."

"You probably will, but that's only because you're an ornery sonofabitch."

"I take that as high praise, coming from you."

"We really need to talk, Yevgeny."

Durov was silent for a moment. Then he asked, "Where are you?"

"In the bosom of my adopted family."

"Ah. As it happens, I am in Washington myself. Perhaps I should allow you to buy me that dinner after all."

"I'll buy you a drink. Dinner depends on whether you have something meaningful to share."

"You drive a hard bargain, Nikolai. Meet me at the bar in the Jefferson Hotel. An hour from now good?"

"Fine. And bring your credit card, in case you disappoint me."

CHAPTER THIRTY

Washington, D.C.

The Jefferson Hotel on 16th Street NW has an intimate bar on the main level, with tables set in alcoves that further enhance the sense of privacy. Located not far from the White House, the hotel's ambiance offers a welcome break from the hectic pace of the nation's capital.

Reagan left the others and went alone to meet with Durov. He knew, if the Russian had anything worth saying, he would only share it in a private discussion. Reagan bypassed the entrance to the hotel lobby and used the door that led from the street directly into the lounge. Durov was already there, his large frame dominating a small table in the near corner.

The Russian did not expend the energy required to get up. He simply extended his hand, said, "Welcome, my friend," then handed Reagan a list of specialty cocktails. "The best mixologists in this city can be found right here," he said, his voice loud enough for the bartender to hear.

The young man behind the bar nodded in appreciation. He was already working on the concoction Durov had ordered.

Reagan told him, "Blanton's on the rocks. Big cube would be good if you have one." Then he took the seat across from Durov. "Every time I turn around lately, you seem to be there."

The Russian shrugged his wide shoulders. "Happenstance, I assure you."

"I think Ian Fleming had something to say about happenstance and enemy action."

Durov showed off his wide smile. "In *Goldfinger*, I believe."

"Go to the head of the class. Didn't think you Soviets appreciated James Bond."

"We're not Soviets, we are Russians again, my friend. And let's just say we like to stay informed about all things western."

The bartender served their drinks, then placed a pewter dish on the table containing assorted nuts and olives.

Reagan lifted his glass and said, "*Nostrovia.*"

Durov smiled at his friend's intentional mispronunciation of the Russian toast. He realized Reagan knew better. "Cheers," Durov replied as they touched glasses and drank.

Reagan said, "Someone told me *nostrovia* is not really a toast, it actually means thank you for a meal or a drink."

"High marks to you, my friend." The Russian paused. "Does that mean you expect me to pay?"

Reagan laughed. "Consider it a wild fantasy." Looking around to ensure they would not be heard, he asked, "Who tried to kill him? And why?"

"I think we can both guess why, although I am not certain what it accomplishes. I suppose that depends on who was behind it, an answer I do not yet have."

"Forgive my bluntness, but are you telling me it was not Moscow?"

"I expect bluntness from you, Nikolai," Durov said with a chuckle. "Otherwise, these get-togethers would be as boring as an embassy dinner." His look became serious. "I have received no indication Moscow had any involvement."

"Is it possible this was a Putin maneuver, but you aren't in the loop?"

Durov pursed his lips for a moment, then said, "I admit I might not have been consulted in advance, but I would've heard something by now. Fact is, I don't see any win in it for us. Putin no longer sees

Mindlovitch as a friend, but he poses no threat. If he has successfully developed the microchip, his death would only tighten Chinese security and complicate matters from our perspective."

"Such as getting your hands on a working prototype."

Durov shrugged.

"That logic works," Reagan admitted, "unless you've already bought off someone in Suzhou to pass you the technology."

"Not impossible, but, again, I know of no such arrangement. And if we bought a prototype, why get rid of Mindlovitch?" Durov picked up his glass and had a long taste of the drink.

"What the hell is that thing?" Reagan asked. "It looks like a Shirley Temple."

"A mix of Stolichnaya, Chambord, and lime." He leaned forward, as if about to impart some important confidential information. "Too sweet for me. Need to finish it off so I can order straight vodka."

Reagan smiled, then drank some of his bourbon. "All right, let's put Moscow aside for the moment. Who would benefit from Mindlovitch's death, whether or not the Ghost Chip is real?"

"That's exactly what I've been contemplating since I heard the news. Neither your country nor mine had anything to gain, not as far as I can see. Likewise, the Chinese would gain nothing. I'm thinking one of those nations you Americans like to call 'state sponsors of terror' as a possible choice."

"Iran? Syria?"

"For example. Or one of the groups we've both been chasing around the world the last twenty years."

"Can you imagine al-Qaeda making a deal in Suzhou to buy a prototype of the chip, then infiltrating Anatole's security team to have him poisoned? Way too subtle for them."

"Agreed, although al-Qaeda can be clever, not to mention forward thinking."

"I said the same thing an hour ago," Reagan told him as he shook his head. "But it doesn't feel right."

Durov responded with a look that said he wasn't disagreeing.

"How about something personal," Reagan suggested, "some sort of vendetta not involving your boy Vlad?"

"Such as?"

"I have no idea, but you know Mindlovitch, you know his history. Anyone that smart and that successful has to have a long list of enemies."

"You think one of them is responsible? I suppose, if you separate this attempt on his life from the research in China, such a thought becomes feasible. But, to borrow your phrase, that notion does not feel right to me. Especially given the timing of your recent visits to his factory and then to his home."

Reagan nodded. "You've come to the same conclusion I have. This attempt on his life and the development of the microchip have to be related. Which means we need to find out how far along they are with the prototype, and who might have bought access to it."

Durov nodded slowly. "As you are so fond of saying, precisely."

* * *

As REAGAN AND DUROV were trying to make sense of what had occurred in California, Anatole Mindlovitch was fighting for his life in the ICU of Cedars Sinai Hospital in Los Angeles. The physicians on his team had already concluded he was infected with some esoteric drug they had yet to identify. His symptoms were inconsistent with any natural medical issue, especially since the man was otherwise in top physical condition.

Mindlovitch was in and out of consciousness. Wired to monitors and connected to breathing and feeding tubes, he was being closely watched by nurses and doctors, including his personal internist, Dr. Kantor, who had been at his bedside since Mindlovitch arrived by ambulance. Kantor was one of Anatole's best friends, and he made sure that access to his patient was restricted to medical personnel with proper credentials.

In addition to his personal loyalty, Kantor had additional incentive to protect his famous patient. Shortly after Mindlovitch was admitted to the hospital, Kantor received a call from Langley, Virginia on his private cell phone. He had never spoken to the man before, but the message was clear. There might be another attempt on his patient's life; assistance with security was being provided; and Kantor was instructed to cooperate with the authorities in not allowing anyone a second chance.

The recovery and good health of Anatole Mindlovitch had become a matter of national security, and Dr. Kantor was instructed—in no uncertain terms—to protect his patient's welfare.

CHAPTER THIRTY-ONE

Baltimore, Maryland

Nahid Jamal received a text instructing him to meet a local contact in the Fells Point area of Baltimore. The message provided an address and time—four that afternoon.

Jamal did not want to go but knew he had no choice. The order had come from the man called Mahdi.

His involvement with these radical Muslims began online. In the beginning, he was inspired by their loyalty to his religion and to the tenets of the Koran. He was pleased when they said he was becoming an integral part of a powerful organization dedicated to their cause. He got caught up in the energy and inclusion they offered. Then, over the course of the ensuing weeks, he came to realize this was more than a spirited exchange of ideas. He learned that their objectives involved much more than mere talk, and he became swept up in the intense emotional pull of their commitment, a fanaticism that resonated with him for many reasons.

Since arriving in the United States nine years ago, Jamal had encountered one disappointment after another, never achieving any part of the American dream of riches and success. Lately, after another long period of unemployment, he landed a job in a pharmacy in Townson, only to be fired weeks later when he was accused of stealing drugs. The Jew who owned the place threatened to go to the police unless Jamal left, never came back, and didn't bother to file for unemployment.

Whether or not Jamal was a thief was irrelevant to him. This was just the latest indignity he suffered at the hands of those who controlled the money, the business, and the appalling American way of life—the same people who had lured his wife away from him with their false promise of more than he could provide.

Falling deeper and deeper into the abyss, he felt rescued by these like-minded brethren, bound together by anger, hate, and a common enemy. It was a bond that transcended family or friendship, a spiritual connection that made him feel alive and important and imbued with purpose.

Until he was confronted with the realities of what was to come.

It became increasingly clear that the murder of others—and likely his own death—was the destiny for which he was being prepared. Suddenly, the rousing words he shared in these secret chat rooms left him with a knot in his stomach. The oaths he took began to feel like psychotic rantings. He worried about what would become of his daughter and wrestled with the dismal specter of his own fate.

In the past several days he decided to be honest about these concerns, writing the group about his doubts, admitting that he had a child, expecting compassion from someone committed to a pious life. He was assured his daughter would be taken care of with money and the acknowledgment that her father had been a hero to their God. When he persisted in expressing his misgivings, the messages took on a different tone. He was accused of blasphemy, of betraying his God and his fellow Muslims. He was reminded of the pledge he had made to Allah and to jihad. There was no explicit threat made against him, but the message was clear—*you are one of us now, and you must honor God by doing your duty.*

Or else.

Jamal stopped confessing his fears. He said that he would do what was expected of him, knowing it was a lie. His passion was gone, the fire extinguished. But he worried that he had already betrayed himself and needed to find a way out, even if he did not yet see a path. For now he would simply go along with them, hoping he would not be one of the chosen to carry out the violent plans being made in the name of Allah.

So today, when he received the message from Mahdi instructing him to meet someone, he had to go.

CHAPTER THIRTY-TWO

CIA Headquarters, Langley

By the time Reagan left Durov at the Jefferson Hotel and rejoined the others at Langley, Bruce Levi had already gone.

"He had to take care of some business," Erin explained, "then he's heading back to California, to see Mindlovitch."

"Understood," Reagan said, then gave a summary of his meeting with Durov.

"You believe him?" Erin asked.

"Yevgeny and I are adversaries, but we respect each other. Not to mention he's saved my life, as you well know." Reagan smiled. "We don't share classified information, and we might play each other a bit, but to lie about this?" He shook his head. "He says he knows nothing of a Russian hit on Mindlovitch, and I believe him."

"He admitted it's something he might *not* know," Cyla Khoury pointed out.

"True, but as he and I discussed, how would Moscow benefit from knocking off Mindlovitch?"

Cyla managed a slight smile. "Putin has been known to hold a grudge."

"I mentioned that," Reagan said.

"Our focus should be the factory in Suzhou," Erin told them.

"Agreed," Reagan said. "If something is going down there, we need to find out what it is."

"After your run-in with the locals," Brandt said, "we can't exactly send any of our people there to knock on the door and ask."

Carol Gellos started laughing. "Alex, I hope Reagan's sarcasm isn't starting to rub off on you."

Brandt began to protest, saying, "I didn't mean—" but Gellos held up her hand.

"Mindlovitch is the one person who could find out what's happening," Reagan interrupted, "but he's out of action, which may be the real explanation for what happened to him." Turning to Erin, he said, "You need to stay in touch with Levi. Find out if Mindlovitch has anything worthwhile to say about all this."

"Will do," she agreed, "but Mindlovitch and his microprocessor may not be our main problem right now. While you were out the DD sent us new information on another possible attack."

"Let's have it," Reagan said.

Erin began describing the recent emails and texts the NSA had intercepted. The pattern of communication was disjointed, as usual, with was no indication of any clear plan. Yet certain words recurred, including boiling water, acid, and rain.

"Some type of manufactured acid rain?" Brandt asked.

"A crop duster filled with some sort of caustic solution?" Gellos suggested.

"That doesn't account for the mention of boiling water," Erin reminded them.

"How do you arrange an attack using boiling water?" Reagan mused aloud.

"Could be a metaphor," Brandt suggested. "Acid tends to bubble up when it interacts with another substance, it can look like boiling water."

"Possible," Erin said. "But then why have those references to boiling water at all? Why not stay with acid?"

"Just adds another layer for us to get through," Reagan said.

"Maybe," she said.

"Whatever it is, we end up chasing the same trail," Reagan said. "Money and supplies. Whether it was the substance they used on the High Line—"

"Something like napalm," Brandt said.

"Right" Reagan said. "Whether it's acid or something else, there's got to be a supply chain for material and money."

"Those sorts of supplies don't require much money," Brandt said, "they just require know-how."

"True," Reagan agreed, "but they also tempt these recruits with cash."

"If not for them, then for the family they're leaving behind," Gellos said.

"The people who carry out these missions are the weakest links in the chain," Reagan said, "and they generally don't have information beyond their limited role. We need to find out who's manipulating them." He stood, and, with the room too small for him to actually pace, he began moving around like a caged animal. "This is such bullshit. With all the talented people and technology we have at our disposal, why can't we put these pieces together?"

Erin knew him well enough not to suggest he cool off. Instead, she said, "While you were with Durov we also received news concerning the recruitment of those four men."

"When you say four men—"

"I mean the two on the High Line and the two who were murdered in Dearborn," Erin said.

He stopped moving. "When were you going to share that?"

"I just did," she replied calmly, then waited for him to sit down. "As you all know, when they send out suicide bombers, they tell them to first destroy any sort of communication device they own. They often take their phone, because they expect them to be destroyed in the explosion, but it gives them the ability to make last-minute contact if a problem arises. They're usually told to get rid of their laptops and tablets. Some do, some don't. In the case of the two men from the

Bronx, they left nothing behind, other than the phone we took from Mustafa Karahan's body."

"What about the two in Dearborn?" Reagan asked.

"They obviously had no idea they were never coming back, so their computers are intact, and we have them." She paused. "We may have a lead on who recruited them."

The others waited.

"As I mentioned in New York, these people go to a lot of trouble to reroute their communications, which makes it difficult for us to pinpoint the original source. Our people say that the initiator of these contacts is using a satellite phone, bouncing the transmissions from one cell location to another. NSA thinks the most recent texts were generated from right here, in Washington."

"Interesting," Reagan said as he leaned back in his chair. "Please tell me they got a location."

"Not that lucky, at least not yet. The origination points varied. Whoever it was is not sitting in their living room when they send these messages."

"But it's definitely Washington?"

Erin nodded. "Seems so. NSA and our team have begun tracking travel patterns for everyone on our watch list who might've come to D.C. recently. It's a longshot, and way too early to know how far we'll get with that, but it's a start. These recruits were all identified, radicalized, and moved around by—"

"Their handler," Reagan said.

Erin nodded. "There's more. The way these attacks are being set up, whoever is behind them is using a method we refer to as planned randomness. They want it to seem as if there's no pattern, but there is."

"So," Gellos said, "find the man doing the planning, decipher the pattern, stop the attacks."

Erin responded with a sad smile. "I wish it were that easy."

"Tell us something we don't know," Reagan said.

"I will." She sat up a bit straighter and pulled three sheets of paper from one of the files. "We've intercepted messages that identify at least one other recruit. His name is Nahid Jamal. Came from Lebanon nine years ago. Lives in Baltimore. Thirty-six, divorced, unemployed. Not on any watch list, by the way." She handed each of the three agents a copy of the data sheet on Jamal. "We need to find him, take him alive, see what he knows."

"When does Kenny want us to make a move?"

She looked at Reagan. "Now," she told him.

CHAPTER THIRTY-THREE

Baltimore, Maryland

Reagan, Gellos, and Brandt went downstairs, grabbed a Company sedan, and headed for Baltimore. As always, Gellos was at the wheel since she couldn't bear to ride with anyone who drove less than twenty miles over the speed limit. Reagan told her more than once, if she hadn't joined the CIA she could've been a cab driver in Rome.

They headed north as Brandt went through the limited dossier they had on Nahid Jamal, reading it aloud.

When he was done, Reagan said, "We start at his apartment."

The other two agents agreed. "With no record of current employment," Gellos said, "there's no place like home."

"Not much here on his ex-wife," Brandt said. "Nurse at Johns Hopkins. Short marriage. One child, a five-year-old daughter."

Reagan nodded. "If we don't find him at his place we'll talk with her."

"Ex-wife. Perfect," Gellos said. "I'm sure she'll be chock-full of helpful information."

"Was that a sexist remark?" Reagan asked.

Gellos responded by stepping on the gas.

They arrived at Jamal's apartment building, which was located in the center of the city slums—not far from the gin mill where the Handler met Mustafa a little more than a week ago. Gellos stayed in the car as the two men got out, had a quick look up and down the street, then headed into the vestibule of the three-story tenement.

Jamal's name was taped to a mailbox indicating his apartment was on the second floor.

When Alex gave Gellos a thumbs-up, she turned off the car, got out, and joined him.

"Second floor," Reagan told her. "You stay here, just in case we have any visitors."

Reagan and Brandt took the stairs to the second landing and knocked on Jamal's door. There was no answer. They waited, knocked again, still no response.

Brandt looked at Reagan, who simply nodded. Brandt drew his weapon as Reagan pulled out some tools and went to work on the lock. In less than a minute he had the door open. Then he also pulled out his gun, and they entered.

It did not take long for them to have a look around the small, poorly furnished apartment. No one was home, but there was an open laptop on the square kitchen table.

"Grab it," Reagan said. "Let's get the hell out of here."

As they left, one of the other doors on the small landing opened slightly. With the chain still in place, a short, older African-American woman peered out. When she saw the two men were armed she went to slam her door shut, but Reagan got his foot in the way first. He holstered his weapon and pulled out his generic federal credentials, which looked very official but said nothing about the CIA. Holding them up he said, "I need to ask you a couple of questions."

"What do you want?" the woman asked in a nervous voice.

Reagan extended his arm a little further, giving her a closer look at his identification. "Federal agents, ma'am. You know the man who lives in that apartment?"

"Arab," she replied, as if that explained everything.

"When was the last time you saw him?"

The woman still had not offered to remove the chain from the door, nor did Reagan ask. "Maybe yesterday." She replied. "Don't think he has a job, just comes and goes."

"You haven't seen him today?"

She shook her head. "Not today." After a slight pause, she said, "He must be in big trouble, feds coming, breaking into his apartment."

Reagan smiled. "The door was unlocked."

The old woman gave him a look that said she was not that easily fooled, federal agent or otherwise. "I don't want no trouble."

"You've got no trouble with us," he assured her. "We just need to find this man, soon as possible. You know his name?"

"Jamal," she said. "Can never remember his first name, some Arab thing."

Reagan motioned to Brandt, who pulled out a card. It had a federal seal on it, his name, and a phone number. "If you see him, please give us a call."

She took the card.

"You don't need to tell anyone you spoke with us," Reagan assured her.

"Me? Tell anyone I talked to the feds? Young man, that is the last thing in the world I'd ever do." Then, as soon as Reagan pulled his foot back, she slammed the door shut.

On the way downstairs, Reagan turned to Brandt. "Let's find his ex-wife."

* * *

It was just after four when Jamal approached the address he had been given, an old brick building along the water in Fells Point. It once housed a factory and had since been converted to offices, without much success. From all appearances, including the "For Lease" signs out front, it seemed almost completely vacant. There was no elevator, so he climbed the stairs to the second floor, found the room number he was given, and knocked on the door.

A tall, dark-skinned Saudi opened the door, smiled, and said, "Nahid Jamal."

Jamal nodded, feeling too nervous to speak.

"Allah be with you," the man said.

"And with you."

The man held the door wider and motioned for Jamal to enter.

Stepping inside, Jamal saw that the room was unfurnished, except for a few chairs and a table set in the middle where two other men were seated. They got to their feet and offered warm greetings, to which he responded in kind.

"Sit," the first man told him, pointing to a chair.

Jamal did as he was told, and the other three took seats around the table.

"The day of retribution is near," the Saudi told him.

"Allah be praised," Jamal said.

"We are told you have questions." The man's tone was calm, even compassionate. "We are about to undertake serious actions, and a crisis of faith is not unusual. We want you to know that we are your friends and that we are here to address your concerns. We would never ask our brothers to do anything they're not prepared to do, even in the name of our God. You understand?"

Jamal felt himself relax lightly. He nodded, then said, "Brothers, I am committed to our cause."

The Saudi smiled slightly as he said, "I believe you, but it sounds as if there is more you want to say. Feel free to speak openly."

Jamal took a moment to look at the other two men. Their eyes did not share the empathic look of the Saudi. "There are many ways to serve Allah, are there not?" he asked.

"Of course," the Saudi replied. "Are you saying you have doubts about your commitment to serve Allah as you had promised?"

Any hope Jamal might have had that this could go well evaporated with that simple question. It was an accusation, and he was left no choice but to say, "I have given my word to God, and I will do what I must."

The Saudi sat back slightly, having a good look at Jamal before he spoke again. Then he said, "You are lying."

CHAPTER THIRTY-FOUR

Baltimore, Maryland

As Gellos drove, Brandt was on the phone, trying to determine in which of the numerous buildings that comprise Johns Hopkins Hospital Jamal's ex-wife worked. It was more a small city than a medical complex, with locations all over Baltimore. After the switchboard transferred him twice, Brandt finally convinced a man in H.R. that he really was a federal agent and that he really did need to speak with Mrs. Jamal.

"She's presently assigned to the General Practice facility on North Caroline Street," the man told him, which is all he was willing to say.

Brandt gave the address to Gellos, which was not far from Jamal's apartment. Gellos made a quick left turn, sped through the maze of city streets, and in short order pulled to a stop in front of the building. The two men jumped out and hurried to the front desk, where Brandt flashed his credentials. After a brief discussion, Sari Jamal was summoned downstairs. By now, Gellos had joined them, and the three agents waited in front of the lobby.

Stepping out of the elevator, Mrs. Jamal was wearing nurse's blues and a worried expression. She looked to be in her early thirties, dark skinned, dark haired, and petite.

Not bothering with an introduction as she approached, the young woman asked, "Is this about my daughter?"

"No," Reagan assured her. "This has nothing to do with your daughter."

"What's happened then?" she asked with obvious relief.

"Nothing has happened," Reagan assured her in a calm tone, "we just have a few questions." He told her that they were federal investigators, then suggested they move to a quiet corner where they could have a measure of privacy.

When they were standing off to the side, she said, "This is about Nahid." It was a statement, not a question.

"Why would you say that?"

She frowned. "Three federal agents come to see me at work, telling me it's not about my daughter and that nothing has happened. Why else would you be here?"

"Has your ex-husband done something that would lead you to that conclusion?"

The frown remained in place as she said, "I have no idea *what* my ex-husband does, other than not paying the child support he owes me. But I can't think of anyone else who would do anything to cause federal agents to come looking for me."

"When was the last time you heard from your ex-husband?"

She looked to each of the three agents in turn, then pulled a cell phone out of her pocket. "I don't hear from him often. He calls when he wants to see Tatiana, and when he does I ask him about the money he owes me. As you could imagine, that tends to cut down on his interest in contacting me." She paused. "But this morning I received an odd text from him." She opened the phone and brought up the message. "Here," she said, handing the cell to Reagan.

The text read, *I have a meeting at 4. In case I do not call later, here is where I am going.* Then it gave an address in Fells Point, on Thames Street, with an office number on the second floor.

"You say this is odd," Reagan said.

"Very. As I said, he almost never texts me, except to see our daughter. Why would he send this, telling me about a meeting? Giving me an address in case he doesn't call later? He never tells me where he's going or what he's doing. And he doesn't even mention Tatiana in the message. Very odd."

Reagan studied Sari Jamal for a moment. She appeared to be a serious person, not likely to overreact to things, especially given her profession. "What do you think it means?"

She shook her head slowly, staring down at the phone as Reagan handed it back to her. "I think he's in trouble. That would seem the only reason he wanted me to know where he was going." She looked up again, the frown having returned. "I think he's scared."

Reagan looked at his watch. It was just after four. "He obviously has not called since you got this."

"No."

Brandt handed her one of his cards and said, "Please let us know if you hear from him."

"I will," she said.

"It would be best," Reagan added, "if you didn't tell him about our discussion."

"I understand," she told them, although her expression made it clear she was not sure she understood any of this.

The three agents thanked her, then hurried out to their car and headed for Fells Point.

Thames Street in Fells Point is at the end of a straight run from Caroline Street, and, even with afternoon traffic, Gellos got them there in only a few minutes.

During the ride, Brandt said, "I agree with his wife, that was a scared message."

"Ex-wife," Reagan corrected him, "and yes, it was."

When they reached the building identified in Jamal's text, Gellos drove past and parked just down the block.

"We have to assume we're walking into trouble," Reagan said. "I'll go in the front entrance, you two come through the side door over there."

"His text said his meeting was on the second floor," Gellos reminded him. "That's where we'll need to be careful."

"Even so," Reagan said, "someone may be posted inside the lobby. Who the hell knows what we'll find?"

"All right," Gellos said. "let's go."

Reagan went straight for the front and, like Jamal earlier that afternoon, found things quiet inside. There was only one staircase, so he waited until he heard Gellos and Brandt enter through the side, then the three of them quietly headed up to the second floor.

They found the office number mentioned in Jamal's text, and Reagan motioned for the others to take positions on either side of the door. Once they were set, he pulled out his automatic, then knocked three times and waited.

They heard some scuffling sounds from inside, so Reagan tried the doorknob, surprised to find it unlocked. He swung the door wide, standing off to the side. From his position, he saw a man drop to his knee, about to fire. Reagan got off two shots as he moved to his left, while Gellos and Brandt also opened fire.

The building was a sturdy old brick structure, but the interior work that divided it into offices was finished with basic sheetrock and metal studs. Bullets began piercing the walls they were using for cover, so Gellos and Brandt dove to their sides, away from the fusillade now being unleased from inside. Reagan followed Gellos to the left.

"What'd you see?" Gellos asked as they crouched on the ground, side by side.

"One shooter, another man sitting at a table, not moving."

"There's clearly more than one guy shooting at us now, Nick."

Reagan nodded. "Let's see if they want to live or die." In a loud voice, he called out, "We're federal agents with backup outside. Toss your weapons, and come out with your hands on your heads."

The response was a string of Arabic profanities, followed by another barrage of shots.

Reagan held up his hand, telling Brandt to hold his fire for now.

"We going to wait them out?" Gellos asked.

"From the look of the room, I don't think they were expecting company. And the door was open," Reagan said. "Their supply of ammunition is probably limited."

"Not our style to just sit here," she said.

Reagan smiled. "No, it's not."

Brandt signaled to them. He had moved down the corridor to the right, where he was pointing at another door, and they immediately understood. These offices probably had side entrances, for tenants looking for a suite of rooms. Brandt was telling them he would enter from the side and outflank them.

Reagan nodded and motioned for Gellos to try the same thing on the left.

Another round of gunfire from inside the office covered the noise the two agents made as they broke through the doors to the left and right. A few moments later, Reagan heard the sound of doors being kicked in, followed by an exchange of shots reverberating from inside. He was on his feet again, moving toward the open doorway, firing into the room, the three agents hitting the men inside from three different vantage points.

It was soon over, silence replacing the deafening noise, the smell of smoke and death hanging over them.

Reagan entered, seeing three Arab men on the ground. Brandt and Gellos were retrieving their weapons, just in case.

A fourth man was seated at the table, his ankles bound to the legs of the chair, his hands tied behind him. He was obviously dead.

"Jamal," Gellos said.

"Afraid so," Reagan said.

They had a closer look, seeing that his eyes had been gouged out and his throat slit.

Gellos shook her head. "Would have been helpful if we could have spoken with him."

"Any of them," Brandt said as he pointed to one of the men on the floor who was still breathing.

Reagan walked over and kneeled down. The man was panting heavily, struggling with almost certain death.

"Why did you kill Jamal?" Reagan asked.

The man ignored him, staring up at the ceiling as he desperately clung to life.

"I can call an ambulance."

The man turned to look at Reagan. "You lie. All of you infidels lie," he said, then gasped for air. "I am going to meet my God."

"Uh huh. Well, for a guy in a hurry to meet his God, you certainly seem to be working hard to hang on. Why not tell me why you killed Jamal?" He pulled out his cell. "Answer that one question, and I'll call for help."

The man looked like he was about to spit in Reagan's face, but the effort led to a long coughing jag. When he was done, he clutched at his chest, breathed one last breath, and was dead.

"Damn," Reagan said as he got to his feet. "We need to get a team down here, figure out who they are, how they knew Jamal."

Brandt said, "First the two men in Dearborn, now Jamal. Why are they killing their own recruits?"

"Don't have a clue," Reagan said, "but I know one thing."

The other two looked at him.

"If we can figure it out, we can get to whoever is running this operation."

CHAPTER THIRTY-FIVE

New York City

Bob Nelson's magazine series on terrorism was still winning rave reviews. In fact, the latest installment was already creating buzz about a possible Pulitzer. The articles were well written, well reasoned, and extremely well informed.

That last part was receiving most of the attention.

Like other members of the Fourth Estate, Nelson was sensitive about his First Amendment rights and adamant about not giving up his sources. Nevertheless, when a reporter is writing in-depth articles that include credible stories from inside al-Qaeda, people become curious about where the information is coming from. In Nelson's case, the curious included the NSA, Homeland Security, and a host of other agencies.

More dangerous to Nelson, however, was the attention he was arousing from the other side.

While Reagan, Gellos, and Brandt turned the bloody scene in Fells Point over to the forensic team that arrived, Nelson was receiving yet another threatening phone call at the office.

He had received a number of these messages, his private line recording them all, but if his tormentors suspected they were being taped, it was not stopping them. They treated him to the usual insults, calling him a filthy American, lying infidel, and so on. Nelson was numb to that sort of diatribe, having the sort of toughness one acquires over the years working as a beat reporter in New York City. At first, he wrote off the calls as the work of cranks and oddballs. Lately, however, the frequency and intensity had increased, and there were now threats of physical recrimination. His boss suggested they provide him some sort of security, but, up to now, Nelson waved it off.

The call he received today, however, was different. For the first time, they mentioned his wife and children, referring to Claudette, Lauren, and Peter by name, then saying, "Remember, we know where you live."

That was when he called Reagan. Catching his friend on his way back from Baltimore to Langley, Nelson described the latest threat.

"With everything that's already been written about al-Qaeda, it's hard for me to believe I'm provoking this sort of reaction," Nelson said.

"Don't be naive, pal," Reagan replied. "Your series is hitting a nerve. They're more concerned about a turncoat in their ranks than they are about you."

"This may seem an obvious question, but concerned how?"

"The stories you're writing about the activity inside their camps, the way they train, the methods they use to recruit—they can't be happy someone is feeding this information to you. Might even be someone high enough in their ranks to really worry them. Maybe someone who became disillusioned enough to give you details that could cause them problems. You might expose their cells here in the States. Identify leaders, the places they hide, or where they build their explosive devices. Any of that make sense?"

"Are you asking if I believe those concerns are possible?"

"That's what I'm asking," Reagan said.

Nelson took a moment, clearly not the first time he had considered the issue. "I see all that. But as I've said, there's already so much information about al-Qaeda out there, can I really be such a thorn? I mean, they post propaganda online themselves, and their internal security is about as tight as a sieve. If they didn't spend so much time running from cave to cave, we would've wiped them out long ago."

Reagan laughed into the phone. "I haven't seen that in your articles."

"I haven't written that yet," Nelson admitted. "As inflammatory as that will be, I'm saving it for the final piece."

"Another little tidbit your source is sharing with you?"

"We're not going there, Nick."

"You called *me*, remember?"

"I called my best friend for help."

"All right," Reagan said, giving it a moment. "How about you just tell me if your source is safe."

"Are you asking if he's reliable, or if he's in any immediate danger himself?"

Reagan uttered another throaty laugh. "Do you have to keep rephrasing my questions, Bob? Damn, I thought you were a reporter, not a lawyer."

"Sorry."

"Okay. I meant the latter."

Nelson shook his head. "No, I don't think he's in any imminent danger."

"Do the two of you meet in person?"

"Not anymore," Nelson admitted. "We did in the beginning. Once the articles came out, we agreed it would be best not to risk it."

"And you're not going to tell me who this is, or where I can find him."

"You already know that answer."

"Look, Bob, you called to tell me they've started threatening your family. That raises the stakes."

"I know."

"Tell me what you want me to do."

"I'm not sure. I realize you can't provide a one-man security detail."

"I would if I could, but it wouldn't be effective. You need a team to be watching your family twenty-four seven."

"Which means private security. Or looking to the government?"

"I don't see asking the authorities. They're going to accuse you of shielding a terrorist informant who could have valuable intel."

"I get it."

"I'm sure your magazine has security people they work with."

"They've offered, but I turned them down."

"But now that they've mentioned Claudette and the kids, it's a different story."

"Yes, it is, which is why I called you. I don't want the magazine hiring some rent-a-cop outfit." He paused. "You know people in the private sector."

"I do."

"Serious people, who know what they're doing?"

"That's right."

"Can you set it up?" Nelson asked.

"I can, and I will."

"Whatever it costs, Nick. I'll work something out with the magazine, but I want this done right, and I want it done now. This is about my family."

"Understood. I'll take care of it."

Reagan hung up and turned to the other two agents in the car.

"We got the gist," Gellos told him. "They're threatening Bob's family because of the articles."

Reagan nodded. "Got to make some calls."

CHAPTER THIRTY-SIX

Washington, D.C.

The Handler's caution had turned to paranoia. Angry messages were coming from Syria and Kabul, and he did what he could to limit his responses while maximizing the encryption techniques available to him. He warned the emissaries of al-Zawahiri about reckless exchanges, whether via text, email, or phone, but he could do nothing to stop their flood of demands.

The planned suicide bombings in New York, although people were killed and injured, were ultimately judged by the hierarchy as a failure. Much more had been expected from the attack. The mistakes made in recruiting Yousef Omarov, the young man from Dearborn, were further evidence of incompetence. How could the Handler have chosen someone whose judgment was so flawed, who failed to control his emotions in the face of minimal provocation? The need to dispose of him, and his friend Fariq Homsi, heightened the risks already being taken by loyal members of their cause.

Now there was the matter of Nahid Jamal. The error in selecting him was bad enough, but added to it was the loss of three loyal men when the Americans intervened. Which raised other troubling questions. How had they been located? What might their enemies have discovered before those three men were murdered? Assuming Jamal had betrayed them, how much information had he already shared?

The Handler was furious. He was a loyal and ardent devotee of jihad, dedicated to achieving a bloody revenge that knew no bounds. *How could they doubt my commitment to the cause?* he asked himself.

But al-Zawahiri and his lieutenants were becoming ever more intolerant of any sort of failure and increasingly concerned with the rise of ISIS.

The former leader of ISIS, Abu Ibrahim al-Hashimi al Qurashi, despised al-Qaeda and was determined to replace them as the true leader of the *jihad*. Since his suicide the rivalry had become even worse, including actions by the splinter group known as ISIS-K. Led by a young man known as Shahab al-Muhajir, or his alias Sanaullah al-Sadiq, their faction was even more reckless and hateful. While these cultural adversaries were not something al-Zawahiri could blame on Mahdi, they required a show of force, and his recent missteps would only make their work harder.

As the CIA learned over the past several years, the competition between ISIS and al-Qaeda was something that should not be under-estimated and might well be exploited. It was a rivalry driven by a competition to enlist young men and women willing to fight and die, and the need for the money and materials required to carry out those missions. While both ISIS and ISIS-K had been routed from their strongholds by the prior American administration, those devoted to Allah were turning their loyalty back to the terrorist organization that had repeatedly demonstrated its ability to carry out dramatic attacks that drew the world's attention.

The image of ISIS was eroding, appearing to be more a disor-ganized source of street attacks rather than a serious organization. Al-Qaeda, on the other hand, was known for its willingness to bide its time—as Reagan had pointed out in his controversial memo, they were pursuing a multi-generational view necessary to fulfill the exhor-tations of the Koran.

Now, however, despite their strategy of long-term terror and domination, they were determined to step up their game or lose their relevance in the fight against the infidels. The Handler was being told it was time to seize the higher ground, and his recent mistakes were raising questions about his ability to get the job done.

Mahdi was enraged by this indictment, thinking about the sacrifices he had made in his life and the risks he had taken—and was continuing to take—on behalf of their cause. Yet he knew better than to interpose any sort of defense. It would sound weak and only embolden his detractors. His job was to ensure that the two remaining missions of the three-pronged attack he had been working on would be successfully completed. Nothing short of that would satisfy his superiors, prove his worth, and shield him from the fate that awaited him if he were to fail again.

After the latest warnings, he sent a message to Ahmed in Chicago, asking whether arrangements for the truck had been completed. Then he sent an encrypted text to his top operative in Shanghai, asking whether they had secured the prototype of the Ghost Chip.

CHAPTER THIRTY-SEVEN

CIA Headquarters, Langley

Sasha Levchenko was one of the agency's most talented computer experts. He was in his early thirties, tall, thin, with straight dark hair and angular features. He always seemed to look tired and almost always sported what appeared to be three days' growth of beard.

Sasha had previously earned a decent living as a consultant for small companies in the private sector. In those days, he used his spare time to hack into government websites.

As Reagan came to learn, many techies who wreak electronic havoc do not do it for profit, they do it simply to prove they could. Bored with helping clients on their computers—people they generally regarded as morons for their inability to use the most basic software or install standard upgrades into their systems—they enjoyed the challenge of breaking codes, finding ways around protective firewalls and otherwise outsmarting others playing the same game. Ultimately they would be caught and, depending on the damage they had done, punished accordingly. In Sasha's case, his reckoning came after he took a run at the CIA.

The Company's specialists detected the attempted intrusion, found the location of the server, and identified the user. That's when Sasha received a visit from Nick Reagan and Carol Gellos. They were dispatched to pick him up at his apartment, where they seized his four laptops and brought him in for questioning. This was a matter of national security, and Sasha was given no warning of the arrest. Reagan and Gellos had no warrant, and there was no offer of a lawyer.

The young man was left to cool his heels in a holding pen overnight as his hardware was examined by experts on the second floor. The consensus was that he had not done the agency any harm, at least not yet, but his other work—invading various bank and credit card sites as well as the Social Security Administration—was potentially damaging and quite impressive. With Kenny's approval, his two agents sat with the young man and made him an offer—a long jail term or a job with the agency.

"It doesn't appear you stole any money when you were hacking these sites," Gellos said.

Sasha gave his head a vigorous shake. "Never."

"This was all about the challenge?"

"Yeah," Sasha said, "it was about the fun."

Reagan stared at him. "You think a ten-year stretch in a federal prison will be fun?"

Sasha blinked but said nothing.

"We have a better idea."

That was four years ago, and Sasha had been with the Company ever since. He was assigned to a unit that monitors cyberattacks, but this evening he had been brought in to address the possibility of a more violent assault.

When Reagan, Gellos, and Brandt got back to Langley, they provided a report to the deputy director on the events in Baltimore that afternoon, then all four of them joined Erin and Levchenko in a conference room down the hall.

"Haven't seen you since you helped us with our problems in London," Reagan said to Sasha.

Levchenko nodded. "You woke me up two days in a row at four in the morning to get that help."

"Sleeping through the night is overrated," Reagan replied. "What've we got?"

As the group took their seats around the large table, Erin asked Kenny, "We have a few items to cover, where would you like me to begin, sir?"

"Start with the new intel," Kenny told her.

Erin turned to the digital screen against the wall and hit the remote. The monitor lit up, displaying an array of various data. "We've received some leads from the NSA and pieced it together. It appears we're looking at a particular type of structure. Sasha will explain."

Looking up from his laptop, Sasha said, "We've been studying buildings with clear roofs supported by metal struts."

"Such as?" Reagan asked.

"A domed stadium. A modern office or apartment building. An enclosed mall. Train station that's been updated. Not so many of those, though."

Looking at the screen, Reagan said, "Seems there are a lot of the others."

Sasha used a remote, and a group of large, recently constructed buildings appeared on the monitor. "Each of these designs has a clear roof or center atrium to allow the light in."

As the group turned to the screen, Sasha took them through a number of photos.

"This is endless," Reagan said. "Can we narrow it down?"

"Not sure yet," Sasha admitted, "but we're working on it. If this is the sort of attack being considered—and combined with the interrogation of the three scientists in Pakistan, we believe it is—an explosion would be particularly devastating to this sort of structure."

"You're saying these buildings are more vulnerable than other types of construction?" Gellos asked.

"Absolutely," Sasha said. "If the explosives are placed and detonated properly, the ceiling itself would become a weapon. Thousands of shards of thick glass and heavy plexiglass would come raining down on anyone inside. Along with the metal supports."

"My group has a lot of work ahead of us on this," Erin said. "We'll be looking for anything that might identify the target, discuss the movement of explosives, and so forth."

"Got it," Reagan said. "You said we had a few things to cover."

"Yes. Anatole Mindlovitch spoke with Bruce Levi."

"I don't suppose he mentioned anything about—"

"At the moment, all he wants to know is who tried to kill him," Kenny interrupted. "He's asking Levi to help."

"He intends to conduct a private investigation, have a renowned criminologist head the team?" Reagan asked.

"We believe so," Erin told him.

"So where does that leave us with the chip?"

"Mindlovitch has no reason to believe the United States was behind the attempt on his life," Kenny said, "and we've taken steps to protect him since it happened. He may become more sympathetic to our concerns."

"Something you hope Bruce Levi can help with," Reagan said.

"Exactly," the DD replied.

"What do you want us to do in the meantime?" Reagan asked.

"That brings us to topic three," Erin replied. Then she turned again to Sasha.

"You may have left four bodies in Baltimore," Levchenko said, "but the axiom that 'Dead men tell no tales' is not true in the modern era."

Kenny frowned. "I already have one inept comedian on my team," he told Sasha, followed by a quick glance at Reagan. "Get to the point."

Sasha nodded. "The forensic team has already identified the three shooters. DHS has sent people out, collecting anything they can from their homes, questioning spouses, significant others, the usual drill. They're also working on their cell phones, and you brought us Jamal's laptop, which could be helpful."

"Our intention," Kenny said to Sasha, "is to have you track all communications any of them had back to the source."

"To identify their superior numbers in the al-Qaeda chain of command," Reagan said.

"I've got Jamal's laptop, and I'm working on it. Hoping DHS will share the cell phones with me soon," Sasha said.

"Which may raise another political dilemma," Kenny said. "Suppose we develop proof that an attack is being planned, such as the one Sasha described. We have the style of building but not the location."

"Which means someone has to decide how much of this the government is obligated to reveal to the public?" Reagan said.

"That's the problem," Kenny agreed. "Until we have possible targets, it would be irresponsible to air any of it."

"Not our issue," Reagan said. "Our job is to find the place."

Kenny nodded. "While Sasha and Erin coordinate their efforts on the laptops and phones, I want you three working on whatever leads are developed. And Reagan."

"Yes, sir."

"We do not want to get into any jurisdictional disputes. Proceed with total discretion."

Reagan smiled but said nothing.

CHAPTER THIRTY-EIGHT

New York City

After hearing from Bob Nelson earlier that afternoon, Reagan had immediately made two phone calls. That was all he required to arrange a protection detail for his friend, as well as Nelson's wife and children. Reagan chose men he had worked with before, all former military with combat experience, all of whom he trusted, and all who were talented and ruthless when the need arose. Reagan told them to be invisible but vigilant, to stay close to each member of the Nelson family, and not to leave anything to chance.

The leader of the detail was Liam Burke, a former Navy SEAL who had served with Reagan in a joint military operation and had helped him since. He was tough and skilled and completely reliable. When Reagan told him, "This job is personal," Burke did not have to ask what that meant.

While the small team arranged to take up their positions, Reagan knew the one person they could not protect was Nelson's source. They did not know who he was or even where to start looking.

As it turned out, they could have begun at the Sloan Kettering Medical Center.

Tarek Shawi was a fifty-six year old Syrian. He had volunteered to travel to the United States several months ago, ostensibly to scout potential targets for al-Qaeda attacks and to assist in domestic

211

recruitment. Unknown to those who sent him, he had learned he was suffering from lung cancer.

He took an apartment in lower Manhattan near the World Trade Tower, the irony not lost on Shawi. Many of the first responders who had rushed to the scene of the attack on Nine-Eleven had died from this same disease or were still suffering its effects. Now Shawi had chosen New York as his new home in the belief he would get life-saving treatment there.

Before he left Damascus, traveling through the open-gate policies of Germany and Sweden, he decided he was done with the terrorist network and saw his journey as part salvation, part escape.

It was not only the confrontation with his own mortality that led him to this decision. He had become increasingly disappointed with the actions of those to whom he had pledged his life. They began as crusaders but had since become indiscriminate butchers, confusing the real tenets of jihad with mass murder and pointless carnage. Tarek had come to realize that he knew the Koran better than any of those he worked with in Syria and Iraq. He understood the teachings of Mohammed and the true meaning of the religious movement he had sworn to pursue. He was frustrated with meaningless attacks that did not promote the word of Allah; killing innocents as well as their own people, without purpose or reason; and destroying mosques and irreplaceable religious artifacts with no thought of what these centuries-old relics meant to the Islamic world.

The new al-Qaeda leadership was following the path ultimately walked by every violent autocrat—blood feeds power, murder ensures fear, and the noble purpose which informed their cause in the beginning was corrupted by the need to preserve control. They had become as bad as the infidels they despised, proving the adage about power corrupting the powerful.

Tarek was supposed to visit Chicago, to interact with the cell established by the Handler. Instead, he landed at JFK and promptly lost himself in the multi-ethnic diversity of Manhattan. He brought a large sum of cash and arranged in advance to set up a bank account to which he transferred enough money to guarantee he would be comfortable for the rest of his life, however long that might be.

Using false identification, he kept to himself, pursued a solitary existence, and made weekly rides uptown to Sloan Kettering for chemotherapy treatments and checkups. He was enjoying his anonymity, dressing in an inconspicuous manner, and dining in his apartment or in places crowded with locals and tourists. Those he passed always seemed to be busy in the way people in New York are busy—preoccupied with themselves, not taking any notice of him. He was one of the nameless people no one sees as they hurry back and forth on the city streets.

Today was a treatment day, which he welcomed and dreaded in equal parts. He realized it was the path to survival, but he felt he was just regaining his strength from the devastating effects of the previous intravenous injection of poisonous chemicals into his system. Now he would have to go through it again, then make the taxi ride back to his apartment where he would lie in bed for two days, staring at the television, waiting to recover.

Before he left his apartment this morning, he pulled out a burner phone and called Bob Nelson's private line.

"Good morning," he said.

Nelson did not recognize the incoming number, but he knew the voice. "I'm glad you called. How are you?"

Tarek had never told Nelson anything about his illness, but from their earliest meetings it was obvious to the reporter that the Syrian had a health issue. "I'm well," he said. "Your latest article was quite good."

Nelson did not respond to the compliment. Instead, he said, "I've received some more of those phone calls."

"I see," Tarek replied.

"No, you don't," Nelson said. "They're threatening my family."

"Typical," Tarek said. "It's me they want, not you, but you should take steps to protect yourself."

"I have," Nelson told him. "Are *you* safe?"

"As safe as I can be," the Syrian replied.

"Is there any way for you to arrange protection of some sort?"

"Not without risking exposure."

"Isn't your survival more important than the possibility you'll be identified by someone on our side?"

Tarek was endlessly fascinated by the naïveté of Americans. They seemed to believe "their side" always occupied the higher moral ground. "You think my capture by federal agents will be any better than my own people finding me?"

"Of course I do."

Tarek smiled. "All right, I'll be especially careful. You please do the same."

"I will."

"I'll phone you in three days," Tarek told him, then ended the call and made ready for his ride uptown.

As Tarek finished his brief discussion with Nelson, two men were waiting in a car on Washington Street, outside the rear of Tarek's apartment building. A third stood on West Street, near the front entrance. They had been watching their prey for the past two days, since his location was discovered.

It had taken some time to find him, but in the end there were electronic and financial footprints to follow, as well as his contact with the reporter Robert Nelson. They began looking for him shortly after Tarek did not arrive for his initial meeting in Chicago. It was obvious he had turned, but no one knew why. Was it for money? A woman? Some crisis of faith? In the end, the reason did not matter, he had to be found and punished.

Through their recent surveillance, they knew he was most likely to use the back exit when leaving his building. They had been there for less than an hour when the Syrian emerged, looking for the car he had called. Before Tarek could head down the street to where a small SUV waited, the two men emerged from their sedan and approached him, one moving to each side. The man on his right grabbed Tarek by the arm, preventing him from taking another step.

"We can kill you here, or you can come with us and be given an opportunity to explain yourself," the other man said.

Tarek looked from one to the other. "An opportunity to explain myself," Tarek repeated. "That is an offer I believe I must decline."

The man on his left did not hesitate. He pulled out the knife he was holding in his pocket and drove it into the Syrian's side, the sharp steel sliding through Tarek's clothing and into his flesh.

The pain was so intense all he could do was gasp.

Then the two men dragged him the few paces to their car, opened the back door, and shoved Tarek inside. He lay across the seat, bleeding as they drove off, another invisible moment in New York City.

CHAPTER THIRTY-NINE

New York City

Reagan received an urgent voicemail from Nelson and called right back.

"What's up?"

"I just got a text."

"Everything okay with Claudette and the kids?"

"They're fine. This was something different. It says, 'The traitor is ours, and you are next.'"

"The 'traitor' obviously referring to your source."

"What else could it mean?"

"If you know where he lives, his real name, anything we could check out, now's the time to tell me."

Nelson drew a deep breath. "Don't have any idea where he lives. He said his name is Tarek, don't know if that's true or not, don't even have a last name. I have a feeling it won't matter anymore."

"Because of the message?"

"I have an emergency cell phone number for him. I called him as soon as I got the text. Someone else answered, called me a lot of names, made another threat, and hung up."

"Which means they do have him."

"And he may dead already, according to what they said."

"Maybe not. They'll be likely to try and get information from him first. Give me the emergency number, I'll have the phone traced."

Nelson did not hesitate.

"I've already got my people watching you and your family. You'll be fine."

"Will we?"

Reagan did not respond.

"We need to talk."

"I'm listening," Reagan said.

"Not on the phone. Are you in New York?"

"I will be tonight, coming back with Erin."

"Can we meet when you get here?"

"Consider it done. I'll pass this phone number to someone, let you know what I find. Get in touch with me if anything changes in the meantime."

"Good."

"And, Bob—"

"I know. Be careful."

"Precisely."

That evening, Nelson met with Reagan and Erin at Shun Lee, a Chinese restaurant on West 65th Street, not far from the Nelsons' apartment.

"Claudette stayed home with Peter and Lauren."

Reagan nodded. "Something tells me you didn't want her to hear this conversation."

"No," Nelson conceded, "I didn't."

"What does she know about your source?" Erin asked.

"Nothing, she knows nothing."

"Where does she think you're getting your information?"

Nelson had a taste of his hot and sour soup, then placed the ceramic spoon on the table. "After all these years together, she understands there are things she is better off not knowing."

"So, she doesn't ask about your anonymous tips," Reagan said.

"No," Nelson said, then allowed himself a slight smile, the first one all day. "That's what I live for, anonymous tips."

"Have you told Claudette we have people keeping an eye on her and the kids?"

He shook his head. "Is that wrong? I don't want her to worry any more than she already does." After a slight hesitation, he added hopefully, "Especially if it amounts to nothing."

But Reagan was not hopeful. "They grabbed Tarek, which means this is serious. Claudette deserves to be warned, so she can be alert to anything suspicious."

"She's a New Yorker, Nick, she's already suspicious."

Before Reagan could reply, Erin said, "Tell her, Bob."

Hearing it from Erin left him no choice. "I will, I promise."

Reagan then shared what Sasha had found by tracking Tarek's phone number and triangulating various calls he had sent and received, several of them with Nelson. "We located Tarek's apartment building. I had someone speak with the doorman, but he was inside when Tarek was taken this morning and didn't see much. Said Tarek seemed to know the two men who were speaking with him. Couldn't see the car they got into from where he was, but assumed they drove off together."

"Damn."

"From there, Tarek's phone showed he was traveling south and then east through the Brooklyn-Battery Tunnel. That's where the signal ended. Whoever grabbed him destroyed the phone after they got what they wanted from it."

"They might have my personal cell number," Nelson said.

"They likely had that already."

"What about Tarek, no way to trace him beyond that?"

"Not without the locator signal from his phone," Reagan said. "They probably broke into pieces and tossed it out the window inside the tunnel. We're working on an I.D. of the car, a description of the two men, the usual. Sasha did find out one thing that might be helpful when he hacked into Tarek's phone records." He paused. "Your friend called Uber for a ride uptown, to Sloan Kettering. We followed up, found out he has cancer, was due for a chemo session today."

Nelson began nodding his head slowly. "He never told me, but I guessed he was dealing with something like that."

Reagan picked up his spoon and started in on the spicy soup. "That's my report, but you called the meeting."

"Right," Nelson said, then looked from Reagan to Erin. "The recent attack, the one on the High Line."

"We remember," Reagan told him.

"I think Tarek knew it was coming."

"Bob—"

"Take it easy. I knew nothing in advance, that's something I would have warned you about. But he did say some things I didn't understand at the time, things he wouldn't explain. Then, after it happened, I began to put things together."

"You still didn't call me."

"I had nothing to tell you. It wasn't as if he told me about another attack."

"But you think he knew that one is coming."

"I do, and I confronted him about it afterward. He denied knowing anything about the High Line, but from what he said I'm convinced he knew there were attacks being planned."

Erin stared at him. "You have anything more specific than that?" she asked.

"Wish I did, but I got the impression that whatever they're working on comes from the Koran."

"He said that?" Reagan asked.

"Not exactly, more like it was a mandate or a prediction, something like that."

"No details?" Erin asked. "No reference to a section of the Koran?"

Nelson shook his head. "You read my articles, you know about this perverse competition between al-Qaeda and ISIS. The rise of

Sanaullah and ISIS-K also threatens the power base that's eroding underneath Zawahiri."

"We know," Erin said.

"That was one of the reasons Tarek left al-Qaeda. He felt they were losing their sense of purpose."

"Other than killing and maiming innocent people," Reagan reminded him.

"I know it sounds ridiculous to discuss spirituality when we're referring to terrorists who randomly slaughter people."

"Yes, Bob," Reagan said, "it does."

"All the same, there's a sense in the Arab world that al-Qaeda has a purer understanding of the Koran and *jihad*. According to Tarek, al-Qaeda is having difficulty finding qualified recruits and maintaining its influence. They're taking on young men and women with profiles more appropriate to psychiatric commitment than religious commitment."

"If you're trying to convince me that al-Qaeda is populated by a bunch of homicidal lunatics, I'm already a true believer. What has this got to do with the plan Tarek referred to?"

"That's the thing," Nelson said. "He gave me nothing specific, and I'm not sure he actually knew. What he did say, was that al-Qaeda was turning to the Koran for guidance in their fight against the infidels."

Erin was feeling as frustrated as Reagan. "Not exactly a news flash," she said.

"It wasn't a general comment," Nelson told them. "I think they're planning a series of attacks based on the word of Mohammed."

"Tarek actually said that?" Reagan asked.

"More or less."

"And that was it?"

Nelson paused. "I wish I had more to give you. I pressed him, believe me, but that's the gist of what he told me."

"That their next assault is going to be something predicted in the Koran?"

Nelson nodded. "I believe so. I only wish I could figure out what it is."

Reagan felt his jaw tense up as he said, "That's precisely what we're going to have to do."

CHAPTER FORTY

New York City

Reagan excused himself, stepped out onto Sixty-Fifth Street, and called a secure line at Langley. He asked the operator to transfer him to Sasha.

"Working late?"

"I prefer working late," Sasha said, "as long as no one is going to wake me in the middle of the night."

"I'll keep that in mind," Reagan said, then described what Nelson just told him. "I'd like you to have a look."

"At what? Like you said, there's not much to go on."

"The starting point is obviously the attack at the High Line. We need to analyze every aspect of how it was carried out and what they intended to accomplish there, try to match it up with something in the Koran." Reagan paused. "Actually, there is something about it that's been bugging me."

Sasha waited.

"The material they used in those suicide vests. The bulk of it was closer to napalm than dynamite. Why? If they were looking for maximum damage, why not use the typical plastique, or some other combustible recipe they typically go for?"

"I see your point."

"I was there, and couldn't help thinking of the expression, 'raining fire.'"

"You think that's what they were going for."

"I do. And it's clear their target was the fashion show. Maybe there's a connection."

"Raining fire on scantily clad women, something like that?"

"Something like that."

"We should get our Muslim scholars looking at this," Sasha said.

"I'll leave that to you. I also want you to do key word searches through the Koran, see what you can come up with on your own."

"Got it."

"Thanks," Reagan said, rung off, called Carol Gellos on her cell, and filled her in.

"It's a theory worth testing," Gellos agreed.

"Let Alex know what we're looking for. The more eyes we have on this the better."

"Done," Gellos said. "I'll also have Sasha read us in on anything he finds, so we're all up to speed."

Back inside the restaurant, Nelson gave his friend a curious look, but Reagan did not share his thoughts or discussions. "Better this way," he explained.

Nelson frowned. "This information highway just became a one-way street?"

"It's a matter of your safety. The less you know from me—" he began to say, then felt the phone vibrate in his pocket. Pulling it out, he saw the call was from Liam Burke, the man heading the protection detail for the Nelsons. Reagan connected, then said, "Go."

"We've got activity on the street," Burke told him.

"Hostiles?"

"My guess is affirmative."

"How many players?"

"I see three."

"How many you have on site?"

"McShane and me."

"Any action yet?"

"Not yet."

"I'm nearby, on my way."

Erin and Nelson saw the look of concern on Reagan's face.

"I've got to leave," he told them as he got to his feet.

Nelson also stood. "It's about my family, isn't it?" When Reagan hesitated, he said, "Don't lie to me, Nick."

"There's activity on your street," Reagan admitted.

"I'm coming with you."

"The hell you are."

"The hell I'm not."

Reagan looked down at Erin. "I guess you're buying dinner. I'll call as soon as we know what's going on."

"You want me to phone for backup? NYPD?"

"I'll take care of that once I have more information," Reagan told her. Then he and Nelson hurried out of the restaurant.

CHAPTER FORTY-ONE

New York City

Nelson's apartment was only a few blocks away, and, given the heavy traffic that time of day, Reagan decided to go on foot. As they ran up Broadway, he called Burke for an update.

"Looks like they're casing Nelson's building."

"Enough certainty to take them out?" Reagan asked.

"Negative. If I'm wrong, it would be murder. Once they make their move, I'll make my mine."

"Copy that. I'm less than three minutes away on foot. And just so you know, I have Nelson with me."

"Bad idea, Nick. If this goes sideways we don't need a civilian to worry about."

"Understood, my responsibility. Details please."

"Two men in an SUV drove by, slowed as they went past the Nelsons' brownstone, then came around the block and made another loop. Not unusual in this neighborhood, as you know, parking spaces are tough to find, but they're not looking for a parking space. There was one not far from me, and they went right by it. A couple of minutes ago they pulled up to a hydrant down the block. That's where the third man showed up, on foot. Met them there."

"Are they moving?"

"Not yet, they seem to be talking things over."

"Where are you?"

"Directly across the street from Nelson's apartment, in front of a basement entrance, just below street level."

"You have a clear sight line?"

"I do. I'll move down another couple of steps, keep out of view if they get close."

"What about McShane?"

"He's across the street, a couple of buildings to my right. Hostiles are to my left."

"Okay, I have the picture, keep this line open so I know what's going on."

Reagan and Nelson reached 69th Street, one block south of the where the Nelsons lived.

"It's likely they'll know you by sight," Reagan told his friend. "I'll go ahead, but you have to hang back. Burke sees three of them, but there's no way of knowing if they have other lookouts in the area."

"It's my family, Nick," he protested.

"And you won't be doing them any good getting yourself shot on the street."

"Tell me what to do."

"Head to Central Park West, then come up and around to 70 from that direction. You'll be against the flow of traffic, so you can see what's coming at you if their SUV moves. Stay close to the buildings, walk at a normal speed. According to Burke they're on the far west end of the street. It won't be that easy to make you from that distance, so you may provide a helpful distraction."

"You're heading up Columbus, coming at them from behind?"

"I am. Let's hope they don't have anyone on their rear flank." As Nelson hurried off, Reagan put the phone to his ear. Burke was still there. "What've we got?"

"Movement. One crossed over to my side of the street, walking slowly this way. Another is keeping pace with him on the other side."

"On the side where their brownstone is?"

"Affirmative."

"You think McShane can see them from where he's standing?"

"Clear line."

"Third man stayed with the car?"

"Lights off, but it appears he's at the wheel, and the SUV isn't moving."

"All right, I'm coming around the corner now, from your left." Reagan stopped at the edge of a building and had a quick look down 70th Street. He saw the SUV, which was sitting curbside, just thirty yards ahead of him on the north side of the street. He could also see the two men moving away from him toward Nelson's brownstone, just as Burke had described. "I'm going to take care of their transportation first," Reagan said into the phone, then pocketed the cell and pulled out his Walther PPK.

Checking to ensure that no one was behind him, he crossed to the north side of the street, moving casually, as if he would be continuing up Columbus Avenue. Then, as he got behind the line of parked cars, he ducked and reversed direction. Staying low, Reagan moved between two parked sedans into the street, using the car directly behind the SUV for cover, coming up along the passenger side. Guessing that the driver would not have locked up—he was obviously positioned to drive up the street and provide a quick getaway—Reagan pulled on the handle, yanked the passenger door open, and jumped into the seat, driving the barrel of his automatic into the side of the astonished man.

Reagan said, "Make a move, and I'll kill you where you sit."

The driver's look was a mixture of anger at his own stupidity and loathing for this man who had gotten the drop on him. "You are the one who will die," he said through clenched teeth.

The threat was all Reagan needed to confirm that Burke was right. "Not sure how you make that calculation, pal," he said. Then, without warning, he used the butt of his Walther to smash the side of the man's head four times in rapid succession.

The driver slumped onto the steering wheel, and Reagan quickly opened the man's coat and removed his automatic weapon, cell phone, and identification. Then he pulled out his own phone, which was still connected with Burke.

"Driver is neutralized. Give me a sit-rep."

"The man opposite has stopped in a doorway, one building short of the Nelsons. The guy on my side is still moving my way, fifteen yards from me. My guess is that he's going past here and circling across the street so they can come at the brownstone from both sides."

"These are hostiles, the driver made that clear," Reagan told him. "Take them."

"Copy that," Burke said.

As the man drew closer, Burke climbed the three concrete steps that brought him to street level. He was just a few feet from the approaching man when he asked, "You have a match?"

Before the man could respond, Burke drove forward with all his weight. He was much taller and stronger than the Arab, and he easily knocked him backward onto the ground, using the man to cushion his fall, his arms wrapped around him. The man had been walking with one hand in his jacket pocket, and Burke was giving him no chance to pull out a weapon or fire a shot.

The takedown was witnessed from across the street, both by the other assassin as well as Brian McShane. The second hitter instantly made his move. Drawing his gun, he began across the street to aid his fallen accomplice, but he only managed to advance two steps before McShane stepped out from the shadows and said, "Drop the weapon. Now."

When the man began to turn, McShane moved forward and shoved the barrel of his M1911 into the broadest part of the man's back and pulled back on the hammer. The sound was unmistakable. "Last warning. Drop it now."

The man let go of his weapon, and it clattered to the ground.

The first shooter had been dazed by Burke's full-body tackle. Burke turned him face down on the pavement and cuffed his hands behind him. Then he removed the automatic from the man's pocket, lifted him to his feet, and exchanged high signs with McShane across the way. Pulling out his phone, he told Reagan, "We have both men."

"On my way," Reagan said.

Reagan dragged the unconscious driver into the back of the SUV, drove up the block, and got out of the car. Nelson had arrived on the scene and was silently staring at the two dark-skinned men who stood with their hands bound behind their backs.

For a moment no one moved. Then Nelson took a quick step forward and hit the man nearest to him with a right cross that crushed his jaw.

McShane caught the Arab as his knees buckled, while Burke grabbed Nelson from behind.

"Enough," Reagan said, stepping in front of Nelson before he could go after the second shooter. Then he had Burke load the two would-be assassins into the back seat of their SUV, McShane climbing into the passenger seat, facing backward with his gun trained on them.

"They were going to kill my family," Nelson said.

"Or take them hostage, as a way to get to you," Reagan told him.

"But they already have Tarek," Nelson said, shaking his head. "What could they want from me?"

"Maybe Tarek didn't tell them anything. Or maybe they just wanted to confirm whatever information he fed you."

"And then kill me."

Liam Burke nodded. "They'd want to shut you up for sure," he said. "And then there's revenge. They're big on revenge."

* * *

THE OPERATION TO TAKE Tarek and murder Nelson was one of the few recent al-Qaeda actions inside the United States not conducted under the supervision of the Handler. It was an obvious sign Mahdi's concerns were justified—leadership confidence in him was waning. When he received a message that evening describing what had happened, there was nothing for him to do about that now. He was focused on another al-Qaeda group, doing the work he had assigned to them for the second part of his three-part plan.

Their success would be his vindication.

Hydrogen chloride—chemical symbol HCL—is a simple compound comprised of two elements. It has various uses, from household cleaning detergents to commercial applications.

Mixed with water it becomes hydrochloric acid.

Hydrochloric acid can be created in many different concentrations, depending on the intended purpose. Once the HCL approaches or exceeds 30 percent it becomes a hazardous substance. At these higher levels it is extremely dangerous to handle and can become life-threatening. The effects of its acrid odor alone can cause irreversible damage to the lungs and intestines, but the most common injuries result from contact with the skin, which is burned away as quickly and disastrously as if lit by fire.

It is not difficult to create hydrogen chloride, but the Handler needed a large supply. He had Ahmed and Talal arrange for the purchase of industrial sized drums from various locations, using different identities and various claims of intended use. They chose Bahir, who looked least like an Arab from those in their group, to rent a truck and deal with the suppliers. He was of mixed birth, and, if he could not pass as a Caucasian, at least he did not raise any unnecessary concerns when he engaged in these transactions.

Bahir had also leased a commercial garage near the airport in Denver, Colorado. That was where they would keep the truck and store the chemicals as they prepared to embark on their deadly journey, further to the west.

As the Handler communicated with Ahmed about their progress, he also received a new piece of information that piqued his interest— sources in New York City reported that one of the men involved in stopping the squad assigned to murder the reporter Nelson and his family was none other than the CIA's Nicholas Reagan.

CHAPTER FORTY-TWO

CIA Headquarters, Langley

Deputy Director Brian Kenny was spending the early part of his evening participating in a secure video conference with representatives of several federal agencies and a top aide from the White House. They were reviewing recent intel on domestic threat levels.

"What's the latest on this microchip?" Matt Fitzgibbon of the FBI asked the group.

"You all heard about Mindlovitch?" Kenny asked. The others confirmed they had been brought up to date on the attempt on the Russian's life. "A friend of his has been working with us. Bruce Levi, expert on terrorism, on the faculty at Stanford. As soon as Mindlovitch regained consciousness he asked to see him." Kenny paused. "Levi just told us there was a breach at the factory in Suzhou where this so-called Ghost Chip is being developed."

Andrew Lipman was representing the White House in this conference. "What sort of breach?" he asked.

"Several of the prototypes are missing," Kenny told them.

"When you say several—"

"At least a dozen, possibly as many as twenty."

"Kind of loose with their inventory," Fitzgibbon said.

"With Mindlovitch out of the picture the past couple of days, maybe someone saw an opportunity to make a move," Kenny suggested.

"How would attacking Mindlovitch in California have any impact on the security at his Suzhou factory?" Fitzgibbon asked.

"Levi mentioned the possibility," Kenny explained. "Says this man is notoriously hands-on with everything he does, particularly a project this sensitive. Checks in with his top people there a couple of times a day."

"Bit of a stretch," Fitzgibbon replied, then thought it over. "Unless they purposely removed him before the theft was carried out."

"That's possible," Kenny agreed. "There was also the likelihood Mindlovitch would die from the attack. Levi thinks the sudden loss of leadership might have delayed discovery that the microchips were stolen."

"That's a better working theory," Fitzgibbon said. "Take Mindlovitch out of the picture, buy some time."

"That's our assessment too," Kenny said. "He has a number of enemies, which is well known, but for now we're working on the assumption that the attack on him relates to the chip."

"I don't really care about motives," Lipman interrupted, "I just want to know if the prototypes are operational."

"The word from Levi," Kenny said, "is that they're not perfect, but they are working. Mindlovitch authorized him to share that."

"How generous of him," Fitzgibbon said. "Especially since he now has our government protecting his Russian ass."

"Then the net result," Lipman interrupted, "is that the wrong people may now have technology where they can communicate without any chance of being located, tapped, or whatever."

"Correct," Kenny said. "Our hope is that whoever took them needs to develop the know-how to use them properly, then distribute them and train their people."

"If it was an inside job, they may already have that expertise," Fitzgibbon suggested.

"Agreed," Kenny replied. "But they've still got to figure out how to make them interface with their computers and cell phones, then get them out of China, all while keeping beneath the radar."

The group was quiet for a moment, the implications of the impending problem lost on no one.

"We've already got our hands full tracking these terrorists," said Fred Carbonaro from the NSA. "If we lose the ability to pick up their chatter, we'll be flying blind."

"The President thinks there's already too much intel slipping between the cracks," Lipman told them. "We barely avoided a catastrophe in New York just over a week ago. Now Homeland is telling us that might have been the first of a series of strikes planned in the States."

No one disagreed.

"It's a manpower issue," Fitzgibbon said. "We've been through this arithmetic before. First there's the problem of identifying who's worth watching and who isn't. They recruit online, in the streets, in mosques—as their numbers grow, surveillance becomes increasingly difficult and takes our resources."

"When we walked out of Afghanistan and the Taliban freed thousands of prisoners, that complicated things as well," Carbonaro complained.

"You're right," Fitzgibbon agreed. "And even when we narrow the field, it takes dozens of agents to monitor a single suspect twenty-four seven. We have to work three shifts a day, seven days a week, watching multiple sites. These are full-time stakeouts, not babysitting."

Lipman was not pleased. "You want me to tell the President that his top people in national security are still grumbling about Afghanistan? Or that protecting our country has become a budgetary issue?"

After a quiet moment, Carbonaro spoke up. "Tell him what you like, whether he wants to hear it or not, but all of this is true."

"All right," Lipman said. "What about the chatter that there's some mastermind on our home turf orchestrating these attacks? Is the data credible?"

"Seems to be," Fitzgibbon said. "We think the two murders in Dearborn and the one the other day in Baltimore are connected.

They're becoming more aggressive in their recruiting, which means they're also willing to prune the ranks when they believe it's necessary."

"Pruning. You mean killing their own people," Lipman said. "Unbelievable."

"It's not unbelievable at all," Fitzgibbon disagreed. "We've done complete background checks, and there is no question all three of those men had been tapped to do something for al-Qaeda."

"Such as what?"

"I wish we knew," Kenny said, "and if al-Qaeda has these microchips it's going to make finding out even more difficult. The point is, those three were no friends of ours, but it's evident al-Qaeda decided they were expendable. The question is, why?"

"Well find out, and find out who's behind it," Lipman said, then ended the conference.

CHAPTER FORTY-THREE

New York City

Reagan and his team had custody of the three men who had gone after Bob Nelson and his family. He brought them to an apartment in an old brick tenement on East 84th Street where three FBI agents from the anti-terrorist task force were waiting. The detail was led by Jonas Wright, an old friend who had worked alongside Reagan more than once. It was for that reason alone, as Wright explained to the other two agents, that he was allowing Reagan what he called some "private time" with the suspects.

Reagan took them into a bedroom where Burke and McShane strapped two of them to chairs and tossed the driver, still unconscious, on the bed, his wrists and ankles bound with tape. Left alone with his prisoners, Reagan paced back and forth until finally saying, "One of you going to speak up, or are we going to keep this staring contest going all night?"

"We have rights," one of them said.

Reagan stopped and pulled up a chair facing the man with the swollen jaw, courtesy of Nelson's right cross. "What rights might those be?"

The Arab did not reply, he just glared at Reagan.

"Come on, you say you have rights. You must have something in mind. A free flight to Guantanamo, for instance?"

"We don't have to speak with you," the man said through clenched teeth. "We have a right to speak with a lawyer. To speak with our embassy."

Reagan began laughing. "Your embassy? What country might that be?"

The man resumed his silent stare.

"What were you doing on 70th Street tonight?"

"We were just walking. Your men attacked us. We are victims."

"Only because we got there in time, otherwise the victims would have been an innocent woman and her children, am I right?" Reagan stood and went to the table where their wallets had been placed. Opening one, he said, "Sayed Mizrah, that your real name?"

"Go to hell."

"Eventually, but not tonight." Reagan dropped the wallet back on the table. "So, Sayed Mizrah, you're asking for a lawyer. You an American citizen?" When Mizrah did not respond, Reagan said, "No, of course not. I'm guessing you're not even in this country legally, correct?" The man did not reply. "You've got as much chance of getting a lawyer as your friend on the bed there has of getting a doctor."

"He may die without medical attention. You are a murderer."

"No, actually the three of you are murderers, you're just really bad at it." Reagan sat again. "Here's the drill. You don't appear to be suicidal. If you were, you would have shot it out with us on the street. You're just three incompetents who got caught, gave up like the cowards you are, and now you're trying to figure a way out of this."

When Mizrah did not answer, Reagan turned to the second man. "You guys don't know who I am, but believe me, I'm prepared to shoot you both and pile you on top of your unconscious friend there for the cleanup squad to carry out in the morning." He pulled out his Walther, then reached in his jacket pocket and removed a suppressor which he slowly inserted into the barrel. When he was done he looked at the second man again. "So what's it going to be? We going to have a discussion, or am I going to start taking you two apart one shot at a time?"

Mizrah spoke up. "You Americans are not allowed to threaten such things."

Reagan nodded. "I just happen to be one of those Americans who thinks the ends justify the means, especially when I'm dealing with scum like you. As an example, I thought nothing of bashing in your friend's head, right?" He waited a moment, then fired a shot between Mizrah's legs that blew a chunk of the chair away. "Damn, I missed," he said, then stood and pressed the warm end of the silencer against the top of Mizrah's right hand, which was taped to the arm of the chair. "How about we do this a little at a time. I think a count of three is appropriate. One."

Mizrah looked up at him, arrogance having been replaced by fear. "Two."

"What do you want from us?" Mizrah asked.

Reagan pulled his weapon back and stepped away. "Let's start with who sent you, and why."

For the first time, the two men looked at each other. Up to now it appeared they meant to weather this interrogation, whatever it took. As soon as Reagan fired that first shot, the game changed.

Mizrah said, "We don't know who sent us. We receive our instructions by text."

"Who sent the text?"

Both men began shaking their heads. "We don't know."

"We have your phones, we'll find out."

"You may find the source, but we do not know his identity."

"It's the truth," the second man said.

Reagan nodded. "All right, I'm going to give you the chance to spare yourself some pain and save me some time." He went to the door and called to the FBI agents. "Bring in their phones." When the agent appeared in the doorway, Reagan turned to his prisoners. "Give this man your access codes."

When that was done, and they were alone again, Reagan sat back in the chair facing Mizrah. Aiming his gun at the center of the man's forehead, he said, "Why don't you tell me what you were supposed to do tonight."

Mizrah did not hesitate. He said they were to force their way into the Nelson apartment, tie up Mrs. Nelson and her children, then call her husband and offer to exchange his family for his cooperation.

"Cooperation? Now there's a euphemism if I ever heard one."

Neither man responded.

"Assuming Nelson agreed to *cooperate*, what were you to do with his family?"

For the second time, they looked at each other, but neither responded.

"I asked you a question."

"We were to take this man Nelson with us and set his family free," Mizrah said.

Reagan smiled. "You're lying."

Neither man disagreed.

"You were ordered to murder his family, right?"

"Not until Nelson was in the car," Mizrah admitted, "and only his wife. We were to keep the children alive, to be sure he told us what we wanted to know."

"Which was what?"

"The information he received from a traitor in our group."

"Who was the traitor?"

"We were never told. We had no need to know."

Reagan stared at these two butchers in disbelief. As they discussed the slaughter of his best friend's family as if it were just another day at the office, he felt the bile rise up in his throat, felt the desire to get to his feet and beat them both to death. Instead, he asked, "Where were you taking Nelson?"

When Mizrah gave him an address in Brooklyn, Reagan decided he was done for now. As he stood, he still had the urge to lash out at them, just one good crack each, smashing in their faces with the butt of his Walther. But he knew he couldn't leave that sort of mess for the FBI agents, not after Wright had given him this first chance to interrogate them. He would forego the impulse, at least for now.

He left the prisoners, went into the living room, and told Wright and the other two agents what he had learned. The most important information, for the moment, was the address where they were taking Nelson. Wright agreed to have their three prisoners transported to a secure location where they would be held incommunicado for now.

"One of them needs medical attention," Reagan said.

"We noticed," Wright said. "We'll handle it."

"You guys are up to speed on the Syrian that was abducted?"

"Tarek Shawi," Wright confirmed. "We've got a BOLO out on him."

"You probably know his phone was traced from downtown into the Brooklyn-Battery Tunnel. That's where the signal was lost."

"That's what we were told," Wright said.

"The address these two just gave me is near the Bensonhurst section of Brooklyn. The tunnel would have been a good way to get there."

"You're thinking Shawi was taken there?"

Reagan nodded. "You know me, Jonas, I don't believe in coincidences."

"We'll have these three taken downtown, then we're on our way," Wright told him.

CHAPTER FORTY-FOUR

New York City

Reagan took a cab back to West 70th Street with Burke and McShane, left them outside, and made his way inside the Nelson apartment.

Bob and Claudette were seated together on their living room sofa, being comforted by Erin who was on the loveseat facing them. The children had no idea what had almost occurred and were watching television.

"You all right?" Reagan asked Claudette as he took a seat beside Erin.

She was a pleasant looking woman with long auburn hair, fine features, and hazel eyes that presently bore a frightened look. "I don't know," she admitted, then stood. "I better put the children to bed."

After protests at being sent to sleep early, they finally relented. Peter and Lauren said their goodnights to Nick and Erin and followed their mother into their bedrooms.

Once his son and daughter were gone, Nelson said, "This was entirely too close." When neither Erin nor Reagan responded, he said, "You're the experts. What do you think I should do?"

"Not sure," Reagan admitted. "I'd like to be able to say you should leave town for a while, but that's not a solution."

"What is?"

Reagan looked at Erin, then back at his friend. "We're looking for the group that was behind this. They're undoubtedly the same people that took Tarek Shawi. They'll want to know everything he told you in case there's anything that could compromise them or their plans. If we can find them and shut down whatever they're working on, they'd have no need to come after you anymore."

Nelson managed a slight smile. "That's kind of blue sky, coming from you, Nick. You've told me more than once that these people have long memories, and your friend outside said they believe in revenge. If you break up their scheme, whatever it is, they'll think I helped you do it. They likely to leave me and my family alone after that?"

Reagan took a moment before responding. "All we can do is knock down one pin at a time. I'll have these men keep an eye on you for now. You have Burke's number in case you see anything suspicious. We have a lead on where they took Tarek Shawi, I'm heading there now."

"All right," Nelson said, "but please let me know what's happening. Good or bad."

Erin and Reagan left together, stopping to have a brief conversation with Burke.

"Get anything from our three friends?" Burke asked.

"Two of them," Reagan said, "the driver was still out when I turned them over to the Bureau. I have a lead on an address in Brooklyn."

"Good." Burke nodded toward a parked car across the street. "That's mine, I'll be spending the night here, second shift coming in the morning."

"Thanks, pal," Nick said. "You know how much I appreciate this."

"All over it."

"There's no doubt you saved their lives," Reagan said. "Just wanted you to know."

Burke smiled, then headed for his Jeep Cherokee.

"Come on," Reagan said to Erin, "I'll get you a cab, then I'm heading out to Brooklyn."

Erin didn't say anything as they walked toward Columbus Avenue.

"You all right?" Reagan asked her.

"I guess so. The question is, will *they* be all right? This isn't just about Bob, it's about Claudette and the kids too."

"I know."

"Makes a big difference, when you're not just concerned about yourself."

Reagan smiled. "One of the reasons I'm such a lousy prospect for you."

"That should be up to me."

He stopped and turned to her. "They have a beautiful family, don't they?"

"Yes, they do."

"Something you'd like for yourself?"

"We've discussed it enough."

Reagan nodded. "You know how I feel about you."

"It's not only what you feel about me, it's what you feel about *us*."

"We're in a lousy business to be thinking about us."

"Other people make it work. Look at Kenny, for instance."

"I love the man, but he's a desk jockey now, not a field agent."

"We're coming to that time when we're going to have to make a decision," she said with a sad smile. "Be realistic, Nicholas. You can't keep doing what you do forever, and I can't continue this on-again, off-again romance."

"You're going to throw the biological clock at me?"

Erin managed to laugh. "If the clock were big enough, I might consider hitting you over the head with it."

Reagan reached out and drew her to him. After they kissed he began to speak, but she reached up and gently placed her finger across his lips.

"Don't say anything right now," she told him, her eyes moist. "I'm willing to live the life we've chosen. Together."

Reagan nodded.

"But as usual," Erin sighed, "with everything going on, this is a rotten time to have this conversation."

Reagan smiled. "Later."

"When things calm down, right? Which is never." Erin flagged down an approaching cab. "You take this one, you need to get to Brooklyn. I'll find my own way home."

"A discussion for another day."

Erin managed another sad smile, then watched as he got in and rode away.

As soon as he climbed into the back of the taxi, Reagan pulled out his cell and called Carol Gellos in D.C. "I'm heading to an address we got from the polite little group that was about to murder Nelson's family."

"You think they told you the truth?"

"No reason not to, given the circumstances. If they lied, I'll be paying them another visit tonight, and it won't go quite as well for them."

"What can I do on my end?"

"Just stay tuned."

His next call was to Jonas Wright, who picked up on the first ring.

"You there yet?" asked Reagan.

"On our way, twenty minutes out. It's a commercial building off New Utrecht Avenue, behind a lumber yard."

"Your show. Don't wait for me, I'm a few minutes behind you."

The taxi driver made good time, and Reagan had him stop a block short of the address. As Wright told him, it was near a large lumber yard, and the street was quiet this time of night. He told the cabbie to make a U-turn and leave the way he came, so he would not pass the target building. Then Reagan hurried toward the side of the four-story structure, keeping watch for any movement at ground level or on the roof.

He saw nothing.

He took out his phone and sent a text to Wright, telling him he was here. His phone immediately buzzed back with a message that said simply: *Going in.*

With Wright and his men heading inside, Reagan tried to find an entrance in the rear or on the side that might give them flank support from a different angle. He found an alley between the old brick building and the fence along the edge of the lumber yard. Moving quickly down the narrow passage, he found a fire door, but it was made of reinforced metal and locked tight from the inside. As he looked around for another way in, he heard the first shots fired.

There were no windows at street level in the rear of the building, but there were on the second story. Reagan climbed the chain-link fence bordering the lumber yard, then leapt across to the fire escape attached to the building's rear wall. The exchange of gunfire had intensified, and he did not hesitate. He drew his weapon, kicked in the nearest window, and had a look into a dark corridor.

It was empty.

The sound was coming from above him, so he climbed through the window, found the staircase, and hustled up to the landing on the third floor. Cautiously peering around the corner, he saw a man with his back to him, standing beside an open door on the left side of the hallway. He had an automatic submachine gun and was firing toward the other end of the corridor.

Even in the dim light, it was clear this was no FBI agent.

"Drop it," Reagan hollered.

The startled shooter spun in Reagan's direction and opened fire, one of the rounds grazing Reagan's left arm, just as Reagan dropped him with three shots to the chest.

Wright, who was positioned at the far end of the hallway, raised his hand, and Reagan acknowledged him with a quick wave. Wright then gestured for Reagan to stay put as he sent two men toward the open door off to Reagan's left.

Before the agents could make their move, two other hostiles began firing, one in Wright's direction, the other toward Reagan. Neither was as rash as their friend, both keeping cover inside the doorway. They were firing blindly into the open space.

Reagan barely felt the wound to his arm, the heat of battle masking the pain. He took a deep breath, then dove across the corridor, rolling over and coming up on his right knee. He was protected by the far wall but with a line of sight at the open doorway that was much closer to him than to Wright.

For a moment there was a pause, and Reagan waited. They could not possibly have seen his move, not from where they were positioned inside the doorway. This time, when they reached out to resume their two-direction fusillade, Reagan fired, catching enough of one man's arm to cause him to drop his weapon, the other falling backward.

That gave Wright's men the opening they needed. They rushed forward, one taking a stance on the near side of the open doorway, the other at an angle from the right side of the corridor. Both opened fire. Reagan scrambled to his feet and moved forward, creating a pincer move as they shot at the two men in the opening, both of whom had gone down. Neither was moving, their bodies preventing anyone else inside from shutting the door.

Reagan and the FBI agents had no way of knowing how many people they were fighting, but however many they were, it was evident they were not going to give up as easily as the shooters who had come for Nelson's family. Gunfire was still being returned from inside, and the agent who had crouched against the far wall took a shot to his leg and toppled onto his side.

Reagan replaced the magazine in his Walther as the man beside Wright pulled the pin on a smoke grenade and tossed it into the open door. Soon the sound of gunshots was replaced by men gagging and choking.

"Come out with your hands raised," Wright shouted, "or the next thing we toss inside won't be filled with smoke."

Reagan could not suppress a grin. One thing he always liked about Jonas Wright was that he was certainly not a by-the-book FBI agent, which suited Reagan just fine.

But the gunfire continued. As Reagan understood only too well, not all Islamic extremists are the same, and some really are willing to die for their genocidal cause, even when it made no sense in a world already short on logic. That was the message delivered from one of the hostiles, who had responded to Wright's warning with a shout of, "*Allahu Akbar.*" The shooter must have been at the far end of the room, since some of his rounds were actually hitting the inside walls and door.

Wright responded by having two of his agents rush forward and remove the injured agent from the scene, then fusillade into the smoke-filled room.

CHAPTER FORTY-FIVE

New York City

By the time reinforcements arrived at the warehouse in Brooklyn, including members of the NYPD and an agent from Homeland Security, the fight was over. As calm descended, Reagan knew there was no chance of finding Nelson's source alive. Two injured hostiles were taken into custody, two had been killed in the shootout, and Tarek Shawi's body was discovered in the back of the room. It was not unlike the scene Reagan encountered when he, Gellos, and Brandt found Nahid Jamal in Baltimore.

The man had been the victim of grisly torture, then murdered with a single shot to his forehead.

Wright saw the look of frustration on Reagan's face. "We're making progress, Nick, it's all we can do."

"Shoveling sand against the tide is not progress."

Wright disagreed. "None of our intel suggests this is a large cell. You took out three in front of your friend's apartment. Four more here. We have their phones. We'll identify their other contacts and chase them down."

"If we can get to whoever is pulling the strings, then it'll mean something. How's your man?"

"He'll be all right, took a shot to the leg." Wright noticed the blood running down the sleeve of Reagan's shirt. "We need to get that looked at."

"Only grazed, didn't hit anything important."

247

Wright shook his head. "Get the hell downstairs and have that treated."

Reagan nodded. Then, as he was about to turn away, he said, "You'll keep me in the loop?"

"I will. And you do the same," Wright said. "You going to need a ride?"

"That'd be good."

It was after one in the morning by the time the EMT finished with Reagan. He opted for Steri-Strips rather than stitches, had an injection to fight a possible infection, then followed one of Wright's men to a car. It had been a long night; he was tired and sore and ready to head back to his Manhattan apartment. The last thing he expected, as he climbed into the sedan, was a phone call from Sasha.

"I thought you didn't like to be disturbed early in the morning."

"This isn't early in the morning," the young computer technician replied, "it's still late at night."

"Perspective is everything," Reagan said. "What made you think I'd be up?"

"I didn't care," Sasha replied. "Maybe you're rubbing off on me."

Reagan sighed. "What've you got?"

"You were right about the Koran," Sasha said. "Did a word search, as you suggested, and had another look at the messages texted to the two High Line bombers the day it happened."

"I'm listening."

"There were all the usual catchphrases to act in the name of Allah, but there were also numbers that key into passages in the Koran. Passages that encourage death to the infidels."

"Just the numbers of the verses, not the actual quotes?"

"Right. And you remember our discussion, about how the High Line attack used incendiary materials."

"It's late Sasha, but I'm with you."

"Right. Anyway, those scientists who were abducted, they said they were questioned at length about modern buildings, with roofs made of metal piping and glass."

"I'm still listening."

"I found something in the Koran, 22:19. I believe it could be the connection."

"I'm not carrying my pocket edition with me."

"Okay. Here's what it says, in rough translation: Punish the unbelievers with garments of fire, hooked iron rods, and boiling water to melt their skin and bellies."

"The plan at the High Line was to use incendiaries to set the models' clothes on fire."

"And everyone around them," Sasha said. "Garments of fire."

"You think the reference to hooked iron rods could have something to do with those translucent roofs."

"That's what I'm thinking. They're held up by metal pipes. Blow up the ceiling and what comes crashing down?"

"Huge pieces of glass and twisted metal."

"Hooked iron rods?" Sasha said.

Reagan thought it over. "What do you make of the boiling water?"

"Don't have anything on that one yet," Sasha said, "but I'm working on it." He paused, then said, "Reagan, I think we're onto something."

CHAPTER FORTY-SIX

En route to Las Vegas

The Handler's henchmen, Ahmed and Talal, were inside the commercial garage they had leased near Denver International Airport, preparing for the next leg of their journey. They were joined by two others, Bahir—the fair skinned Egyptian who had fronted their rental of trucks, this space, and their purchase of the chemicals—and Sayyar, selected for the mission to replace Yousef Omarov. He was not as large and strong as the younger man had been, but he was all they had.

The four of them worked together, moving forty large barrels of hydrogen chloride into the back of the rented vehicle Bahir had just brought them. Another truck had been used to pick up the HCL from various chemical plants, but it could be too easily described later on by people working in those places. As they traveled west, they would be in this new truck that none of those suppliers had ever seen or could identify.

They handled the heavy containers with caution. In powdered form the compound was far less dangerous to the casual touch than when liquified, but they were warned to be careful.

It was a warm day, and the temperature inside the windowless garage was over a hundred degrees. The stagnant air was oppressive, and Sayyar had been complaining all afternoon. Finally pulling off his shirt, he said again, "This makes no sense. At least open a door."

Ahmed had enough of his grousing. Turning to the man, he said, "No door will be open until we are done. Now shut up and finish loading the truck."

But Sayyar refused to shut up. "What kind of fool chooses a garage in this heat with no air conditioning? There's not even a fan."

Ahmed stepped forward until they were face to face, then demanded, "Who are you calling a fool?" Then he gave him a forceful shove.

Sayyar fell backward, tripping over one of the barrels, stumbling into another, and toppling to the ground, causing that last drum to fall over, the top coming off.

Sayyar was drenched with sweat, and some of the powder that spilled from the container immediately clung to his skin. The dry compound instantly became hydrochloric acid, eating away at the man's back, shoulders and arms.

He shrieked, the pain as intense as if he were being burned alive. He scrambled to his feet, reached for his shirt, and tried to wipe away the acid. But it was too late.

The others had no idea what to do, standing back as Sayyar implored them to help. Desperately rubbing at the deadly moisture with his shirt, he only spread the acid, making it worse.

"What should we do?" an anxious Talal asked Ahmed.

"He needs a hospital," Bahir said as Sayyar's screams grew louder and more frantic.

"A hospital?" Ahmed responded. He turned to Sayyar and waited, not wanting to touch the man as he writhed in pain in the rear of the garage, looking for something to end his agony. When Sayyar managed to get to his feet and stagger toward him, Ahmed lashed out with a powerful sideways kick into the man's chest, sending him crashing against the wall and back onto the floor. Moving forward, he placed his foot on the man's chest. Then he pulled a dagger from his belt, leaned down, and, in one fluid motion, slit Sayyar's throat.

"What have you done?" Bahir asked with a look of revulsion.

Ahmed calmly cleaned off his knife and replaced it inside his belt. "What do you think I've done? I've protected the three of us and our mission. You wanted to take him to the hospital? Bah! He was half dead already. And what would we have told them about the acid? Now get back to work."

"What are we going to do with the body?" Talal asked.

Ahmed looked around the small garage. "No place to hide him here. We'll have to put him in the back of the truck, dump the body when we have the chance."

Talal responded with a solemn nod. "I suppose you had no choice."

Bahir stood there, gaping down at the dead man. "No choice? Look what you've done."

Ahmed also looked down at Sayyar. "Who is the fool now?" he asked.

It was dusk by the time they finished loading the drums and cleaning the mess. First, they carefully did what they could to clean up the spilled HCL and bloodstains, then waited for night to fall before they finally rolled up the main door, climbed inside the truck, started the engine, and pulled out, closing the garage behind them.

Their planned route was west on Interstate 70, then southwest on 15 toward Nevada. The ride would take roughly twelve hours, not counting a couple of quick gas station stops. They would move with the flow of the other commercial traffic on those roads, their vehicle unlikely to arouse any attention or suspicion as they traveled to their ultimate destination, South Las Vegas Boulevard, commonly referred to as the Strip. In the event anyone came looking for them because of their large purchases of HCL, their search would end up with the empty truck they left parked in the garage in Denver.

Large vehicles moving in and out of Las Vegas, both on the highways and the Strip itself, were not unusual. Deliveries to the numerous hotels happened all through the day and night, and one more truck would not be suspicious, even early on a Sunday morning.

Their challenge was twofold. Since the Handler's people in Dearborn had been unable to hack into the software program that operated the hotel water show, they would have to get access to the control booth where the computers were located. Second, they needed time to dump the contents of forty heavy barrels of hydrogen chloride into the water system that supplied the fountain.

Sunday featured the earliest show of the week, at 11:00 AM. There were obvious risks in making their move in daylight, but acting in the middle of the night might draw even more attention. Then there was a timing concern. The longer the HCL remained in the system, the more it would be diluted by recirculation and the more time the corrosive compound would have to damage the pipes. Given the enormous volume of water involved, it was also critical to ensure the maximum concentration was used to wreak the greatest damage.

They needed to coordinate their efforts, poisoning the water before the angle of the nozzles was altered and the show began. Only then would the jets rain lethal acid onto the unsuspecting crowd of spectators standing along the perimeter of the fountain.

CHAPTER FORTY-SEVEN

CIA Headquarters, Langley

It was after two in the morning by the time Reagan got back to his apartment. He took a shower, careful not to disturb the bandages stretched across his left triceps. He pulled on black slacks, a white shirt, a gray cotton sweater, and rubber-soled loafers, then arranged for an agency car to bring him to CIA headquarters. He decided he needed to join his team, but it was too late to arrange a flight, and he needed a few hours of rest. Whatever sleep he would get was going to come in the back of the company SUV as the driver made his way through the night from New York to Virginia.

When he arrived at Langley, just before dawn, Deputy Director Kenny was not there to greet him, but Reagan had called Carol Gellos and Alex Brandt, and they were waiting for him.

They met in the cafeteria, where they caught up on the events of the past two days over eggs, bacon, and hot black coffee.

"Heard you got winged in the gunfight," Gellos said.

"Didn't think you cared."

"Really, you okay?"

"Nothing an I.V. of Jack Daniels wouldn't fix," Reagan said. "You've spoken with Sasha?"

"We have," Gellos told him.

"What do you think of our theory?"

"The Koran says to punish the unbelievers by setting their clothes on fire, pouring boiling water on them, and attacking them with hooked iron rods?"

"That's it," Reagan said.

Gellos nodded. "They set garments on fire, that's for sure, and Sasha is convinced the iron rods relate to the roof design we've been looking at."

"What kind of buildings have you been focusing on?"

"Domed stadiums. Modern train stations. Shopping malls. Contemporary office buildings with open areas in the middle and glass tops," Brandt told him. "Blow the roof of a crowded stadium or shopping mall, just think of the damage."

Reagan nodded. "How many actually fit the narrative?"

"Few dozen stadiums. Less than a hundred large malls," Brandt told him. "We're discounting other buildings because they would be smaller and have less people in harm's way."

"An attack there wouldn't cause as much death and injury," Reagan said.

"That's how we see it," Brandt agreed. "They're aiming for a bloodbath."

"Same could be true in a train station with that sort of ceiling design," Gellos reminded them.

"You two have just named a lot of potential targets."

Neither of them disagreed.

"All right, what about the other component of this triad of horror?" Reagan asked.

"Boiling the skin off the infidels," Gellos said.

"We've been looking at that," Brandt told him. "Actually, Sasha has some ideas."

"Such as?"

"To start with, the literal use of boiling water is probably not a plausible or efficient way to commit mass murder. But there are some frightening alternatives."

Reagan thought it over. "Steam?"

"That's one. Find a way to fracture a major steam pipe, maybe inside an industrial plant. Anyone nearby would have their skin melted off, just what the Koran calls for."

"Not easy to guarantee where the intended victims might be standing when the pipe blows," Reagan said.

"No," Brandt agreed. "We also discussed the extreme temperatures in a steel mill."

"Detonate some sort of smelting mechanism?"

Gellos nodded. "Unthinkable, huh?"

Reagan blew out a deep lungful of air. "This is a sick game to be playing at this hour of the morning. What else have you got?"

"We've been looking at other places that deal with high temperatures," Gellos told him.

"Please don't tell me you're thinking of a nuclear power plant."

"It was a thought, but we don't believe they have the resources for that sort of attack."

"If they tried, they wouldn't be targeting the superheated water," Reagan said. "They'd go after the reactor itself."

"That's how we figured it," Brandt agreed.

Reagan sat back and looked at his two friends. "How low does this world have to sink before we climb out of the mud?"

A voice from behind them said, "Very low, it seems."

The three agents turned to see Kenny. He was wearing his usual gray suit, white shirt, red tie, and serious look. "Let's take this to my office."

Upstairs, Sasha Levchenko was waiting for them. As they took seats around the conference table, the DD said, "Tell them what we've got."

"Hydrogen chloride," Sasha said. "Not a controlled substance, but something various agencies keep an eye on. OSHA and DOT, for example. DOT requires identification on shipments when it's liquefied, uses the classification 1789."

"Liquified as in—"

"As in hydrochloric acid, one of its primary uses," Sasha explained. "OSHA has rules about handling it, to protect workers."

"What's your point?" Reagan asked.

"HCL is easy to manufacture, and in small quantities it's difficult to monitor. But when there are larger, industrial size transactions, databases maintain information on who manufactures it, who buys it, what type of businesses they operate, and so forth."

"But you've already said it's not a controlled substance," Reagan pointed out.

"That's right," Sasha admitted. "There are any number of commercial uses, and it's not illegal for companies to sell the compound on the open market. However, a number of large containers were recently purchased under unusual circumstances."

"Unusual how?" Gellos asked.

Sasha pulled out some notes. "Large drums of the compound were bought from several different suppliers in and around Arizona. The reason it's unusual is that the company making the purchases is newly formed, and, when we ran a standard check, their address turned out to be an empty warehouse in Illinois."

"Which means," Reagan said, "we can't link any legitimate use for the material to the outfit buying it."

"That's it in a nutshell," Sasha agreed. "We checked all available information on the buyer, and it's not much. Limited liability company formed online just two weeks ago. The signatory appears to be a phony name, and the email address that was used to file the paperwork has already been shut down."

"Welcome to the world of cyberterrorism," Gellos said with a rueful shake of her head.

"How many barrels did they manage to buy?" Reagan asked.

"We're still working on it," Sasha said, "but it's at least thirty, could be as many as fifty."

"How big are these barrels?"

"Fifty-five-gallon drums," Sasha told him.

"Assuming it's going to be used to create hydrochloric acid—"

"You're looking at one helluva lot of acid," Sasha finished the thought.

"This may seem an obvious question," Brandt said, "but since the address they filed in Illinois is empty, do we have any leads on where they're storing the chemicals?"

"It's actually a very good question," Kenny said. "We've just learned that this same LLC rented a truck several days ago in Phoenix. We have information on the vehicle and confirmed with two suppliers that it fits the description of the truck used to pick up the chemicals from their plants. Then we learned the same LLC rented a garage last week, near the airport in Denver."

"Based on this passage you've found in the Koran," Gellos said, "they could be converting all of this HCL to hydrochloric acid—"

"And using it to melt the skin off the infidels," Reagan finished the thought.

"Dealing with hydrochloric acid is very dangerous," Sasha reminded them. "It's all about how concentrated you make the mixture. The stronger it is, the more toxic, but the harder to handle. It'll eat right through metal if the percentage of HCL is high enough."

"Which means they're not likely to liquefy the compound before they reach their target, wherever that is," Gellos said. "Moving the containers filled with the dry compound is much safer. Once it's converted to acid, they would need a special tanker to carry the liquid."

Reagan nodded. "The next question is whether they're going to use it passively or actively."

"Meaning what?" asked Kenny.

"Take a simple example," Reagan replied. "Let's say they're going to dump the powder in a public swimming pool. I would call that a passive approach. They walk away and wait for people to jump into the water. Or they might use it to pollute a small reservoir. Either one of those is an awful scenario, but not likely to be very effective.

It would be detected too quickly, the use of the water stopped. The more active approach would be to liquefy it, then spray it on people or actively mix it in a water system that allows them to use it as a weapon of attack."

Kenny had a grim look on his face. "We need to imagine a way they would use these chemicals to inflict maximum damage with minimum chance of things going wrong."

Kenny's private line rang. It was Erin David, calling from her office in New York, and he brought her up on the video monitor.

"At work early on a Sunday?" Reagan said, but Erin was all business.

"We have an update," she told the group. "We had locals check out the garage that was rented by that LLC last week near the airport in Denver. The truck they rented is still there, but it's empty. Forensics is on the way to see if there are any traces of HCL."

"NSA picking up any chatter?" Gellos asked.

"Nothing solid," Erin admitted, "but we do have one possible lead."

"We're listening," Kenny told her.

"Remember the computer that was owned by one of the two young men murdered in Dearborn last week, Yousef Omarov? Well it may seem a longshot, but in addition to all the al-Qaeda blogs he followed, he also downloaded several maps and websites about Las Vegas."

"Vegas?" Reagan asked.

"Correct," Erin admitted. "From what we've learned, he was almost never outside Dearborn, and there's no indication on his laptop that he looked up flights or anything else that suggests he was going to book a trip. So why was he so interested?"

"Go on," the DD said.

"We've assumed he was part of a planned mission, then taken out for reasons we still don't know."

"But we might assume Vegas is a possible target," Reagan said.

No one in Kenny's office disagreed.

"Then there's the geography," Erin told them. "If you draw a line from Illinois, where the LLC was formed, to Arizona, where most of the chemicals were bought, to a garage in Denver, where do you think they're going from there?"

"West all the way," Gellos said.

"To Vegas?" Reagan asked again.

"Swimming pools in every hotel," Brandt agreed.

Reagan shook his head.

"What is it?" Gellos asked.

"Vegas makes sense, but I'm back to my question. Are they going passive or active?" He looked to the image of Erin on the large monitor. "You think they're going to pour the HCL into swimming pools around town, make it look like they're adding chlorine?"

Erin thought it over. "Not likely. The first person dips a toe in and gets burned, word will spread throughout the city in a flash. After the mass shooting, the communications network in that town is phenomenal. They'll shut down every pool in half a heartbeat."

"Agreed," Reagan said.

Gellos sat back and ran her fingers through her short, sandy-colored hair. "Las Vegas is in the desert. Other than swimming pools, how else are they going to turn their powder into acid?" Turning to Reagan, she said, "You said they might try to contaminate the drinking water?"

"No way," Reagan said. "That could be horrible, but it wouldn't melt the skin off anyone's body. And why drive all the way to Vegas to do that?"

"What then?" Brandt asked. "You obviously have an idea."

"You would need to spray it, somehow get the acid in the air and then rain down on people."

"Water attractions," Sasha said.

"That's what I'm thinking," Reagan agreed. "There are active fountains and water attractions all over Las Vegas. You start spraying people with hydrochloric acid, and I promise you'll see their skin melting off."

Kenny stood. "Reagan, you get to Andrews now. Brandt will take you. Gellos, line up whichever of our jets will get him to Las Vegas fastest. I'll alert the task force out there and update the White House. I want Reagan there as our liaison. Erin, you keep him posted on any new intel."

Reagan was on his feet. "Who do I see when I get there?"

"We'll handle that when you're in the air. Now go."

CHAPTER FORTY-EIGHT

Las Vegas

When Reagan landed at McCarron airport, with the change in time zones and a flight of less than five hours, it was just after nine in the morning locally. The day was typically hot and sunny and dry, and Reagan pulled off his sweater and rolled up his sleeves before climbing into the agency car that met him and headed for the address Kenny had provided. It was the office where the Las Vegas Police Department, Nevada State Troopers, and local FBI office maintained a centralized team charged with keeping the city safe and monitoring threats, terrorist or otherwise. By now they had already been alerted to the possibility of an attack, and representatives from key federal departments were also on the way to lend their support.

Reagan arrived, a couple of quick introductions were made, then he was shown into the main room outfitted with an array of computers, monitors, and telephones, much like the setup at the NYPD. They were on high alert and only had just begun to send an alert to all the hotels linked to their communications center.

Unfortunately, none of them knew that the Handler's men were already approaching their destination, nor what their plans were for the next two hours.

* * *

The water show at the enormous fountain in front of the Bellagio Hotel has long been among the most popular tourist attractions in Las

Vegas. Huge jets of water pulsate, twist, and explode into the sky, their perfectly timed aquatic choreography lit from below and matched to musical scores chosen for these spectacles.

The fountain is set on eight acres, receiving its water from a freshwater well that was created many years ago for a golf course that previously occupied the site. The flow is controlled through a maze of underwater pipes with over a thousand nozzles, and there are more than four thousand lights to illuminate the display. Working together by means of elaborate computer software, the nozzles and lights are coordinated with an outdoor music system that together provide the magic of the programs that take place.

There are four types of jets that force the water to cascade upward. One class of nozzles can send the spray more than two hundred feet into the air, while another group shoots the water more than four hundred feet high. The important category, dubbed Oarsmen by the manufacturer, is more sophisticated, enabling a full range of spherical motions. They send up the streams of water that gracefully wave back and forth, smoothly changing height and spin, all in rhythm to the music.

There are more than two hundred Oarsmen installed in the fountain, and these were the devices that were critical to the Handler's plan.

* * *

AHMED WAS AT THE WHEEL of the truck when they reached the city. He made a right off the Strip onto West Flamingo Avenue, bypassing the main entrance to the Bellagio Hotel. Guiding the truck around the side of the sprawling complex, he stopped in a loading zone opposite the small, square building where they housed the computers and personnel that operated the outdoor fountains. It was attached to the main structure, but, at the moment, the only person in the area was a burly security guard in a dark gray uniform with a sidearm at his hip.

Leaving Bahir at the wheel, Ahmed and Talal climbed out and approached the guard.

"Can I help you fellas?" the man asked.

"We have a delivery, not sure where to drop it off," Ahmed said, pointing to the truck. "Some kind of dye to color the water in the fountain, something about a special celebration."

The guard responded with a suspicious look, then turned toward the truck. He was about to say something, but that sideward glance was all they needed. Ahmed, who was gripping the handle of his dagger under the cover of his jacket, swiftly drew it out and drove it with a powerful, upward thrust into the man's gut, then yanked the blade higher. The only sound the guard made was a raspy inhalation as he grabbed for the handle of the knife with both hands, his eyes open wide with pain. Talal stepped to the side, pulled the gun from the guard's holster, then took hold of the man so he did not collapse to the ground.

Ahmed hurried to the door and began pounding on it. "We have a problem," he hollered. "Man out here is having a heart attack or something."

He repeated the words until the door opened slightly, and a tall, lanky, bespectacled man of about forty peered out. He saw Talal holding onto his co-worker, but with the guard's back to him he could not see the blood or what had happened. "What's going on Jimmy?" he asked.

Ahmed did not respond. Instead, he pushed on the door, shoving the man backward as he entered. Talal followed, dragging the dying guard with him.

"What the hell," the man asked as he struggled to keep his balance.

Ahmed lashed out with a backhand across the man's face, knocking off his glasses and sending him sprawling onto the floor. "If you want to live, you will not say another word unless I tell you to."

They were in a small vestibule. Behind was the door them leading outside from where they had just come in. On the other side was a door into the main room of the facility. It was closed. Ahmed drew the automatic from his waistband and moved forward.

Talal had dropped the security guard to the carpeted floor and wiped his bloody hands on the dying man's shirt. Still holding the Colt automatic he had taken from the man's holster, Talal pointed it at the technician, motioning for him to stand up. "How many of you are in here?"

The man replaced his glasses and stared into Talal's cold, dark eyes as he got to his feet. "Two."

"Let's go."

Ahmed, Talal, and the technician were standing at the closed door leading to the main room.

Ahmed, in a quiet voice, said, "Only one other man inside?"

The technician shook his head, then managed to say, "A woman."

"Just one?"

He nodded again.

"What is your name?"

"Roger."

"There must be security cameras inside. I don't see any in here."

Roger said nothing.

"Are there any?" Ahmed demanded.

"No, not here," Roger stammered. "There are inside."

"If you or the woman lie to us, just once, you will both die. Understood?"

Roger nodded repeatedly.

"What did you say the guard's name is?" When Roger hesitated, Ahmed poked the barrel of his Glock into the man's side.

"Jimmy, it's Jimmy."

"You open the door and call to the woman. Tell her something is wrong with Jimmy, and to come out here right now. You understand?"

He nodded.

"Do it now."

The technician did as he was told, and a woman of about fifty came rushing out to see what was wrong. Talal had been standing behind the door and slammed it shut as soon as she reached the entry area. Her eyes widened with fear as she took in the scene—Jimmy on the floor covered with blood, and two men holding automatic weapons, one pointed at Roger, the other at her.

"Say nothing," Ahmed told her. "If you and your friend want to live, you will say nothing unless I tell you to speak. Just nod if you understand."

The woman slowly nodded.

"Good," Ahmed said. "Now listen carefully to what I want you to do. If you fail to do as I say, if I believe you are trying to warn anyone watching you on your security cameras inside or if I see you trigger any sort of alarm, you will both die here and now. I want you both to nod if you understand me and believe what I am saying."

They each nodded, and the woman said, "But what do you want from—"

"Silence!" Ahmed growled, followed by a sharp slap across her face. "Now, are you ready to hear what I need you to do?"

This time, as they both nodded slowly, neither spoke.

"Which of you is the more experienced in operating these fountains?"

The man and woman turned to each other, sharing a look that admitted fear was gripping every ounce of their being.

"Sharon," Roger finally managed to say.

Ahmed turned to the woman. "Is this true?"

She nodded.

"Good. Now I will tell you what I need you to do. First, people monitoring your security cameras may become concerned that no one is sitting in the control room." He turned to Roger. "You go inside to your station. Do nothing and touch nothing. My friend here will have his gun trained on you in case you make a single unwanted move. You understand?"

Roger nodded his understanding, then, with a shove from Talal, he opened the door, went inside, and sat at his computer.

Ahmed took his time explaining in detail how he wanted Sharon to reprogram the Oarsmen jets in the fountain. He wanted her to arrange it so their upward spray, when it undulated back and forth, would move an additional thirty degrees in each direction. When he was done giving her these directions he asked if she had any questions.

She appeared genuinely puzzled. "An additional thirty degrees will cause the water to fall on the spectators standing on the edge of the fountain. Is that what you want?"

"That is exactly what I want," Ahmed admitted, knowing the information would do her no good. All that was important now was that she do what she was told. "Your friend inside will know whether you are properly adjusting the fountains as I have directed. We will be standing here with him watching you, and if he thinks you're doing anything other than what I have told you to do, we will kill you, and then we will kill him." Ahmed checked his watch. It was almost ten. "Go inside, tell him he can take a break, say it in a normal manner, then do what I have told you to do."

Sharon nodded, stepped past Talal, and entered the control room. She spoke to Roger, after which he came out to the foyer.

"Good," Ahmed said to Roger. "Now you come with me."

The anxiety in Roger's eyes was clear, as he said, "I thought you wanted me to watch what Sharon is doing?"

Ahmed offered a cruel smile in response. "She believes you are watching. That, and Talal remaining here with a gun pointed at her head will be enough."

CHAPTER FORTY-NINE

Las Vegas

Ahmed and Roger left the building and walked toward the parked truck. Ahmed made it clear to the tall, thin technician that he would not hesitate to use the automatic if he felt the need. Bahir was waiting at the wheel as Roger climbed in the passenger side, followed by Ahmed.

"Everything all right?" Bahir asked.

Ahmed nodded, then said to Roger, "We know where the main valves are for the fountain. They have security there this time of the morning?"

The look in the technician's eyes made it plain he was thinking only of his own survival. "I'm...I'm not sure."

Ahmed showed him the barrel of his gun. "You're lying. I already know they have at least one man posted there round the clock."

"I'm...uh, not involved in that part of the operation. I don't know everyone there."

"But the people there, they know who *you* are?"

"Yes," Roger admitted. "They do."

"Good. Now, no one else needs to get hurt if you do as I say. You understand?"

The man nodded.

"We're going to drive around the corner and pull up to the pump house. You're going to get out with me and explain to the guard that I am here to add some special dye into the system."

"What sort of dye?"

Ahmed's instinct was to hit the man across the face, but he could not afford to have him looking injured when they met with the security guard at the pumping station. "That is no concern of yours," he said through gritted teeth, "and you are not to speak other than to say what I have just told you. If they ask, tell them the dye is being used to color the water for this morning's display."

Roger was shaking his head before Ahmed had finished. "They won't believe you. They would have received written instructions."

"I understand," Ahmed said as calmly as he could. "You just leave that to me." Speaking to Bahir, he said, "Let's go."

The pumphouse was just around the corner, less than a block away. Bahir pulled to a stop in front.

Ahmed shoved his automatic back into his waistband, pulled his jacket over it, and turned back to Roger. "Remember, no one else needs to be hurt. What happens next will be up to you."

They climbed out of the truck, Bahir remaining behind the wheel. The structure that housed the main valves for the fountains was slightly larger than the building from which they had just come. As they got to the door, it opened, and a man, in the same style of gray uniform Jimmy had worn, stepped out and greeted Roger.

"Hi, Lucas," the technician replied.

"What brings you over here?" the guard asked.

Roger glanced to his side, then said, "Seems we have—," but before he could finish, Ahmed stepped forward, gun raised, pointing it directly at the security guard's eyes.

"Do not speak," Ahmed told the guard as he removed the gun from the man's holster. "Let's all go inside."

Roger had a quick look over his shoulder at Bahir, who was still in the truck, just a few steps away from where they stood. Whatever thought of escape the technician may have had, it was clear there was no place to run. Ahmed made a gesture with his weapon, and both

Roger and Lucas stepped inside. As they did, Bahir turned the truck around and backed up to the door.

The inside of the pumphouse contained several huge water pipes that led out the back of the building to the fountains. Large valves operated by metal wheels controlled the main flow of the water, which passed through three enclosed holding tanks. There were also a number of electronic gauges showing various measurements, including water pressure, rates of flow, and temperature.

"This is going to be simple and fast," Ahmed told them. "We have a number of barrels containing dye in the back of the truck. You are going to open the three holding tanks. Then you will assist us in dumping the contents into them. Do what you are told, no one will be hurt, and my friends and I will be on our way. Do you understand?"

Roger and Lucas turned to each other, then looked back at Ahmed but said nothing.

Ahmed, speaking slowly, said, "I will not ask again. Do you understand?"

The two men shared another look, then both nodded.

"Good. Now this is how we will work. There are two hand trucks which my friend is removing from the truck. It will take two men to carry each barrel off the truck, then one man to wheel it in here and two men to dump the dye into the holding tanks. At no time will both of you be allowed out of this room together. If either one of you fails to give his full cooperation, I will kill you both. If either of you attempts to run, to contact someone passing by, or to make any other move contrary to my instructions, I will kill you both. Do you understand?"

The men nodded again, each realizing that if they made a run at this man, at least one of them would be shot, leaving the other to face the man outside. For now, they felt as most captives do, that time was on their side, and that help would ultimately come.

For Ahmed, the loss of Sayyar had created a tactical problem. He had to leave Talal with the woman at the control room. That meant he only had Bahir outside to coordinate the offloading of all these drums from the truck. He sent Roger out first, feeling the technician would be less likely to make an attempt to escape than a trained security guard.

The first two barrels were brought in by Roger and Bahir, using the hand trucks, and all four men were back inside. Ahmed told Bahir to take out his weapon and use it if necessary. Then he pulled on the gloves he had in his pocket, opened the first drum, and instructed Lucas to assist him in dumping the contents into the nearest holding tank.

Ahmed and his men had not even bothered to disguise the labels or cover the warnings on the containers. As soon as the chemical hit the water the tank became a bubbling cauldron, and a mist began to rise into the air.

"What the hell," Lucas asked as he jumped back.

Poisonous gas was a byproduct of turning the HCL compound into hydrochloric acid, and, in this confined space, none of them were going to survive the mixture of chemicals and water as they continued to bring in barrel after barrel. Ahmed already felt his own eyes burning and knew they could not remain in such confined space without protection. He turned to Bahir, nodded, then drew his weapon.

They had no choice but to go with the backup plan.

Bahir fired two shots into Roger's chest. Ahmed shot Lucas twice in the head. Both men died almost instantly.

Shoving his gun back in his waistband, Ahmed said, "Let's get the gas masks."

CHAPTER FIFTY

Las Vegas

It took longer than expected, but Ahmed and Bahir had brought a total of sixteen drums inside and emptied their contents into the three holding tanks. As a result the atmosphere in the pumphouse had become almost as lethal as the acid itself. With a poisonous cloud hanging over them, they kept their gas masks on, even when they went outside to pull down two new barrels.

Bahir had backed the truck as close as he could to the door. The road was more than thirty yards away, so the risk of them being seen by someone in a passing car was slight. As for pedestrian traffic, Las Vegas has very little of it this time on a Sunday morning, especially at the back end of a hotel.

Ahmed's principal concern was remote surveillance. When the Handler made his plan, he learned there were cameras inside the computer control room but was unable to determine what sort of devices were in place at the pumphouse. They had to proceed on the assumption there were unseen cameras, both outside and inside, meaning they had to act swiftly. If they still had Sayyar with them, Ahmed could have done a better job of forcing the security guard and technician to assist, rather than having to kill them.

Now, with only Bahir to help him get this done, offloading the containers was simply taking too long. Ahmed knew they were running out of time and that soon someone would be on their way to see what was going on.

He and Bahir stepped outside, where Ahmed pulled off his mask and phoned Talal.

Talal connected on the first ring. "Problem?" he asked.

"It's taking too long," Ahmed told him.

"Do what you can, and get out."

Ahmed nodded to himself. "What about the woman?"

"It appears she has done what she was told. Since then, she has been sitting at her station with her hands in her lap."

"Has anyone called her?"

"No."

"Good," Ahmed said. "Bahir and I are going to bring in a few more barrels, then we will have to leave."

"Understood. What should I do with the woman?"

"Wait five minutes. Then call her out and ask if she has done what she was told. You will know if she is telling the truth. Then kill her so she cannot change anything once you are gone."

"Understood."

"By then we should be there to pick you up."

They ended the call, and Ahmed turned to Bahir. "No matter how incompetent their hotel security may be, someone is sitting in front of a monitor somewhere inside the main building, and they're eventually going to notice something is wrong. Let's dump in a few more barrels and get out of here."

* * *

AHMED'S LOW OPINION of hotel security was misplaced, but his fear that time was running out was not. There were already two people on duty in the central monitoring station of the Bellagio who had begun to suspect there was a problem.

There were no active security cameras inside the pumphouse, but Sharon's actions in the control room—or, more accurately stated, her lack of action—were unusual. She was a friendly, animated person who was known to regularly engage with her co-workers in the main computer center as well as inside the hotel via the monitors. This morning, she had uncharacteristically been sitting for a very long time without moving, hands in her lap, staring straight ahead.

"Hey, Brian, have a look at this," said Antonio to the other guard on duty.

Brian studied the screen for a moment, then said, "Sharon looks like she's in a trance."

"That was my thought," Antonio agreed.

"Maybe we should give her a call. Tell her to 'Snap out of it!' like in that movie. What was the name of it?"

Antonio was still watching the screen. "I know this'll sound nuts, but I think she's trying to send us a signal."

"A signal?"

"Like something's wrong, but she can't call us to say what it is. It's been more than ten minutes, and the only time I've seen her move was when she had a few looks over towards the door that leads to the entry area."

"We don't have a camera out there," Brian said.

"No we don't, and I'd like to know what she's looking at. And where the hell is Roger? If he went to the john, it's been way too long."

Brian stared at the image of the motionless woman on the screen. "You think there's some reason she can't call us, she doesn't want us to call her, but she's trying to tell us there's a problem?"

"Hey, if I'm wrong, what does it cost to have someone check it out?"

With that, the phone tied directly to the head of hotel security began to ring. Brian picked it up, identified himself to the director, Ken Thompson, and listened to what his boss had to say about a possible security threat. When Thompson was done, Brian said, "Sir, I have some information that might be relevant."

When he finished telling Thompson about Sharon and their concerns about the control room for the fountains, the director gave him a couple of quick instructions. When Brian hung up he turned to Antonio. "We're on high alert. And this is not a drill."

CHAPTER FIFTY-ONE

Las Vegas

By the time hotel security spread the word that they were under some sort of attack, Ahmed and Bahir had dumped the contents of four more drums into the tanks. Stepping outside again, Ahmed pulled off his mask and said, "Let's go."

Bahir did nothing to hide his surprise. Ahmed was not someone who gave up on a mission until it was done. "That's less than half of what we brought," he said.

Ahmed nodded. "The longer we stay, the more likely we get caught. If they find us here, they'll see what's in the truck and turn off the fountains. Everything we have done will be for nothing." He checked his watch. "The first show is in twenty minutes, and there's already enough HCL in the water. We can pick up Talal and get away."

"We needed more men," Bahir said as he pulled the back of the truck closed.

Ahmed did not want to hear anything more from him about murdering Sayyar. "Drive," he told him, climbing into the passenger seat as Bahir got in the other side and started the engine.

As soon as they began to back up, they could hear the sound of approaching sirens.

"What should we do?" Bahir asked.

"Don't turn right. Go left, away from the control booth, let's circle the block and see what's happening."

"What about Talal?"

Ahmed shook his head. "If they're heading there, we have no way of helping him now. Drive around past the front of the hotel, and let's find out."

* * *

THE LAS VEGAS TASK FORCE was scrambling to piece together the intel they were receiving from D.C. about a truck filled with HCL.

"They couldn't intercept the damn truck?" one of the sheriff's men asked.

"We had no I.D. on the vehicle," Reagan said. "By the time we learned they switched trucks it was too late."

Las Vegas has an early warning network that provides every hotel in the city with notice of imminent danger, from theft, to card counters, to threats of violence. Warnings were now being sent out, telling them all to be on the lookout for any suspicious trucks or deliveries.

Ken Thompson, head of security at the Bellagio, had just ended his cell phone call with Brian, and turned to the group. "I've got a problem," he said, then described what he had just heard.

"There are a lot of potential targets in this town," Reagan said. "Pools, water parks, all of that. But if they get access to your pumphouse and dump the chemicals into the water system, those jets are going to be spraying hydrochloric acid into the air next time they go on."

Thompson stared at him.

"I'm hoping I'm wrong," Reagan told him.

Thompson nodded. "I've got to get my people."

"I'm coming, if that's all right."

"What agency did you say you're with?" Thompson asked.

Reagan responded with a brief shrug.

"Let's go," Thompson said.

A local police officer was assigned to provide them a ride, and, on the way, Thompson phoned the head of his squad of armed men and women, ordering them into action.

"Follow the emergency protocols," Thompson told his top lieutenant, Peter Rancellet. "We have every reason to believe we're facing a lethal threat. Body armor for everyone. Bring a vest for me and one for a federal agent I have with me. Proceed with appropriate caution and be prepared to respond with deadly force."

Thompson had served two tours in the Marines, ten years as a police officer, and for the last six years had been the director of security operations for the Bellagio. He had the respect of everyone who knew him, especially his staff. When he gave those general warnings, followed by specific assignments, Rancellet did not question a single thing he said.

The task force center was only a mile down the Strip from the Bellagio, and moments after Thompson finished his call, they reached the front of the hotel. The group designated as team one was already outside, where Rancellet handed vests to his boss and Reagan. Then he gave Thompson an earpiece with mic, which he fixed in place.

"Listen up," Thompson told everyone tied into the audio link, "Teams one and two are heading to the building that houses the fountain's control booth. I want teams three and four at the pump station, pronto. Team five stays at the front of the house, contact us if you see anything, and start moving people away from the fountain. I'm counting on you to manage the chaos. Let's move out."

Team one was comprised of Thompson, Rancellet, a man they called Zak, and a woman named Brittany.

Reagan followed the four of them as they raced off. By now, sirens were blaring along the Strip as vehicles of all kinds began to converge on the hotel, but Thompson knew the fastest way to the control booth was through a narrow passageway that ran beneath the outdoor restaurant plaza.

As the five of them ran, he saw the crowd gathering on the walkways around the fountain for the morning's first water show. Calling into his microphone, he asked, "Can anyone provide a sit-rep?"

"Approaching the control booth," the leader from team two said. "Also got word there was a truck parked outside the pumphouse for the past twenty minutes or so."

"And no one said anything?" Thompson hollered into his radio. "Goddamnit! Teams three and four, get your asses to the pumphouse. Now!" Thompson then addressed himself to the men in the security monitoring center. "Brian, what are you seeing?"

"Sharon just got up from her desk," Brian told him. "The way she turned her head and stood up, it looked like someone called to her. She walked to the door, camera lost sight of her. Roger still hasn't come back, the control room is empty."

Thompson pulled out his cell and called the conference number that tied him into the task force. "This is Thompson at the Bellagio. I have new information," he shouted into the phone. "We have word there was a truck outside the pumphouse that handles the water flow to our fountain. Might have dumped the HCL in there. Let's find that damn truck."

The lead FBI agent responded. "We're coming around the back of your hotel now."

"Trooper Chelworth here," another voice jumped in. "I'm tracking a vehicle, think it might be the one that was outside your hotel. Anyone have a description?"

"Negative," Thompson said, "just pull them over whoever they are."

"I'm on it," Chelworth said.

"Be sure you have enough firepower," the FBI agent told Chelworth. "We still have no idea what we're dealing with."

"Roger that," the trooper said.

"The next show is in less than five minutes," Thompson told everyone. "We're out of time."

"If the truck left the site, the chemicals are probably already in the water," Reagan hollered, loud enough to be heard on the conference call and Thompson's mic.

"Team five," Thompson yelled, "get everyone away from the fountain. Now!"

"Is there any way to turn the entire system off?" Reagan asked.

"Only if we get into the control booth in time," Thompson told him. Then barking into the mic again, he said. "You all get that?" Thompson asked. Then, just to be sure, he repeated everything, especially the need for someone to get to the kill switch in the control room. Then he raised Brian and Antonio again. "Listen up," he said. "We have reason to believe the water supply to the fountain has been contaminated. We're going to do all we can to turn off the system, but you need to get your butts out onto the plaza, grab any staff you can along the way, and work with team five to disperse that crowd. Take the bullhorns with you, tell the front desk to start running a continuous announcement over the P.A., do anything you can to get everyone away from the water."

"Should one of us stay here to monitor the video feed?"

"Screw the video. Get down there, and move those people away from the fountain."

Brian and Antonio grabbed the battery-operated bullhorns and raced for the door, Brian using his radio to notify customer services that they needed every available hand outside to tell people to back away from the water.

* * *

WHILE ACTIVITY AROUND the hotel intensified, Talal was standing with Sharon in the vestibule outside the control room. Several minutes had passed since Ahmed called, but he and Bashir had not come for him. Left on his own, Talal dialed the emergency number for the Handler.

"Mahdi," he said, "it's Talal."

"Why are you calling me?" the voice demanded.

Talal gave a concise report on the situation, then asked, "I want to know what you want me to do."

"You should not have called me," the Handler admonished him again, then softened his tone, knowing from what Talal had described that he was speaking to a dead man. "Here's what you do," he said, gave a few instructions, then hung up.

Talal had not murdered Sharon as Ahmed had instructed, not yet. The Handler suggested she might become valuable as a hostage, knowing it was a lie, knowing that Talal was not going to live out the morning and neither was the woman. For now, however, he told Talal to use her as a human shield and hold out until help arrived.

* * *

THOMPSON'S GROUP OF FIVE reached the building that housed the control booth just after team two arrived. There were only three minutes left before the first water show of the day would begin. They had to get inside to turn it off, and everyone in hotel security was listening to the radio transmissions and knew what was at stake.

"We need to get in there and shut down the system, right now," Thompson bellowed.

"Just checked, the door's locked. We pounded on it, no response," the team two leader told him. "Based on what we know, we assume there are armed men inside."

Thompson had already pulled out his master key and was approaching the metal door. "There are also hundreds of innocent people about to get an acid shower if we don't get the hell inside. Pull out your weapons and let's move."

Thompson unlocked the door, and, when he pulled it open, gunfire immediately erupted from within.

CHAPTER FIFTY-TWO

Las Vegas

Talal was clutching a handful of Sharon's hair and holding her in front of him as he began firing.

Thompson was protected from Talal's initial shots by the metal door but had no way of looking in to see how many hostiles were inside. He hollered toward the opening, "Drop your weapons and come out. Now!"

The response was another series of shots that ricocheted off the door and concrete stones at the entrance to the building. Then a voice said, "I have the woman. Make a move to come in, and I will kill her!"

Reagan positioned himself on the other side of the open door. He and Thompson exchanged a look that said everything men with combat experience had no need to voice. They did not want anything to happen to Sharon, but they had no time for a hostage negotiation, not with the lives of so many other people at stake.

Thompson yanked the door all the way open and Reagan charged in, Thompson right beside him, each man firing his weapon as they moved. Rancellet, Zak, and Brittany followed close behind, guns ablaze, all of them doing what they could not to inflict any damage with friendly fire.

The small entry area was filled with the ear-splitting noise and the distinctive odor of gunfire. When silence suddenly replaced the clamor, Talal was on the ground bleeding to death, all of the ammunition in his weapon having been spent. Reagan leaned down and grabbed his gun, then stood over him, keeping his weapon trained on the Arab's face.

"You want me to get an ambulance here," Reagan said, "you better start talking."

Talal looked up at him, his eyes blank as he drew his last breath.

"Damn," Reagan said, then rushed over to Jimmy, the guard Talal had stabbed and left bleeding in the corner. He was also dead.

Thompson and Rancellet were kneeling beside Sharon. She had taken three rounds, one in the shoulder, one in her side, and one in her neck. It wasn't clear who had fired which of those shots, but right now it did not matter.

The two men tried to stop the bleeding as Sharon stared up at them with the vacant look of someone who knew she was about to die.

"I didn't do it," she said, her voice a raspy whisper.

"Don't talk," Thompson said, "we're going to get you help."

Reagan also crouched beside her as Sharon said, "It's important, just listen." Mustering all of her remaining strength just to speak, she said, "They wanted me to change the path of the jets. I didn't do it. I made changes, but not what they wanted. The people will be safe." Now Sharon stared up into Thompson's eyes, grabbing at his shirt as she said, "Do you understand what I'm telling you?"

"Yes," he said as his eyes filled up.

"They wanted me to change the path of the jets," she told him. "They wanted to spray the crowd with contaminated water."

"But you didn't do what they wanted," Thompson said, not bothering to wipe at his tears.

"Yes," she said, "yes." After a painful breath, she said, "He made a phone call. A name. Sounded like Mahdi." Then she let go of his shirt and let out a long sigh.

"God bless you," Thompson said.

Sharon managed a slight smile and died in his arms.

The room was silent for a moment, then Thompson spoke up. He had been hit with one shot to the chest, which was protected by his vest, but a second caught him in the shoulder. Brittany and Zak saw the wound and began to work on him, but he pushed them away. "Someone get in there," he hollered, "and turn off the damned fountain! I don't want this woman to die for nothing."

* * *

JUST AROUND THE OTHER SIDE of the hotel, state trooper Chelworth was working with two other cars to force the suspicious truck off the road.

When Ahmed saw the vehicles coming at them with sirens blaring, he told Bahir to run through them. He stepped hard on the gas.

Once it was clear the truck was not going to stop, the three state cars and an LVPD black-and-white had too much combined power and maneuverability for Bahir to break through. Two came at the truck from the sides, the third angling a collision off the front passenger side of the truck's cab.

The multi-vehicle impact that ensued sent the truck careening off to the left. Bahir jammed on the brake, but their momentum carried them head-first into a concrete divider. Ahmed, who had not strapped on his seatbelt, crashed into the windshield when his airbag failed. Bahir was not as badly hurt when the bag exploded from the steering wheel, but, by the time the two terrorists could get their bearings, the truck was surrounded by armed law enforcement, all of whom had their weapons drawn and aimed at them.

Ahmed, still in a daze, raised his automatic and pointed it through the broken glass, but never got the chance to fire. As soon as he showed his weapon, he was riddled with shots from both the front and the side of the truck. He was dead before he could make another move.

Bahir was hit in the arm by a bullet that had ricocheted inside the truck's cab but raised his hands over his head, screaming, "I am not armed, I am not armed," until two officers yanked the driver's door open and dragged him facedown onto the pavement and cuffed his hands behind him.

* * *

By now, Reagan and several of Thompson's men had rushed into the computer control booth, heading for the kill switches for the various jets in the enormous fountain outside.

Two other teams had reached the pumphouse and made their way inside, where they found the bodies of Roger and Lucas. Before they could get to the tanks, the group was overcome by the noxious fumes of poisonous gas that filled the place and were forced to retreat. With no time to go back for gas masks, they ripped off their shirts and used them to cover their noses and mouths, three of them rushing back in, struggling through the overwhelming haze to shut off the pipes.

By the time all that was done, in the control room and pumphouse, it was already too late.

Despite the courageous actions of Thompson's men and women, and the ultimate sacrifice made by Sharon, the water show had already begun and lasted four minutes before the jets cut out.

Antonio and Brian were outside on their bullhorns, along with team five and more than two dozen customer service personnel, all of them running through the crowd shouting warnings, straining to be heard above the loud music that accompanied the display. Repeated public address announcements were also being drowned out, and there were too many people there and too little space for everyone to safely back off in time.

Sharon had told the truth, she hadn't done what Ahmed and Talal had demanded. She had not changed the trajectory of the main jets to rain directly on the spectators standing beside the fountain. The changes she did make, however, created an issue with the crossing paths of the cascading water. When combined with the morning breeze, some of the spray reached people positioned on the eastern edge of the fountain, near the Strip.

No one who witnessed the event would ever forget the agonizing shrieks of those who were hit.

The effect was not immediate. At first, people were either amused or annoyed at getting wet. Only moments later, the burning sensation began to take hold as the hydrochloric acid ate through their clothes and began to burn away their skin.

It was far worse for those who looked up and were hit in their face, or hair or hands.

A boy of eight, dressed in shorts and a t-shirt, was visiting with his parents from Kansas City. When he first felt the water sprinkle his face, he instinctively rubbed his eyes. Now it would take a miracle to save his sight.

A young woman from Detroit had been up all night celebrating her birthday with four of her girlfriends. They were supposed to leave town today and wanted to make the most of their final hours in Las Vegas, so they came by for the show. Now they were all trying to pull their own hair out at the roots as the acid dripped down onto their scalps. The pain was unimaginable.

Three men from Los Angeles had stopped by, doing their best to deal with their hangovers and gambling losses from the night before when they were hit by the acid. Now they were running in circles, not understanding what had happened to them or what to do.

Scores of others were stumbling around or writhing on the ground, all screaming for help, none of them knowing what was going on or how to stop the pain.

Those around them, whom the spray did not reach, were unsure of how to react. Some attempted to aid their friends and family, only to find their hands burned when they came into contact with the acid. Others were too frightened to act at all.

Within minutes, every available ambulance and EMT in or near Las Vegas was on their way to help. All responding medical personnel had been warned that they had to wear gloves and proceed with caution. Acid burns to dozens of people was not something they were accustomed to handling or equipped to deal with, but every one of them did their best to relieve the anguish of the victims.

It was all they could do.

CHAPTER FIFTY-THREE

CIA Headquarters, Langley, Virginia

The events unfolding in Las Vegas were being monitored in a conference room at Langley by Gellos, Brandt, Levchenko, and Kenny. They had access to live feeds, including a satellite link that displayed the police apprehending the truck. They also witnessed the entry of Reagan and Thompson's people into the control booth, although they could not see the battle that took place inside.

Worst of all was the view of the catastrophe at the fountain, those four minutes when acid poured from the sky, spreading injury, mutilation, and pain.

The four of them sat in silence as they watched in horror at what a deranged group of zealots would inflict on unsuspecting, innocent people who had never done them the slightest harm.

Their collective sense of helplessness was overwhelming as they watched the ambulances and emergency rescue trucks arriving, the doctors and nurses and technicians, all wearing gloves and goggles and some in hazmat suits, rushing to attend to the afflicted. The medical teams worked quickly, administering alkaline powders and ointments. Others carried away the most severely injured on stretchers, poor souls who continued to thrash about, some beginning to respond to the massive painkillers being administered, others not.

Unable to watch anymore, Gellos finally stood up. "This bullshit has got to stop," she said, her voice breaking with rage and despair.

"Yes it does," Kenny said quietly.

Gellos looked down at Levchenko. "Sasha, I want everything you can put together on any building, anywhere in this country that uses the sort of design those scientists were questioned about."

Sasha said, "You'll have it."

Gellos turned to Kenny. "Sir, I say this with all respect for who we are and what we do, but Reagan and I can't listen to anything more about jurisdiction, or inter-agency authority, or any of that. We want the sonofabitch who's behind these attacks, and we're going to get him."

* * *

THE STORY ABOUT THE ATTACK was all over the news, providing the Handler his first opportunity to see actual footage of what had occurred.

Television correspondents described the damage that had been caused, estimated the number of those injured, and the current casualty count, including the five hotel workers who had been murdered by Ahmed and Talal. The reporters found innumerable ways to say how the nature of the assault was unthinkable and how the people behind it were reprehensible monsters.

The Handler nodded at the screen. It was not all he had hoped for, but it was better than the results at the New York High Line.

For the third phase of this operation, he would have to accelerate the timetable. Ahmed had died when his truck was intercepted. He had enjoyed the fate of a warrior in the name of Allah, as had Talal. Bahir was a coward who had given himself up and was now a risk to provide information that might compromise the Handler's plans.

Fortunately, Bahir did not know as much as Ahmed had known, or even Talal, but he still presented a problem. They would have to assume he would turn on them, and they would proceed accordingly.

When one of the newsmen began lauding the heroism of a woman, Sharon Ashford, who had prevented far worse damage by duping the terrorists, the Handler angrily switched off the television and left for dinner.

PART THREE

The following evening...

CHAPTER FIFTY-FOUR

CIA Headquarters, Langley

Reagan returned from Nevada the next afternoon and went straight from the airport to Kenny's office at Langley, where Gellos, Erin, Brandt, and Sasha were gathered. After a debriefing of the events in Las Vegas, Erin quietly asked Reagan if he needed to rest.

He waved it off. "Later." Turning to Levchenko, he asked, "What've we got on these buildings?"

Sasha had compiled a digital list of all buildings constructed with translucent roofs supported by metal crossbeams. His data confirmed that the design was not limited to covered sports arenas and shopping malls, but the team agreed they would make better targets than an apartment building or office tower with that sort of atrium.

As Sasha took them through a series of images on the wall monitor, Reagan, said, "This sort of design is obviously not new."

"It's decades old," Sasha agreed.

"Is it logical to think that older buildings would be more vulnerable to an attack?" Reagan asked.

"It's not illogical," Sasha conceded, "but you have to view these on a case by case basis. There are other factors to consider, such as the height of the building, the nature of the materials used for the roof, the design of the supporting structures, and so on."

"There's obviously no time for us to send people around the country to inspect all these locations," Reagan said. "The attacks in New

York and Las Vegas were just a little more than a week apart. If a third assault is coming, it may be coming soon."

Kenny agreed. "We have to assume their planning is pretty far down the road."

Reagan looked from the monitor to the DD. "Who's analyzing the phones they took from the three men in Vegas?"

"FBI and DHS," Kenny replied, "they're working together on it."

"How the hell do they work together decrypting a phone?" Reagan asked, then looked at Sasha, who was shaking his head in mute agreement.

"It's their show," Kenny said.

Reagan turned to Erin. "You have friends in both agencies that work in forensics. Any chance you can get us a preview?"

"I'll make some calls," Erin said. "Anything specific you're looking for?"

"A clue to whoever is behind this would be nice," Reagan said, "but we'll take whatever you can get."

"We already know they were using burner phones. Probably only used them to stay in contact with each other during the operation," Erin told him. "Sorry to be so negative."

"You never know who else they might have spoken with in those last few hours," Reagan said.

"Just find out what you can," Kenny told her.

"I'll get on it," Erin said and left the room.

"As to these sites," Sasha said, "the only efficient way for us to review the architecture and uses of all these buildings would be through virtual tours. Bring them up on the screen, check them out, evaluate their likelihood as targets."

"Even that's going to take too much time," Brandt said.

Reagan agreed. "We'll never figure this out by looking at videos of ballparks and shopping malls."

"We might get some help," the DD said. "Those three scientists from California are still in Washington under the care of the FBI."

"We could also bring in a few of Sasha's friends from the second floor," Reagan suggested, "have them join the search."

"Let's do it," Kenny said.

In their interviews with the FBI, the three scientists who had been abducted in Pakistan described the various subjects their interrogators had touched upon, much as they had when Reagan questioned them on their way home. Their captors had grilled them about infrastructure, the impact of earthquakes and subterranean explosions on building foundations, and the possible destruction of translucent roofs supported by metal piping. They were also asked about water flow and the engineering that determines optimum pressure flows within utility pipes.

When Kenny phoned Matt Fitzgibbon at the Bureau, he was given a summary of those discussions.

Kenny told him, "We've developed some information we can share with them, might be more valuable helping us look ahead, rather than reviewing the attacks that have already happened."

"What sort of information?"

"A theory that we need to keep eyes-only."

"Understood," Fitzgibbon replied.

Kenny described the section of the Koran that called for the murder of nonbelievers by three different methods, and how two of the three had now occurred during the past ten days.

"The Koran calls for these attacks?" Fitzgibbon said.

"Verse 22:19 directs the followers of Allah to punish the infidels with garments of fire, hooked iron rods, and boiling water that will melt their skin and bellies."

There was silence until Fitzgibbon said, "What kind of world is this?"

"You tell me," Kenny replied. "I preferred the army. At least I knew who we were shooting at."

"No argument there," Fitzgibbon said, followed by a loud, deep breath. "So your take on this is that New York was an attempt to set garments on fire, and Las Vegas was about melting the skin off innocent spectators."

"That's our read. An acid bath is close enough to boiling water."

"What have you come up with for these hooked iron rods?" Fitzgibbon asked. "Sounds medieval."

"That's where the three scientists come in. How about you bring them here so we can all talk?"

"I'm on my way," Fitzgibbon said.

CHAPTER FIFTY-FIVE

Los Angeles

Anatole Mindlovitch was still confined to a private hospital room in Cedars Sinai in Los Angeles but was becoming feistier by the day.

"They tried to kill me," he said for the twentieth time that evening. "Over a microchip?"

Bruce Levi, one of the few friends Mindlovitch agreed to see, was perched on the windowsill. There were only the two of them in the large room. "I think we both know it was about more than that," he said.

Mindlovitch, who was sitting up in bed, fell back against the pillows stacked behind him. "I suppose you're right. What's got me crazy is that someone on my security detail sold me out." He sat up again. "I treat them like family. I overpay them. I'm not like one of these asshole celebrities who act like their employees are invisible."

"Might not have been security. Could have been someone on your household team."

"Even worse," Mindlovitch said.

Levi did not respond.

"Now they're all being questioned, which is an insult to the loyal people on my staff. Some of them have been with me since Moscow."

"If they're really loyal they'll understand."

Mindlovitch nodded glumly. "Until we straighten this out, I've had to hire new bodyguards, men I don't even know."

"That's a good thing," Levi assured him. "They've all been vetted by our friends at Langley. They have no history with you or Moscow. The chance any of them would be compromised is negligible."

The Russian managed to laugh. "Negligible to you, maybe. I'm the guy who doesn't want to have his stomach pumped again."

When it appeared that his friend was done ranting for the moment, Levi said, "We should discuss the theft of these prototypes."

Sitting back again, Mindlovitch asked, "Why?"

"For starters, it's a national security issue."

"So I'm told. The feds have already displayed their characteristic lack of tact, forcing their way into my room while I'm on my deathbed, demanding answers I don't have."

"Their timing may be lousy," Levi admitted, "but I'm sure you understand the concern. After the attack in Vegas, there's a heightened level of anxiety. From everything you and Nick Reagan told me about this Ghost Chip, I can certainly see the problem."

"I'm an innovator, not a policeman. What do they expect me to do?" Mindlovitch sighed. "You make it sound like a car manufacturer is responsible when a driver gets drunk and runs someone down."

"Not a very apt analogy, Anatole. And what about the other functions of the chip? High frequency transmissions that can be lethal. The ability to remotely detonate them?"

Mindlovitch shrugged. "How do you expect scientists to make advances if they're going to be held responsible for every unforeseen consequence of their creations?"

"You sound like a poster boy for the NRA. Guns don't kill people, people kill people."

Mindlovitch responded with a frown. "There's a point to be made there. If someone develops a more efficient weapon, are they accountable for how it's used. Or by whom?"

Levi smiled. "A clever argument, although Einstein said he regretted his involvement in the creation of the atomic bomb."

"People forget that Einstein was wrong about any number of things," he said with a wave of his hand. "The point of the Ghost Chip is to develop a means of enabling communication that cannot be intercepted by those not entitled to listen. After living in Russia, my motive was about privacy, about combatting Big Brother and the way government intrudes into our lives."

"Do I hear Putin's name in there someplace?"

"Yes," Mindlovitch conceded, "but things are not much better in this country. Look at your NSA and Homeland Security, the information gathered from citizens not even aware their lives are being violated. Can any of us make a phone call anymore that isn't being overheard by someone who has no right to be listening? Not to mention the private sector. Facebook and Google and Twitter and on and on."

"All good points," Levi admitted patiently, "but if you want to debate morality, there's another imperative at play. Let's say you developed a chemical that had valuable, practical applications, but was also toxic if used improperly. And let's say the chemical falls into the wrong hands, and you're the only one who has the antidote. Do you have a responsibility to provide that antidote to an innocent person infected with the chemical?"

"The answer is obvious. I would provide the cure." Mindlovitch said. "But I have the sense there's a trick to your question."

Levi smiled. "Now let's suppose that by providing the antidote, you're neutralizing the effectiveness of your chemical. Or worse, giving information that could lead someone else to duplicate your valuable creation."

"Aha!"

Levi leaned forward. "I know you very well Anatole. I know how people in Russia betrayed your friendship and what you've done to rebound from that. I also know you're extremely protective of your innovations, and inclined to deal with problems yourself, rather than allowing others to help."

"Because, as you say, they might then be able to copy my technology," he finished the thought.

Levi laughed. "Your recovery seems to be going quite well. At least there's no sign of mental impairment."

"I haven't become a blithering idiot if that's what you mean. Do you expect me to throw open the doors to my factory in Suzhou? Invite your friend from the CIA into my research and development laboratory?"

"Nothing quite that drastic, but I do expect you to cooperate."

Mindlovitch grunted.

"I'll tell you something," Levi said.

"Please do."

"There's been an attempt on your life, and once you leave here, you may still be at risk. In the category of possible new friends, you could do worse than Nick Reagan."

"And what do you suggest I do to earn that loyalty?"

Levi paused, then said, "I suggest we call him and tell him whatever you know about the theft of the Ghost Chip."

Mindlovitch responded with a sheepish grin. "If you insist. Which would mean I should also tell him that I not only created the chip, but I also have the so-called antidote. I have the means to remotely disable all of those functions you're so worried about."

Levi stared at him without speaking for a moment. Then he said, "You son of a bitch."

"Call him," Mindlovitch said.

CHAPTER FIFTY-SIX

CIA Headquarters, Langley

Kenny was still in the office with his team when his assistant came in and told him he had a call from Bruce Levi. "He's with Anatole Mindlovitch, they want to speak with you and Reagan."

"Tell them to hold on," the DD said, then sent the rest of the team to the conference room. Once he and Reagan were alone, he took the call.

"Deputy Director Kenny here, on the speaker with Reagan."

"Bruce Levi, in Anatole's hospital room. Just the two of us, so I'm also going to put this on speaker."

There was a pause, the sound of a muted debate in the background, until Levi said, "Anatole wants your assurance it's just the two of you."

"You have it."

When both speaker functions were activated, Reagan asked, "How are you, Mr. Mindlovitch? Very sorry to hear what happened."

"I'm doing better."

"Any progress on the source of the problem?"

"If you're asking if they know what poison was used, the answer is yes. Some sort of snake venom. As for who's behind it, we don't know which snake it was, but my people claim they're getting close."

"Good," Reagan said. "If we can help, we will."

"As I understand it, you already have, but I'll keep it in mind." He paused. "So, the reason for my call."

Reagan and the DD waited.

"When you came to see me at my home, Mr. Reagan, you were interested in an item our company has under development."

"Very interested," Reagan agreed.

"I was not as candid as I might have been."

Reagan looked at Kenny as he said, "I think we all knew that."

Mindlovitch managed a brief chuckle. "You were aware we've been working on a prototype of the item."

"Yes," Reagan said. "There's also a rumor that the prototype was recently stolen."

"That's true, although it's not as if we only created one," the Russian told him. "Numerous versions were assembled. Some work, others don't. Of the ones that work, some work well, others not so much."

"Then you know what I'm going to ask," Reagan said.

"Which were taken?"

"And how many," Reagan said.

Mindlovitch paused again. "A tray holding two dozen of our best samples are gone. There is no evidence of a break-in, which leads to the obvious conclusion that they were taken by someone inside."

"And without help, no thief could have known which were effective and which were the clinkers."

Mindlovitch laughed. "We prefer to think of the less successful models as the building blocks of progress, rather than clinkers."

"My apologies," Reagan said with a slight smile. "So what steps are being taken to investigate the theft, and what's being done to secure the remaining prototypes?"

"The other samples are secure. As for the investigation, I'm relying on private resources, for reasons I'm sure you understand."

"Forgive my bluntness, but that didn't work so well for you personally. Do you believe the theft and this attempt on your life are unrelated?"

"Bruce and I were just discussing that issue, which is one of the reasons I called. This awful occurrence in Las Vegas has me concerned."

"You're wondering if the stolen chips were used by the people who planned the attack?"

"Yes," Mindlovitch admitted.

"We have no way of knowing, but if it helps, I can tell you the planning for the Las Vegas attack was well before the theft in Suzhou. It's what happens next that concerns us."

"Of course," the Russian said.

"You have any suggestions that might help?"

Mindlovitch thought it over. "When the prototypes are not in use they have no sort of independent homing device in them, nothing like that. But I created a failsafe that is known to very few people. Bruce has persuaded me to share that information with you."

"A failsafe?"

"There is a process by which I can jam the signal from any device utilizing the chip."

Kenny, who had remained quiet up till then, asked, "How close would you have to be to the device to interfere with the signal?"

"I could be on the other side of the world," Mindlovitch told him. "These chips rely on the use of a proprietary frequency, it's part of what makes them effective. When they're using that frequency, I have a means of overriding the connection and cutting off the communication."

"But you can only do this when the device is in use?" Reagan asked.

"Correct," Mindlovitch said. "Since I know which microchips were taken, I already have their electronic fingerprints."

Reagan said, "I thought the point of the Ghost Chip is to prevent *any* sort of interception."

"Any sort of interception but mine." Mindlovitch uttered another weary laugh. "No one should ever design a bomb without some sort of circuit breaker. You obviously recall that terrorist incident, when Apple claimed they had no way of bypassing a customer's encryption, then changed their story? Once I know a connection is made, I can stop the transmission."

Bruce Levi prodded his friend with a simple, "And?"

"Yes," Mindlovitch responded, "here's the part you're really going to like."

"We can hardly wait," Reagan said.

"Once I identify the use of the frequency and override the connection, *then* I can pinpoint the locations of both the sender and receiver. There is no encryption that can prevent it, no caroming the signal off a dozen satellites, nothing like that. I can create a digital map leading me directly to the source."

"Forgive me if this question sounds ungrateful," Kenny said, "but why are you sharing this with us now?"

"Selfishly, I want your help in recovering my property. I would never want to have these chips fall into the wrong hands, and I believe you have the resources and motivation to retrieve them." He paused. "Then there is the matter of my personal safety. As you pointed out, I have reason to be worried, and, as Bruce has advised, it is valuable to have you on my side."

"Then you'll give us your full cooperation," Kenny said.

"I will," Mindlovitch replied, "and we have solid information about who was likely responsible. But first, I have one condition. Once we recover the prototypes—and we will recover them—they will be returned to me. All of them. Intact. Uncopied."

Kenny said, "I am a man of word, Mr. Mindlovitch, so I will not guarantee we can find them, even with your help. And I certainly cannot assure you they will be intact. What I can promise, is that whatever we find will be returned to you. But I also have a condition."

"Which is?"

"You will not sell the technology to anyone before offering it exclusively to my government."

After a brief silence, the Russian said, "A right of first refusal?" He sounded amused by the notion.

"After your unfortunate incident, you know who provided an additional level of security for you, in the hospital as well as your home?"

"Yes, my unseen protectors from Langley. Bruce told me you've been very generous in that regard."

"We didn't do it in expectation of some quid pro quo," Kenny told him. "We did it because, under the circumstances, it was the right thing to do."

"As it turns out, for you as well as for me," Mindlovitch said with one more brief laugh.

There was a knock on Kenny's door. His assistant looked in and said in a quiet voice, "Agent Fitzgibbon is here."

Kenny nodded. Then he said, facing the speakerphone again, "Mr. Mindlovitch?"

"All right, I agree."

"Good. You can begin by sharing what you have on the theft. I'm going to turn this call over to one of our agents, Alex Brandt, and one of our top analysts, Erin David. Bruce has met Brandt, and he knows Erin quite well."

"I do," Levi spoke up.

"I'll have Brandt and David get back to you. Say, ten minutes?"

"Fine," Mindlovitch replied.

Before they hung up, Reagan said, "Just to be clear, you'll give us *everything* you know about the theft."

"Yes, Mr. Reagan," Mindlovitch said. "Everything."

CHAPTER FIFTY-SEVEN

CIA Headquarters, Langley

Reagan followed Kenny down the hall to one of the secure conference rooms used for visitors. Unlike the antiseptic working spaces elsewhere in the building, this room was well-appointed with comfortable leather chairs, walnut furniture, and a large monitor on the wall.

Waiting there were Matt Fitzgibbon of the FBI and the three men from California. Carol Gellos was playing hostess—a role she generally resented—while Sasha worked on the audiovisual system.

Kenny entered, introduced himself, then took a seat at the large, rectangular table facing his guests. "I apologize for the delay. Can I get you anything? Coffee, water?"

"Your assistant has already taken our requests," Fitzgibbon told him.

Reagan walked around the table to greet Fitzgibbon and shake hands with each of the three professors. "You're all looking a lot better than last time I saw you."

Schapiro, the geological engineer, said, "Thanks to you and Ms. Gellos. Not to mention, Washington has been far more hospitable than Islamabad."

"Not if you're a member of the minority party in Congress," Reagan said with a grin. "As you've no doubt guessed, you're here because we still need your help."

"Whatever we can do," the professor told him.

As Reagan took a seat beside the DD, Fitzgibbon said, "You said you have something you want us to see?"

"First we need to go over a couple of items," Kenny said, then turned to the scientists. "I understand that when you were in custody there was an area of particular interest you were questioned about."

"There were a few," Reynaud replied.

"I'm referring to a specific architectural design, and the interest these people had in the potential effects of a roof collapse."

"More than a collapse," Reynaud told them. "They grilled us about what would happen in the event of an earthquake, an explosion, or any event that could impact the stability of that sort of building."

"When you refer to *that sort of building*," Kenny said, "I was led to believe they were focusing on the ceiling rather than any other part of the structure."

"That's accurate," Finerman agreed.

Turning to Levchenko, Kenny asked, "You ready?" When Sasha nodded, Kenny said, "Gentlemen, please have a look at the slideshow we've put together. It is by no means a comprehensive review, but we want to know if you believe these are the sorts of buildings they were asking about."

Sasha began the presentation, and, from the first few images, the reaction from the three men from California made it clear these were precisely the type of structures at issue. Modern design. Roofs that were translucent or transparent. Domed stadiums, modern train stations and shopping malls, office buildings with atriums. All of them featuring weight bearing beams and joists made of interconnected metal pipes.

Hooked iron rods.

After more than fifty images quickly came and went, Reynaud said, "These are exactly what we took them to mean, and all of them are excellent examples of the style." Then he turned from the screen back to Kenny.

The DD began rubbing the bridge of his nose between his thumb and forefinger. "We'll have to read you into a situation we're studying."

Reagan smiled at his use of the word "studying." He said nothing.

"You will need to keep this in the strictest confidence. Time is short, so all I can do is rely on your integrity."

"You have my word," Schapiro said.

The other two men voiced their agreement.

"When you say situation, Brian—" Fitzgibbon began, but Kenny was not going to waste time circling about the issue.

"Another possible attack," the DD replied. Then he provided the three engineers the background on the theory of a three-part assault. "The first two attacks match the exhortations in that section of the Koran. Based on the nature of your interrogation and our analysis of the available information, we've concluded there will be a third target."

"A building like one of these?"

"Given the questions you were asked and the mention of hooked iron rods, that's our working theory."

"There must be hundreds of these structures around the country," Fitzgibbon said.

"Not that many fit our profile of logical targets," Levchenko told him.

"Do we at least have an idea of what part of the country they might hit?" Fitzgibbon asked.

"Not yet," Kenny admitted. "But we think it will be a retail building, such as a shopping mall, or a domed stadium."

"That makes sense," Reynaud said.

They all turned to him as Fitzgibbon asked, "Why do you say that?"

"Because of the questions they asked us." Reynaud glanced at his friends for a moment, then turned to Fitzgibbon and said, "The three of us have obviously discussed all of this since Reagan and his people pulled us out of there. Our captors thought they were being clever, trying to make it sound as if they were interested in how that sort of construction would respond to anything from a seismic event to a misguided military strike. They were ridiculous. We figured they had some idea about planning an attack, and we understood what they were after. They wanted details on what would happen to the metal struts in the event of an explosion. We did everything we could to confuse the issue."

Reagan nodded. "Did they ever mention a specific type of building?"

Finerman nodded. "There was some discussion about different uses, but if they want maximum damage, blowing up the roof over an atrium in an office building isn't likely to inflict much in the way of personal injuries."

"Or death, if we're going to be blunt about it," Reynaud added.

"Right," Finerman agreed. "At any given moment, how many people are standing in the lobby in an office building?"

"If you want to create serious harm," Reynaud told them, "hit someplace where there are a lot of people directly below the roof."

"My next question will be obvious," Kenny said.

"Did they ever mention a specific building or location," Schapiro replied.

"Exactly. Anything at all?"

The three men looked at each other, each of them shaking his head.

"Wish we could help with that," Reynaud said, "but as clumsy as their questions might have been, they weren't that stupid."

"Looking back," Schapiro interjected, "I doubt any of them would have known. These men did not seem to be high enough on the food chain to have that information. One of them was definitely an engineer, and he was on a fact-finding mission, but if there was a plan to blow up the glass pyramid at the Louvre, my sense of it is that none of them would have known."

Kenny sat back and looked to Fitzgibbon. "Now what?"

"We get to work, keep tracking the chatter," the man from the FBI said.

"You may want to consider the types of explosives they would use," Reynaud suggested. "These structures are not made of Legos, they're meant to withstand hurricane winds and other compromising events. A couple of sticks of dynamite or a pocketful of plastic explosives is not going to get the job done."

"When you say compromising events—" Reagan began.

"I'm not suggesting they're going to survive a major earthquake, but the construction design takes into account subtle seismic shifts, burst water mains, that sort of thing. You're not going to bring the ceiling crashing down with a simple shove. You're going to need to position enough explosive material at critical support joints that will create a sort of chain reaction."

"And you believe they understood that much?" Kenny asked.

Once again, the three scientists looked to one another.

"I'm afraid so," Reynaud conceded.

* * *

WHEN THEIR MEETINGS WRAPPED up after nine that night, Reagan met Erin, and they took the elevator down to the underground garage where he kept his Porsche Cayenne. From there they headed off to the home he kept on the shore of the Chesapeake.

Reagan had owned this small, gray cedar-shingled house on the water for several years, but almost no one knew about it. Using a shell company, he purchased the place, set on nearly two acres, as his personal retreat. Other than Erin, he never brought visitors. There was no name on the mailbox, and the only thing he ever found there were throwaway advertisements addressed to "Occupant." It was a completely anonymous sanctuary.

Along the way they stopped for some groceries, a couple of bottles of wine, and a large steak. Reagan prepared their dinner on the outdoor grill, and they ate at the teak table set on the rear deck overlooking the water. Following the events of the past several days, and making their way into the second bottle of cabernet, they were both exhausted and happy to go inside.

In the bedroom, when Reagan stripped down, she could see the blood that had stained the dressing on his left arm. They headed for the shower, holding each other as the warm water cascaded over them, then helped each other dry off. Erin carefully cleaned the wound and applied new bandages. Still naked, they got into bed.

Reagan held her in his arms as they shared a passionate kiss.

Then Erin said, "Get on your stomach."

He smiled. "Should I ask why?"

"You need some serious attention," she said.

He did as he was told, lying face down with his arms at his sides as she straddled him and began a deep tissue massage, from the shoulders down.

After a few minutes of this sublime treatment, feeling the soft skin of her firm legs spread across his him, Reagan said, "Tired as I am, it's much more likely you're going to drive me crazy with desire than relax me."

Leaning down, she pressed her breasts against his back as she kissed his neck. "Turn over," she said, "we can sleep later."

CHAPTER FIFTY-EIGHT

CIA Headquarters, Langley

With Mindlovitch instructing two company executives in Suzhou to cooperate, Alex Brandt was informed of a crucial lead on the whereabouts of the stolen microchips. Mindlovitch's men were careful not to say anything they should not, but when Brandt asked the most obvious question—had any people who worked in research and development stopped coming to work in the past several days—he received their reluctant reply.

The answer was Xia Chen, a young woman personally recruited by Mindlovitch from the University in Shanghai where she completed her graduate studies just six months ago. Chen came from a poor family, was extremely bright and ambitious, and Mindlovitch had welcomed her aboard. He liked bright and ambitious women, especially those who had not come from a privileged background. He believed hunger was a great motivator.

Unfortunately, Chen's ambition was apparently not paired with loyalty, deciding the best way to benefit from her contributions to the new microchip development would not involve a bonus or pay raise. At first her co-workers did not want to believe she was behind the theft and did what they could to cover for her, but it had now been days since anyone had heard from her—not since Mindlovitch was poisoned and the microchips went missing. There were no phone calls or emails explaining her absence, and no one could reach her. She had simply disappeared.

"She's the thief," Brandt told Levi and Mindlovitch.

"Has to be," Levi agreed, "but knowing that doesn't help identify who bought the prototypes from her or where they are now."

"Sasha found the address in Shanghai where her parents live with her younger brother," Brandt told him. "We're having our local assets check it out."

"Xia?" Mindlovitch said. "Incredible." After a pause, he asked, "What if we find that her family is also gone?"

"One person on the run, presumably with a lot of cash, poses special problems," Brandt said. "A family of four, assuming they're together, will be a lot easier to track. The PRC is a huge country, but it's a totalitarian state. They're pretty efficient keeping an eye on things."

"Meaning passport control, for instance," Levi suggested.

"For instance," Brandt agreed. "The key may be your relationship with the Chinese government, Mr. Mindlovitch. As we've all said, they're pleased to have you maintain this factory in Suzhou. If one of their nationals is responsible for this theft, they're likely to provide some serious assistance in locating her."

"Especially since they want the chip," Mindlovitch said.

"And all the more reason to suspect she's already left the country," Levi suggested. "You may need to get the State Department involved."

Brandt agreed. "We need to find this Chen woman, then we'll find out who paid her for the prototypes."

No one asked how they were going to persuade her to tell them.

CHAPTER FIFTY-NINE

CIA Headquarters, Langley

The next morning, Reagan and Erin joined Gellos back at Langley. They were sifting through the latest intel when Sasha rushed into the secure conference room.

"I think we have something," Levchenko said. "Just spoke with a friend at NSA. They've been working on that cell phone you guys found in the computer center in Vegas. Belonged to Talal bin Abdullah, a Saudi national."

"There was no phone found on him, but the woman who died, Sharon Ashton, said she heard him make a call," Reagan explained to Gellos and Erin. "We found two phones on the body of the security guard."

"And one of those belonged to Talal," Sasha said. "Must have tried to hide it there, just before the shooting started."

"Thank you, Sherlock, so what've you found?" Reagan asked.

"Not many calls made or received on it, and all but one of them were with his two buddies in Vegas. It's that last call that's interesting. It was outgoing, made by him minutes before the shootout, to an encrypted number. The signal was bounced around a bit, but NSA is convinced he reached someone in France."

"France?" Gellos asked.

"As sure as they can be at this point," Sasha replied. "Now get this. With his photo and prints we got a positive I.D., ran it back through our system, and guess where he lived?"

"Not in the mood for—"

"Chicago," he interrupted Gellos.

"That'll connect some dots," Reagan said.

"Oh yeah it will, because there's more. We've been able to confirm that he rented a car in Bloomington—the night those two guys went missing in Dearborn."

"And I'll bet he dropped the car off in Chicago."

"No, even better than that. The car was found abandoned on a street in the north Bronx. Not far from where one of those two men who attacked the High Line lived."

The door opened again. Kenny walked in and asked if Levchenko had brought them up to speed. When the others said he had, the DD said, "Gellos. Reagan. Come with me."

Alone in his office with Reagan and Gellos, Kenny said "Based on the current intel, if we want to get to the source of the planning, there are only a few logical starting points."

"Paris or Suzhou," Gellos said.

"Or Chicago," Kenny suggested.

"Suzhou would be a waste of time and resources," Reagan said. "The prototypes are gone, probably out of the country by now. Brandt and Erin can follow those leads, but that investigation is a lateral move, we need to get ahead of the curve."

"The trail in Chicago will also be cold," Gellos said. "Talal and Ahmed are dead, and the FBI is working on Bahir. Far as my contacts can tell, he's a bit player, doesn't know enough to make himself a deal."

Kenny nodded. "Which leaves Paris, maybe our best chance to identify whoever is organizing these attacks."

Reagan agreed. "When Talal made that final phone call from the Bellagio, it was an act of desperation. Whether he was providing information or asking for help, we'll never know, but he wasn't phoning a friend for spiritual comfort."

"He had to be calling his boss," Gellos said.

"Which means we need to find whoever it was that he reached out to," Reagan said.

"I think you're both right," Kenny said. "We'll continue to work with Homeland and the NSA deciphering any new messages they intercept, but we need to be proactive if we're going to prevent another attack."

Then he sent his two best agents hustling to the airport for a flight to Paris.

CHAPTER SIXTY

Paris

Sasha's connection at NSA had been correct. The last person Talal called was in Paris.

After spending time in Washington, New York, and Baltimore, The Handler was pleased to have returned to France. The move made just a few days ago seemed especially prudent in hindsight, since Bahir was now in custody, along with the spotter from the High Line and the three assassins who were caught trying to take out Bob Nelson and his family. One of them was eventually going to talk, and, although they were all at the lower tiers of the al-Qaeda information chain, it was impossible to be sure how much each of them knew.

Bahir, for instance, may have learned about future plans from Talal or Ahmed. Those two had been trusted and discreet members of his operation, but men in battle together form a special bond that can often transcend loyalty to their leaders. There was no way to know how much Bahir had been told of the coming attack or what he might have gleaned about Mahdi's identity. The Handler had laid enough groundwork for the third phase of his mission, and he had decided there was no need for him to take the risk of remaining longer in the United States. If necessary, he could return, but not at the present time.

For now, he was working to ensure there would be no mistakes in the implementation of the next attack. The first stage, in New York, had been the simplest. He had armed two young men with suicide vests containing incendiary devices. It was the meddling of some law enforcement officers who happened onto the site that prevented the maximum damage being inflicted.

The operation in Las Vegas was more complicated and had therefore been assigned to Ahmed and Talal, with Sayyar and Bahir chosen to assist them. Ahmed explained that Sayyar's insubordination and injuries gave him no choice but to eliminate the man, leaving three of them to complete the work of four. Now, as the Handler sat at the table in his sparsely furnished office near Parc Monceau in Paris, he shook his head as he reviewed what occurred. The plan was clever and well thought out. According to that last phone call from Talal, they were only minutes away from inflicting the ultimate devastation they had worked toward. If Sayyar had been there to assist, things might have gone differently.

He managed to console himself with the press coverage of the damage done, television correspondents repeatedly describing the extravagant nature of the plot.

Only one aspect of the reportage irritated him, the attention being paid to the woman who was being hailed as a hero. Although her efforts had not been completely successful, she was being praised for limiting the carnage and frustrating the intentions of these loathsome terrorists.

"A woman ruined everything!" the Handler heard himself say aloud. "Bah!" *And what of his men, who had died for the jihad in the name of Allah? Where was their recognition?*

He smiled grimly as a reporter rattled on about the courage of Sharon Ashford. *What did she do, other than die?*

Finally, there was the unsettling possibility that Nicholas Reagan had participated in the rescue effort. Although Reagan had turned away from every television camera on site, the Handler was certain he spotted him with the hotel security team in two of the on-air reports he watched. Interference from Reagan was the last thing he needed now.

Switching off the television, he turned his thoughts to the final stage of his Koran-inspired attacks. He knew this mission would be the most difficult of the three to complete, but the results would be far more spectacular. He had been in touch with his people in Dearborn as well as Minneapolis. They assured him they were prepared to go forward, that they were about to receive the full shipment of C-4 plastique, and that they were finalizing the intelligence on the placement of those charges.

The Handler nodded to himself, shut down his laptop, and stood. He had not seen his wife for days, she had just arrived back in France, and he was joining her for coffee before she went to her office. He could not bring his computer, it might prompt her to ask questions he did not want to answer, so he left it in the office. He would be meeting with his assistant that afternoon about an overseas delivery he needed her to handle. She could pick up the laptop and deliver it to him then.

CHAPTER SIXTY-ONE

Paris

Aboard one of the Gulfstream jets available to the CIA, Reagan and Gellos reviewed all the intel they had to date, then both did their best to grab a few hours of sleep. They were trained to operate on little rest, even while traveling through multiple time zones. When they landed early that morning, at the private airfield at Paris Le Bourget, they were refreshed and ready to go.

After making their way through customs they found their driver, a young woman sent by the local company office. They introduced themselves to Agent Sanchez, then Reagan turned to his partner.

"Should we stop for some espresso and croissants at the Café de Flore?"

Gellos smiled. "Much as I'd love to, how about we get to the office."

The CIA Station was on the Left Bank, just off the Boulevard Saint Germain. They were acquainted with a couple of the agents there, one of whom Reagan knew very well, who was waiting to usher them into his office.

It was Chris Weber.

"I didn't know you were here," Reagan said. "Haven't seen you since I dragged your ass out of the PRC."

Weber frowned. "Remind me never to have dinner with you unless I pack a suitcase first."

"What are you doing in France?"

"Temporary assignment, till they figure out what to do with me."

"Get any pushback from the Chinese?"

Weber shook his head. "Not in the States and not here, at least not yet."

"You must've run into someone from their MSS over the past couple of weeks."

"I have, but if there's a target on my back they haven't taken the shot. You're the one I'm worried about."

Reagan shrugged. "I have no plans to visit Shanghai anytime soon, believe me. Although you might think they would show some appreciation for the fact I didn't take out that entire group. I left them all breathing and even called for an ambulance."

Weber looked to Gellos. "He's such a Boy Scout."

"You know why we're here?" Gellos asked, getting down to business.

"The attack in Las Vegas. A call was made from one of the perps to someone here in Paris."

"You have a fix on the location yet?" Gellos asked.

"We've zeroed in on an address near Parc Monceau, in the Eighth Arrondissement."

"Nice neighborhood," Reagan observed. "Residential area."

"There are businesses there too. What we've identified is an office building on the Avenue de Valois," Weber told them. "What are we looking for?"

"Hard to say," Reagan admitted. "The call was probably a distress signal, not a scheduled communication."

Weber handed Gellos a single sheet of paper. "This is what we've developed so far. After pinging the nearest towers, we feel confident this is the place."

"All right," Reagan said. "Let's get fitted up, then we'll go have a look around."

After they were armed with Glock 23 handguns, additional magazines, and disposable cell phones, Weber, Reagan and Gellos followed their driver back downstairs.

"I guess we're still passing on the espresso and pastries," Reagan said as they crossed the Seine and headed north.

"I'm feeling wide awake, how about you?"

"Adrenaline is the breakfast of champions. Let's go find this snake."

Agent Sanchez let them out of the car at the southern entrance to the park, two blocks from the address Weber had identified as the place Talal's call had been received.

"You want me to wait here?" she asked.

Reagan, who was standing by the driver's window, entered her number in his cell. "Stay three or four blocks from here." Leaning down, he said to Weber, "If this goes sideways, we'll call you for backup.

"Can't wait," Weber said, then Sanchez drove off.

Parc Monceau is one of the many beautiful spots in a beautiful city, an oasis of greenery popular with young and old alike. Parents push their toddlers in strollers, lovers walk hand in hand, retirees move slowly along the tree-lined lanes, and performance artists put on shows, especially on weekends. This was an early Wednesday morning, and things were relatively quiet.

"This place is for locals. We stand out like a couple of rubes," Gellos said.

Reagan was dressed in his customary dark colors—gray slacks, black long-sleeved cashmere polo sweater, and black suede shoes with rubber soles. Gellos was wearing tan pants, a cream-colored sweater with cowl neck, and what Reagan called her "sensible shoes"—saddle brown leather with low heels and a front strap that would allow her to run when the need arose.

"We're just a romantic couple, checking out the scenery."

Gellos shot him a sideward glance but said nothing.

"Might help if we held hands," Reagan said with a grin.

"Fat chance," she told him. "Let's have a look at the Avenue de Valois."

They exited the park to the right and made their way to the address Weber had provided. It was a four-story building with a main door that required a code to enter. Alongside the keypad was a directory of the businesses inside.

After a quick look at the entrance, they strolled past, Reagan giving his head a short nod toward the top of the door at the CCTV camera.

Gellos took his lead as they continued to slowly move on, not stopping until they were around the corner on the busy Boulevard Malesherbes. None of the pedestrians walking past took any notice of the American couple staring into one of the shop windows.

"That closed-circuit video is a problem," Reagan said.

She nodded. "Doesn't appear another way inside."

"You get a good look at the tenant list?"

Gellos held out her phone, having taken a picture of the directory as they passed by.

"Nice," Reagan said, "didn't see you do that. Let's have a look."

Most of the names were nondescript, revealing little about the nature of their businesses.

"A couple sound like investment firms," Gellos said. "These two may be some sort of tech companies."

"Nothing with al-Qaeda in the title?"

Gellos frowned. "What now?"

They returned to the park and sat on a bench, Reagan pulled out his phone, and said, "Let's Google some of those names."

They searched for websites of the companies, rejecting the first three—one was too large, there was not enough information about the second, and the third was a brand name they recognized, not a likely front for terrorists. The fourth was one that Gellos had initially guessed was involved in technology. Turned out that Fortris Services was a small company providing computer support, its website listing the key personnel.

"That's the one," Reagan said. "Let's come up with a story, and give it a try."

After taking a couple of minutes to organize a strategy, Gellos returned to the front door of the building, where she hit the intercom button for Fortris.

Posing as a sales rep was an easy cover, since it was generally the NOC she and Reagan used when they traveled. Using passable French, she convinced the woman on the speaker that she was with a software firm from the United States, had a business opportunity to present, and asked to be allowed in.

Reagan was watching from the front of the neighboring building. When the buzzer finally sounded, Gellos entered, moving slowly enough to allow Reagan time to hustle to the entrance and slip inside behind her. Whether someone was watching the video feed remained to be seen.

As Gellos went to the second floor to find Fortris, Reagan used the staircase to reach the top floor and have a look around. It was not a large building, but he was not about to start knocking on every door. Since the entrance had a remotely controlled lock and live camera feed, there were likely to be other security measures in place. Eventually, someone was going to be asking about an American running through the halls like a door-to-door salesman. He had to choose wisely.

Logic told him that he was looking for one of the smaller suites. If one of these workplaces was being used as a communications center by al-Qaeda, there was no way they would need or risk a large group of offices.

The easiest way to assess the size of a suite was to check the distance between its front door and the next one down the corridor. Reagan quickly ascertained that the fourth floor was occupied by only three companies, all large suites, so he headed down a flight.

He repeated the process on the third floor without a likely candidate, then hurried down to the second, where Gellos was already visiting Fortris. He ran into a man in the hallway, apparently on his way to the men's room. Reagan responded to his curious look with a slight nod, doing his best to appear as if belonged there. When the man disappeared into the lavatory, Reagan continued his search for a smaller office, without success. That left only the ground level. Rushing downstairs, he found two possible candidates. They were at opposite ends of the building, small corner spaces with no visibility from the main corridor. From the sign on the first door, it appeared to be a small import-export company. Reagan walked the length of the building to the other door, which featured an inexpensive looking plaque that read "HST Enterprises."

Reagan nodded to himself, figuring this was as good a guess as he was going to make. Taking a moment to adjust the grip of the Glock in the back of his waistband for easy access, he rapped on the door.

There was no answer.

He knocked again with the same result, then had a look over his shoulder to be sure no one else was in the hallway. Pulling out the small, metal strips he carried in a leather case, he unlocked the door.

If an alarm went off, silent or otherwise, he would have to take his chances.

Entering the space, he found one large room divided in two by a drywall installation, leaving a small entry area up front and a larger office in the rear. The furnishings were spare, the anteroom with only a small table and chair, no telephone, and no computer. The back office had four chairs, a desk, and a television monitor on the wall. There were two street level windows secured by exterior vertical steel bars and covered with venetian blinds. Reagan had a quick look outside, finding a view of a back alley, then pulled the blinds shut.

There were no papers of any kind in either room. The only thing of interest was a laptop that sat atop the desk in the main office.

After all the time he spent in the field, all the battles he fought, all the life and death moments he endured, Reagan had an intuition that could neither be learned nor taught, it could only be earned. As he stared down at the small computer, those instincts told him he was in the right place.

He picked up the laptop and turned to leave when he heard the front door opening.

Moving quickly to the near corner of the room, he gripped the computer in his left hand while drawing the Glock out with his right. A moment later, a tall, slender, dark-skinned young woman walked in, then stopped, staring at the empty desk.

She had not taken off the tweed jacket she was wearing over her gray skirt and beige top. She had not put her purse down. She was obviously there only to pick up the laptop.

"Looking for this?" Reagan asked as he stepped forward, the weapon aimed at her head.

She could have screamed, or fainted, or turned to run. But she simply glared at him with coal-dark eyes and said, "Who are you? What are you doing in here?"

"Since I'm the one holding the weapon, how about I ask the questions?"

She said nothing, ignored the gun, and continued to gaze directly into his eyes.

"At least you speak English, it'll simplify things. My French is lousy." When she remained still, he said, "My Arabic is not bad though. So tell me, what sort of business you run here?"

"You break into our office, point a gun at me, then ask what sort of business we run?"

Reagan could not suppress an admiring smile. She was a tough bitch. "This your computer?"

There was an almost imperceptible hesitation before she said, "Yes, it is," which told him she was lying. Then she said, "Why don't you give it to me and get out of here before I call the police?"

"The police. Now there's an idea. I think you should call them. Where's your cell?"

When she glanced at the purse she was holding in her left hand, Reagan stepped closer and pointed the gun directly at her dark eyes.

"Have a seat," he told her, gesturing with the Glock toward the chair to the left of the desk.

She turned, as if she was going to sit, then suddenly pivoted back, swinging her handbag up at his gun while trying to drive the knuckles of her right fist into his neck. Reagan was surprised, but he was also larger, stronger, and faster. He reacted by sidestepping the attempted chop shot and, using the butt of the Glock, hit her in the jaw with a vicious jab that knocked her backward.

But she was not done. Managing to keep her balance, she lunged forward, once again going for the Glock.

Reagan was still holding the computer in his left hand, and he was not about to risk dropping it. Turning sideways, he responded to her charge with a kick to the chest, this time sending her sprawling onto the floor.

Not knowing what she might have in the purse that now lay beside her—and not interested in finding out the hard way—Reagan drove the hard toe of his shoe into her ribs, then stomped down on her neck before kicking the purse out of her reach.

Gasping, she stared up at him with hate in her eyes.

"Enough," he said. "You make another move, and I'll break your neck."

"That's your weakness," she snarled, trying to catch her breath. "All of you think death is something to be feared. We welcome the chance to die in the service of Allah."

"I'm so tired of hearing that bullshit, you have no idea. So believe me, you don't answer my questions, you'll get the chance to meet your God."

She tried to spit at him, but her damaged jaw made it impossible. Reagan rewarded the effort by kicking her in the side again.

While she dealt with the pain, he placed the laptop on the table and pulled out his phone. Gellos answered, and he said, "Hope you're done with your sales call. I'm on the main floor, last door to your right as you get off the elevator. Get down here right now, I'm calling Sanchez. We'll be having a guest for lunch."

CHAPTER SIXTY-TWO

Paris

Weber phoned Reagan as soon as he and Sanchez pulled the car in the front of the building on the Avenue de Valois. Moments later, Reagan and Gellos emerged holding both the computer and the woman. She made one futile attempt to pull herself from Reagan's grasp, but she was no match for him. He shoved her into the back of the sedan, and Gellos bound her wrists with the plastic handcuffs Weber provided. Then they sped off to a small flat in Les Marais.

They arrived, and Sanchez waited in the car as the other three agents brought the woman upstairs. Inside the apartment, they sat her on the couch and secured her ankles. Before Gellos placed a large strip of duct tape across her mouth, the woman said, "I think he broke my ribs."

"Then you got off easy," Gellos told her and applied the adhesive.

Reagan had gone through her purse on the ride over. In addition to a small handgun and her cell phone, he found a driver's license and credit cards, all of which identified her as Rima Vaziri. Turning to her, Reagan said, "I'm going to make this simple. All you have to do is nod your head for yes or shake it for no." He pointed at the laptop which was now sitting on the coffee table. "You lied when you told me this is your computer. You want to tell me who really owns it?"

Her dark eyes glowered at him. She did not move.

"All right. I assume that means you are also not going to tell me where you were going to take it."

Once again, the question was met with a stoic silence.

"Come on," he said to Gellos, "let's toss her in the bathtub until we figure out what to do with her."

They lifted her from the sofa, carried her into the bathroom, and deposited her in the tub. While Reagan attached her bound wrists to the faucet, Gellos got a length of cord from the kitchen and trussed her ankles, then connected that rope to the base of the sink. When they were done, Rima Vaziri was uncomfortably stretched out in the porcelain bath.

Then they returned to the living room.

"What now?" Weber asked.

Reagan sat on the couch and pointed at the computer. "Whatever is in there will obviously be encrypted. We need our top people in Paris to break through, and I mean right away."

Weber nodded. "What about her cell phone?"

"I'd like to hang onto that for now. The way she came into the office and went to the table, she wasn't there to stay. She was there to pick up the laptop for someone. Maybe when she doesn't show up that someone will call."

"Makes sense," Weber said.

"We'll also need cooperation from the local anti-terrorism task force," Reagan told him.

"When you say local—"

"I mean the GIGN."

The GIGN was one of the most experienced and respected anti-terrorism task forces in the world. Since its formation, in 1974, it was reported their agents had been involved in nearly two thousand missions and managed to rescue some six hundred hostages—numbers that had never been confirmed because of the extreme secrecy under which they operated. They ran their clandestine service from headquarters just outside Paris, in Versailles-Satory, and were often called upon to assist the National Police in covert operations.

"If anyone can find out who rents that office right now, it's that group," Reagan said. "They'll also have jurisdiction to canvass the building without wasting time getting a warrant, see who goes in and out of that office, other than our girl Mata Hari. Maybe they can get some descriptions and, if we're really lucky, a few names. No one in Paris is going to speak to a bunch of Americans flashing US creds, we need the GIGN on this."

"You're right about that," Weber agreed.

"There's also the CCTV," Gellos reminded them. "We need to know if it's only a live feed or if they have a video archive. The call made from Las Vegas was just a few days ago, maybe we can find a picture of someone coming or going from that office around the time Talal had his little chat."

"Can you handle all that on your end, Chris?" Reagan asked.

"Getting cooperation from the French authorities is not always easy," Weber said, "especially when they see us as trespassing all over their sovereignty. You know all about that Gallic bullshit."

"Bad as the Chinese?"

"Worse," Weber said with a smile. "But once I convince them this is about terrorism, they'll be all over it."

"We can get you help from State if you need it," Reagan told him. "I let Kenny know what we're up to, and he texted back, told me our liaison for this mission just arrived in town, which could be useful."

"I'll get right on it," Weber said.

"The laptop will be key," Reagan said. "If it's owned by the person we suspect it is, it might contain information about the next attack. That may be optimistic, but it's possible."

"If you want the best people we have in Paris, we'll have to go outside the Company."

"How far outside?"

"There's a task force working at our embassy," Weber told him. "Staffed by NSA analysts and cryptographers."

Reagan shrugged. "As long as the French don't ask for the computer. Everything points to another attack in the US, we need to have the first look."

"I'll tell the French something to get them involved, but I'll hold back on the computer as long as I can." Weber took out his cell, went to the other side of the room, and began making calls.

Gellos looked at Reagan. "Whatever they can find in the laptop, our best lead at the moment is the woman."

Reagan let out a long sigh. "She already told me she thinks it's an honor to die for Allah."

"Talk is cheap," Gellos replied, "and as you've often said, there are things worse than death."

Reagan responded with a grim smile. "We've got to get Chris out of here. I don't want him implicated in anything we do. I caused him enough grief in Shanghai."

They waited for Weber to finish making his arrangements.

"I'm going back to my office," he told them. "I've put things in process, now I have to get in front of our French counterparts to make sure it all happens."

"That's your part of the show," Reagan said. "We're going to stay back, have a little chat with Miss Vaziri, then we'll see where we go from there. Can you leave us the car and the keys to this place?"

"My first call was to have an agent pick up Sanchez and me. We'll leave you her ride."

When he got a text saying his driver was downstairs, Weber stood to leave. "Please remember, Nick," he said, "this is France." He nodded toward the bathroom.

Reagan smiled. "I appreciate the concern, but Carol and I will be fine. We have to deal with the gap between politics and reality every day."

"Then you know what I'm talking about. We don't know who this woman is. You've got to tread lightly until we find out more."

Reagan's smile vanished as he looked at his friend. "I was on the High Line in New York when they tried to torch hundreds of innocent people, and I was there when they sprayed acid on children in front of that fountain in Las Vegas. I don't give a rat's ass what the French think of my methods. I'm not going to stand by and let these bastards take another run at us if there's any way I can prevent it."

Weber hesitated before saying, "Do what you have to." Then he left.

Reagan and Gellos immediately headed into the bathroom, where they found Rima Vaziri struggling against her restraints.

"Easy there, Rima," Reagan said, then bent down and roughly pulled the tape from her mouth.

She launched into an angry tirade in her native tongue, to which Reagan responded by slapping her across the face, making sure to hit her directly on the bruise he left when he struck her with the butt of his Glock back in the office.

"This is how you treat a woman?" she demanded angrily.

"You gave up any claim to chivalry when you took a swing at me. Just shut up and listen." Reagan knelt on the floor beside the tub and got in her face. "You want to die, we can arrange that. But it's not going to happen quickly, and there will be no honor in it. You understand?"

She said nothing.

"There's no one coming to rescue you. No one knows where you are. By the time your friends start wondering what happened to you and their laptop, you'll be in so much pain you won't remember your own name. Am I making myself clear?"

For the first time, a hint of fear was visible in her ebony eyes. She began to say something, then stopped.

"Good," Reagan said. "Let's begin by cleaning you up a bit." He reached out, lowered the drain stopper, and turned on the cold water. "This may be a little chilly, but at least there's no acid in the water. Know what I mean?"

The tub began filling as she twisted and turned, her teeth clenched against the cold.

"If you think I'm going to drown you, you're wrong," Reagan told her. "That would be too fast and easy. No, I'm just going to get you all wet and freezing, then I'm going to cut you in a few delicate places. When you start to bleed I'm going to pour enough salt on those cuts to really get your attention. And that's just the beginning."

"You animal," she said through gritted teeth.

"Your English really is excellent. You spend time in the States, did you?"

She glared at him. "What do you think you'll get from me?"

Reagan and Gellos exchanged a quick glance. They knew, as soon as anything close to that question was asked in an interrogation, the game was over.

"Everything," Reagan said. "Who you work for, where they are, and who owns that laptop. To start with, I'll take the password to the computer as a show of good faith. Then I want to know who you were going to meet, and when and where." Without waiting for a reply, he removed a jackknife from his pocket and flipped it open. He cut away the front of her blouse and sliced her bra, exposing her breasts. Turning to Gellos, he asked, "Where do you think we should start on Ms. Vaziri? She's a good-looking young woman, and the way she dresses I can see she takes good care of herself." Turning back to Vaziri, he said, "Vanity is not very devout of you."

Gellos knew Reagan well enough to realize this was all a bluff, but their prisoner was not so sure.

Rima Vaziri stared up at him, the fear visible in her onyx eyes.

CHAPTER SIXTY-THREE

Paris

Cyla Khoury had just returned to her office at the embassy in Paris when she was greeted by a phone call from the President's aide, Andy Lipman. She was told to provide whatever assistance was requested by Brian Kenny of the CIA and his people. That was followed almost immediately by a call from her old friend Erin David.

"What's going on?" Khoury asked.

"Things are evolving quickly," Erin told her, then furnished an authorized rendition of the search for missing microchips and their interest in an office near Parc Monceau that might be an al-Qaeda station. The less detail Khoury had, Kenny reminded Erin, the better. She was with State, and there were things she did not need to know. Erin painted the picture with broad strokes.

"How can I help?"

"First," Erin said, "you cannot share this information with anyone other than my agency and the White House. No one else, no exceptions."

"That's a bit awkward for me, Erin. I'm relatively low on the totem pole here, despite President Harmon's relationship with my parents. There are people I report to."

"It's not a request, Cyla, it's an order. You can confirm it with Lipman."

"Already got a call from him, but he never mentioned that. I will have to confirm, no offense."

"That's fair," Erin said. "You should also be aware that we have an agent stationed in Paris, Chris Weber. Don't think you know him, but you'll be hearing from him."

"All right."

"He's already contacted the French anti-terrorism squad. Asked for their help in conducting an immediate investigation of the office building in question. There may be some pushback from the French State Department. If that happens, we want you to intervene, handle those communications, then report them directly to me. Assure the GIGN that this is an active inquiry based on credible threats of a terrorist strike, not a fishing expedition. We need their help, and we need it right away."

"I'll see if we've had any contact from them on this yet."

"I need to be blunt here, Cyla. People in your department might resist you taking the lead, but they'll be told you're taking orders directly from the White House. Play that card if you need to."

"Lipman did tell me that."

"Good. Find out what you can, and get back to me right away."

"Will do," Khoury said, then hesitated. "Can you tell me anything more about the missing microchips?"

"When I have more, I'll let you know," Erin said, "but I can tell you this—we think the theft of those chips may have been engineered by the people behind the recent attacks. We're concerned they might try to use them in planning their next move. That's why we need to keep the loop small for now."

"Does that loop include Reagan?"

"It does. Why do you ask?"

"Lipman told me that I should assist Deputy Director Kenny and his agents. I had a feeling Reagan would be involved." When Erin said nothing, Cyla asked, "Is he already in Paris?"

"He is," Erin told her, "and he'll be in touch."

* * *

334

RIMA VAZIRI DID NOT KNOW whether the American was really prepared to slice up her breasts, but given the way he had treated her up to now, she was not interested in finding out. She began by admitting the laptop was not hers, then told them she did not have the password to open the computer. She said she was only retrieving the computer for someone.

"Who might that be?" Reagan asked.

Vaziri claimed she knew him by only one name, Mahdi, which she told them was Syrian for "guided."

Reagan and Gellos looked at each other. Mahdi was the name mentioned in various intercepted calls and text.

When Reagan asked what the man looked like, Vaziri provided a verbal sketch that could have described any one of ten million middle-aged Muslim men.

"You're going to have to do better," he told her. She was still bound and lying in the tub, and, although he had turned off the cold water, her entire body was already soaked, leaving her wet and shivering.

"Let me up," she demanded for what was at least the tenth time.

"You're not going anywhere till you convince us you're telling the truth," Reagan said. "Where does this Mahdi live?"

"I have no idea."

That reply was greeted by skeptical looks from the two agents.

"He calls me," she said. "He usually has me meet him at the office. There is no regular schedule. Sometimes I do not see him for weeks. I know nothing of his personal life."

"Uh huh. And when you meet him at the office, what do you do there?"

"I run errands for him."

"What sort of errands?"

"Mainly I deliver messages or packages."

Gellos was standing above her, leaning on the sink. "To where and to whom?" she asked.

She paused. "If I tell you—"

"Spare us the melodrama," Reagan said, "and answer the question."

Vaziri looked from Reagan to Gellos, finding no comfort in the eyes of either agent. "Different locations. Here in Paris. In London." There was a slight pause. "Sometimes the United States," she added with obvious reluctance.

"And where were you taking the laptop today?" he asked.

Vaziri was still looking up at Gellos, who responded with a glare that said she had better answer.

"The Hotel Bristol," Vaziri said.

"What time?"

"One," she replied.

Before Reagan could look at his watch, Gellos said, "It's already ten after."

Reagan stared at Vaziri. "Your friend must be looking for you by now. And for his computer." When she did not respond, he asked, "Where, exactly, were you making the delivery at the Bristol?"

When she did not reply, he held the knife up to her eyes where she could have a good look at the blade.

Discomfort from the cold water had turned to pain as she remained stretched out in the tub. "In the bar, in the rear of the lobby."

"Were you taking it to your boss or some third party?"

"To Mahdi."

Reagan glanced up at Gellos, then turned back to Vaziri. "Why would he risk leaving his laptop in the office, then have you deliver it to him?"

"I don't know," she told them.

Just then Vaziri's cell phone, which Gellos had placed on the vanity, began ringing.

Gellos picked it up, looked at the screen, then showed it to Reagan. It read, *No Caller ID.*

"That has to be him. He's looking for her, which means we may still have time to catch him," Reagan said. He took the phone and shoved it in his pocket. "I'll tape her mouth and pull the drain. Make sure those ropes are secure, throw a blanket over her, and let's get the hell out of here."

CHAPTER SIXTY-FOUR

Paris

With Gellos at the wheel, weaving in and out of traffic, they made it to the Hotel Bristol in less than ten minutes. Pulling the car to a stop in front of the hotel, she and Reagan immediately jumped out and headed for the entrance. Before the doorman could voice an objection to her leaving their car on the street, Gellos tossed him the keys and handed him a twenty euro note.

"We're picking up a friend, we'll be out in five minutes," she told him. Then she and Reagan hurried inside.

The hotel lobby was large and grand and seemed to have as many staff bustling around as it did guests relaxing in the lounge area and tearoom. But none of them looked anything like the man Vaziri had described—which meant there was a chance he was still waiting for her in the bar.

They rushed toward the rear of the spacious main floor, entered the cocktail lounge, and quickly scanned the room. There was a collection of small tables, comfortable armchairs, and a long bar off to the left. Roughly half of the tables were occupied, but, again, they saw no one close to Rima Vaziri's description of Mahdi. There was a young Parisian couple seated at the near end of the bar, so they approached the far side, where a young woman was fixing a pair of colorful cocktails.

"Good afternoon," Reagan said.

She looked up, eyed Reagan with a warm smile, then gave Carol Gellos a disapproving once-over. Turning back to Reagan, she asked, "May I help you, monsieur?"

"I'm hoping you can. We're looking for a friend of ours. We were supposed to meet him here, but we were tied up in traffic. Looks like he left."

She shrugged and said, "*Quelle dommage*," then poured the pink concoction she had just completed into a pair of elegant martini glasses.

"Yes," Reagan agreed, "we're sorry we missed him." Then he provided the vague description Rima Vaziri had given them, not even certain any of it was true. "Did you see him?"

The young woman took her time answering, focusing on Reagan, apparently trying to figure whether he and his companion were some sort of romantic item or if it was just business. The hard look in Gellos' eyes told her it didn't matter.

"I'm not sure," the young woman replied.

Gellos had no patience for the flirting or the waste of valuable time. She pulled out a hundred euro note and passed it across the bar. "Just answer the question," she said in French.

Reagan smiled. "What my friend means, is that we're *very* sorry we missed him."

Picking up the note, the woman took a minute to show Reagan her lovely smile again. "Ah yes, I remember now. He was sitting over there," she told them, pointing to an empty table in the corner. "I noticed that he looked at his watch more than once, then he asked for his bill and left."

"How long ago?" Reagan asked.

The bartender stuck out her lower lip in that pouty way French women have mastered. "Ten, fifteen minutes ago?"

"*Quelle dommage*," Gellos said.

Ignoring his partner, Reagan asked, "When he paid his check, was it cash or credit card?"

"Cash, monsieur." The young woman hesitated. "I did notice that he made a phone call. It was right after that he signaled for his check. All he had was one Balvenie scotch," she said with an appropriate scowl reserved for customers who did not drink enough to earn her large tips. "He placed his money on the table and left."

Reagan shook his head. "I don't suppose you have a name."

"How would I, monsieur?"

"Maybe he's been in here before?"

"If so, I do not recall," the young woman said. Then, with a skeptical look, she added, "If he is your friend, don't you know his name?"

"Just wanted to be sure we're talking about the right guy," Reagan said with a smile. "By the way, what's your name?"

"Yvette."

"All right, Yvette, thanks for the help."

Trying one more smile on him, she said, "If you need something else, you know where to find me."

As they headed back through the lobby, Reagan pulled out his phone, called Weber, and brought him up to date. Then he said, "We're leaving the Bristol now. The description the bartender gave us matched what Vaziri said, so it seems she was telling the truth. Our boy was here all right. He was alone, had a scotch, looked like he was waiting for someone, made a call, then got up and left. The timing of the call matches the one Vaziri got on her cell, around one-ten."

"Anything else to identify him? Credit card receipt or something?"

"I asked." Reagan said. "He paid in cash so we don't have a name, but there are CCTV cameras all over the place, they must have footage."

"That could work," Weber said.

"I think we can still get this guy, Chris, but Gellos and I have no credentials that'll get us access to their closed-circuit tapes. You need to work with the locals and get a photo."

"I'm on my way," Weber said.

"We ran out of the apartment when we got the call, Chris, left our guest where she was. You may want to get someone over there to babysit."

CHAPTER SIXTY-FIVE

United States Embassy, Paris

When Reagan and Gellos were shown to Cyla Khoury's office at the embassy, they were reminded that she still held a junior position at State, even if she was a presidential favorite. The room was not only small but was not anywhere near the Ambassador's suite.

After an exchange of polite greetings, she sat behind her desk, and the two agents took the two other chairs. Reagan provided a brief, sanitized version of what they had been up to since arriving in Paris early that morning. There was no reason to upset her with stories of kidnapping, enhanced interrogation techniques, or the developing manhunt for an al-Qaeda mastermind.

"Tell us about this high-tech task force you have here," Reagan said.

Cyla explained that it had been formed on a confidential basis, by NSA, DHS, and State. "They wanted technical capability somewhere outside the US comparable to what we have back home. Not to replace anything we have there, just to be sure there was a team that could act quickly on site, in Europe, in case of any unfortunate developments."

"Why Paris?"

Cyla smiled, and Reagan noted again that she was much better looking when she abandoned her serious demeanor. "France is our oldest ally," she said with a hint of irony.

"With allies like France—" Gellos began, but Cyla cut him off.

"Alliances are complicated," she told them, sounding very much the diplomat she was becoming. "I think you would agree that Saudi Arabia is our strongest ally among the Arab countries in the Middle East. Have you had a look at their record on women's rights recently? Or humanitarian issues? See what they teach in their classrooms about the United States, the non-existence of the Holocaust, and so on. I know the two of you live with this every day, but international relationships are complex. And remember, France has been targeted by both al-Qaeda *and* ISIS several times in the past few years."

"Fair enough," Reagan said. "So how is this team of high-tech operators working out?"

"They've been effective, far as I know, and very helpful to the French anti-terrorism efforts."

"That's good news. I hope they're effective in breaking into the laptop we delivered to them today."

Before Cyla could reply, Reagan felt one of the two cell phones in his pocket vibrate. It was the burner Weber had provided. "Excuse me a moment," he said, then got up and went out to the hallway. "What's up?"

"I'm here at the Hotel Bristol with one of the French agents from the GIGN. When he flashed his I.D., security became instantly cooperative. They played the video from the bar, got us two grainy head shots, best we could do for now. I'm texting the pictures to you."

"I'm at the embassy. I'll let you know if they find anything on the laptop."

"Get back to me when you can."

"Will do," Reagan said and signed off, then waited for the photos to come through. When he opened the attachment, he felt as if someone had just punched him in the gut. After looking carefully at both pictures a second time, he closed the phone and shoved it in his pocket. Back in Khoury's office, she and Gellos were still debating the vagaries of international relations.

"Sorry to interrupt this meeting of the General Assembly, but can we get back to the task force here?"

"Of course," Cyla said. "Should I know anything else about what's going on here in Paris?"

"You don't need to know," Reagan said, "and I mean that literally and respectfully."

"All right," she said, "but I understand you're trying to prevent an attack back home. Something related to the incidents in New York and Las Vegas."

Reagan was surprised she had received that much intel, but his face remained impassive as he said, "We obviously know you're Muslim, so this sort of discussion may be a bit uncomfortable."

She smiled. "Uncomfortable for who, Nick, you or me?"

"Maybe both of us."

"I'll be fine," she said. "Try me."

Reagan glanced at Gellos, who nodded. "Okay. I'll start by admitting I have no idea how devout you are, or how familiar you are with the Koran."

"My parents are Muslims, born and raised in Lebanon, moved to the United States soon after they were married. I was born there, and they raised me as a Muslim-American. As I think you'll recall, I'm married to a Lebanese man, who is also Muslim. I think it's fair to say I'm very familiar with the Koran." Before Reagan could reply, she sat forward and added, "I'm also familiar with your views about my faith. I know you believe that there is no such thing as a moderate Muslim."

Reagan was surprised at the challenge. "The Koran teaches that the Muslim faith is the only way to heaven. It also encourages hate, violence, and death to anyone not practicing your religion. So yes, I have doubts about anyone claiming they have a moderate view of those teachings."

She surprised him again, this time by offering another smile. "What about the Catholic church? Unless I missed a recent Papal Bull, they don't believe anyone practicing another faith will be admitted past the pearly gates. And what about the mention of stonings and violence and other exclusionary teachings of the Bible?"

"Point taken," Reagan said.

Cyla nodded in appreciation. "So, you have a question about the Koran?"

"Specifically, a section dealing with infidels. I'm referring to 22:19. If you need me to remind you—"

"That won't be necessary. As I recall, it's one of a handful of those troubling sections of our holy book, calling for the death of non-believers."

"Several passages call for their death, but this one actually prescribes the methods to be used."

She thought it over. "I'm sorry, but if you could remind me—"

"Garments of fire, that's one."

"The High Line attack in New York."

"Correct. A second is boiling water that will melt off the skin of the infidels. A bit of a stretch, but melting off the skin—"

"Sounds like the acid used in Las Vegas," Cyla finished the thought.

"Right again. The third is trickier. It speaks of hooked iron rods."

"Ah yes," she recalled. "Something more suited to an attack that would have taken place five hundred years ago."

"That's our thought," Reagan said.

"You don't believe al-Qaeda is going to send a group of pipe-wielding men and women into a crowd."

"No," Reagan agreed. "We figure this is going to involve a bit more ingenuity than that."

"Such as?"

"Something we can get to later, as needed."

"As I said, I'm here to help."

"It's important the GIGN cooperates with us, and that you do whatever you can to hold off any interference from their State Department. Time is short."

Cyla said she understood and promised to do her best as their liaison.

"Thanks," Reagan said, then stood up. "We'd like to visit with that task force you have here."

"Of course," Cyla said as she got to her feet. "What's next for you after that?"

"We have a few items to take care of here, then back to D.C.," Reagan said.

"Will you let me know what you come up with, before you leave town?" she asked.

"We will," Reagan told her.

Cyla gave them directions to the tech unit located in the basement, then called ahead to arrange access for them. After saying their goodbyes, the two agents headed for the elevator.

Riding down in the lift, Gellos asked, "What was all that about?"

"What?"

"Pressing her about the Koran and the hooked iron rods, then dropping it without saying anything about the buildings we're looking at?"

Reagan stared at his partner without speaking.

"You obviously didn't want her to know. But—"

Reagan tilted his head slightly toward the camera in the upper corner of the elevator, then scratched his ear.

Gellos nodded her understanding—the rest of their discussion would have to wait.

CHAPTER SIXTY-SIX

Paris

Reagan and Gellos were admitted to the secure basement office that housed the task force. They quickly learned that, thus far at least, the team had not cracked the encryption code to the laptop Reagan had taken. One of the women there said they were close, but, as the team leader acknowledged, once they broke through there was no assurance there would not be another line of cyber defense, multiple firewalls, or that they would even find anything useful.

Gellos handed them the phone she had taken from Vaziri. Since the woman had given them the PIN, this would be an easier task—find out who was calling, texting, and emailing Vaziri and to whom she was sending texts and emails and making calls. After an exchange of contact numbers, Reagan and Gellos left them to their work.

Outside, they picked up the agency car Weber had loaned them; Gellos took the wheel and drove them swiftly beyond the Avenue Gabriel into the Place de la Concorde.

"Now can you tell me what's up?" Gellos asked.

"Yes," Reagan replied. He pulled out the burner phone and brought up the two photos Weber had sent him of the man they believed to be Mahdi. Holding up the cell so Gellos could see the images as she drove, Reagan asked, "This guy look familiar?"

It only took a moment for Gellos to say, "You're kidding me."

"Wish I were, but you saw the framed picture Cyla had on the credenza behind her. Photo of her arm-in-arm with someone who looked a lot like this. I never met her husband, but I know from Erin that he's older than she is. Had to be her husband, right? Who else's picture would she have in her office?"

"Let me see those photos again," Gellos said, taking the phone from Reagan's hand. The images were granular, taken from the distance of a CCTV camera from behind the bar to a cocktail table in the corner of the room at the Bristol, then converted to a still. Even so, Gellos could do nothing but shake her head. "What do you know about him?"

"When we were in the basement just now, I shot a text to Langley. Sasha confirms his name is Walid Khoury. Lebanese. Some sort of international banker. Travels a lot."

"Does Erin know you're asking about him?"

"I hope not."

"And your religious discussion with Cyla?"

"Just testing," Reagan said. "Wanted to see where she'd go with it. I certainly wasn't going to tell her anything about a possible attack on glass-roofed buildings."

"I get it."

"What do you think?" Reagan asked her.

"If she was acting, she's awfully good."

"You're guessing she has no idea who her husband might really be?"

"I realize love is blind, and all that, but I don't know enough about her to make that judgment," Gellos admitted.

Reagan shook his head. "She's been a friend of Erin's for almost fifteen years. Kind of unthinkable she's any part of this."

"I get the conflict, but let's put that aside and make a plan. For starters, did Sasha have a lead on where this guy is now?"

"He's in Paris. Passport check shows he arrived two days ago. Sasha sent me the address of the apartment they keep here."

"Let's go."

"I've got to let Weber know what we're up to."

"You talk, I'll drive," Gellos said.

"What else is new," Reagan said.

CHAPTER SIXTY-SEVEN

Paris

Walid and Cyla Khoury lived in an apartment just to the west of Parc Monceau, less than six blocks from the office where Reagan met Rima Vaziri a couple of hours ago. That did not bode well for the likelihood this was some unfortunate case of mistaken identity. Reagan had been willing to consider the possibility that Cyla's husband and the blurry shot of the man in the bar at the Hotel Bristol were not the same person. As he told Rima Vaziri, after she gave them her description of the man she called Mahdi, it could have fit any one of a hundred million middle-aged Arab men.

But Reagan hated coincidences, and when Brandt texted him the Khourys' home address, so near to the office, he knew they had their man.

The questions that remained were obvious. Would they find him at home, or had he gone to ground? Rima had not delivered his computer and did not answer his phone call. Those two facts might cause him to run. If they did find him, what were they going to do with him? They had no authority to arrest him in France, which meant whatever they did would violate one or more international laws, starting with kidnapping. That was all right with Reagan, as long as they had the right man and could persuade him to tell them what they needed to know—where and when the next attack was going to take place, and how they could prevent it.

Gellos drove past the front of the apartment building. With no legal spaces in sight, she pulled into a no parking zone thirty yards down the street.

She turned off the engine, and Reagan said, "Let's move."

They each checked their weapons, making sure a round was chambered in the Glock 23s Weber had given them. Then they got out of the car and walked back down the street.

It was a classic, high-end Parisian building, with a large wooden door that opened into a cobblestone-paved courtyard. They did not have to check the directory, Sasha had told Reagan the Khourys' flat was in the rear of the second floor, apartment 2D. They wasted no time, hurrying up the stairs to the left, then walking quickly toward the back of the building.

Without exchanging a word, they took positions on either side of the apartment door. Having worked enough missions together, each could anticipate the other's moves. Gellos reached out and knocked.

There was no answer.

After knocking again and receiving no response, Reagan went to work picking the lock. Once again, he was not concerned about alarms. If Khoury was their man, they needed to get to him before he disappeared from Paris.

When they heard the tumbler *click*, they raised their weapons and made their way inside.

They were met there by silence but proceeded with caution. Moving slowly from one room to the next, it did not take long for them to search the place and confirm that no one was home. A well-furnished living room, two bedrooms, a kitchen, dining area, two bathrooms, and powder room were all empty.

"Damnit," Gellos said as they made their way back to the entry foyer.

Reagan already had his burner phone out and was calling Weber. "Chris, we've got a lead, but there are collateral issues." He filled him in on what they had learned, including their belief that their man was the husband of their State Department liaison.

"You're kidding."

"Wish I were, "Reagan said. "You send someone to watch Vaziri?"

"I sent one of my guys, Brophy. Still holding her in the apartment."

"Good."

"At some point we're going to have to pull her out of the tub, Nick. Not only that, but we're going to have to tell the French we have her. GIGN is going to insist on speaking with her."

"She talking to your guy at all?"

"The usual claptrap," Weber told him. "Demands we release her. Wants a lawyer. Going to sue the entire United States government."

"Can't wait to see how that one plays out," Reagan said. "Tell your agent Brophy that her friend Mahdi knows something is up. I'm guessing he's already on the move. See if she'll make any kind of deal to tell us where he might go."

"Already on it. She claims that office is the only place she knows of, otherwise they meet at different drop spots around the city, always a different location. Sounds credible."

"It does," Reagan grudgingly conceded. "She told us she runs errands that take her to the UK, the States, wherever he sends her. Which means he moves around freely himself. If Walid Khoury is our guy, being married to someone at State gives him incredible flexibility."

"Assuming your guess is right."

"Yes, assuming that."

"We can try to get the French to issue a BOLO," Weber said. "I'll get on it with Interpol. For all we know, he's already on his way to Mecca."

Reagan looked to Gellos and shook his head. "See what you can do and keep us informed. You know where we have to go."

"I don't envy you that discussion. You said she's an old friend of Erin's."

"Not for long, I'm afraid."

By the time Reagan and Gellos made it back to the embassy, they had already alerted Kenny. He made the necessary calls to have Cyla

Khoury isolated. When they arrived upstairs, they were shown to a small room where she was being held with no access to a phone or computer, an armed guard posted outside.

As the two agents entered the room, Cyla stood. "Nick, what's this about?"

"Sit down," he said, then he and Gellos took seats across the table from her.

"Nick—" she began again, but he cut her off.

"Right now, you should say nothing except to answer our questions."

She fell back into her chair, a look of utter bewilderment on her face.

"Where is your husband?"

"My husband?"

"Where is he right now?"

"I have no idea. He just got back to Paris. He's been in New York, while I was shuttling back and forth to D.C."

"You've seen him since he's back?"

"Of course. We had coffee this morning, at a café near our place," Cyla said. "Then I came to the office. Haven't heard from him since."

"Is that unusual, or do you tend to be in touch during the day?"

"He has his career, and I have mine. Why are you asking me—"

"Just answer my questions. Where is his office, here in Paris?"

"Walid doesn't have an office in Paris. He works from home. He has an office in Washington."

Gellos leaned towards her. "Are you aware that he maintains an office on the Avenue de Valois?"

She looked from Gellos to Reagan. "What?"

"It's a simple question," Gellos said.

"No. He has no office in Paris, I would know if he did."

"Do you know a man called Mahdi?"

She appeared to be thinking it over. "It's not an unusual Arab name, but no, I can't think of anyone."

"You ever hear your husband referred to by anyone as Mahdi?"

Cyla shook her head, as if the question was absurd. "No, never."

"Do you know a woman named Rima Vaziri?" Reagan asked.

Once again, she responded with a look of utter confusion. "Who?"

Reagan repeated the name, then held up his phone, showing her the picture of Vaziri he had taken back at the apartment.

"Never laid eyes on her," Cyla said as she shook her head again. "Please, you have to tell me what this is all about."

Reagan got up, opened the door, and asked the guard to have someone bring him Cyla's cell phone. When he sat back down, he asked, "How do the two of you usually communicate when you're apart? Phone call, text, email, what?"

"We usually text," she told them.

There was a knock on the door, and a young woman entered, handing Gellos the cell.

When she left, Reagan said to Cyla, "We want you to send your husband a text. Tell him you are getting done early today, ask if he would like to get together for a drink. Is that something you might normally do?"

"He's Muslim, more devout than I am. He almost never drinks alcohol."

Reagan exchanged a quick look with Gellos. *Scotch on the rocks at the Hotel Bristol.* "What would you usually do, then? Meet for a late lunch, an early dinner?"

"We like to meet at an outdoor restaurant, when the weather permits."

Reagan sat back and had a good look at her. "Your husband is a person of interest in the investigation were conducting."

"Walid? But—"

"Just listen to me, Cyla. This may all come to nothing, but right now we need to speak with your husband, and we have not been able to locate him. He is not at his office, and he is not at your home. We need you to reach out to him and set something up as soon as possible."

She responded with a blank look. "A person of interest?"

"That's right, and I repeat, we need to speak with him as soon as possible."

"You're talking about my husband, Nick."

Reagan suddenly slammed the table with the palm of his hand. "Listen to me carefully," he said through gritted teeth. "At the moment I am proceeding on the assumption that you are unaware of whatever is going on here, and as Erin's friend I am extending you every possible consideration under extremely difficult circumstances. But if you don't cooperate, this is not going to go well for you. Am I clear?"

She stared at him without speaking.

"If he has done nothing wrong, we'll clear this up straightaway. Now," he said, holding up her phone, "give me the password to open your phone, point me to his contact information, and tell me what sort of message you would send to get him to meet you. Now," he demanded again.

Cyla nodded slowly and gave Reagan the information.

"You two ever go to Farnesina? It's not far from here, has outdoor seating."

She nodded.

"Good," Reagan said, then opened her phone and typed a text, asking Walid if he would like to meet for a late lunch at Farnesina. After reading it to her, he asked, "That sound like something you would write?"

Cyla nodded again, and Reagan hit *Send*.

CHAPTER SIXTY-EIGHT

Dearborn, Michigan

Rashid Jalloud was in Dearborn when he received the text from Mahdi the previous night, the communication he and his men had been waiting for. It was a simple message—*Proceed*—which meant the operation was going forward. The explosives had been gathered in a warehouse behind one of the largest Mosques in Dearborn, not far from the building where Ahmed and Talal had murdered Yousef Omarov and Fariq Homsi.

Transporting the men and materials from Michigan to Minnesota would not be difficult. They would travel in two cars and a panel van. The dynamite and C-4 would be secreted behind interior panels in the back of the small truck. Even if they were stopped for some traffic infraction, their deadly cargo would not be visible. Unless someone had a reason to strip down the vehicle from the inside out, or bring in bomb-sniffing dogs, they would reach their destination without incident.

Once there, they each had an assigned task. They knew there was security on-site twenty-four seven, but it was not the sort of defense one would find at a more vulnerable installation, such as a chemical plant or other high-risk target. The guards there were generally focused on garden variety disturbances such as theft, burglary, the safety of patrons, or disorderly conduct. The sort of violent attack planned by the Handler was not likely to be on their radar.

The biggest issue Mahdi's men would face arose from the complexity of the assault itself, and what had to be done to position the explosives without being detected.

As the leader of the mission, Jalloud would be driving the van. He was a Syrian who had entered the United States illegally, coming by car across the Canadian border with forged documents. Since his arrival three months ago, he had been kept safe by associates in the Islamic community in Dearborn. He had been handpicked to carry out this last phase of the Handler's mission. An expert in explosives, he had fabricated numerous IED's in Damascus as well as in Iraq, where he was assigned to battle the Americans. Now he would take the fight to their homeland in dramatic fashion.

Plotting their journey west, Jalloud figured if they stayed within the speed limits, it would take about twelve hours to travel the seven hundred miles to their destination, allowing for two rest stops. They would drive throughout the day, arrive in the evening, check into separate motels, and then set out to implement their instructions before dawn.

In addition to overseeing the others, Jalloud had the responsibility of organizing access to the catwalks that led to the roof. This had to be accomplished in sufficient time to plant the charges without being detected, then detonate them after reaching safety without being stopped. He had mapped out exactly where the explosives would be placed and how their ignition would be coordinated. After much study, including some help from the three American scientists who had been interrogated in Pakistan, he was confident of what was needed to accomplish their deadly objectives.

Unaware that a manhunt was underway in Paris to find the Handler, Jalloud began their final arrangements.

CHAPTER SIXTY-NINE

Paris

There was not much time to arrange for the manpower needed to trap Walid Khoury, but time was a luxury they did not have.

Within minutes of sending Cyla's text, her husband responded via email. He said he would be pleased to meet her at *Farnesina* in an hour.

"Just remember," Reagan reminded Cyla as he got to his feet, "if your husband has done nothing wrong, nothing will happen to him."

She responded with a look of utter incredulity. "You've asked me to set a meeting with my own husband so you can arrest him, Nick. If he's innocent, as I know he is, he'll never forgive me."

Reagan shook his head. "He'll never know you were involved. We'll say that we've been following you all day. You knew nothing and told us nothing. We'll never say that we set the meeting."

She uttered a bitter laugh. "I see. You not only have me betraying him, you want me lying to him as well."

He stared down at her. "That'll be up to you."

She responded with a helpless look but said nothing.

Reagan felt sorry for the woman, but he was out of patience. "If your husband is not who we think he is, you'll work out your marital problems. But if he is, then he's the murderer of innocent people, and we need to stop him. I can't be any clearer than that." Without another word, he and Gellos left the room. Outside in the corridor, he said, "I'm surprised he got the text. I thought he would have ditched his cell by now."

Gellos agreed. "Once he saw it, he might have guessed we got to her. Sent the reply then trashed it. He probably keeps more than one phone anyway."

"You're right."

"Notice that he responded by email."

"Tougher to track on short notice," Reagan said. "Could have sent it from a device other than his phone."

"Right. So you think he'll show?" Gellos asked.

"I wouldn't order his lunch just yet, but my guess is he'll be somewhere nearby, have a look around."

Gellos nodded. "Let's go set up the welcoming party."

Reagan had good reasons for choosing Ristorante Farnesina. It was just a few blocks from the embassy, which made it a logical place for Cyla to meet her husband. It also set up perfectly for their purposes. It was on the narrow Rue Boissy d'Anglas, located midway between the Rue de Faubourg Saint-Honore and the juncture of the Avenue Gabriel and the Rue Rivoli. With agents posted at both ends of the street, once Khoury made his way toward the restaurant he would have no chance to escape. Farnesina was also situated directly around the corner from various government buildings and the Élysée Palace, which meant there were always armed soldiers present, and Khoury would have no reason to be surprised to see security details on duty.

Reagan was pleased to learn from Weber that the French were offering their full cooperation. Once they were persuaded the target may have been behind the two attacks in the United States, there was no way they wanted him running free in Paris.

All Mahdi had to do was show up.

Reagan had Cyla request a table in the outdoor café, where she could easily be watched from the street, and where her husband could be seen when he arrived. Two GIGN operatives got there early and took a table inside, near the door, where they had a good view of anything happening outside. They could also grab anyone attempting to make their way through the restaurant and out the back.

Cyla arrived and was shown to her seat by the maître d', who had no idea he had been cast as a bit player in this drama. He asked if she would like an aperitif, but Cyla said she would just like some Perrier for now.

Weber and one of his men were on the south end of the Rue Boissy d'Anglas, standing on opposite sides of the street across from the Place de la Concorde. Reagan wanted as few Americans in evidence as possible, so he relied on the GIGN and the state police to provide surveillance from the north end of the street, on the Rue de Faubourg Saint-Honore.

With all the official buildings in the area, CCTV installations were everywhere, and Reagan's phone had been linked to a live feed from the camera that was set up directly across from the restaurant. He and Gellos were seated inside a small bar just a couple of doors from the restaurant, when an attractive woman walked in and strolled up to them.

"Mr. Reynolds," she said with a wry smile.

Reagan grinned as he got to his feet. "Amanda Whitson. Imagine running into you here."

"You really do get around," she said.

"I suppose we both do." Turning to Gellos, he said, "Carol, meet Amanda, one of our British cousins. We were in the middle of an interesting conversation in Shanghai when the Chinese authorities rudely interrupted."

"Yes," Amanda said, "I believe we were discussing foreign relations."

"Something like that," Reagan said, noting that she was even more striking in the Parisian daylight than the Shanghai night. Her dark pants-suit, minimal makeup, and pulled-back hair suited her well.

"I believe I owe you a Walther PPK," she said. "Although I suppose if I send it to a 'Nick Reynolds' it will end up in the lost and found."

He shrugged. "Did I say my name was Reynolds? Must have been confused by all that vodka."

Looking him in the eyes, she said, "From what I understand, it isn't that easy to confuse Nick Reagan."

He smiled. "Keep the gun as a remembrance. I try not to form emotional attachments to weapons."

Amanda nodded. "Any sign of our man yet?"

Reagan shook his head, then held up the phone where she could see Cyla on video, nervously fidgeting with the silverware, waiting for her husband to appear.

"Hope you don't mind me crashing your party."

"Delighted," Reagan said. "Won't even ask who sent you the invitation."

Then the three of them sat and waited. As in most stakeouts, the moments passed slowly, tension growing as the appointed time approached.

* * *

WHEN WALID KHOURY RECEIVED the text from his wife, he was not sure what to make of it. He trusted Cyla. He was convinced she had no idea about his work with al-Qaeda. Still, there were undeniable indications that something was wrong.

First, Rima had not shown up at the hotel with his computer. Then his call to her went unanswered, which told him it was time to immediately leave the bar at the Hotel Bristol. Once he was out on the street, he destroyed the cell phone from which he had called Vaziri, depositing its various parts into different trash bins as he circled the block. He ended his stroll outside the modern art gallery on the boulevard directly opposite the hotel entrance, pretending to admire the paintings on display.

And waited.

It was not long before a car sped down the street and came to a stop at the hotel entrance. Turning his back to them, he watched in the reflection of a plate glass window as a man and woman, obviously American, got out and hurried inside, leaving their car with the doorman.

He did not recognize the woman, but, even from a distance, even using the window as a mirror, he was sure the man was Nicholas Reagan.

Whether through torture, threats, or simple betrayal, Rima had certainly revealed where she was delivering his laptop. Leaving their car out front meant they did not expect to be inside for long, and so, when they discovered he had already gone, the obvious question was—where would they go next?

He hailed a cab and gave the driver an address across the river. There, he took a table inside the rear of the small café on a side street where he used the time to assess his situation.

It was evident he needed to leave Paris. *Let them spend their time and resources chasing me*, he told himself. The important thing was that his men carry out their deadly mission without interference. Rima Vaziri knew nothing of his plan, she could not provide them any help with that. Khoury smiled, the irony delighting him for the moment, the thought that they would be focused on finding him rather than stopping the mission. Then, as he sat contemplating his options, he received that text from Cyla. It was an unwelcome surprise.

He knew the meeting was not her idea, they never got together for a "late lunch" as she called it. He felt Reagan's fingerprints all over the message. *But how had they connected me to Cyla so quickly?* Rima Vaziri did not know his real name or anything about his personal life. She had no way of even knowing he was married to Cyla.

However it happened, he was forced to assume his pursuers, not his wife, had issued the invitation and that Reagan was leading the operation. Which meant the best thing he could now was pretend to accept. No questions, no hesitation. Then he would disappear.

He headed for the men's room and responded to his wife with a short email saying he would meet her at the restaurant. He was then obliged to destroy a second cell phone in less than an hour, leaving only the one he carried with a number no one else on earth knew.

He left the café, hailed another cab, and headed east along the Seine. He could not return to his apartment, or his office, and he certainly would not be keeping that lunch date with Cyla. He considered walking past the Rue Boissy d'Anglas, just to confirm his belief that they had set a trap for him, but he knew he would be flying too close to the flame. The reward did not justify the risk.

The Handler then returned to the issue of his assistant. He knew where Rima was when he called her, having tracked her location before he ended the call. He knew it was time for him to leave town, but where he should go was a matter for which he would seek guidance. He powered up his remaining cell phone, entered the encrypted number, sent a text, and would now wait for a response. Meanwhile, he gave the driver the address where Rima was being held.

* * *

A LONG AND ANXIOUS twenty minutes had passed since the time Khoury was to meet his wife. Although others suggested they wait a while longer, Reagan knew their plan was blown. None of the units in position had seen anyone remotely resembling their target. They had to assume he suspected something and was not coming.

"It's your call," Reagan replied to the head GIGN agent through his earpiece. "We'll stay in place a while longer."

As soon as he signed off, Gellos received a call. Looking at the number, she said "Sasha," and connected. "We're on a stakeout," she told their tech expert at Langley.

"I know," Sasha told him, "but we've got some news, and the DD wanted me to get it to you pronto."

"Go."

"We've been in contact with the task force at our embassy in Paris. They've gotten into this guy's laptop."

Gellos looked at Reagan. "They're into his computer," she said, then told Sasha, "I'm listening."

"There's no clear road map to his plans, and there are more encryptions once we got past the initial security wall."

"I'm sure they're doing a great job, Sasha. Can you give me a headline or two?"

"I can give you one," Sasha said. "We are definitely on the right track. There are emails referring to several high-profile targets, although many of them don't fit the model we've been working on. A few of them do, and we think we know where they're going." Before Gellos could ask where, Sasha added, "The DD wants to know where you stand on your search for Khoury?"

Sasha handed the phone to their boss, and Gellos recognized Kenny's voice as he asked, "What's the sit-rep?"

"We think he made us, sir," Gellos told him. "We're more than twenty minutes past the meet time. We have video on Cyla, she has her phone on the table in front of her. She's had no incoming messages, no calls. And there's no sign of him on the street."

"Let the GIGN take it from here, they can work with Weber and his team. I want you and Reagan back here right away."

"But—" Gellos began before her boss cut her off.

"We'll talk when you're in the air. I've booked you a ride on a government jet, it's ready to go at Orly. Get there ASAP."

* * *

JUST AS KENNY RANG OFF, the video feed to Reagan's phone showed Cyla making a move for her cell.

Speaking into his mic, Reagan asked the GIGN team leader, "What's happening?"

He was told to hold on. A few moments later the French voice was back. "She just got an email from her husband, claims he got tied up in a meeting, won't be able to make lunch."

"Can we trace it back to the source?" Reagan asked.

"Appears to be a public site."

"When you say a public site—"

"One of those café computers."

"Do we have a location?"

"Working on it, but you can be sure he's on the move by now."

Reagan signed off and turned to Amanda. "Time for us to move. I guess we'll always have Shanghai."

She smiled. "Maybe London next time. I know you have your hands full at the moment, but I'd love to continue our conversation. Perhaps we could discuss Anatole Mindlovitch."

"Perhaps we should," Reagan said, then looked at Gellos. "Let's go."

*　*　*

LEAVING HIS SMALL AUTOMATIC in his pocket, Khoury knocked on the door to the apartment. He had no idea how many people were inside, but Rima was probably in restraints, and no more than one agent was likely assigned to keep watch over her.

A wary voice from inside asked, "Who is it?"

"I'm with the GIGN," he said in English with a French accent. "Reagan sent me."

Agent Brophy opened the door slightly, gun in hand. "Why are you here?" he asked, noting that the man's hands were empty.

"We're supposed to move the prisoner," Khoury said.

Before Brophy could react, the Handler drove his shoulder into the door, not hard enough to knock the man down, just enough to move him backward and momentarily lose his balance. Then he came forward, and with a single, swift motion, lashed out with the sharp, curved blade he had hidden in the cuff of his jacket, cutting the agent's throat.

Brophy fell against the wall, clutching at his throat as Khoury came forward and hit him with a second, lethal gash. As Brophy crumpled to the floor, Khoury quickly picked up the man's weapon and swept the small apartment to see if anyone else was there.

He found he was alone, except for Rima Vaziri, who was still bound, laying in the bathtub, covered in a blanket, her mouth taped shut.

Khoury stood there, automatic pistol in hand, staring down at her.

At first, upon seeing him, the woman's eyes displayed a sense of hope. But as he stood there without speaking, that look turned to one of dread.

"You betrayed me," he finally said.

Vaziri began vigorously shaking her head, trying to speak through the tape.

"They came to the Bristol. There was no way they could have known I would be there unless you told them." He bent down, pulled the blanket away, lowered the drain stopper and turned on both the hot and cold faucets full blast. Then he made a show of looking her up and down. "It does not appear you have been harmed. Did they threaten you?" When she began nodding her head, he stood and held up his hand. "Or did they promise you some great reward if I were captured?"

Vaziri shook her head again, straining against the ropes as the tub filled around her.

Khoury ignored her protests.

"What else might you have told them, I wonder?" He gazed down at her with a sad look, as if he had just received some heartbreaking news. "A beautiful woman, giving her life for no purpose," he said. Then, his teeth suddenly clenched in rage, he growled, "A woman I trusted."

He waited as the water rose above her legs and chest until, though she writhed and twisted against the restraints, it covered her face.

Khoury watched as her eyes widened with terror, the tub continuing to fill. Finally, when it was about to overflow and she was completely submerged, he reached his hand down into the water and ripped the tape from her mouth.

Her next move was reflexive and lethal. Her lungs cried out for air, and she was not able to close her mouth despite being fully submerged. Her restraints kept her from rising above the water level, leaving her with no choice but to engage in a grotesque combination of a scream and a gasp for life, as she swallowed a large mouthful of water.

Then Khoury turned off the water and walked away, leaving her there to drown.

CHAPTER SEVENTY

En route to Bloomington, Minnesota

Sasha had been on the right track about the type of building being targeted. Unfortunately, there were too many structures that fit the model—any number of domed stadiums, retail locations, and transportation hubs with translucent roofing supported by metal struts. Now they had Khoury's computer, however, and it was a matter of breaking through the firewalls and interpreting the coded language to find a pattern that would lead them to the precise location.

The task force in Paris found several possibilities, recreating the Handler's short list. Geography apparently played a role in his selection process, perhaps based on the available resources they had in the United States necessary to implement the attack.

Reagan and Gellos were on an agency plane, tied into a video-conference with Levchenko and Brandt, trying to decipher the new information.

It was Sasha who pointed to a decoded email from less than a week ago. It was apparently sent from D.C. to someone located in Dearborn, Michigan. It read, simply:

America will suit our needs. Proceed now.

"He's obviously not referring to the United States of America," Reagan said. "It's already a given that the attack is in the US."

Brandt did not disagree. "What are you thinking?"

"Another text talks about getting there. They're already in the United States, and the exchange was with someone in Dearborn, so when they're told to proceed, they mean—"

"Someplace with the word 'America' in it," Brandt suggested.

"Which only describes thousands of places," Sasha said.

"Not necessarily," Reagan told them. "Not if you limit a search to the type of building they're targeting. Have look at the list the task force put together from Khoury's computer."

"Which suggests it's not a stadium, it's a mall. With the word 'America' in its name."

"Right," Reagan said. "Then, when you pare it down to a mall with the word America in it—"

"Are we all thinking the same thing?" Sasha asked.

"We are, if you're all thinking the Mall of America," Reagan said. "It's not much of a stretch, once you tie it all together."

Sasha nodded. "The Mall of America is within driving distance from Dearborn."

"And consider the importance of the target," Brandt said.

"And it's in the Midwest," Gellos agreed. "New York on the East Coast, Las Vegas out west, now the Mall of America in the heart of the country."

"It was the subject of a terrorist threat just a few years ago," Reagan reminded them. "Something that was never carried out."

"Right," Sasha said. He brought the mall's website up on his screen, with photos of the various sections, then posted it to their screen. "Look at the design at the center. Check out the ceiling and all the activities available below. It's exactly what we've been talking about."

"The text you found also says 'Proceed Now,' which means they're already on the move."

Brandt and Sasha got to their feet. "Guys, we're going to see Kenny."

* * *

"Looks like we're changing our destination," Reagan told the pilot.

Both men in the cockpit nodded their understanding, the co-pilot telling him, "We just got word."

Reagan returned to the comfortable leather seat of the well-appointed Gulfstream. He and Gellos were the only two passengers, although there had been discussion about bringing Cyla Khoury back to the States with them. Ultimately, they agreed it made more sense to have her taken to D.C. by her own security people for questioning which, as it turned out, was for the best. Reagan and Gellos needed to get to Minnesota as soon as possible.

Reagan was pleased to find his weapon of choice aboard, the Walther PPK, with several additional magazines. Gellos opted for an M1911.

Working on a laptop, Gellos said, "The Mall of America deserves the name. By any reasonable measure, it's the largest shopping mall in the country. Has been for more than a quarter century." Reading from the website, she went on. "The MOA, as it's known, covers almost a hundred acres, with more than five hundred stores. It has indoor amusement parks, theme parks, all sorts of rides. The place is enormous."

"Been there," Reagan replied. "Back in early 2015, when al-Shabaab made his online threat against the place, then expanded it to include malls all across the company."

"I remember that," Gellos said. "Nothing came of it."

"No, but it gave me a chance to meet the MOA security staff, and, let me tell you, these are not your typical mall cops. They have their own anti-terrorism task force. Every one of them goes through training with the Mossad and Israeli military. They learn techniques for identifying suspects, dealing with crisis intervention, engaging in rapid response. When a recruit passes the course, which takes six full weeks in Israel, they get certified as Behavior Detection Officers. Impressive for a retail operation."

"Didn't they run into some trouble with their tactics a while back?"

Reagan frowned. "Some of their staff were accused of racial profiling, stopping customers without probable cause. Threats of that attack by al-Shabaab were credible, but people at the mall were shopping and didn't want to be bothered with reasonable efforts to protect them."

Gellos responded with a short nod.

"Let's call Alex back, see what's being done to coordinate with the locals."

Brandt was already on a flight from D.C. to Minnesota. They reached him on a satellite link, and he gave them an update on their communications with the security force at the mall. "Guy in charge is all business. Happy to have support from the authorities, but clearly feels he can run his own show."

"I remember. That's how he rolls," Reagan told him. "Have they seen any unusual activity?"

"None. Which raises another concern," Brandt said. "Without more to go on, the locals aren't about to make any sort of statement or set up roadblocks or do anything else that might cause a panic. This is not just a safety issue, there's an economic component. This mall employs thousands and is the biggest draw in the area. We've made an educated guess, but if we're wrong—"

"This is more than an educated guess," Reagan said.

"Understood," Brandt replied, "but again, if we're wrong—"

"A bunch of people are going to be unhappy with us," Reagan finished the thought. "I get that a lot."

"What about the jurisdictional question?" Gellos asked. "I assume Homeland Security and the FBI have been read in."

"Fully on board," Brandt said. "They're taking the lead, but the DD still wants us on site. We just have to keep our involvement limited."

Gellos broke into laughter. "And Kenny knows how discreet Nick can be."

"Precisely," Reagan agreed with a smile.

"So, it's just the three of us from the company?" Gellos asked.

"That's it," Brandt said. "I'll be waiting at the private terminal when you arrive. The mall is only ten miles from there."

"Any news on Khoury?" Reagan asked.

"Nothing that we've heard," Brandt told them. "Seems to have evaporated into the ether. They confirmed that last email he sent his wife was from a café near Notre Dame Cathedral. They've issued the BOLO nation-wide, hoping to spot him at an airport or train station."

"Unless he's hiding in Paris," Reagan mused aloud, not happy that they had been so close to the man but were forced to move in the opposite direction. "I want that bastard."

CHAPTER SEVENTY-ONE

En route to Marseilles

Walid Khoury was comfortably ensconced in the privacy of a first-class compartment on the late afternoon train from Paris to Marseilles. He sent the text stating that he needed immediate exfiltration, and travel arrangements were handled for him by Mahmoud, an al-Qaeda lieutenant he knew well. Mahmoud told him which train to take, what compartment had been reserved, and that upon his arrival in Marseilles he would be met by two men selected to escort him out of the country. Their top priorities were to provide him safe passage and to ensure that nothing interfered with the last phase of the three attacks mandated by 22:19 of the Koran—*Death by hooked iron rods*.

Khoury sat back, sipping a Macallan 18, watching the countryside whiz by at breakneck speed. Soon he would be safely out of France, probably transported by ship and then ground to Damascus. Once there he could enjoy praise for the fruits of his labors, then regroup and embark on another assignment.

He thought of Cyla as he tasted the whisky. *The things she believed,* he thought to himself. He had only a few regrets about the way he had used her to obtain the information he then passed on to the leaders of al-Qaeda. His stories about international banking were an elaborately crafted cover, the lies he had to live. Now he wondered, *How she would deal with his betrayal?* She was a loyal and trusting person. At first she would not believe what the Americans said about him. Eventually, when she realized he was not returning, she would know the truth.

He would never understand why she had such loyalty to the Americans. Now, he hoped, she would see them for who they really were. They would suspect that she was part of his conspiracy, or at least that she knew enough to cause her serious legal trouble. Her personal life was ruined, and her career destroyed. *What a fool she was to trust them.* As the train pulled into the Lyon station—the only stop this express would make en route to Marseilles—he consoled himself with the knowledge that, in waging war against the infidels, compassion had no place, and she had earned her fate.

Just a few minutes after the train ground to a halt, there was a knock at the door of his cabin.

"*Privée*," he told whoever was there, the entire four-person cabin having been booked for his use.

A voice from outside his locked compartment responded with a single word. "Mahdi."

Khoury got to his feet and opened the door, finding two muscular young men standing there.

"We are here to safeguard the remainder of your journey," the taller of the two told him.

He let them in, locked the door behind them, and they exchanged the blessings of Allah.

"I thought you were meeting me in Marseilles," Khoury said. "Is there a problem?"

"Not at all," the taller man assured him.

Khoury had a good look at him, judging him to be Syrian. "Damascus?"

"Aleppo," he replied.

Khoury nodded, not revealing it was the city where he lost his first wife and their beloved young daughter. Instead, he asked, "Why the change in plans?"

"Mahmoud thought we had time to meet your train here," the shorter, stockier man replied. He appearance and accent were Lebanese. "We were told to keep you safe. We will meet our brothers when we arrive in Marseilles."

Khoury nodded again. The stopover in Lyon would be just over ten minutes. He had the curtains drawn, so people passing on the platform could not see inside. "Make yourselves comfortable," he told his escorts.

The Syrian eyed the glass of scotch on the table but said nothing. Instead, he turned to his companion and said, "I will call to tell them we have arrived in time."

The Handler thought there was something odd in how he recited this statement and how the Lebanese reacted. It sounded like some sort of signal.

Walid Khoury had not survived this long without superior instincts, both for appraising a situation and for survival. From the moment they entered his compartment he felt something was wrong—their claim that the plans had changed was something Mahmoud would have communicated directly to him; the stiffness of their demeanor; his sense that the things they were saying had been rehearsed; and now the mention of a phone call that felt like some sort of code.

When the Lebanese pulled a long-bladed knife from inside his jacket and came toward him, Khoury had already reached his right hand into the pocket of his slacks, taking hold of his Rohrbaugh R9S, a hammerless 9-millimeter gun with no safety that was barely larger than his palm. The result, although both men were younger and stronger, was that the Handler had time to react to their assault, countermoves he had trained for many times.

Khoury sidestepped the thrust of the knife, deftly pulling out the small automatic and firing two quick shots into the man's side, sending him lurching backward onto the floor.

As quickly as he had dispatched the first assailant, there was still the taller man to deal with. He was behind Khoury, now also with a knife in hand, and he managed to slash the Handler's left arm before Khoury could spin away and fire three shots directly into the man's stomach. Gasping in agony, the Syrian dropped his knife and fell back onto the seat, grabbing at his gut as if there were some way to undo the lethal damage.

But the Rohrbaugh was a 9-millimeter, and the close-range damage ensured that both men were as good as dead, regardless of how desperately they clung to life.

Khoury stepped forward, standing over the man from Aleppo, pointing the small automatic at his face. "Who sent you?"

The man did not reply, choking with pain.

When the Handler asked the question again, the man looked up, panting as he managed to say, "Too many mistakes, Mahdi." Then he exhaled a final, uneven breath and was gone.

Khoury had a quick look at the Lebanese man. He was on the floor, not moving.

The Handler knew that even in a noisy train station like Lyon, the gunshots would be heard. He had to move quickly.

Pulling off his sport coat he had a look at the gash on his arm, blood already running down the torn white sleeve of his shirt. Removing his tie, he did what he could to bind the wound, wiped his hands on the pants of the dead Syrian, then pulled on his jacket.

Checking the compartment to make sure he was taking what little he had brought with him, he opened the door to see if anyone was in the corridor. It was clear, so he left the cabin, pulled the door shut behind him, and moved into the busy station at Lyon, leaving two corpses to complete their journey to Marseilles, wondering where he could go with both the Americans and his own people hunting him.

What echoed in his head as he disappeared in the crowd was the Syrian's haunting phrase, *Too many mistakes, Mahdi.*

CHAPTER SEVENTY-TWO

Bloomington, Minnesota

Every available FBI and DHS asset within driving distance of Bloomington was poised for immediate action, while local police and state troopers were put on high alert.

The Security Director at the Mall of America had been alerted and his team was ready—in addition to the full complement of staff on hand, he also called in men and women who would have been off for the day, doubling up on patrols.

What none of these people could possibly envision was the sheer depravity of the Handler's plan.

Not wanting a repeat of al-Shabaab's aborted threat to attack the MOA in 2015, Walid Khoury had made meticulous preparations. The van that carried the explosives, and the cars transporting the men assigned to complete this mission, had arrived from Dearborn last night. Everything was already in place for the assault, which would occur in two waves.

Size would become both the strength and weakness of the Mall of America.

* * *

By the time Reagan and Gellos landed in Minneapolis and met with Brandt, all three agents had been fully briefed on the current situation.

They were also told that John Ekey, the MOA Director of Security, had declared to anyone listening that he would be in charge of coordinating all efforts. Ekey was former military, having served as an officer in Special Forces. He was then selected to succeed the legendary Special Operations Security Captain at MOA, who was responsible for turning his staff into the highly trained and well-respected unit it had become. As Ekey announced on a call with representatives from the FBI, DHS, and local law enforcement, "This is my house, and I have the primary responsibility to keep it safe."

For now, at least, no one argued.

Since Reagan and his fellow agents had no real jurisdiction, the locals had not been notified that they were approaching the scene.

"Which means we don't have anyone to answer to," Reagan said.

Gellos laughed. "Not buying that one partner."

"They may have the authority, but we have the experience to deal with these bastards in real time."

Brandt reminded him that Kenny expected to be kept up to speed.

"We'll call as soon as we have something to tell him," Reagan replied as they climbed into the sedan Brandt had arranged for their ride to Bloomington. Gellos was at the wheel, as ever.

"Something came through a little while ago that you two might not have heard yet," Brandt told them. "Walid Khoury is still at large."

"Details?" Gellos asked.

"He was in a first-class compartment on a train from Paris to Marseilles. Looks like a couple of his friends got on in Lyon, must have tried to take him out. Sound of gunshots brought in the locals, the two men were found dead."

"But no Khoury."

"No."

"Damn," Reagan said. "No one spotted Khoury leaving the train?"

"The train only made that one stop, in Lyon. He probably got off there. The locals are working on it. Also checking Marseilles."

Gellos shook her head. "Why would they come after one of their own, especially someone so highly placed?"

"Al-Qaeda is not a big fan of loose ends," Reagan said. "Once they realized he was on the run, he became a liability."

"True," Gellos said.

"I admit, it happened awfully fast," Reagan said. "I'm guessing they had doubts about him before yesterday."

Gellos nodded. "Maybe New York and Vegas didn't get them enough of what they wanted. Al-Qaeda is also not big on failure."

"You're right," Reagan said. Turning back to Brandt, he asked, "What about the CCTV system in those two train stations, they pick anything up?"

"As I said, they're working on it," Brandt told them.

Reagan shook his head. "He's on the loose, and we need to get to him before his own people do. An hour in a room with him could be extremely valuable."

They were all quiet for a moment. Then Gellos said, "Right now we need to concentrate on what he's got lined up for Bloomington."

"Right," Brandt said. "What's our plan for when we get to the mall?"

"Unless we're all wrong," Reagan said, "they're going to try to blow the roof off some part of the place."

"That's the theory," Gellos agreed as she sped along the highway, "but let me remind you that *the place*, as you call it, is huge."

"True, but only certain roof sections are built with the design we're looking for," Reagan said. Turning again to Brandt in the back seat, he asked, "The locals doing any aerial reconnaissance?"

"Kenny said they're not sending up any choppers until they have more information. If the threat is imminent, they want to deal with it now. Sending up air support could scare them off, no telling when they might try again."

"Everyone is convinced this is happening soon?" Gellos asked.

"Almost everyone," Brandt said. "There have been additional intercepts coming out of Dearborn that make it sound that way."

"And the fact they tried to take Khoury out so quickly could mean the same thing," Reagan reminded them.

"That's what all indications point to," Brandt agreed.

Gellos asked, "Soon meaning—"

"Today, tomorrow, soon."

"All right," Reagan said, "I buy the analysis, but that gets us back to Alex's question. What do we do when we get there?"

"We could do the righteous thing and check in with this guy Ekey," Brandt suggested. "He's running the show."

"I'm sure that's just what he's hoping for, three more feds crawling up his ass." Reagan thought it over, then said, "Let's have a look around first. You never know what we'll spot that others might miss. Not to mention all the friends we've made in the Middle East over the years. Is it insane to think we might recognize someone?"

"Recognize, or racially profile?" Gellos asked.

Reagan ignored her as he opened one of the floor plans of the MOA Brandt brought with him. "Let's start by checking out this food court."

"You hungry?"

"No, but I'm interested in this large, open area right next to it," Reagan said as he poked at a spot in the center. "We can start there."

CHAPTER SEVENTY-THREE

The Mall of America

There is nothing one can read, have someone else describe, or even view online, that can possibly capture the sheer enormity of the Mall of America. In addition to the seemingly endless array of large and small retail stores, it features dozens of restaurants, bars, and movie theatres and even connects to a major hotel. As if that were not enough, it houses a sprawling theme park at its center, complete with all manner of rides, including a full-scale roller coaster.

The food court Reagan pointed to on the floor plan was near that entertainment area—just beneath a large translucent roof several stories up.

When the three agents reached the MOA, Gellos parked the sedan, and the three of them walked toward one of the many entrances.

"I don't see anything to suggest this place is on alert," Reagan said as they passed through the glass doors leading inside.

Gellos agreed. "Impressive security, keeping it under the radar." As they strolled down the wide corridor and made a right toward the amusements, she said, "So far, we're the three most conspicuous people I've seen—and we're supposed to be clandestine agents."

Reagan laughed. "When we reach that department store ahead of us, let's split up. I'll keep to the left, you stay right, Alex can walk down Main Street, or whatever it's called."

The other two nodded, and, after a few yards, they branched off without another word.

They had each studied the floor plan and photographs they were provided, along with the MOA website. It was obvious the ceiling above the amusement park and food court was a perfect example of the architecture they believed the terrorists would target. It was also a logical spot to cause the sort of mayhem al-Qaeda favored. Women, small children, teenagers.

"Just what these scumbags would aim for," Reagan had said, and neither of his fellow agents disagreed.

Although the three of them had diverged, they were proceeding toward a common destination, each coming at it from different directions as they had a look around.

* * *

As THE THREE AGENTS NOTED when entering the mall, the joint task force was indeed taking a low-key approach. They were determined to prevent the attack, and, in the process, they wanted to avoid any sort of panic.

John Ekey was running the show from his large basement office, where one wall was covered with twenty monitors, giving him rotating, real-time views of every part of the mall, both inside and out. Each screen changed its camera source every thirty seconds, so nothing could escape his notice. The constant bombardment of images might drive someone else to distraction, but this was Ekey's talent—sorting a wide range of information, staying on top of what was happening, then reacting without hesitation.

The mall was essentially laid out in four areas named for the directions on a compass, with the amusement park in the middle. There were personnel from law enforcement agencies and the MOA security staff assigned to each section. Their job was to observe, report, and intercede if necessary. Men and women from the state police, the FBI, and Homeland Security were dressed in plain clothes posing as customers moving in and out of stores, sampling coffee from the various shops, and otherwise trying to remain unobtrusive as they covered the interior of the mall, as well as the parking lots and other outdoor areas. There was a constant flow of information being exchanged as they spoke with their respective superiors, using hidden earpieces and microphones, describing anything unusual they witnessed. All of this was distilled down to the important data, then passed to Ekey.

At one point, staring at his monitors, Ekey said to his second in command, "We're missing something. I know we are."

His lieutenant, last name of Michaels, was standing beside his boss. He said, "We've got every square inch of the place under watch. Maybe they spotted something and left."

"I don't think so," Ekey said, his gaze still fixed on the wall of monitors. Then, as casually as if he were commenting about a smudge on one of the screens, he lifted his hand and said, "There, take a look."

Michaels turned to where his chief was pointing. It was an image on the middle screen of the left row of monitors. A young man, walking alone, had just entered the mall.

How Ekey could identify the first of Jalloud's suicide bombers that quickly was not clear. There was nothing obvious in the young Arab's appearance that should have drawn Ekey's attention. This was Bloomington, and people of Arab descent populated various surrounding areas and would not be out of place at the mall. As far as his clothing, when Khoury drew up the details for this attack, he was insistent that the men wearing the explosive vests be trim, so their deadly cargo would not be obvious. Minimum reveal, maximum firepower.

But Ekey saw something. Hitting the speaker function on the phone connected to the various team leaders of the operation, he said, "Possible lone player, just entered at West Market."

The head FBI agent immediately responded. "We've got eyes on someone in our sector, just entered through the North Garden."

Then one of Ekey's men said, "Copy that. We also have a suspect on South Avenue."

Ekey was staring at the screens where he now had views of all three of these men, all wearing COVID masks, each moving at an unhurried pace toward the interior of the mall. "Coordinated attacks," he said, more to himself than anyone listening. "Would have been useful if they were stopped outside."

No one was about to make any remarks about racial profiling, but Ekey's agent, who reported on the man who entered at the West Market, spoke up. "Our guy was dropped off right at the door, there was no time to make him or stop him."

"We'll get the outdoor team to grab the vehicle that brought him here," Ekey barked. "Probably the same M.O. for all three. Track down their transportation. Now."

"FBI here," the lead agent weighed in again. "I'm reading this the same way you are, control, none of them look like shoppers. I think we need to move fast, take them all down."

"If they're wired, they could detonate on approach," Ekey said.

"Agreed," the federal agent replied, "but we have no choice. We can't just shoot them, we're not sure if they're rigged up. If they are, the further inside the mall they go, the more people at risk."

"All three of them seem to have their hands free," Ekey observed. "No sign of detonators, no hands in the pocket."

"True for our man," the FBI agent agreed, "but it only takes seconds to reach in his jacket and hit a button."

"Could be on timers," Michaels suggested.

"DHS here," the lead agent from Homeland Security said. "We're letting you run the show, control, but we can't just sit by and let them get to the crowds. Right now all three are in still making their way down the entry corridors, am I right?"

"You are," Ekey said.

"Then we're at the point of minimum civilian damage. I've got to give the order to engage."

Ekey took a deep breath. Neither he nor his predecessor had ever suffered an explosion inside his house, and he didn't want to see it happen today. He took a moment to exhale, then said, "You're right. Move on them."

* * *

THE THREE CIA AGENTS were not tied into that conference line, so they had no way of knowing what was happening at three of the four main entrances to the mall. By the time DHS gave the order to stop the three suspicious men, Reagan, Gellos, and Brandt had all reached the perimeter of the amusement park, in the heart of the sprawling complex.

The first thing Reagan did was look up at the ceiling. More than four stories above them he could see daylight through an intricate mesh of large metal piping and translucent ceiling.

"Damn," he said aloud to himself, signaled to Gellos and Brandt, and all three headed toward a set of escalators off to the side. When they converged there, the other two agents did not hesitate, following Reagan up.

"What gives?" Brandt asked.

"It's obvious," Reagan told him. "You want to blow that roof, you're not going to do it from down here."

"Agreed," Gellos said, "so what's our play?"

"When I studied the plans, I looked at all four levels," Reagan told them. "The top has a passageway connecting to the hotel and a multi-plex movie theatre that's been under renovation during the pandemic. A few restaurants. Not much else."

"Meaning that there's not much happening on that level," Gellos said.

"Not compared to the activity down here," Reagan said. "Unless someone is trying to get to the roof."

"Don't you think the task force has people stationed there?" Brandt asked.

"Assume nothing," Reagan replied. "You'll live longer."

The three of them got on the escalator and headed upstairs.

* * *

THUS FAR, THE TIMING was working well for Jalloud and his men. He received texts confirming all three suicide bombers had been dropped off without incident and all three were now inside the mall. He had convinced each of them that they were decoys, that their explosive vests were merely props, and that there was little or nothing the law could do to them if they were arrested. Once they were apprehended—and he told them he wanted them stopped within five minutes of entering the MOA—they would create a distraction that would allow the others to carry out their plan. Where was the crime in wearing a contraption around the chest that contained no combustible material?

What these three young men did not know was that their vests carried large amounts of C-4 plastique, along with nails and ball bearings, all of which were connected to a device that Jalloud could remotely trigger. The distraction they would provide was going to be much more than an encounter with mall security guards.

Jalloud was seated with one of his men in the coffee shop at the top level of the hotel attached to the MOA. Two others on his team were at a table across the room. They had already paid their checks when Jalloud looked at his watch, then nodded and stood. After he and his companion left, the other two men soon followed.

Moving in pairs, the four men exited the hotel and walked along the skyway that connected to the open area of the mall's fourth level. Jalloud and his partner stopped just outside the closed multiplex while the other two continued on, pretending to look into the restaurants as they passed.

Jalloud reached into the outside pocket of his jacket, feeling for three small devices. Moving toward the railing in the center of the floor, he looked down at the amusement park below. Children were screaming as the roller coast rocketed up and down its tracks. The sky ride zipped around the open space just beneath him. A crowd of people, young and old, were involved in all sorts of activities. Having fun. Enjoying themselves. None of them had the slightest notion of the gruesome deaths that would soon befall them.

CHAPTER SEVENTY-FOUR

The Mall of America

Members of the task force had moved in to confront the three young men Jalloud had sent to die. All of these law enforcement officers were taking the same actions, all by the book.

First, they told the young men to stop where they were. Then they warned nearby shoppers to clear out. Finally, with guns drawn, they approached their targets slowly, keeping as much distance as they could, ordering them to drop to their knees and open their jackets.

The first young man, who had entered the mall through the western entrance, began laughing. The sound was not mirthful, it was the nervous reaction of someone in a tense situation who had no idea how it would end. He stood there, seeming unable to stop his idiotic cackling.

The second, who had arrived from the south, believed he had a critical role in an important event. He played his part to perfection, doing exactly what he was told. He got to his knees and pulled open his jacket, exposing the package strapped to his chest that he still believed to be fake.

The third, who had strolled in through the northern entrance was defiant. He was the only one of the three who had come to suspect he might actually be carrying a live charge, and he was not about to succumb to the orders of his sworn enemies. He would not fall to his knees, he told them, but he did open his coat, shouting at the officers, "Come closer, you cowards, and die with me in the name of Allah!"

Upstairs on the fourth level, Jalloud was too far from any of this to see or hear anything, but he knew it was time. The devices in his pocket each contained a single button protected by a plastic cover. One by one, without removing them from his pocket where they might be seen, he flicked back the covers with his thumbnail and pressed the buttons.

The sound of the three explosions, one after the other, reverberated throughout the huge expanse of the Mall of America.

The bedlam that ensued was horrifying. All three young men were instantly ripped to shreds, their body parts dismembered, blood and human debris sprayed about in a grisly shower of death.

The force of the initial impact drove the approaching officers backward, some of them badly injured, one of them dead from the force of the blast that drove him through a shop window, broken plate glass slicing him to ribbons.

Numerous other windows were also destroyed, shards of glass covering and cutting shoppers both inside and outside those stores.

The ball bearings and nails that had been packed tightly against the C-4 explosive rocketed out in all directions, the makeshift shrapnel hitting lawmen as well as dozens of customers.

The screams of pain and terror were deafening as people ran this way and that, not knowing where to go or what might come next, searching desperately for a way to escape the carnage.

* * *

REAGAN, GELLOS, AND BRANDT were on the escalator leading from the third level to the fourth when they heard the three blasts.

Brandt's first impulse was to run up the moving stairs so they could turn back and head downstairs to wherever these sounds had come from.

Reagan grabbed his arm. "I admire your instinct, to run to the trouble, but that's not our job. There's nothing left for us to do about whatever happened down there. Believe me, they've got enough men in place."

"But they set off—"

"I understand," Reagan told him, "and if that was the only attack they planned, then our analysis was wrong, and we failed."

Brandt stared at him. "What do you mean *if*? You heard the explosions."

Reagan nodded. "Which means we were too late to stop them down there. But what if that's not the end? What if we've been right all along? What if the main attack is going to happen above us?"

"You think they've used suicide bombers as a diversion?" Brandt asked.

Reagan did not bother to reply. They had reached the top landing, where people were running out of the restaurants, not sure what to do or where to go. Some were leaning over the glass partition that allowed a view of the amusement park below. Most were rushing toward the skyway leading to the hotel.

No one was riding the escalator down to the direction from where the noise had come.

Even with the chaos unfolding around him, Reagan remained composed as he assessed what was happening. The multiplex was closed, and there was very little retail on this top level, which meant there were far fewer shoppers here than anywhere else in the mall. Reagan spotted a man, near the closed theater entrance to the left. He had his back to Reagan and was apparently working on the lock of some sort of service door. Two other men were walking towards him.

Reagan tapped Gellos on the arm, subtly pointed her toward the man at the door, then pulled out his Walther PPK and took off, weaving through the restaurant patrons who were struggling to find a path to safety.

Before Reagan could reach him, Jalloud sprung the lock, opened the door, and hurried through with the other two men right behind him. What Reagan could not see was that Jalloud had another accomplice, positioned out of view behind a large floor plan directory, which was off to the right. Reacting to Reagan's move, the man drew his weapon and also began running.

At the sight of two men rushing through the crowd brandishing automatic weapons, several people began yelling, trying to move out of their way, but there was one person who held her ground. Carol Gellos turned slightly, as if she also meant to get out of the way of Jalloud's man. She then quickly spun and took out the man's legs with one sweeping kick. He went sprawling across the floor, losing his grip on the gun, which went sliding off to the right.

Meanwhile, Reagan had entered the passageway, racing up the stairs in pursuit of Jalloud and his two men, with Brandt on his heels.

Outside on the fourth floor, as Carol Gellos was driving her knee into the back of the fallen man, two plainclothes members of the MOA security force, a man and a woman, came rushing out of the crowd, weapons drawn.

"Easy there," Gellos said as she put her hands in the air. "Federal agent. Cuff this creep and call for help."

The woman bound the man's hands behind his back as the other officer said, "Show us an I.D. And go easy, please."

Gellos pulled out her credentials, then pointed to the door across the way. "Where does that lead?"

"Outside. It's access for maintenance and roof cleaning."

"Get everyone you can up here. We've got three hostiles heading up there to set explosive charges. Two of our men are in pursuit."

The woman got on her radio and told Ekey what was happening on level four.

"Any other way to the roof?" Gellos asked.

"Several," the man said.

"Get people heading up every way that intersects with that passage," Gellos told them. "And do everything you can to clear the amusement park below. Right now."

CHAPTER SEVENTY-FIVE

The Mall of America

Jalloud was no suicide bomber. Like so many senior members of al-Qaeda, he felt it was his duty to inspire young recruits to give their lives in the pursuit of terror and mass murder. Jalloud preferred to live for Allah rather than die for him—his role was to have others provide that service.

Now, however, he was trapped.

He and his two men intended to place their explosives in strategic locations, then set the detonators with enough lead time so they could safely return to the fourth level. From there, they would take the walkway back to the hotel and safety. He realized they might encounter security personnel after the charges were set, and they were armed and ready for that possibility. What he did not anticipate was being engaged in this race for their lives even before he positioned the C-4 charges.

He could hear the two men in pursuit, knew there were probably others behind them, and realized his choices were limited.

They could turn and fight, perhaps buying time to plant the charges. But he realized, even if they were successful, that they would ultimately be apprehended, or worse, die in the explosion.

They could stop and give themselves up, but he was well aware of the fate of anyone who failed the caliphate. Even in custody, they would not be safe from the retribution of his superiors.

Their best hope was that they had enough of a lead to position the explosives, then escape through the passageway on the far side of the roof.

As he was considering these options, he continued to race up the stairs, leading his men as the sound of his pursuers echoed behind him.

* * *

REAGAN HAD MADE THE SAME analysis. He was prepared for an ambush at one of the landings of these steep, metal stairs that led to the roof. Every time he and Brandt approached a turn, they proceeded with caution, listening for the footsteps of the three men above them.

He had concluded that these men would not surrender, meaning confrontation was inevitable and only a matter of timing.

His job was to get to them before they had the chance to detonate the explosives they were carrying, to prevent the awful consequences of huge chunks of thick glass and large, metal pipes cascading onto the people below.

* * *

WHEN JALLOUD AND HIS MEN reached the last access door, the one leading outside, they did not hesitate. They opened it and climbed out onto the catwalk that provided a means for cleaning and servicing the enormous translucent roof panels. There, he and his men began pulling out the packages of C-4 plastique and dynamite they had secured in the linings of their jackets and inside their shirts. Without speaking, Jalloud pointed to the three locations where they planned to set the explosives, then took out the detonators and started to set the timers.

Rigging the explosives was not a sophisticated matter. All they had to do was secure the packages to the clear panels with two-sided tape and attach the triggering devices. With the timers set, they would continue across the catwalk to the other side of this section of roof in the hope of reaching the second passageway that would lead them to safety.

As they went about setting the explosives, they heard the door behind them open, the one through which they had just passed. At the same time, they heard the sound of approaching helicopters.

* * *

UP TO NOW, EKEY and the law enforcement agencies involved in this operation had agreed to hold the choppers back, certain they had enough manpower on the ground to prevent an assault.

But they were wrong.

Using three suicide bombers as a lethal distraction was more depraved than any of them had imagined. Now they were determined to make up for that error in judgment.

There was a frenzy of communication among the authorities. In the midst of that, Carol Gellos used her cell to reach Kenny, who was immediately patched through to the task force. The DD explained that he had two federal agents in hot pursuit of hostiles who had entered the service passageway leading outside to the roof. He said the men they were chasing were almost certainly carrying explosives and intended to blow the panels above the amusement park at the center of the mall.

The FBI helicopters, which had been waiting for orders, had immediately gone airborne, with sharpshooters in position as they neared a range where they could take out Jalloud and his two men. They were also warned not to fire at the two feds who were now out there as well.

Meanwhile, various personnel from the different agencies were racing to the fourth level, then flooding all passageways heading up to this section of the roof. Carol Gellos led a charge through the entry-way directly across from the one his fellow agents had entered.

At this point, Reagan and Brandt still had no audio connection to any of this activity and were completely on their own when they opened that door and spotted the three men taping their explosive charges in place.

Reagan fired first, two shots, hitting one of the men in the shoulder and chest. He fell over the iron railing of the catwalk, slid down the side of one of the glass panels, then tumbled the remaining four stories to the ground.

Jalloud and his remaining accomplice turned and fired back, but they were exposed, out there in the open, while Reagan and Brandt had cover behind the door. In the next exchange of gunfire, Jalloud was hit in the leg by a shot from Brandt. As he lost his balance, Reagan hit him with a round in his throat, knocking him backward, onto the metal walkway.

The last of Jalloud's men turned and began running for the far door, but, after only a few steps, one of the snipers in the helicopters fired a series of shots that tore into his back, sending him tumbling forward, over the railing, to the ground fifty feet below.

Reagan and Brandt came into the open and began waving to the helicopters. Knowing the agents up there would be watching through binoculars, they holstered their weapons, held up their hands, then hurried forward to where the three charges had been placed.

At that moment, Gellos and a contingent of law enforcement emerged through the opposite door.

"Get the hell out of here!" Reagan began yelling at them as he continued to move toward the explosives. "I see three charges, no telling how they're rigged. If they blow, we don't all need to be up here," he hollered. "Please, Carol, unless they've got an explosives expert there, get them back down the stairs."

With the others not sure what to do, Brandt stayed right behind Reagan. Before his senior agent could say anything, Brandt said, "I'm not going anywhere."

Reagan nodded then hurried forward to the first package, Brandt got to the second.

"Timer," Brandt said.

"Damn," Reagan said. "Rip the tape away, no time to play with them."

As Reagan pulled the first explosive device from the roof, Brandt grabbed the second and then the third.

"Timers," Reagan shouted to the men still standing at the door. "The digital display says they're going to blow in a little over two minutes. I can try and pull the detonators, but that might set them off. Or I can try and heave them over the side into the parking lot."

A young man, wearing a bullet proof vest, pushed his way around Gellos and hurried toward them. "FBI. Phillips. Bomb squad."

Reagan nodded and handed him the first large package he had removed from the panel.

"Primitive," Phillips said after having a look. "This timer appears to be loaded with nitro. Once it's ignited, that sets off the plastique which then triggers the dynamite. Kind of a chain reaction. Pulling the detonator away shouldn't set off the charge."

Reagan stared at him. "Shouldn't?"

Phillips shook his head. "There could be a failsafe underneath that we can't see. That might cause it to blow. Can't be sure."

With that, two other men came out, carrying a huge loop of nylon rope and a large, heavy metal box.

"How much time?" one of them asked.

"Ninety seconds," Phillips told him.

One of the men began securing an end of the long rope to the catwalk while Phillips and the other agent carefully placed each of the three charges inside the box and secured it shut with four bolts.

"Only one way to do this," the other man said. "The fastest way is down. We're going to tie someone to this end and lower him along the side of the building. It'll have to be a fast drop, but we've got the PSBD truck below. If we get there in time, they'll toss the box into the truck and let these suckers go off in there."

"I'll take it," Reagan said.

"Why not just lower the box?" Brandt asked.

"Too risky. There are so many ledges and angles on the way down, the bumps might set it off. Then there's the possibility it gets stuck on a ledge or a pipe or whatever. Then we're screwed."

"*We're* screwed? What about Reagan?" Brandt hollered.

Reagan held up his hand. "Nothing to this," he said. "Rig me up."

No one argued since there was no time for discussion and no other volunteers.

As they secured the rope around Reagan's waist and under his arms, Brandt asked, "What if he doesn't get there in time?"

"Then they detonate in this reinforced chamber," Phillips said. "It'll blunt the explosive force somewhat, but the man carrying it—" He didn't bother to finish the thought.

"Enough talk," Reagan told his fellow agent, "we're out of time. You guys ready?"

Phillips lifted the thick leather strap on the box over Reagan's head. It was incredibly heavy.

"This weighs a ton," Reagan said, worried he might lose the package as he rappelled down the angular side of the mall.

"The rope will hold," Phillips told him. "Use your hands and legs to keep pushing away from the building. The faster you get there, the better—"

"I get it," Reagan said. "Let's go."

* * *

THE ENTIRE DRAMA WAS BEING witnessed by Brian Kenny, Erin David, and Sasha Levchenko on the video screen in the DD's office. The three of them were standing, watching as the rope was being tied around Reagan's chest.

Erin suddenly felt as if she could no longer breathe. "Why him?" she finally asked.

In a rare display of physical affection, Kenny placed his arm around her shoulders. "Because this is what he does, Erin."

Erin did not respond and did not wipe away the tears that now flowed freely down her cheeks. In that moment she knew how much she loved Reagan, and that Kenny was right.

* * *

PHILLIPS AND BRANDT HELPED lift Reagan over the side, then each grabbed a piece of the thick nylon cord, along with two other security agents, and the group of them began lowering him down.

This first section of the roof was somewhat like a geodesic dome, with angles and struts Reagan had to push away from, just as Phillips had told him. Reagan was already moving fast, which was fine with him, even if it was going to be the longest sixty seconds of his life.

The thickly lined metal box was heavy, over a hundred pounds, and he felt it straining against his neck and shoulders while he kept pushing and kicking as he dropped lower and lower. It was not quite a free fall because of the angle of the roof, but they were letting out the rope faster than he could react to every new impediment. His arms and legs were being battered and cut by the metal supports.

Halfway down, with his back to this section of the roof, he managed a quick look through the thick glass at the enormous amusement park beneath him and all the people still down there. He kicked harder, straining to get to the bottom as soon as possible.

With two more powerful leg thrusts against the glass panels, he finally got past the slanted portion of the roof and found himself staring down at a straight thirty-foot drop. After all of the shoving and pushing, it now felt as if the men above had let go of the rope, and he braced himself as he prepared to hit the ground.

The team waiting for him below were all on their radios, giving progress reports to the men on the catwalk above. After a frightening twenty-five-foot drop, Reagan felt a sudden tug, coming to a stop just a couple of feet from the pavement.

He heard someone yell, "Move it," and a group of people in hazmat suits rushed forward, yanked him to the ground, and pulled the strap from around his neck.

In a matter of seconds, they raced to the public safety bomb disposal truck, shoved the box inside, and secured its door. This entire area of the parking lot had already been roped off, and now someone hollered, "Everyone back!"

But Reagan did not move. He figured he was far enough away, sitting on the ground with his back to the wall, the rope still around his chest. All he did was count off the seconds from the moment he hit the pavement until three successive blasts rocked the large, heavy truck, each of the explosions lifting it a foot off the ground. Then a brief quiet was followed by the men and women around him breaking into loud cheers.

Seventeen, Reagan told himself. He had counted off seventeen seconds from the time he hit the ground until that first blast. *I guess I found myself a new lucky number.*

As he got to his feet and pulled off the rope, Reagan began thinking, not only about the people they had saved today, but also the people they had not—those murdered and injured inside the mall. He shook his head, reminding himself that his job was never really done.

CHAPTER SEVENTY-SIX

New York City

Three days later, Reagan, Gellos, and Brandt were sitting with Bob Nelson at a corner table in Il Mulino on East Third Street, waiting for Erin to join them for lunch.

When she arrived, she greeted each of them in turn, getting to Reagan last. "You're a lunatic," she said. Then, before he could respond, she added, "But I'm so proud of you, Nicholas." Then she gave him a tight hug and a kiss on the lips.

Reagan smiled as he stepped back and held out a chair for her. "If I had more time to think about it, I might've tied that rope around Alex," he said as they all sat. "I really do hate heights."

Erin laughed. "I thought about that when they were lowering you over the side."

"I swear," he admitted. "I didn't look down until the end."

"Now the Flying Wallendas are going to want you in their act," Gellos said.

"No chance," Reagan told her.

"We watched the whole thing in the DD's office," Erin told them. "I can't remember Kenny ever looking so tense. As soon as you hit the ground he called John Ekey, barking instructions, telling him under no circumstances were they to keep any video of you."

Reagan laughed. "You've got to love the DD, always thinking a step ahead."

Gellos laughed too. "You wouldn't be very effective as a clandestine agent if your picture was all over the evening news."

"They gave credit to one of Ekey's men," Brandt said, "and that's the story everyone is going with."

Nelson said, "I'm just a lowly reporter, but it seems to me there ought to be some heroes being praised in this group."

"This is not a game for glory seekers," Reagan said, then lifted his glass and turned to his friend. "If you want to write about a hero, how about Sharon Ashford?" Reagan had a taste of bourbon. "That technician in Las Vegas died trying to protect a lot of innocent people from the deadly spray those bastards were going to unleash on them. Maybe people should hear her name again."

The others were silent for a moment.

Reagan nodded slightly as if confirming a thought, then looked to Gellos and Brandt. "For us it's all about results, and, sadly, we didn't get enough done."

"We did what we could," Gellos told her partner. "If we hadn't been at the High Line and Vegas and Bloomington, believe me, it would have been a lot worse."

"There is that," Reagan conceded, then called the waiter over and ordered Erin a glass of wine. When the man walked away, Reagan asked her, "How's Cyla doing?"

"I spoke with her this morning, first time since this all happened. She's devastated of course. Learning her husband is a terrorist, overseeing attacks in the US. The whole thing is unimaginable to her. On top of that, she had to spend two days being interrogated. Her career is obviously in shambles, and so is she."

"It's hard to reconcile," Reagan admitted. "A woman that bright, not seeing any of this in the man she lived with."

"I suppose, 'Love is blind' doesn't get it done," Erin said.

"That's what I told Nick back in Paris," Gellos said.

After a quiet moment, they let the subject go.

"Well," Nelson said, "it seems you dismantled the cell this fellow Khoury was running."

"Not necessarily," Brandt replied. "We've identified the men involved in the attack in Bloomington. Every one of them was living in Dearborn, still a hotbed of radical Islam. When one leader goes down, another replaces him."

It was not the response Nelson was looking for, and Reagan saw the look on his friend's face. "You and your family will be fine," he told him. "Your series on al-Qaeda is done."

"It is for now, I can promise you that."

"And your source is gone. They have no reason to bother with you again."

Nelson forced a smile. "I wish you could say that with a bit more conviction. I still recall your man Burke saying they're big on revenge."

"Don't worry, Bob, we still have people keeping an eye on you," Reagan assured him.

"And we'll be there too," Gellos added. "The FBI and DHS are looking into Khoury's associates and contacts. They've raided several homes in Dearborn, and Khoury's computer is yielding some valuable information. There are a lot of leads now, and more will be coming."

Nelson nodded. "But it never ends. That's the awful truth, isn't it?"

Reagan looked to Gellos and Brandt, then said, "It doesn't end for us, that's for sure. Especially since there are still huge chunks of the puzzle missing."

They could not mention the Ghost Chip in front of Nelson, and he knew enough not to ask what Reagan meant. Chen, the young woman who had stolen the prototypes from the Suzhou factory, was still missing and the samples had yet to surface on the black market.

Then there was the matter of Walid Khoury, who was still at large, being chased by the French, the Americans, his own people, and probably ISIS as well.

"Organized hate is a powerful adversary," Reagan said. "All that's left for us is to keep fighting it."

THE END

ACKNOWLEDGMENTS

It must be remembered that this is a work of fiction, and, although the locations where the three attacks central to the plot occurred, it should go without saying that most of the details are sheer fabrication. Taking them in order, the assault on the High Line could never have occurred as written. I have far too much respect for the New York City Police and the various other federal, state, and local agencies that protect the city.

The Bellagio is one of the most beautiful hotels in the world, not just in Las Vegas, and their outdoor fountain and shows are not to be missed. Yet all the information and description of the pump house and control room are mere invention, and I do not have any reason to believe there is the slightest chance of polluting the water as I have described in this novel.

If you have never been to the Mall of America, it is well worth visiting. Mammoth, active, ingenious, and vibrant do not begin to describe the facility. As with the Bellagio, the nature and details of the terrorist attack portrayed in this book are the product of my imagination and have nothing to do with reality.

There are numerous other real places depicted in the story, including CIA Headquarters, the Hotel Bristol in Paris, various restaurants, One Police Plaza, and on and on. Though all of these exist, I have simply borrowed them and created details that aided me in shaping the narrative. I can only hope no one has been offended, since no offense was intended.

This book could not have been written without the input and expertise of Larry Garinger. Once again, he has provided the insight, criticism, encouragement, and suggestions that have helped shape the story. Any failures in delivering a compelling plot to the reader are mine, not his.

Ryan Steck, editor extraordinaire, has provided his usual steady hand in guiding my progress, especially when it comes to pacing and authenticity. Once again, if I have sounded any sour notes, I was the one at the keyboard.

Thanks to my wife, who is always the first to read whatever I write; my sons, who are next in that line; and all my dear friends, including Ed Scannapieco, Scott Sumner, Steve Weisblum, Eric and Melissa Thorkilsen, Michele Poretto, and so many others who provide endless support, advice, and encouragement.

My gratitude, as well, to Anthony Ziccardi and his entire team at Post Hill Press who continue to endorse and back my efforts as a novelist.

Finally, it is important for me to express my admiration for the real heroes who work tirelessly, in and out of the shadows, to keep us and our great country safe—some of whom I have been privileged to know. They are the ones who inspired this story about the fight against the forces of darkness. I also want to again make it clear, as I did at the outset, that I do not believe all Muslims are evil. There is a point to be made, however, when terrorist organizations continue to exist, like al-Qaeda and ISIS. They slaughter innocent people while advocating a rule of law that subjugates people, marginalizes women, and calls for the death of all those people who do not agree with them. Making things worse, there are nations that actually support these barbarians, or at least look away from their atrocities. All I ask of the Muslim world is to speak out against these massacres and injustices. Only when the good rise up and raise their voices will the wicked be defeated.

God Bless America.

AUTHOR'S NOTE

The following comments on Islamophobia are solely the views and responsibility of the author.

The use of "phobia," when combined with another word, comes from the Greek and refers to a fear or dread of that other thing. Examples are "hydrophobia," which is a fear of water; or "agoraphobia," which is a fear of going outside; or "ophidiophobia," which is a fear of snakes.

Some phobias are irrational while others are experientially based. For instance, if you have been bitten by a poisonous snake and survived, a subsequent fear of snakes would seem to make sense.

Islamophobia is a word that has become distorted by misuse, as some suggest it refers to an irrational "hate of" or "prejudice against" Muslims. Neither this writer nor any of the characters in this novel feel that way toward the vast majority of Muslims in the world.

Nevertheless, there have been two major attacks on the World Trade Towers, the second leveling them and murdering thousands of innocent Americans. There have been assaults on the USS Cole, the Boston Marathon, and many other lethal terrorist attacks in the United States and abroad too numerous to list, all of which were perpetrated by Islamic extremists who have not only been properly blamed for these atrocities, but who have actually taken credit for them in the name of Allah.

Therefore, I submit that Islamophobia, meaning the fear of these extreme and dangerous people within the Muslim community, is a rational and reasonable response to the state of the world—at least until the moderate leaders of Islam take responsibility and control these forces of evil. As we wait for that day to come, I think it is also fair to point out that not all snakes are venomous, but we must be ever vigilant with regard to the few who threaten our existence.